MIME

A SUPERNATURAL THRILLER

MIME

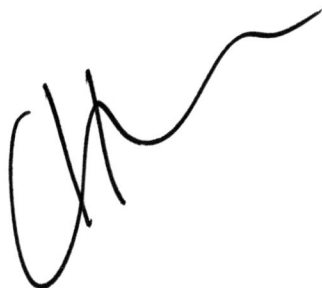

CHRISSEY HARRISON

Matador
9 Priory Business Park,
Wistow Road, Kibworth Beauchamp,
Leicestershire. LE8 0RX
Tel: 0116 279 2299
Email: books@troubador.co.uk
Web: www.troubador.co.uk/matador
Twitter: @matadorbooks

ISBN 978 1838593 605
Also available as an eBook: ISBN 978 1838595 890

British Library Cataloguing in Publication Data.
A catalogue record for this book is available from the British Library.

Printed and bound by CPI Group (UK) Ltd, Croydon, CR0 4YY
Typeset in 11pt Garamond by Troubador Publishing Ltd, Leicester, UK

Matador is an imprint of Troubador Publishing Ltd

MIX
Paper from
responsible sources
FSC
www.fsc.org
FSC® C013604

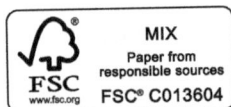

2009

BRISTOL

I

Oily and bitter, the lingering odour of burnt flesh lodged in the back of Elliot's throat. If he hadn't known where the smell came from, he might not have thought anything of it.

Fifteen minutes had passed since the first reports had hit social media. Ten minutes since "spontaneous combustion" had started trending and flagged up on Elliot's searches. Mostly third-hand accounts, but he'd found enough supposed eyewitnesses to convince him it was worth investigating.

Seven minutes since he'd left the *Weird News* office to drive down Whiteladies Road and across the city centre to the scene. Now, as he approached the waterside edge of Castle Park, that hint of charred human on the breeze made the whole situation more real. He pressed his lips together, swallowed, and headed closer.

A couple of patrol cars were parked on the roadside, alongside a grey Ford Mondeo he suspected was an unmarked police vehicle from the radio equipment visible on the dashboard. Rows of curious people gathered behind railings strung with blue-and-white striped tape. Some held phones above their heads like digital periscopes, trying to glimpse the focus of all the activity before the daylight faded. People loved a morbid circus.

Elliot pushed closer to the front.

Beyond the cordon, blue lights flashed from the roof of a police car parked near the bandstand – no sirens though, which left the park oddly quiet against the background hum of the city. Further in, another police car, two ambulances and a white van were parked in a rough circle around a brightly lit white tent, which presumably hid the remains. A large presence, but then Bristol had been on high alert for violent crime since the shooting last week.

He'd missed the initial frantic activity. Now, quiet tension held sway.

At a break in the railings where a cycle path entered the park, the police tape looped between several bollards. There, a police officer wearing a stab vest stood with his hands clasped in front of him, chin tilted up as if daring anyone to try something. Elliot sized the man up from a distance. In his forties, maybe even early fifties, and stuck with guard duty? Couldn't be an ambitious sort, but probably dependable, stoic. The onlookers were certainly giving him a wide berth. Elliot doubted he'd get more from him than an official line, but if he could get the man flustered something might slip. He extracted himself from the press of bodies and skirted the rear of the crowd.

The constable gave him the evil eye as he approached. "Should have known you'd turn up at some point."

Elliot tried for a friendly but professional smile. "Have we met?"

"No, but the inspector warned me about you."

"Detective Inspector Yates?"

The man nodded. Now Elliot realised where he'd seen that particular grey Mondeo before. He could do without crossing paths with Yates again, but he wasn't going to let that stop him. It had been weeks since a story with genuine supernatural potential had broken so close.

"Well, PC…" He looked for a name tag.

"Reynolds."

"Right. Elliot Cross." He held out a hand, which Reynolds briefly shook. "I'm sure he'll have told you I'm just a reporter. Right?"

Reynolds' jaw twitched. "That wasn't the word he used," he muttered.

Elliot kept his expression bland, pretending he hadn't heard. "I'm only after the facts. Is there a theory on how the fire started?"

Reynolds widened his stance and straightened up. "You've wasted a trip, I'm afraid. We're not releasing any details at this time."

"I appreciate your investigation has barely begun, but surely there's a basic statement you can give me?"

The man folded his arms. "DI Yates will be issuing a press statement tomorrow morning. You'll have to wait till then."

"Right, right. But you see there's already a lot of speculation flying around. Maybe you could help me put a few rumours to bed before they get out of hand." He took his notebook from his pocket, flipped to a fresh page.

Reynolds frowned and said nothing.

"Are you treating this as an act of violence? An attack?"

"I can't disclose that information," Reynolds said, but at the same time he shook his head.

"Alright. Is there any truth to reports of the man getting angry before the incident? Any evidence he was making a phone call?"

Reynolds shifted his feet. "What's that got to do with anything?"

"What about unusual phenomena in the lead-up? Strange silences, animals acting unpredictably…?"

"Unusual… A man died from burns. There's nothing *unusual* about it! Have a little respect."

"I apologise, I meant no disrespect. I'm sure there's a clear, rational explanation for what happened."

"Of course."

"Which is?" He held Reynolds' gaze, letting him see a hint of a challenge.

"We don't… You'll have to wait till the press statement."

"Fair enough." Elliot made a show of jotting down a few notes.

Reynolds huffed. "Are you done?"

"Did the victim work with flammable chemicals at all?"

"Not that we know of. Now I'm serious, you'll have to wait till tomorrow. Move along."

"I understand. Thank you for your time."

Elliot finished noting down his thoughts as he returned to the crowd.

The number of people didn't seem to be decreasing. Why were they here, really? He could still taste that bitter taint on the back of his tongue. Had any of them even noticed it? Of course, some of that bitterness might have come from realising how much his reputation had spread among the Avon and Somerset constabulary.

Police withholding information was to be expected, but Reynolds' unsettled demeanour suggested that whatever had happened wasn't clear cut. Otherwise they'd have wrapped up faster and at least issued a basic statement to forestall any hysterics. He was certain they didn't have a theory, but that didn't mean much. As a rule, he didn't accept a lack of evidence as proof, especially when it came to the supernatural. For all that *Weird News* drew a fairly sensationalist readership, it was a matter of principle that he stuck to the same journalistic standards he always had.

What he needed now was a first-hand witness.

He backtracked along the cordon. About fifty yards from the cycle path the road dropped below the level of the park; it turned ninety degrees to the right along the base of a four-foot retaining wall topped by dense shrubs. There was *technically* no access into the park this way, and no police guarded it. With the daylight fading quickly it should be easy to stay hidden. Elliot checked no one was looking, then hoisted himself onto the wall. He scrambled through the overgrown bushes, picking up a few scrapes and almost losing his glasses when a stray branch flicked in his face.

He crouched behind the fence at the top of the slope and paused, giving any details a chance to leap out at him from this new vantage point. Three shadows moved around inside the tent, silhouetted against the canvas by work lights running off a portable generator. Still gathering evidence.

The rear doors of one ambulance stood open. Inside, a paramedic moved around a person sitting on the stretcher. Elliot could only see the edge of a knee and arm, but anyone being treated must have been involved. He checked Reynolds was still facing the other way, then climbed over the fence.

As he approached, it became clear the patient was a young woman. The harsh fluorescent lights washed the colour from her pale complexion, and greasy soot stained her blonde hair. The paramedic was applying dressings to her hands.

Behind the ambulance, the central tent stirred as those inside emerged. Elliot darted round to the far side of the vehicle, out of sight.

"… but they're not looking in the right place," the girl was saying.

"I wouldn't worry," the paramedic said. "The police will go over every inch of the park if they have to. If it's important, they'll find it."

"But they won't. Everyone's walked all over it now; you can't even see where it was." She sighed, then sucked in a pained breath through her teeth.

"Sorry, nearly there."

Elliot leaned against the side of the vehicle, listening to see if she'd elaborate further before he put his head in to introduce himself.

"All done," the paramedic said. "We'll get you up to the hospital as soon as we can. I'll be back in just a tick." She stepped down from the ambulance and Elliot waited until she'd moved away. Inside, the girl with the burned hands sniffed like she was crying.

He was about to step round to talk to her when a hand settled on his shoulder and squeezed tight enough to make him wince.

"You'd better have a damn good explanation why you're on this side of the tape," a deep voice said near his ear. The hand on his shoulder pulled him round and he stood face to face with a man he unfortunately recognised.

"Detective Yates. I hoped I might—"

"Cross! What a surprise." A sneer pulled at the detective's mouth, replaced quickly by a rigid scowl, which deepened lines that clearly saw a lot of use.

Elliot had started off on the wrong foot with Yates not long after he moved to Bristol. He'd published a piece debunking one of the detective's cases while it was still going through court. While his article hadn't affected the proceedings, the scandal had escalated in ways he hadn't anticipated. Talk of positive discrimination, and questions about whether Yates had been promoted on merit or because the colour of his skin helped someone, somewhere, meet a target.

And that wasn't the only time they'd clashed.

Yates stepped closer, invading Elliot's personal space to the point where Elliot could smell the mint of his gum tainted with tobacco. "Always got to push your luck, don't you? Poking your nose in where you shouldn't."

The frustration radiating off the detective couldn't only be about him. Nosey reporters were a fact of police life; and although Yates made no effort to hide his distaste for the press in general, he was usually more subtle. No, this was because what lay in that white tent defied explanation.

"No nose poking," Elliot said, retreating several steps and raising his hands in placation. "Just after the facts."

Yates followed. "Facts are my business." The detective glanced at the ambulance. "I hope you weren't planning on approaching a vulnerable witness."

Elliot fought to keep his expression neutral and his mouth shut.

"Come on, piss off. This is a crime scene, for Christ's sake." Yates gestured towards the barrier tape and Reynolds, who was watching them in the fading twilight. The constable reached for the radio clipped to his vest.

Elliot turned to face Yates. Over the detective's shoulder he could see the girl sitting in the ambulance. She briefly made eye contact, then Yates stepped closer, blocking the view.

Elliot refocused on the detective. "So this *is* being treated as a crime?"

Yates blinked, then scowled. "What did I just say about pushing your luck? Leave. Now. Or I will physically escort you out of the park."

When Elliot hesitated, the detective made to grasp his arm.

Elliot jerked out of reach. "Alright, I'm going." With one last frustrated look towards the ambulance, he started walking.

"Freak," Yates muttered behind his back.

He swallowed the jab and kept moving. There was nothing more he could do here anyway. The girl would be the key; somehow he'd have to identify her and find her again.

2

When Sam arrived at work, she turned her key in the lock and pushed, but the door wouldn't budge. An experimental shove only yielded an inch. She crouched down and peeked through the letterbox.

"Elliot? Can you let me in?" She could see all the way down the hallway to the back door. There was no sign of movement. The door to the main office on the right was closed though, so maybe Elliot couldn't hear her. She swung the old iron knocker, twice. Still nothing. It was unusual for him not to be in first. Maybe he'd gone for a run before work.

Puffing out her cheeks, she put her bag down on the front step, set her shoulder to the heavy door and pushed until she could squeeze through the gap.

Three stacked boxes of printer paper stood on the doormat with a delivery note on top. This morning's, so Elliot must have been here earlier and gone out again. She moved the boxes out of the way, collected her things from outside and hung her coat on a hook beside the door.

Weird News occupied the ground floor of an Edwardian townhouse, the latest in a long line of metamorphoses. Each chapter of the building's history was imprinted into its fabric, like half-remembered past lives: ornate plaster ceilings, woodchip wallpaper, seventies' patterned carpet, and a vintage cigar-smoke fug they could never fully clean out. Despite the damp problem in the back room and all its other imperfections, Sam loved the place.

Today though, the acrid tang of burnt coffee masked the office's familiar musty odour.

In the pokey kitchenette, left of the hall, scorched brown sludge steamed in the coffee pot on the machine's hot plate. She'd cleaned it out before she went home yesterday, so Elliot must have refilled it then left it all night. Lovely. She tipped the contents into the sink and chased it down with fresh water.

A cupboard door creaked behind her. She flinched and fumbled the coffee pot. Her heart seized, waiting for the glass to shatter, but somehow she managed to cushion it with her hand.

She spun round. "You made me jump!"

"Sorry." Elliot reached into the cupboard, crumpled white shirt sleeves rolled up to the elbow, and lifted a mug down. His eyes homed in on the coffee pot in the sink.

Sam flattened herself against the cheap white kitchen units as he tried to squeeze past her. "I thought you were out."

"No."

"But you didn't hear me calling?"

"What? Oh, no, I was busy."

He reached for the pot, but she put her hand over it to stop him. "Busy with what, our resident poltergeist?" With her other hand she reached across the counter for the jar of instant coffee.

"No, spontaneous co— What poltergeist?"

"You know, the one that barricaded the door this morning?" She pressed the jar into his hands.

His frown deepened, then lifted when the penny dropped. "Ah. I was going to move those. Sorry." He paused, then looked from her to the empty mug on the counter to the jar in his hand, and round again. Sam could see the request forming.

"Give it here," she said, to save him from saying it.

He flashed a smile and returned the jar. "Thank you."

She rolled her eyes behind his back as he retreated to the main office across the hall.

While the kettle boiled, she tried to shift her brain into work mode. Keeping the crazy stories they dealt with separate from her personal life was deliberate. To Marie and her other friends, *Weird News* was all just make-believe and con men. Granted, a lot of it *was* con men, and hoaxes, history, folklore – and don't forget coincidence – but occasionally it was more than any of those things. Maybe she should have buried the fact she knew that at the back of her mind and gone on living her life in wilful ignorance, but she preferred to know there were ghosts and monsters in the closet and sleep with a knife under her pillow. Metaphorically speaking.

She stirred a half spoon of sugar into Elliot's coffee then took both mugs through to the office. Originally a sitting room, there was plenty of space for the two of them, despite Elliot's habit of spreading out. His desk filled the corner facing the door and, as she entered, she noted the empty take-out cartons stacked on the edge.

"You were here all night again."

From the three-day stubble on his jaw and the dark circles under his eyes behind his glasses, she wondered if he'd spent much time at home at all this week. He certainly hadn't been for a haircut in months; there was this mad-scientist curl going on behind his ears.

"There was something I had to follow up." He followed her gaze and nudged the cartons into the waste basket beside the desk.

She handed him his mug and set hers down on her own desk by the bay window. "What could possibly be so important that you couldn't go home and sleep?"

"Spontaneous human combustion. Possibly. Right here in Bristol," he said, eyes glued to his laptop screen.

She watched him for a moment, an uncomfortable tightness in her gut. He didn't lack empathy, but sometimes he lacked perspective. He was a wide-angle lens person; he looked at the whole picture, and the fact that the people in the picture were human beings got a bit lost sometimes.

"Someone died?"

He looked up. "Well, yes. But we can't do anything about that now."

"Go on, then."

"Right, so last night a number of people started tweeting about someone catching fire in Castle Park."

"What time?" Sam asked as she wheeled her desk chair over.

"Evening. About ten past nine. I picked it up about ten minutes after the first mention and headed straight there."

"What makes it spontaneous combustion and not regular combustion? Like, I don't know, some freak barbecue accident?"

"All the reports say the same. The man was walking and then he was on fire. Just like that." He stared at his screen for a moment, clicking. "There are inconsistencies. Initially people were describing it as a real inferno, then others started to argue that there were no flames."

"That's weird."

"Yes. But the end result was clear enough." He frowned at the screen. "There was a picture somewhere... I can't seem to find it now."

Sam inwardly thanked whoever had removed the picture. It was too early to be looking at something like that.

Elliot shook his head. "Anyway, the body was thoroughly charred."

"Who was it who died? Could it have been some kind of attack?"

"I'm not sure yet. The police haven't released a name. They were treating it more like a crime than an accident, but every account I've seen agreed there was no one near him." He paused, frown deepening, and focused on the screen. "But the girl had to be close," he muttered, talking to himself. "And there was that mention about him arguing with someone before it happened. Maybe she knew him, and that's why—"

"Elliot?"

His head snapped up. "Hmm?"

"Do you need me?"

He blinked, then closed his laptop. "Not yet. There's a witness I need to track down – a girl I saw last night." He rummaged in his desk drawer for a notebook, unplugged his iPhone from the charger beside his desk, and pocketed both. "I shouldn't be too long."

Sam returned her chair to her own desk.

Elliot paused by the door. "Will you be alright here?"

"I'm sure I'll survive."

A moment later the back door slammed closed and Sam exhaled a long, slow breath. Spontaneous combustion. She really hoped this one was one of those strange coincidences and nothing more.

———•———

An empty crisp packet whipped across the path as Elliot entered Castle Park from the edge of the city centre. The summer heat of the day before lingered as uncomfortable humidity, but the sun hid behind dark, threatening clouds.

He'd expected the park to be closed, but apparently the police had wrapped up the situation overnight. He followed the tarmac path between the fences surrounding the scant remains of the castle and earth banks topped with plane trees, their thick summer foliage creating deeper shade on the overcast day. The path curved to the right, and the flat area beside the octagonal bandstand, where the white tent had stood the night before, opened before him.

He paused and stepped aside to let a woman with a pushchair stride past. The park always served as a thoroughfare, a shortcut, but today no one seemed inclined to dawdle.

Apart from a large black scorch mark on the grass, and the scuffed tyre tracks of the emergency vehicles, there was little evidence of last night's drama. Elliot had spent most of the night trying to find any hint of the girl's identity in the reports on social media, but, while a few mentioned a blonde girl trying to put out the fire, no one knew who she was. His only slim lead was the speculation that maybe she knew the victim.

Floral tributes already clung to the railings of the bandstand. Elliot walked over and discreetly inspected a few cards. The deceased's name was Samik Chaudry, but he was clearly known to most as Micky. Not a common name, which would make him easier to trace. Elliot stepped under the canopy, leaned on one of the posts as he made a quick search on his phone and pulled up Facebook and Twitter accounts. Lots of photos, smiling teenage friends on nights out.

"It was right here," a voice said.

Elliot glanced up. About fifteen yards away, a lanky lad with ginger hair and a petite blonde girl walked towards the bandstand, heads down as if searching for something. The girl pointed, revealing a hand wrapped in bandages. Elliot pocketed his phone.

"It went this way." She paced several steps away from the scorched circle where the unfortunate Mr Chaudry had died. The sleeves of her oversized hoodie came down over her bandages. She hunched her shoulders and kept her hands close to her body; still in a lot of pain, no doubt. The boy with her was a similar age – about seventeen or eighteen. Freckles dusted his cheeks under thick-rimmed glasses, and he wore skinny jeans and a plaid shirt.

Elliot stepped off the bandstand. The girl looked up and he saw recognition in her eyes.

"You," she said. "You were here last night."

"So were you." He indicated her hands with a nod and she hugged them to her middle, wincing.

"Who are you?"

He approached closer. "Elliot Cross. I'm a reporter. What are you looking for?"

The girl's friend stepped between them. "Hey, she doesn't have to talk to you."

"True. But is anyone else listening?"

The lad frowned, and the girl warned him back with her bandaged hand on his upper arm. "It's okay, Harry. Maybe he can help us."

Harry looked Elliot up and down. "You work for a paper?"

"In a way. I specialise in certain types of stories."

"What kind of stories?" the girl asked.

"Unusual ones. Like this one. You knew him, didn't you?"

Her lips parted. "How did you—"

"Gut feeling. You tried to help and now here you are searching for something because you care about the truth. Because you cared about him."

She nodded slowly.

"I care about the truth too," Elliot continued. "It seems to me like the police aren't offering many answers."

"No, not at all," Harry said. "They won't even tell his family whether it was an accident or not."

Elliot nodded towards a bench at the side of the path. "Do you have any reason to believe it wasn't an accident?"

Harry shrugged. "Micky didn't have enemies, everyone loved him. But, well, you hear about people getting beat up over nothing in the news sometimes. Especially when they're, you know, not white."

"It wasn't an accident," the girl muttered, her eyes filling with tears.

"Becky saw something," Harry said. "But the police won't listen."

The three of them reached the bench. Becky sat while Harry stayed standing behind her.

Elliot took the opposite end. "What did you see, Becky?" he asked, making eye contact.

"It's going to sound crazy." There was a fragility to her voice, like she couldn't bear for one more person to tell her she was imagining things.

"Not necessarily. Go on."

"There were no flames." She shook her head. "There was smoke, and heat, and he turned black, but there were no flames." She regarded him with narrowed eyes. Was she testing him? Using this to work out whether she could trust him further?

"I know. You're not the only one to have said that. There's more to it though, am I right?"

Becky stared into space. He watched the way she cradled her burned hands in her lap. Maybe it would be easier if they circled back round to the heart of the matter.

"How did you know Micky?"

Her eyes stayed vacant. "We're friends. We go to college together. Went to college. I… I liked him."

"I'm sorry. Were you with him at the park, before it happened?"

"No, I was just hanging out with some other friends."

"And when did you see Micky?"

She blinked and frowned. "Umm, I was going to get some drinks. It must have been about nine, maybe. So I was walking the other way." She glanced along the path in the direction of the shops.

Elliot followed her gaze. "You were walking this way." He pointed in an arc across the grass. "And he was facing away from where we are now?"

She nodded.

"Can you tell me what you saw?"

She took a deep breath and sucked her bottom lip.

Harry leaned forwards. "It was—"

"It's alright." Elliot glanced up, warning him off. He could see Harry only wanted to help, protect his friend, but he needed the first-hand story. "He was just walking, alone?" he prompted Becky.

"Yes."

"Could you see his face?"

"Kind of. I did recognise him, if that's what you mean."

Elliot paused while she wiped her eyes with her sleeve.

"Did he see you?"

She shook her head.

"Did he look angry, upset?"

She raised her head, focusing on him as if the question had pulled her out of the nightmare and made her *think*. "No. Maybe a bit at first. I think he had headphones in, and he was talking, or singing along maybe."

Now he had her engaged he could push forwards. "Did anything strange happen before the fire? Anything unusual?"

"He stopped." She closed her eyes and tilted her head. "I remember because I was about to shout hi, and he stopped and looked down at his clothes. He patted himself, like maybe he was trying to find something in his pockets. That's weird, right?"

"Maybe. Is that when it started? The fire?"

"I was a way off still, but I'm sure I saw it, in the grass."

"Saw what?"

Becky glanced at Harry. "This line, in the grass, moving towards him. The grass turned black and smoked and it went right to him." She gestured towards the scorch mark. "Then I heard him screaming for help and loads of smoke started coming off him. I started running, but…" She pressed her lips together, eyes tearing up again.

Elliot gave her a moment and used it to pull his notebook from his pocket and jot down what she'd told him. No one else had mentioned a black line in the grass, but he didn't doubt her. Unlike all the other witnesses, she'd been paying attention to the victim *before* it started. "This black line in the grass, you think that's what started the fire? Like a fuse?"

She nodded. "But no one believes me. I tried to show the detective last night, but after all the chaos and everyone walking over it you couldn't even see where it was anymore. He just said they'd investigate. But it was definitely there. I saw it." There was a hint of defeat in her voice, like she didn't know what else to try.

"Where did it come from? How far, what direction?"

"Over there." She twisted in her seat and pointed towards the earth bank on the far side of the path. A few trees cast shadows that might have been deep enough to hide someone in the twilight.

"Was there anyone there?" Elliot asked.

"I don't know, I was looking at Micky. I ran and tried to tell him to roll around. And he did, but he just kept burning, like the flames wouldn't go out, even though there weren't any. I know that sounds crazy. I… I tried to pat them out." She wiped her streaming eyes on her cuff again, above her bandages. "He just kept screaming and screaming." She tailed off into a sob.

"There was nothing more you could have done."

Becky shook her head, although it hadn't been a question.

"I'm sorry," Elliot said. "It must have been very difficult."

She knuckled her puffy eyes with the edge of her bandage. "I keep seeing it, every time I close my eyes, you know?"

Elliot nodded. "I can understand that. Thank you for talking to me."

Harry put a hand on Becky's shoulder. She glanced up, then nodded and stood. Elliot rose and fished a couple of business cards from his wallet; plain ones, with his name, rather than *Weird News*. "If you think of anything else, please call me."

Harry looked down at the card. "Here, if it turns out someone did this to Micky, you'll do something about it, yeah?"

Elliot frowned. "I… Of course. I'll do whatever I can."

Other than passing on the information to the police he wasn't sure what he could do. The thought nagged at him as he walked back to his car.

———•———

Sam sipped her second coffee of the morning – from the freshly washed coffee pot – and relaxed in her chair while her elderly office computer reluctantly booted up. She used her laptop for articles and photo editing, but confining the general admin to the archaic desktop kept the clutter, and the crazy, contained. The nature of what they did attracted a lot of… intense people.

So far that morning she'd cleaned the kitchen, opened the mail and finished writing a short commentary on a "scientif-ic"paper entitled *Telepathic Communication Among Red Squirrel Populations of the Isle of Wight*. The results of the study were inconclusive, which was weird enough for her. She reckoned the squirrels probably weren't telepathic, just surprisingly good at faking it. But enough wily squirrels, she'd put it off for as long as possible – it was time.

Inbox: two hundred and forty-three unread messages.

She groaned, but quickly whittled them down by deleting all the spam about male enhancement products and financially desperate relatives in Africa. By the time she'd filed all the subscription updates from news sites and blogs, she had a much more manageable twenty-eight.

Half were submissions and correspondence from what she and Elliot referred to as the "outer circle" – serious contributors they'd worked with before but who hadn't graduated to the "inner circle" of regulars trusted with Elliot's direct line. Even some of the fringe academics and consultants they worked with could be a bit over the top sometimes. She acknowledged each email; they could tackle them more thoroughly later.

Of the remaining half, nine were responses to last month's issue. In dribs and drabs they were manageable, but they could build up all too easily, so she spent a few minutes thanking the positive ones and placating the negative.

The last five emails contained the entertainment for the day – readers and other crazy people with even crazier stories. She fortified herself with another sip of coffee before she leapt into the unknown.

First up, one vegetable photograph from Mr Aberforth, claiming he saw the face of Elvis. Sam tilted her head sideways. As veg portraits went it wasn't bad; there was definitely a likeness. And hey, who doesn't love Elvis on a potato? She sent a quick thank you, saying they might use the photo in a later issue.

Mrs Whelmsley was concerned her dead cat was haunting her. Sam copy pasted their standard animal ghosts response from a template. It gave a list of specific phenomena to watch out for, and then suggested that grief did funny things to the mind.

A local Wiccan coven invited them to attend a Lammas celebration near Cheddar on the first of August. She marked the date and sent a quick "maybe" reply. If nothing else, it might be a way to drag Elliot away from his desk for an afternoon.

The final two were both local to Bristol. Rachel Wells-Evans wanted to know if it was normal for a spirit medium to need a week to meditate in order to contact a spirit, *after* being paid. Certainly fishy, and worth looking into.

The last email wiped the smile off Sam's face. Joyce Perry had lost her son last week, the victim of the shooting near the university. The incident had been all over the news – local and national – with appeals for witnesses. She and Elliot hadn't looked into it; a shooting in Bristol was unusual for sure, but it wasn't *Weird News'* brand of unusual.

Joyce, on the other hand, seemed convinced a policeman had shot her son and they were covering it up. If she was right, there was a story about police corruption to uncover. Sam jotted down a few questions and chewed the end of her pen. It wasn't really within their remit, but a mystery like this might be right up Elliot's street. Closer to what he used to do, before *Weird News*. There'd certainly be no harm in doing a little preliminary digging while he was busy with the spontaneous combustion story.

Mrs Perry had included a phone number, so Sam finished off her coffee, flipped to a fresh page on her notepad, and dialled.

"Mrs Perry?" she asked when a woman answered.

"Speaking."

"Mrs Perry, my name is Samantha McBride. I work for *Weird News*. We received your email."

"Oh goodness." There was a loud scrape and muffled bump from the other end of the line.

Sam nibbled her lower lip, waiting for the woman to continue. "Mrs Perry?"

"I'm sorry, dear, I just needed to move through to the other room." She sounded flustered.

"Is everything okay?"

Mrs Perry lowered her voice. "My husband didn't approve of me contacting you."

"I'm sorry, it must be a very difficult time for both of you. If there has been some kind of cover-up by the police, I'd like to think we can help you find the truth."

"Oh, bless you. I really didn't know where else to turn."

Sam poised her pen over her notepad. "Could you tell me what you know?"

Mrs Perry proceeded to describe the events of her son's death, with dates, times and lots of details that Sam was sure weren't entirely relevant but jotted down anyway. Clearly the woman was channelling what must be very fresh grief into the questions surrounding her son's death. That's what conspiracy theories were, for the most part – people in pain desperately searching for answers.

Finally, the woman got to the heart of the matter.

"They say they're still investigating, but they won't even say what type of gun it was. They say they never found the bullet, but that's impossible."

"Actually, it is possible that they really haven't recovered it," Sam said, cautiously. "I know it's hard to think about, I know we're talking about your son, but a bullet, when it exits a... a body, can still be travelling very fast. It could—"

"Oh no, you don't understand," Joyce said. "The bullet didn't come out."

"What do you mean?"

"There was no – what do they call it – exit wound. The bullet must have stayed inside."

A cold shiver ran up Sam's spine. "How... Can I ask how you know that?"

"It's what she said. The lady who examined Alex, after."

She wrote "coroner's report" on her pad, underlined twice. "That does sound very unusual." Maybe it wasn't a bullet wound at all, but then why would the police state that to the press if they weren't sure?

"I wish they'd just tell the truth!" Joyce suddenly snapped, making Sam jump.

She decided to change tack before Joyce got too worked up. "Tell me about Alex, Mrs Perry."

The woman's breath hitched. "He was a wonderful boy," she said. "He was going to start his PhD next year. He was so smart. Not like me and his father." She continued describing Alex's life, his studies, hobbies and so on; he sounded like any typical student – smart, quiet, law abiding. Not someone likely to get themselves in trouble.

"I'm sure the police have already asked this, but can you think of anyone who might have wanted to hurt him?"

"No. No one. He had such a lot of friends. His girlfriend is such a sweet girl. She's in bits, just like me."

"I'm so sorry, Mrs Perry. I'm sure he'll be missed by a lot of people."

"Thank you, dear."

"We'll do what we can to investigate. Can I call you again if I have more questions?"

"Oh yes, but perhaps it would be better to call my mobile. As I said, Barry thinks I should just let the police handle things."

Sam took down the number and said goodbye. She scanned the notes on her pad. So, it was police cover-up versus mysterious vanishing bullet. Maybe this *was* their brand of unusual.

3

When Elliot returned to the office Sam was out, but she'd covered his desk in three neat stacks of paperwork labelled sign these, pay these, and call these. A sticky note on the desk explained she'd gone to visit someone in Clifton about a medium.

He obeyed the notes – not because she'd nag him if he didn't, but because he hated wallowing in overdue admin. He must have dealt with all the time-consuming daily tasks she took off his hands before she came to work with him, but he couldn't remember how he'd coped.

Eventually he wanted to expand into the back room – which currently served as interview room, break area and storage cupboard – and bring in a bigger team. They relied so heavily on freelancers, especially around publication time. But turnover didn't quite stretch to that yet. The first steps had been moving out of his living room, then taking Sam on full-time. He hadn't needed to ask Jasper for a cash injection for nearly eighteen months now. Not that his (mostly) silent partner would mind – Jasper had money to burn – but it was a matter of principle that he didn't break their profitable streak by overstretching their resources.

There were mugs drying on the draining board, and another note stuck to the now clean, full coffee pot permitting him to use it. This one Sam had signed with a smiley face. He poured a cup, quietly reflecting that she also forced him to take better care of himself than he otherwise might.

He started to add sugar, but changed his mind and took a bitter sip.

The sound of Sam's key in the door drifted through from the hall. Elliot paused in the kitchen doorway.

"Oh hey," she said as she came in. "Did you have any luck?"

"Some. What about you?"

"Uh huh, I've been chatting to Beryl McGrew and her cat Alfie."

"Oh?" Elliot sipped his coffee with one arm folded across his chest, while Sam disentangled her windswept hair from her bag and camera straps.

"And her granddaughter, Rachel." She shrugged out of her coat and hung it up, then tucked her unruly red locks behind her ears, cheeks flushed pink from the fresh breeze outside. "They got conned by this piece of shit claiming to be a medium. Not just them, either, a whole bunch of others in the same neighbourhood. All old people who'd lost someone recently."

"Did you get a name?"

Sam beamed at him. "Of course. He was using the name Henry Blake, but he slipped up. Fake website on a domain name he'd registered under his real name, David Oldham. Gotcha!"

She moved past him into the office.

"Nice work."

He hesitated before following her and took a slow breath. He was under no illusion; she'd be moving on soon. Her potential and enthusiasm had rapidly outstripped the limited salary he could offer, and he knew she struggled living on her own. If they could increase turnover by another thousand a month, he could offer her enough to move out of that shitty little flat in

Bedminster, then maybe she'd stay. But that was some way off, and once she figured out she could do better elsewhere…

"Yeah, well, the guy made it too easy really," she said. "Blagged his way in with info from the obits, then feigned difficulty contacting the spirit. Charged up front, then said he'd have to meditate to re-establish contact." She made air quotes with her fingers around "meditate".

Elliot nodded. Textbook stuff, predictable. "He strung each victim along while he conned others in the area?"

"Exactly. Quick and easy, but a good page filler." She moved round to her desk. "And at least they have something to take to the police now, though whether they'll do anything… Anyway, I'll write it up this afternoon. But come on…" She turned to face him. "… how did you get on? Any more idea about this mystery girl?"

"I found her. Purely by chance."

"And?"

He leaned against the end of his desk and explained about his meeting with Becky and the way she'd described the flameless fire and the fuse in the grass.

"So, do you think it's actually spontaneous combustion?"

He shook his head. "No, not really. It doesn't fit what seem to be the hallmarks. I'm leaning towards a chemical reaction, maybe. I want to see if I can find any other similar cases."

Sam nodded as she sat behind her desk and opened her laptop. "Well, if it doesn't pan out, I may have found something else."

Elliot moved round behind her, took off his glasses and gave them a quick polish with the cloth from his pocket. "What have you got?"

"Vanishing bullet or mistaken identity shooting," she said, glancing over her shoulder. "I'd like to say I'm leaning towards the latter, but I don't see the point. Accidents happen. Usually they just hold an inquiry and someone gets fired, so why try to cover it up?"

She brought up a page from the *Evening Post*. A grinning student in graduation robes. The picture had been all over the news headlines a few days ago. He'd barely paid it any attention. As a rule, the supernatural didn't make use of guns.

"You mean *that* shooting? But there wasn't anything strange about—"

"Not that we were aware of." She ran through what her contact, the boy's mother, had told her.

Neither of them broke the silence for a moment. Ninety per cent of what they published was strange but ultimately mundane. The supernatural was so rare, and so rarely identified as such, that it was a good month when two or three genuine cases reached him from across his global network of contributors. Two deaths with unexplained aspects, in the same city, within days of each other, just didn't happen. These two had nothing in common, and yet...

"It's probably nothing," Sam said.

"Right. Two points don't make a pattern, just a coincidence."

"Yeah." Sam twisted away from the desk. "What if it's not though? A coincidence, I mean."

"We can't assume anything. Right now I doubt it'll turn out that either of them *are* supernatural." Elliot put one hand on the back of her chair. "Have you got a plan?"

"You want me to take this one?"

"For now. If you feel up to it."

She grinned. "No, sure, I've got this. I need to be certain about the body first. Even with Mrs Perry's help it could take weeks to get the coroner's report, so I guess I'll need to go see for myself."

"Good call." He retreated to his desk and let her get on with it. Sure, he could just thank her and say he would take it from here, but it was her story. She was more or less the age he'd been when he'd left London, and there he'd learnt to defend his leads tooth and nail. She'd need the experience, when she started looking for new opportunities.

"One field trip to the morgue coming up," Sam said with a slight tremor in her voice. Elliot glanced over as she reached for the phone. She hesitated, hand hovering, then took a deep breath and lifted the handset.

Meanwhile, he needed to get a better handle on spontaneous human combustion.

———•———

With a quick call to Mrs Perry, Sam explained what she needed to do. Only next of kin could make an appointment to see a body, so it wasn't something Sam could do for her. Joyce rose to the challenge admirably, despite her worries about how to hide it from her husband.

While she waited for Mrs Perry to get back to her, Sam read up on "invisible bullet" myths and the science of gunshot wounds. Talk about tinfoil-hat brigade; there was so much pseudoscience and false logic it made her brain ache. Could you make a dissolvable bullet from ice or – eww – meat? More to the point, *why* would you? If invisible bullets were ever a thing, they were the tools of assassins and shady international organisations. Even the most hardened conspiracy nut would struggle to explain why the great "They" suddenly needed to off an unremarkable physics student from Bristol.

She pulled up Alex's graduation photo again. His broad smile showed slightly crooked teeth and made his eyes shine with pride. He wasn't particularly attractive or distinctive, just… unremarkable. And, from what Mrs Perry had told her, that went for his life as well.

Exit wounds were messy and hard to miss; and from what she'd read, a small calibre bullet to the torso would more likely stay inside. But Mrs Perry's theory about a police cover-up made no sense either.

Sam massaged her temples and pushed her notes to one side. Until she saw the body it was all just speculation. Most likely the police had made a mistake. People liked to think institutions of authority were competent and powerful, because the idea that normal, fallible people ran the world was a frankly terrifying alternative.

Putting it out of her mind, she took a few minutes away from the crazy, sitting on the saggy green sofa in the back room. She texted Marie to see if she was coming to their photography meet-up that evening, then tried to relax and clear her mind. It helped to step back occasionally, and Elliot never objected. He seemed to appreciate she needed a bit of distance, even if he never allowed himself the same respite.

For the rest of the afternoon she focused on Henry Blake, the fake medium. A little case history, some victim reports and several photos – including one of Alfie the cat – combined into a nice double-page spread. It was a little rough, but she could tidy it up later. They still had over two weeks until their next publication deadline.

She shut down her computer at quarter to six. Elliot was still sitting at his desk. She glanced over a couple of times while she tidied up, but it didn't seem like he was winding down. She slid her laptop into her bag and swung it onto her shoulder.

He looked up as she approached his desk, and took in her bag and the empty mug in her hand. "Oh."

"What?"

"You're going?"

"Elliot, it's six o'clock already. I need to go home and have some dinner. And I have Camera Club tonight."

He checked his watch and rubbed his eyes, pushing his glasses askew. "Oh, right." He re-settled his glasses and focused on his laptop screen.

Sam pressed her lips together. "What about you?"

"What about me?"

"Are you going home soon? You know, eat, relax, sleep, that stuff?"

He glanced up. "In a bit. Maybe."

"Please, Elliot. The story will still be here in the morning. Promise me you'll go home tonight."

He gave her a shallow nod but said nothing.

"I'll see you tomorrow."

"Hmm."

She headed out and, as she walked down the steps outside the office, puffed out her cheeks as if she could exhale all the frustration of the day. The wind had dropped from the blustery morning, and only a few soft clouds marred a clear sky, softening to pale blue at the start of a long midsummer evening. It should be a good night for photos.

Her beaten-up red Fiesta waited for her in a street space. The door hinge screeched. She chucked her bag across to the far side and climbed in, driver's seat squeaking. Sometimes it felt like the car was trying to talk, it had so many different creaks, clicks and rattles. Maybe it was falling apart, but it was still hers.

Elliot parked his BMW M5 in the space behind the office. Big, black, with ridiculous alloys, four exhausts, and an engine that growled like a predator, it was, unlike her Fiesta, a complete contradiction. He'd left behind most of the trappings of his life in London, but not the M5. She knew he'd earned a good wage back then, but it couldn't have been astronomical, so she wasn't sure how he'd afforded it. But then, he didn't like to talk about his past and his background much. As she wrestled the Fiesta into first gear, she contemplated that if she could figure out how he and the car fitted together she might understand him a bit better.

———◦———

"Hey, you're late," Marie called from across the road as Sam climbed out of her car.

Sam waved. "Sorry, I was a bit late leaving work." She'd swung home, grabbed a sandwich and swapped out her workwear for a long skirt and crocheted cardigan.

Luckily there'd still been a street space outside the terraced townhouses that overlooked the edge of Clifton Down. "The Downs" stretched south here, between high class suburbs and the edge of Avon Gorge. Large trees dotted the park, and beyond them Sam glimpsed a granite tower – the Bristol side of the Clifton suspension bridge, which was the location and subject for tonight's shoot. Across the gorge on the Leigh Woods side, the tower's twin, with its substantial red-brick footing, stood bathed in warm sunlight, and the famous white cables elegantly joined the two.

About ten members of Camera Club had shown up. Not a bad turnout. They milled around on the grass, chatting. Sam hefted her camera bag and tripod out of the boot, locked the car and crossed the road.

Marie snapped a picture of her as she struggled to lug her kit up the bank at the edge of the park.

"Hey!"

Her friend poked her pierced tongue out, grinning, and Sam couldn't help but smile back. Marie had inherited her glossy dark hair, sultry eyes and the olive tone to her skin from her Eastern European ancestors, but her attitude was all her own.

"So, what kept you late at the office?" Marie asked. She took the tripod, then linked her arm through Sam's.

"Oh, you know, same old crazy."

Another of her friends, Eleanor, fell into step on the other side. Most of the group followed the park towards the edge of the gorge, for a view back up at Bristol's famous landmark, while Sam, her friends and a few others headed directly towards the bridge.

"Crazy as in that crackpot boss of yours?" Marie hugged Sam's arm tighter.

A rebel smile curved her lips. "Don't call him that. And no, he didn't *make* me stay, I was just working on a story."

They joined the flagstone path that followed the road as it approached the bridge. As they walked, Sam took her Nikon D70 out of her shoulder bag and lifted the strap over her head. The camera was showing its age now – the sensor was small and the shutter was a bit unreliable at times – but if she was going to dangle a camera over the edge of the bridge, better this one than her brand new D3X. Especially since Elliot had helped pay for it so she'd have a top-end camera for work.

A few cars waited at the toll gates. Sam smiled at the clinks and clatters as the drivers tossed their fifty pence in change into the hoppers. She dodged around a temporary AA sign for a festival at Ashton Court across the gorge, and paused to take a batch of shots of some backpackers who were headed that way.

Marie and Eleanor skirted the huge stone tower and paused on the walled terrace at its base. Sam followed. The criss-crossed wrought-iron railings of the bridge stretched away with the road, disconcertingly insubstantial. Sam rested her forearms on the sun-warmed stone. The gorge yawned below them, and she was glad for the solid barrier.

She stroked her finger affectionately over the worn shutter button of the D70. In other ways it would be worse to lose this camera. She and the D3X hadn't really bonded yet, but the D70 had been with her through a lot. Not all of it good.

A shutter clicked beside her and she looked up sharply to find Marie's lens pointed at her. Behind Marie, Eleanor studied the city through her own camera.

"What's on your mind?" Marie asked.

"Oh nothing."

"Come on, spill it. Mooning over a certain someone?"

Sam did a double take, mentally dragging herself out of the past. "What? No, you know it's not like that."

Eleanor looked over her shoulder. "Nothing worse than an unrequited office romance," she teased.

"Stop it, both of you. It was a silly crush and I'm over it." She felt her cheeks warming and covered her face with her camera to take a shot of the low sun striking the bridge tower across the valley.

It was all connected, of course. Her past, the D70 and why she first contacted Elliot. Her photography had got her into trouble and, looking for someone to save her from insanity, she'd found him. No, actually she'd more found the *idea* of him.

"There's nothing wrong with a crush," Eleanor said, leaning on the wall.

"How many times? We're just friends, colleagues. Now that I know him, it's… well, it's different."

Marie clicked off another shot. "How?"

"It just is." The crush was before she'd even met him in person, when he was just a name at the bottom of emails that had helped her heal after her life had shattered. It had nothing to do with who he really was – a man with deep issues of his own.

Marie lowered her camera, lips pursed as if planning her next line of attack, but then her eyes widened. Sam braced herself.

"You know what? We should do something." Marie turned to Eleanor. "The three of us. Go away for a few days and do something fun."

"I can't at the moment, we're way too busy," Sam said.

"But you don't work on the weekend! How about it? El, could you leave the kids at home with Mike?"

"Yeah, no problem."

Sam cringed. "Maybe. It's kind of short notice."

Marie hugged her with one arm, still holding her camera in the other hand. "So what? Come on! Let's book an overnight, somewhere with a spa and cool stuff to shoot." She waved her camera for emphasis.

It sounded great, and Marie was right, it wasn't like she was supposed to be working anyway. But Elliot would. She ought to stop by and check on him at some point.

"I guess. But does it have to be *this* weekend? Couldn't we work something out for next month?"

Marie's grin faded. "Sure. Don't think you're getting out of it though." She turned away to photograph a pair of pigeons perched on the bridge railings.

Sam peered over the wall. The deep gorge receded away below, and her stomach lurched at the sight of the terrifying drop.

"He's no good for you," Marie said from behind her view-finder. "We hardly see you anymore."

Sam stared down at the river far below. "It's not his fault." She held her camera over the side and pressed the shutter button.

———•———

"Any chance of a lift?" Marie asked, hugging her patchwork coat round her arms. The rest of the club had headed off at various points, but after the sun set the crystal-clear night offered a creative sparkle that Sam and her friends couldn't resist playing with. Now it was getting very late.

"Of course. El?"

"I'll walk," Eleanor said. "It's only five minutes for me."

Sam loaded her equipment into the boot and then she and Marie piled in. The route to Marie's place took them past the *Weird News* office and, as they passed, Sam noticed the front window still lit up. She slowed the car.

"Sam? Why are we—"

"I just need to… I forgot something at the office. I'll be two seconds." She snagged a vacant space.

Marie's eyes strayed over her shoulder to the lit-up window and she sighed. "Don't let him drag you into his craziness."

"Two seconds, I promise."

She climbed out and closed the door, cutting off Marie's reply.

Hugging her cardigan around her, she hurried up the steps and let herself in, careful to click the door shut softly behind her. The light in the hall was off and she left it that way; there was plenty of light spilling through from the office.

She paused in the doorway. Elliot sat at his desk, slumped forwards with his head on his folded arms, glasses stuck up at an awkward angle. It was like he couldn't put the work down, not for a second. What did he think would happen if he did?

She walked over to the desk, crouched beside him and gently shook his shoulder.

His head jerked up, then froze as if he was working out where he was.

"You promised you'd go home," Sam said.

He sat up, raked his fingers through his hair, rubbed his eyes and re-settled his glasses. "What time is it?"

"Nearly midnight. You must have crashed out. Which is what happens when you hardly sleep all week."

He frowned, not fully awake. "What are you doing here?"

"I was on my way home. I saw the lights on."

"You didn't have to…"

Sam sighed and stood up. "You promised. If you keep doing this you'll make yourself ill. Come on, at least sleep on the couch." She nodded for him to follow her through to the back room. Surrounded by boxes of files and back issues, she stacked up two cushions at one end of the sofa.

"Come on." She pulled the fleece throw off the couch, shook it out.

Elliot kicked his shoes off. "Alright, alright. But you don't need to…" He snatched the blanket from her hands, chucked it in a heap at one end, then sat at the other. He tilted his head back and yawned.

Sam retreated to the door and watched him with her arms crossed.

"Are you going to stand there all night?" he muttered.

"That depends," she said, "on whether you're going to sneak back to your desk as soon as I'm gone."

He chuckled and shook his head, then took his glasses off and set them on the side table. "You can go. I promise I'll get some sleep, alright?"

"Good. I'll see you in the morning." For added measure she flicked the light off and pulled the door closed, leaving him sitting in the dark.

The buzz from the night out with her friends had completely worn off, and all the puzzling thoughts about mystery bullets, people burning alive, and Elliot, crowded back in. She passed through the office, turning off computers, lights, gadgets, then slipped quietly out through the front door.

When she slid back into the Fiesta, Marie stared at the side of her head.

"Not a word," Sam said.

Marie drew her pinched fingers across her lips, zipped tight.

NO REGRETS

Elliot checked his desk drawers for anything important he might have missed. He found a few pieces of personal correspondence shoved to the back, and added them to the top of the archive box sitting on his office chair.

A few heads watched over desk partitions. Some even looked genuinely sad to see him go, but most favoured dark speculation as they tried to work out the real story. Not many believed he'd resigned by choice.

His desk creaked as someone leaned on it behind him and made him jump.

"You can still change your mind," Catherine said. "One call to HR and everything can go back to the way it was."

He watched her inspect her hands, running her thumb across each perfectly French-manicured nail.

"Everything, huh?" he muttered.

"You want me to say I'm sorry? Fine, I'm sorry. I should have given you more space to grieve."

He levelled a stare at her. The fact he'd be walking out the door for the last time in a few minutes made it surprisingly easy to find the words he'd struggled with in the five weeks since James's death.

"What, you mean instead of trying to derail my career because I wouldn't sleep with you anymore?"

Her dark bob swished as she glared at the watchers around the office.

"Elliot," she warned.

"Forget about it. I'm moving on anyway."

She folded her arms and pursed her lips. "Moving on where, huh?" She lowered her voice to a whisper. "I know you don't have anywhere yet. I can make sure you don't find anything. You'll come crawling back in no time."

He added a last couple of things to his box. The lid slid on with a satisfying sense of finality. "You're assuming I care." If his father's disapproval hadn't been enough to undermine his resolve there was no way Cat's vague threats would do it.

"Of course you care."

"I really don't. Don't you get it? None of this matters." He turned, locking eyes with each of the people in the room. "Do you hear me? All of this…" He gestured with both hands to take in the whole office. "… politics and celebrity shit – it's not important."

Cat put her hands on her hips. "So what is this? Throwing yourself on the sword because we're all so despicable?" She scoffed. "You're as bad as any of us."

"Oh, you think I don't already know that?"

He picked up the box and stepped round her.

"It's a waste, you know. You could have achieved a lot here. And now?"

He spun round to face her, walking backwards towards the stairwell, and shrugged as best he could with the box in his arms. "I guess we'll see."

He faced the exit again and kept walking.

A few paces from the lifts, Cat called out, "Elliot, wait."

He paused to let her catch up. Nothing she could say would change his mind, so he might as well let her speak.

"Don't you want this?" She held out a glass block engraved with his name. *Young Journalist of the Year, 2005.* A four-inch cuboid of glass that simultaneously represented the best and worst of who he was.

The sight of it made his stomach boil. He hated that he wanted to keep it.

"No," he forced out. He strode to the stairwell and escaped.

4

Elliot rolled to the side and woke with a start when he nearly fell off the couch. Dim light filtered in round the blind across the window at the rear of the room. He found his glasses, untangled himself from the blanket and sat up. The couch was too short to sleep on comfortably and his back ached, but better than…

He scrunched a corner of the fleece in his hand. Sam had stopped by. He'd dozed off at his desk and she'd woken him up. He realised he hadn't even thanked her – she'd caught him off-guard and he'd grumbled and moaned like *she* was inconveniencing *him*. He'd have to make an effort to tell her he *did* appreciate her concern, even if he found it hard to accept. He rubbed his stiff neck and checked his watch: ten to nine. She'd be in soon.

After he'd set some coffee brewing, he neatened himself up as best he could with the few toiletries he kept at work. Later he'd swing home and grab a shower and a change of clothes. He scratched his cheek – and a shave.

While he sipped his coffee, sitting on the couch, he flicked on the television to check the news and tried to shake the sleep from his head. Not that TV news ever threw up anything of interest. The stories he sought out rarely made headlines.

National news gave way to local, and he zoned out, thinking about Samik Chaudry. If someone had walked across the grass with a container leaking a flammable liquid, it could have ignited by accident. But that wouldn't explain why Samik had caught alight so fast, or why there were no flames. A caustic or acidic reaction shouldn't have generated so much smoke or carbonised the body. None of it made any sense.

"… police are still seeking an explanation as to what caused the injuries that led to the young woman's death less than an hour ago, here, in this popular Bristol market."

Elliot's head snapped up.

The reporter stood under an umbrella against a background of police tape and market stalls. Elliot vaguely recognised him, but he couldn't dredge up a name.

"Conflicting eyewitness accounts initially pointed towards an animal attack, but, after a thorough sweep of the area, police have confirmed no animals were involved. There is thought to be no risk to the public."

He turned the volume up and sat forwards.

"One onlooker captured the incident in this video footage. Sensitive viewers may wish to look away."

After a brief pause the screen filled with a view of a local farmers' market Elliot recognised immediately as Whiteladies Road, not far from the *Weird News* office. A few customers, and teens loitering before school, browsed stalls still being set out. A young woman in the middle of the screen jerked from side to side, her arms outstretched, as if something were buffeting her. The video froze and shrank to a picture in the corner of the screen, while the programme returned to the reporter at the scene.

"Police urge residents to avoid the market area while the investigation proceeds."

"Shit." Elliot shut the TV off and gulped down the last of his coffee.

———•———

The stalls and abandoned produce at the Friday farmers' market and craft fair on Whiteladies Road formed a miniature ghost town. Elliot parked on an adjacent street and walked round. A line of flimsy barrier tape held back a smattering of people. Not many – it was raining, and nothing curbed curiosity like drizzle.

"Do you think we'll see the body?" a young lad said to his friend.

"Nah, the ambulance took it away, but I heard she was already dead when it got here."

Beyond the tape, fifty feet down the road, technicians in white coveralls moved between the stalls as they examined every inch of the scene. Along the cordon, a pair of police officers were moving people on. Elliot retreated before they could reach him.

A couple of television crews had taken up positions to the side of the roped-off area, waiting for police statements or the chance to interview a witness. Elliot spotted the reporter from the local news leaning against the broadcast van taking a quick cigarette break, with his shoulders hunched against the rain. His film crew were probably inside, keeping dry.

"Rough morning?" Elliot asked as he approached, wishing he could remember his damn name.

The man looked up and frowned, but there was a hint of recognition there. A hint was good. "Sorry, do I—"

"Elliot Cross," he said, as if he was mildly insulted that the man didn't remember him.

"Right, right. Jake Aldom." He switched his cigarette to the other hand and offered a handshake. "Remind me. You local or national?"

"National. Heard about what happened but it all seems a bit vague so far."

"Yeah, well, the police are asking everyone to keep quiet till they get a handle on things."

"Has there been any movement?" Elliot joined him with his back to the van.

"Not really, no. I think they're leaning towards the idea that it was some kind of massive hoax."

"But someone died."

"Right, and thirty people all say the same thing about what happened. The video may be a fake, but the eyewitness reports can't all be. I don't know, seems insane."

Elliot turned to face him. "Have you seen the video? The whole thing?"

"Yeah, it's not pretty. I know they can do stuff like that with special effects and all, but not in twenty minutes. The background all matches up; it couldn't have been made in advance." He took a drag on his cigarette.

"Where can I get a copy? Was it released by the police or—"

"Some kid uploaded it online. Police tried to jump on it, but there's a dozen copies going around by now." Jake cast a furtive glance towards the police further down the street, then took a last drag on his cigarette before dropping the butt and stepping on it. "If I send you the link, maybe you could pass me any leads you get?"

"Sounds fair."

He pulled out a Blackberry, and Elliot gave him an email address to send the link to.

"Thanks." Elliot shook his hand once more.

"No worries."

Back in his car, Elliot set up his laptop on the passenger seat. He picked up a Wi-Fi signal from a nearby coffee shop and set the video to download. The progress bar crept along and he drummed his fingers on the steering wheel.

Once it started playing, he found the footage actually began a few minutes before the event – teenagers mucking around. Then a ripple of horrified gasps passed through the vendors and early-bird customers, and the young cameraman swung his phone round to capture the incident. Some unseen force dragged the woman from side to side. If he didn't know she'd died, he'd think she was doing some strange dance.

A tap on the rain-streaked window made him jump. He slapped the screen down on the laptop. Detective Yates glared and tapped again, softer, more deliberate.

Elliot lowered the window. It was still spotting with rain, but not so heavily. "Detective. Can I help you?"

"I must not have made it clear last time. I expect you to stay out of my investigations."

Yates was heading up this case too? Interesting. Elliot put up a placating hand. "Just covering the story like everyone else."

Yates pressed his lips together and huffed. "If that were the case, I'd have no problem, but I know you, Cross. You'll twist it. Like you did with PC Grove. Don't think I've forgotten about that."

Constable Grove had taken his own life, and maybe Elliot should have steered clear, but there were four other people who'd done the same and they'd all previously lived in the same house. A reputedly *haunted* house. He'd just put the pieces together. But he could appreciate how his alternative interpretation of those events looked from Yates's perspective, and that of the late constable's family.

"I'm not looking to twist anything," he said. "Just trying to understand what happened this morning."

"A woman died. That's all you need to know. Maybe, for once, you could show a little respect and not try to exploit that fact for your own ends."

Elliot swallowed, suddenly realising there was no one else around on this side street. No witnesses if the inspector lost his temper. Police were rarely pro-press, but Yates had a particular reputation for limited patience. Where Elliot was concerned that patience wore thin especially fast. Nevertheless, fortune favoured the brave.

"How do you explain her injuries?" Elliot studied the man's face, trying to read him. He wasn't exactly familiar with the moods of DI Richard Yates, but from the muscle twitching on his jaw line and the unsettled look in his eyes Elliot suspected he'd come across something that had left him rattled. He didn't answer the question.

Assuming he'd seen the video, Yates must know there'd been nothing and no one near the woman… just like there'd been no one near Samik Chaudry.

"Have you established a connection between the murder today and the fire in Castle Park?" he asked, watching Yates's expression carefully.

Yates clenched his teeth. "Who said anything about murder? Something you're not telling me, Cross?"

Any sense that the detective might be open to exploring alternative explanations vanished. Elliot could tell he just wasn't ready, and he certainly wasn't ready to hear any theory that Elliot might have.

"I apologise, Detective, I made an assumption."

Yates grunted. "I want you gone in ten minutes."

"No problem."

——•——

It wasn't until Sam sat down at her desk that she spotted Elliot's note on her keyboard. *Following up a lead, back later.*

No mention of where, what or who. It didn't even say what time he'd left. She'd left him sleeping on the couch in the back room and he was still up and working before she arrived. How did he find the energy? She scrunched up the note. If it was stubbornness or zeal, that might be okay, but she knew it was worse. This place, their little publishing empire, was a sanctuary to her – somewhere the monsters in the dark lost their power under the harsh light of understanding – but it was Elliot's prison, the venue to serve out his sentence. He pushed himself to exhaustion because he wanted to suffer.

She set about clearing the email inbox and opening the post like she did every morning. If she didn't keep on top of the daily grind during this, the quiet part of the month, it would quickly overwhelm her come publication time.

Elliot swept into the office like a small, indoor tornado just before lunch. She caught a gust of fresh deodorant, and his smooth cheeks and damp hair proved that at least he'd been home.

"Everything alright? No emergencies?" he asked.

"What? When have we ever had an emergency?"

He unpacked his laptop and switched it on, then crouched behind his desk to hunt for the power cable. "This morning."

Sam rose from her desk. "What do you mean? Where have you been?"

"Home."

"No, before that."

His head appeared over the edge of the desk. "Whiteladies Road."

"And? What's at Whiteladies Road?"

"A murder."

"Elliot, more words, please."

Power cable found and attached to his computer, he clambered up into his desk chair. "We were wrong."

She moved up behind him so she could see what he was doing on the laptop. "About? Come on, talk to me."

He glanced over his shoulder and visibly collected himself. "Sorry. I mean, I think we were wrong to dismiss a link between the deaths. Something is going on. Is *still* going on."

"Something new happened?"

He nodded. "A woman was killed this morning."

"How?"

"Hard to say. It's not the same as either of the others, but there are some similarities. And three unusual deaths, so close together—"

"Is probably no coincidence."

"Right."

He turned back to his laptop and clicked a few times. "There's a video from the one today." He spun the screen, so she could see better, and clicked play.

With no sound from the muted laptop, the woman's silent screams were still deafening. The first few slashes across her body caught mainly clothing, but when one opened her flesh and sprayed blood across the white canvas beside her Sam looked away.

"Turn it off."

Elliot silently closed the laptop.

"It looked like… like…"

"Like claws," he supplied.

"Yeah. But there was nothing there."

He reclined in his chair, fingers laced, elbows on the armrests. "Injuries consistent with mauling, but no animals to inflict them. Burning with no flames. A bullet wound with no bullet." A deep frown creased his forehead. "It could be some kind of possession. Maybe a cursed object changing hands."

She perched on the edge of his desk. "You said it was murder?"

"Gut feeling. Someone or something did this to the victims."

"But we're definitely talking supernatural here?"

He nodded.

"And you're sure there's a link between all three?"

He paused for a moment then shook his head. "I'm not *sure* of anything. But I think at this stage it would be remiss of us not to proceed on that assumption. It's too much of a coincidence. Spontaneous combustion and slash wounds are consistent with demonic activity." He looked up at her. "It's a start at least."

She'd read enough *Weird News* articles to know Elliot was on board with the idea that demons – or something people called demons – really did exist. Having never encountered one personally, she wasn't sure what she believed, but she knew ghosts were real, and demons didn't seem a big leap. "What about the bullet wound though?"

He sat forwards and rubbed a hand across his mouth, elbow on the desk. "That's the one I'm having trouble with."

"Okay. That's okay, I can keep investigating that one while you work on the other two."

The colour had drained from his face and he pressed his lips together.

"What's wrong?" Sam asked.

"If whatever is going on is still happening, there might be another attack. We need to figure this out as fast as possible."

Sam watched him warily as he re-opened his laptop. A nagging feeling that he was going to do something reckless tightened her guts.

"Elliot, you're a reporter, not a detective. The police will have people on this too." She put her hand on his shoulder, but he shrugged it off.

"No. Whatever this is, the police won't be equipped to deal with it. If they even recognise the links."

"Okay, but even if we can figure out some kind of pattern, what exactly are we supposed to do?"

He twisted round to look her in the eye, and she could see the uncertainty in his expression. Uncertainty mixed with a frightening determination.

"I don't know. Whatever we can."

Weird News observed and documented the supernatural and, okay, they investigated and intervened occasionally, like with the fake medium yesterday, but charging off to confront someone or something that might have killed three people was definitely not part of the job as she understood it.

"Elliot, please. I understand you want to make a difference, but this could be dangerous. I know you; you'll keep trying to do more and more until you get hurt or get yourself in trouble, and it's stupid. You don't need to punish yourself."

Elliot's jaw set in a hard line and she edged back, conscious that she'd struck a nerve.

"I'm sorry," she said. "I didn't mean—"

"You have that appointment at the mortuary at two thirty, right?" He turned back to his laptop.

It was hard enough to get him to talk when she approached the subject carefully. Throwing it in his face like that was guaranteed to make him shut her out. Arguing would only make it worse. He'd snap at her and then beat himself up when he regretted it later.

She closed her eyes and took a breath. "Yeah. I'll let you know how it goes."

Frustration radiated off him like heat. She wished she knew how to get through to him.

5

"We need to be one hundred per cent sure about this." Sam climbed out of her car outside the public mortuary at Flax Bourton. "That means we may have to touch him."

Joyce Perry looked at her across the bonnet. "You'll be careful though?"

"Of course."

Secretly she'd hoped Joyce might do it for her, but this was one of those times when she needed to be the adult. She'd met Joyce in town outside the Galleries shopping centre, rather than picking her up from her home. Joyce was still hiding her activity from her husband. The woman's grey-threaded hair had a dull greasiness to it, her skin blotchy and sallow. The loss of her son was taking its toll.

The newly built facility stood across the car park from the historic Coroner's Court. They headed inside. The foyer didn't feel right. It still smelled of new carpet and fresh paint. Everything pristine. Maybe it needed time to settle into its identity, and in the future it would become infused with the subtle odours of death and embalming fluid. The freshly painted walls would take on a mildewed pallor, peppered with yellow-brown flick stains that you hoped were coffee but secretly feared were some unmentionable excretion.

"Mrs Perry?" said a male voice.

Sam jumped, pulse spiking. She rubbed an uncomfortable tingle on the back of her neck.

"Right this way," the attendant said with a sweeping gesture towards a door.

Sam let Joyce go first.

There were dead people on the other side of these walls. Sam had never seen a dead body. She'd seen pictures, sure, but she'd never been up close and personal with a real, freshly corpsified human wrapper. She wasn't entirely sure how she was going to react, and it made her itchy and uncomfortable in her own skin. She hunched her shoulders, skin prickling.

The building presented a false sense of normalcy. She longed for the tatty, mouldy morgue of her imagination, where the deceased would not be so unexpected.

The attendant led Sam and Joyce through a corridor to another door. The room beyond was dark, but a light flicked on as he entered, triggered by the movement, and he held the door for them. To the side of the room, laid out on a stainless-steel trolley and covered with a crisp, white sheet, lay the body of Alex Perry. A simple floral wreath, propped up against the wall by his head, gave a nod towards the humanity of the moment.

Sam moved up closer to Joyce, and the older woman took her hand, squeezing tight like Sam was holding her up. Or holding her together.

Sam squeezed back as the tingle at the base of her skull intensified and jerked hard on a memory she tried to keep buried. She concentrated on keeping her breathing even against the sudden surge of adrenaline. Spirits maintained a link to their earthly remains – Sam knew that first hand – and Alex's presence was heavy in the room. Expectant. She should have anticipated that.

The attendant crossed the room to the corpse and, at a nod from Joyce, turned down the sheet to reveal Alex's pale, blue-lipped face. His eyes were mercifully closed.

"Could we have a moment alone?" Joyce asked.

That was supposed to be Sam's line, and she realised she'd just been standing there doing nothing – except trying to control the urge to bolt for the door – instead of taking charge. The attendant nodded and stepped out. There were no sounds of footsteps in the corridor, so he was likely waiting just outside. They would have to be very careful.

Sam took a moment to acclimatise. The itch creeping over her scalp hadn't progressed further and she tried to calm herself and tune the sensation out by studying the cold contrast of Alex's lifeless face. The utter stillness. Her hands instinctively went to where her camera would be, but she'd left it in the car. Memento mori, photographs of the dead from Victorian times, had always held a chilled fascination for her. Looking at Alex now, she understood why. No matter how they were posed or lit, or made up, the dead never looked alive. They were altogether other.

Joyce stifled a sob and wiped her eyes with her other hand. If Joyce could hold it together, then Sam could do what they'd come here to do.

She released Joyce's hand, stepped up to Alex and took a deep breath. Slowly, she took hold of the sheet and drew it further down, revealing his neck, shoulders, the puckered, bloodless, Y-shaped incision across his chest, and one small hole, an inch to the left of his breast bone.

Sam felt tears threatening but forced herself to focus on the mystery and not the fact that Alex was no longer Alex but a chilled meat bag because an evil thing had ripped through his vulnerable flesh and taken away what had made him Alex.

She took a pair of latex gloves from her pocket and put them on, taking the time to steel herself for the next step. Then, gloved up, she put one hand on his shoulder and the other under his lower back. His arm brushed her sleeve and she tensed. Like an echo, a sensation of fingers on her skin slid up her neck and cheek. She shuddered.

The feeling subsided and she breathed again. Carefully, she rolled Alex's body towards the wall and leaned down to peer underneath. A bullet exiting a body exploded out, ripping tissue as it went, leaving a ragged, mushy wound, far more gruesome than a neat round entry wound like the one over Alex's heart.

But there was nothing. The skin on his back was unbroken, unmarred but for some red blotches like livid bruising. Sam pushed him further onto his side, checking in case the bullet had gone through at more of an angle than the entry wound suggested.

Joyce wasn't mistaken. The bullet must still be inside.

Or it had never existed in the first place, like the animals that ripped up the girl at the market, or the flames that no one could agree were there or not when Samik Chaudry burned to death.

She settled Alex back down. Quietly, carefully. Without saying a word, she replaced the sheet and removed her gloves.

"I was right?" asked Joyce.

"About the exit wound, yes. But I'm not sure that points to a cover-up. I'm not sure what's going on, but we'll find out. I promise."

———•———

Sam returned to the office after dropping Joyce off in town. In the time she'd been gone, Elliot had taped a map of the city to the wall. Three coloured dots marked the three deaths. Sam walked in as he tacked up a set of photos and notes. Alex Perry's image smiled across the room at her and she averted her eyes.

Elliot stood back from the wall, one hand on his hip, shirt sleeves rolled up to the elbow. He rubbed the bridge of his nose with his other hand and then re-settled his glasses.

"Hey," she said.

He flinched, clearly lost in thought, and turned. "How did it go?"

Sam paused before she answered. She couldn't decide whether she wanted her findings to support their theory or not. "There was no exit wound," she said, as she set her bag on her desk. "But, you know, bizarre things happen every day without needing to be magic, right?"

Elliot nodded and turned back to his map. She waited to see if he would share his thoughts on the matter, but he didn't. He was either too engrossed in what he was doing or still upset with her about what she'd said earlier. She decided not to disturb him, and quietly settled at her desk to type up the results of her trip to the mortuary while it was still vivid in her mind.

Reading the visceral descriptions of the boy who burned, even watching the video of the girl at the market, it was still easy to distance herself, but she'd physically touched Alex's lifeless body. Held his mother's hand.

She'd felt the tingle wend its way up her spine and across her scalp in a way she'd hoped never to feel again.

It was too real. She wanted to go home and hide, but she felt an unsettling obligation take shape. She glanced over at Elliot. He slapped a sticky note onto the map beside stills from the market video and started scribbling on another. God, was this how he felt all the time?

She pushed the feeling away. She didn't owe Alex, or Joyce, or anyone, anything. She would do what she could, but this was just work, not her whole life.

As if the universe chose that moment to validate her thoughts, her phone buzzed with a text from Marie: "*You. Me. Tonight. Pizza. Margaritas. Movie marathon. You in?*"She smiled and replied: "*Sounds magic. See you at seven.*"

For the rest of the afternoon she turned her attention to other tasks. There were emails to respond to, stories to review and shortlist for upcoming issues, artwork to commission, contracts to prepare. The more mundane parts helped to ground her thoughts. She'd almost put the memory of Alex's cold, stiff body – and the unnatural tickle on the edge of her consciousness – out of her mind by the end of the day. Almost.

At quarter past five she packed up and cautiously approached Elliot's desk where the wall now resembled a creepy shrine. He sat with a book open on his lap, glasses sliding down his nose.

"Elliot?"

He looked up with a start.

"I'm going home now. I know you probably won't listen to me, but I think you should do the same. I think you should take the weekend off and come back to it fresh on Monday."

Returning his attention to the book he nodded. "I'll consider it."

She narrowed her eyes. "Will you though?"

He glanced up briefly and sighed. "You really don't need to worry about me."

"Too late. I don't like seeing you like this."

"Noted," he said through gritted teeth. "You can go. I'll see you on Monday."

"Elliot, please—"

He snapped the book shut. She jumped and stepped back.

"Do you not get it? It's not about me," he said. "Lives could be in danger. I need to focus on this."

"I know, but—"

"Go home," he snapped. "Go chill out and watch TV, buy shoes or whatever other pointless shit it is you do on the weekend. Do whatever the hell you want, just don't keep telling me to stop, because I *can't* do that."

For a second she stared at him, speechless, then she gathered herself. "I know you don't mean that."

"Go on, go." He turned his back on her and stared at his stickered map.

She knew he was pushing her away again, trying to make her hate him so she'd give up. And right at that moment it was working. She walked to the door.

"Well, I won't be stopping by tonight to peel your face off your keyboard again," she shot back as she left. As she slammed the front door behind her, she squeezed her eyes shut, and a few frustrated tears leaked out.

6

Elliot worked on into the evening, getting nowhere as the pictures and notes on his map began to blur together, until he realised Sam was probably right. He needed sleep. He went home and then returned to the office mid-morning Saturday and tried to view the puzzle with fresh eyes. Now, early on Sunday, he had an idea where they needed to go next.

He parked on the double yellow lines outside Sam's building. A rust-speckled white van and a couple of geriatric Ford Escorts had done the same, either because they knew no one would be issuing tickets today, or because they didn't give a shit.

A couple of boys with mountain bikes and cans of Red Bull loitered across the road.

"Hey, nice car," one of them called as Elliot climbed out.

"Touch it and die," he said, fixing them with a stare as he locked the BMW. They laughed.

Bedminster wasn't the roughest part of Bristol, but it was close. Towards one end of the road some new residential buildings under construction hinted that redevelopment might be imminent, but most of the quiet street was run-down to the point of dereliction. Sam's apartment was in one of the flat-roofed, pebble-dashed, eighties-built blocks that filled the spaces between older brick terraces. Elliot jogged up the front steps to the recessed porch. A crack spider-webbed the glass in the door to the dingy foyer. Only the reinforcing wire mesh held it together. Patches of coloured paint remained on the grubby white walls where someone had tried to clean off some graffiti.

Maybe he could take another look at the budget and see if he could re-jig some expenses so he could give her a pay rise. Even if it wasn't enough for a *better* flat, maybe she could at least move somewhere safer. No, that was unfair. She'd never complained of feeling unsafe. It was just a matter of appearance. And contrast.

He pressed the buzzer for flat five. After a couple of minutes he held it down a second time and rocked on his heels while he waited for an answer.

"Hello?" Sam said drowsily through the intercom.

"It's me. You ready?"

"Elliot? Ready for what?"

"I left you a message."

"What message? Oh, this is stupid. Come in." The door clicked and buzzed green. Elliot entered and took the stairs up to the second floor, two at a time. Sam opened the door before he could knock.

"Elliot, it's Sunday. What are you doing here?" She held the sides of a cream-coloured dressing gown closed across her chest, and her hair was still tangled from bed.

It suddenly occurred to him that maybe she'd ignored his calls on purpose yesterday, after the way he'd acted on Friday. He knew he should lead with an apology, but he didn't want to pick the scab off the wound in case he was wrong. "You didn't get my message?"

Her eyes narrowed and she shook her head.

"Alright, but I really do need your help this morning. I've got a lead – well, sort of. A place to start, and your assistance would be—"

Sam held up her hand. "Fine. Give me ten minutes to wake up and get dressed, okay?" The glare she gave him warned him not to argue.

"Sure. Shall I wait in the car?"

"You can come in if you promise not to tell me to hurry up."

She disappeared through the door to her bedroom, off to the right. Elliot closed the front door. To his left, an arch opened into a small but airy living room, and directly in front of him a beaded curtain, tied to the sides, framed the doorway to the kitchen. A pair of wine glasses and two plates stood among the dirty pots and pans on the counter from the night before. Otherwise it was cluttered but clean.

"Make yourself useful and make me some coffee," Sam called through the bedroom door.

He ducked past the curtain beads and located her kettle.

"So, I was thinking," he called back. "Burning and mauling are one thing, but if there was a gun, someone had to pull the trigger, right?"

"Can't hear you!" she shouted.

While he waited, he hunted through her cupboards until he found two insulated mugs. He filled them with instant coffee, then leaned on the counter.

Sam crossed to the bathroom and the sound of spraying deodorant and a toothbrush reached his ears. A few minutes later she emerged in jeans and a T-shirt, tugging a brush through her hair, and joined him in the kitchen.

"Okay, go on."

"I think we're looking for some kind of street performer."

"What, like a juggler?" she asked, her voice laden with scepticism. "Although an evil juggler is a scary thought."

He chuckled. "Hear me out. What if someone fired the gun at College Green and that same person trailed accelerant across Castle Park and lit it? Ignoring the fact that no one could *see* these things, it's still logical to assume someone was there."

"Okay. Like an actual person, but using magic or telekinesis or something?"

"Exactly. It got me thinking, what if they *have* to be there? So I checked the video again." From the inside pocket of his coat he pulled out a printed still from the video – a grainy, indistinct section of the background which showed a black-clad figure lurking beside one of the market stalls. "This guy watches the whole thing and doesn't react at any point. He doesn't seem surprised, he doesn't try to help or run away, nothing."

Sam took the photo from his hand. "You think he caused it somehow?"

"Maybe. If nothing else, he must know something."

"So, why do you think he's a street performer?"

Elliot pointed to the figure in the picture, specifically the deep areas of shadow around his eyes and mouth. "Look at his face. Even at this resolution that has to be makeup. Anyway, I started thinking how I might approach this if I were investigating a human serial killer. The date of the first murder could indicate when he arrived in the area. It might not sound like much, but that festival at Ashton Court this weekend started setting up right around the time Alex Perry was killed."

Sam lifted her eyes from the picture, lips pursed. "*This* is why you got me up at seven thirty on a Sunday?"

"Uh, well…"

"I'm kidding," she said, grinning. "Just let me get my camera."

She nipped through to the living room. Elliot took his glasses off and rubbed his eyes.

Once Sam had fetched her things, they headed down and climbed into the black BMW.

"Sorry to be a pain," Sam said as she buckled up, "but how are we getting into a music festival at the last minute?"

Elliot glanced over from the driver's seat. "Press passes. I know a guy who can get us in. Should be no problem."

"How come we never get free festival tickets when there isn't an emergency?"

Elliot suppressed a smile and concentrated on pulling out onto the road.

———•———

They took the suspension bridge across the gorge. The river formed a natural barrier to the city's urban sprawl, and on this side the very exclusive community of Leigh Woods nestled on the cliff top, between undisturbed forest to the north and the expansive acreage of the Ashton Court country estate to the south.

It had rained again yesterday but this morning the clouds were breaking up, and they looked set for a bright, warm June day. Elliot followed the yellow AA car park signs through one of the stone gatehouses. Some areas of the estate had been designated as campsites, now a mosaic of multi-coloured canvas. They parked up and, with a quick radio check at the press entrance, security waved them through with passes and a programme.

Sam took her camera from the case over her shoulder. Elliot watched the way she gripped it in both hands, held up slightly. It was something he'd seen her do before, when she was nervous.

"Good plan," he said. "Keep an eye out for anyone in dark clothes. Not that I expect him to be here, but you never know."

They emerged into an area bounded by stalls and catering trucks. The scent of fresh fried doughnuts wafted on the air. Maybe after they'd investigated they could stop for breakfast.

They continued deeper, past tented bars where staff were restocking with kegs and bottles after being hit hard the night before. Trampled cans, paper cups and polystyrene burger boxes carpeted the muddy grass in front of a steel-framed music stage with enormous speakers strung up on either side.

"Where do we start?" Sam asked, turning in a circle.

Elliot consulted their map. The festival seemed roughly split into three areas – this main stage, a huge undercover tent stage, and a more loosely defined area of smaller stages and tents labelled *Cabaret*. He showed Sam, and then set off towards a blue-and-white striped big-top tent. As they walked down an avenue lined with more traders, food vans and alcohol vendors, the distance to the cabaret area seemed to stretch out in front of them. His skin itched with nerves.

"Elliot?"

"Hmm?"

"What do we do if we find something?"

He took a deep breath. He didn't expect the hooded man to be here waiting for him, but if someone here knew who he was, or where to find him… He glanced across at Sam. "Honestly, I have no idea."

The festival goers had churned the field in front of the big top to slick mud over the last few damp days. The sticky ground sucked at their shoes. A few early risers practised juggling outside the main tent. Others browsed the stalls still setting out their wares. A pair of costumed, stilted acrobats strode past, followed by a young woman handing out flyers for a circus somewhere else in the city next week. Sam clicked off a couple of photos.

Elliot scanned the perimeter of the field, hoping for – or maybe dreading – a glimpse of the mystery hooded figure.

A shrill cry to their left made them both jump. A dance troupe burst into an impromptu routine, the leader tapping a drum to keep time.

Sam let out a slow breath, shoulders dropping from a tense hunch.

"Come on," Elliot said. "There's no point standing here, we should start asking questions."

By the big top, the juggling workshop broke up and the participants dispersed. Elliot strode towards the two instructors packing up their equipment. One young woman walking away from the practice ground gave him a friendly smile as she passed.

He approached the lads. "Hello, do you have a minute?"

"Sure, next workshop starts on the hour."

"I'm not here for the workshop. Elliot Cross. I'm a journalist."

"Oh yeah?" The young man glanced over Elliot's shoulder at Sam with her camera, eyes lighting up. "You with a magazine or something?"

"Yes, of a kind. Can I ask, have you seen any performers in dark clothes, hood, black-and-white makeup, maybe hanging around on and off? Maybe arrived here with the festival?"

He shook his head slowly. "Not that I've seen, mate, sorry. What's this guy's thing?"

Sam nudged his elbow. "Elliot?"

"One second, Sam. I'm not sure exactly. Have you or anyone else noticed anything unusual happening around here?"

"Like what?"

"Could be anything. People acting strangely, or strange sounds. Hot or cold spots."

The young man chuckled. "Hard to say. Lots of people acting strange around here." He held his fingers to his lips as if holding a joint and pretended to take a drag.

"Elliot!" Sam tugged on his arm and he turned.

"What?"

"Look." She pointed across the field. The young woman who'd passed them moments before stood shaking her fist. No, not shaking, *hammering*, but there was nothing but open space around her. She felt her way around in a square and came back to where she started, describing an invisible box surrounding her.

"Do you cover mime in your workshop?" Elliot asked, without taking his eyes off the girl.

The circus lads moved up beside him. "Not really, no."

Around her waist her long skirt began to lift, drifting out as if supported by water that was gradually rising around her. There was nothing beneath her but grass. She stared down aghast, eyes wide, and her mouth opened in a cry that didn't reach beyond the box. Elliot glanced at Sam and they both broke into a run.

Within moments the young woman was standing on her toes with her neck tipped back. She scrabbled against the walls of her prison. Her feet lifted off the ground, and any hope Elliot had that this was just some performance piece shattered. The girl waved her arms frantically, trying to hold herself up against rising water that couldn't possibly be there. Her eyes briefly met Elliot's with a silent plea for help.

Abruptly, her ascent ceased, and her head tilted back further. She pressed her palms up and pounded a fist against the invisible ceiling.

Elliot reached the tank, put his hand out and encountered a hard surface. His eyes were telling him there was nothing there, but he could *feel* it.

As Sam joined him beside the invisible water tank, its captive began to drift down again. Her hair fanned out from her face, floating, wraith-like.

"She's going to drown! We have to help her!" Sam cried, feeling her way around the box.

Elliot joined her, tracing the edges of what could only be described as solid air, feeling for any inconsistency – a hatch, a lid – but it was smooth, cold like glass, impenetrable.

A few people, including the two lads from the circus workshop, stood watching. Did they still think it was all a show, and that he and Sam were in on it?

The woman's struggles grew more panicked. Elliot drew back and kicked the box as hard as he could, the impact shuddering up his leg like he'd kicked a concrete wall. Sam set her back to the side and heaved, trying to tip the tank over, feet sliding in the mud, but it behaved like it really contained the full, immovable weight of gallons of water. He kicked again. If he could crack the glass the pressure might do the rest.

The girl jerked and her eyes locked onto Elliot's. She put one hand out towards him.

"No!"

Her eyes unfocused and she hung in the air, drifting. It looked like he should be able to reach out and touch her – the tank and the water were completely invisible – but she was dying regardless.

"Someone call an ambulance, now!" he cried, pounding the glass with his fist. "She can still be resuscitated!"

No one moved. How could they all still believe this was some clever special effect?

A sudden outward rush of thick air knocked him, and the surrounding people, to their knees. The young woman collapsed to the ground like a rag doll.

Elliot crawled to her side, across grass no muddier than before. He flipped her onto her back and checked her breathing. "Who knows CPR?"

The two lads from the circus workshop stepped forwards. "Is she alright?"

"No, she's not breathing!" He shifted out of their way. Out of the corner of his eye he saw Sam making the call to the emergency services.

One of the two lads tilted the girl's head back and tried to blow into her lungs, but he came up gasping. "It's like her airway is blocked."

"Treat her like she drowned," Elliot said. "You have to drain the water from her lungs."

"But... she's dry."

"Do it anyway!"

The lad turned her over and began slapping her back.

"What exactly just happened?" his companion asked.

Elliot pushed himself to his feet and stepped back, giving them space to try to save the girl's life. He raked a hand through his hair. "I don't know."

The little crowd had grown, those who had been knocked down clambering back to their feet. Elliot glanced from person to person, searching each face for black-and-white makeup. The man had to be here somewhere. He scanned the spaces between the stalls. Somewhere close enough to see, but where he wouldn't be seen. The crowd shifted, and by the side of the big top he spotted a pale face under a dark hood. He took a few steps forwards and the man bolted.

"Hey, stop right there!" he cried, launching into a sprint.

Across the open space he gained a little ground, but the man in black angled down the route to the main stage and tore through the sparse crowds without touching a single person. Elliot lost speed as he clipped shoulders and dodged round people. He pushed himself harder, but suddenly the man he was chasing ducked sideways into a marquee – a bar. As Elliot dove through the fabric flap, he collided with a man wheeling two beer kegs on a sack truck.

"Hey, watch it!"

"Sorry!"

On the far side of the tent another flap led out. He skirted around the man with the kegs and darted out into a small compound where several delivery trucks were parked. By the time he squeezed between them to the service road behind, there was no sign of the man.

"Shit!"

Chest still heaving from the run he ducked back into the bar and nearly bumped into Sam.

"I lost him," he said. "Did she make it?"

Sam glanced over her shoulder. "I don't know. I was following you."

They walked silently back to the scene of the attack. That word applied, regardless of what had happened. He was sure of that.

Security personnel turned up and cordoned off the area. The two circus lads continued to pump the woman's chest and breathe for her, but their efforts flagged along with their hopes. Admirably they kept it up until the ambulance crew arrived and took over. Elliot stood with Sam while the paramedics tried adrenaline and other drugs, to no avail.

Police followed shortly after the ambulance. He and Sam both gave statements, describing as much as they could without sounding too much like suspicious crazy people. Elliot suspected the other eyewitnesses were doing the same, and no one was held for further questioning.

After, they walked to the car in silence.

Sam clicked her seat belt in and faced him. "I'm sorry."

"There was nothing more you could have done."

"No, I mean I'm sorry I didn't take it seriously before. You were right; if we have a chance to stop this, we have to try everything." She wiped her eyes with her sleeve. "Sorry, I don't know why I'm—"

"It's alright." He wished there was something he could do to make her feel better. But he couldn't exactly offer her a hug; he was her boss. "You were right too. I was so drained I couldn't think straight."

Sam rubbed her cheeks again and sat back in her seat. She clutched her camera in her lap like a security blanket, hands shaking as the adrenaline drained away.

Elliot cleared his throat. "I think we both need some time out after what just happened. These last three attacks have all happened two days apart. If we're lucky that pattern will continue and there won't be another attack tomorrow."

Sam didn't say anything.

"Let's get some rest, and tomorrow we'll figure it out. Yeah?"

She nodded, but brought her thumb to her teeth and worried at her nail. Elliot glanced at her, then started the car. She'd be alright, once she was home with her TV and a mug of coffee, safe in the world of the mundane.

NO FUTURE

"Do you want a cup of tea?" Elliot's mum asked.
"Sure, alright." He slumped down on the wide leather
sofa, tilted his head back and closed his eyes.

James's funeral had been brutal. Perhaps it was the military
honours, or the way his brother's army friends had stood up and
described a man that Elliot realised he barely knew. Or maybe it
was the creeping feeling that everyone was staring at him. They
weren't, but maybe they should have been. After all, he was the
last one to see James alive.

A ceramic clink as his mother set a mug on a slate coaster on
the coffee table pulled him back to the present. At least it was
over.

"There you go, love."

"Thanks."

His dad emerged, having shed his suit in favour of casual
slacks and slippers, and took up his favourite spot under the
reading lamp with his feet up. He shook out a paper and laid it
across his lap. *The Telegraph*. His parents did deign to buy *The
Tribute*, if and when Elliot pointed out one of his articles, but

they were broadsheet traditionalists and *The Trib* was too tabloid for them now.

For once, Elliot was grateful, because it meant they weren't tracking how little page space he'd had recently. The last thing he needed was a lecture in self-promotion from his dad. Self-promotion was not his problem. He'd promoted every which way until it turned him into someone he didn't like.

"Are you staying the night?" his mum asked, still bustling round the room. She'd been doing that a lot, as if staying still would force her to face the reality of James's death.

"No, if it's alright I'm going to head home tonight."

She perched on the sofa next to him, clearly expecting further explanation. He wasn't really ready to tell them his plans, but they'd find out soon enough anyway.

"Actually, I'm going to look at a new flat tomorrow."

His dad perked up, drawn out from behind the paper by one of his top ten favourite topics – climbing the housing ladder. "Oh?"

"Hmm." Elliot picked up his mug.

"Where are you looking?"

He sipped the tea, once, twice, before he took the plunge. "Bristol."

As the pregnant pause stretched out, his parents' eyes burrowed into the side of his head until the pressure was too much. "I'm making a fresh start," he said. "As soon as I get everything arranged. I need to… I'm going to spend some time on a project of my own for a while."

The silence held.

His mum broke it first. "Well, that's—"

"For heaven's sake, why?" His father tossed the folded newspaper onto the coffee table where it knocked the TV remote spinning to the floor.

Elliot cringed. "It's just something I need to do."

"What about the paper?" his father asked.

"I've handed in my notice."

His father gave him a thin-lipped look of appalled disappointment.

Mum put a hand on his arm. "Elliot, love, are you sure now is the right time to be making a decision like this?"

"Now is exactly the time."

Dad tutted and Mum shot a glare at him. "I know you feel somewhat responsible," she said, "but you really shouldn't. What happened wasn't your fault."

Elliot said nothing. They didn't get it and he'd never make them understand. His brother was dead because Elliot was physically incapable of thinking of anyone but himself, and he didn't want to be that person anymore. A clean break from the London press scene, and the egotistical, elitist creatures it bred, was necessary if he ever hoped to make amends.

"You could have at least talked to us first," his mum said. She was, he could tell, paraphrasing thoughts his dad was itching to express in more colourful language.

"I'm sorry, but it's my decision to make. You've barely supported me in the past; you don't get a say in this."

"Barely?!" His father growled. "What about your tuition, the deposit on your flat?"

"I'm not talking about money," Elliot muttered. "What's fifty, sixty grand to you anyway? All you ever cared about was forcing James into politics. You've never given a shit about what I did with my life." Mum tried to grasp and still his hands, but he pulled away. He slid to the far end of the sofa. "But I suppose that's changed now, hasn't it?"

They both drew in a sharp gasp at that one. He took his glasses off and rubbed a hand over his face.

"I'm sorry, it's been a difficult day."

"Do you think running away is going to make it easier?" his dad asked.

Elliot frowned, put his glasses back on. "Who said anything about running? I'm not running away." He stood. "If anything, I'm owning up to what I did. Running would be pretending everything was fine."

"Don't be ridiculous," his dad grumbled. "What is this if not running away? Damned if I know why though."

Elliot pasted on a bitter smile. "It's not so complicated. I've just decided I value my soul more than the next promotion."

He started for the door.

"Don't expect any help from us!" Dad called after him.

"Don't worry, I wasn't banking on it."

He let himself out into the cold night air. It didn't matter what they thought. There was only one truth that mattered – if he didn't try to make a difference, what was the point? Of anything?

7

The early morning sun formed long, weak shadows from the trees that lined the avenues and paths across The Downs.

Elliot's mind was too full. Running was simple.

The heavy dew soaked into his trainers, but each pace carried away a little stress and tension.

The Downs rose out of the noisy urban landscape like an island of simplicity. Still. Quiet. It was one of the reasons he'd chosen his flat in nearby Stoke Bishop when he moved to Bristol. The park spoke to a part of himself he actually liked.

He picked a route he used often, which circled a little under a square mile of parkland. The cool air chilled the sweat on his back and temples but his skin radiated heat. The stillness of the place and the rhythm of his pace quietened his thoughts.

The illusion, or spell, or whatever it was, had been perfect and impenetrable. He'd never felt more helpless than as he'd watched that girl drown in mid-air, six inches in front of him. No, that was a lie. At least he'd *tried* to save her. Not like with James.

He quickened his pace as thoughts of his brother crowded in, along with old questions about himself that he never had any answers to. Who was he, that he'd been so cold? Was that still who he was? He tried to push the shameful memories back down and think about something else.

Sam had surprised him yesterday. Though she'd gripped her camera like a shield, she'd been right there alongside him the whole time. She'd even apologised for not taking him seriously. A fresh stab of guilt – he should have been the one apologising.

It was hard to stomach when she said she worried about him. If he hadn't cared so much about himself back in London, James would still be alive. Every time she tried to tell him to go easy on himself, the temptation to accept the way out she offered scared him. It made him feel like he hadn't changed, not really. That he was fooling himself.

He was trying to do something positive with *Weird News*. In three and a half years he'd exposed a lot of con men, provided wondrous proof of amazing paranormal phenomena and shone a light into the darker places of the supernatural world.

But had he ever made a *real* difference?

He slowed on the path, breathing hard, and tried to think of one occasion, just one, where his actions had made a significant difference in a genuine, supernatural case. He came up blank.

He set off again at a fast run. Whatever was ultimately behind these deaths was mocking him, or that's how it felt. The man he'd chased from the scene was key. The dark clothes and black-and-white makeup, like a mime artist, had to be relevant given the invisible causes of the deaths. But was he the cause, or was he connected in some other way? Something acting through him, perhaps? Was he human, or something else?

Slash wounds and the burning pointed towards possession or some kind of demonic influence. Maybe even the drowning too. He didn't know enough to say how, or what else it could be, but he had a contact list full of experts who might. Some were even based in Bristol, and all were only a phone call away.

He sucked in ragged breaths, pulse thumping. The past few days he'd been beating himself up for not figuring out what was going on, as if it were some personal challenge. He turned onto a tarmac path and his feet pounded the pavement, sending hard jolts up his shins. He clenched his fists. He should have been kicking himself for not recognising that he needed help. His damn pride held him back, *again*.

Sweat beaded on his forehead and neck, his grey T-shirt clung to his body. He pressed on, pushing himself harder in the final stretch until his legs turned to lead. Panting, he collapsed onto a park bench and sat forwards with his elbows on his knees. He checked his time – three and a bit miles in half an hour – enough for today.

And enough self-pity. There was an explanation. All he needed to do was talk to the right people.

———

He arrived at the office at around half eight, hair still wet from his shower. As he turned his car into the alley at the rear of the terrace, he passed a man standing on the corner smoking a cigarette. Detective Yates.

Elliot cursed inwardly. He didn't like the fact that Yates had once again managed to catch him alone in a place where they wouldn't be observed. Maybe that legendary short patience had finally worn through.

He took a steadying breath as he parked up behind the office and exited the car. Yates approached along the alley.

"Detective," Elliot said, holding up a hand in greeting.

"You certainly know how to find trouble."

Elliot shut his car door and locked the BMW with a beep. "Which particular trouble would you like to discuss today?" He leaned against the side of the car while he waited for Yates to catch up.

"A death. Yesterday afternoon."

Elliot weighed up his options. Yates clearly already knew he'd been at the festival, which wasn't a surprise since he'd given a statement. Evading his questions would simply irritate him. "The woman who passed away at Ashton Court yesterday? Yes, I was there. I saw her collapse."

Yates nodded as if he'd been expecting more resistance. "I have some questions."

Elliot fingered his door keys in his pocket. He couldn't invite Yates in; the information spread across the wall behind his desk would pose more questions than it answered. Ones that Yates might feel compelled to ask in the more official setting of a police interrogation room. He gestured down the alley and started walking. Yates fell into step beside him.

"How can I help?" Elliot asked.

"First, I want to know what you were doing there. You seem to have a habit of showing up where bad things happen."

"I'm a reporter. Bad things make for good stories."

Yates sucked his teeth. "This time you showed up *before* it happened. Which I find very interesting."

Elliot watched him cautiously. The man was a professional, good at his job. No doubt he could spot a liar. "I was investigating something. I had questions for some of the performers there."

"What questions?"

"I wanted to know if they knew someone. It's not really important. I was on the wrong track."

"And you know that how?"

"Because they couldn't help me." He leaned against the wall of the house at the end of the alley, arms folded. "Look, I went to the event to research a story I'm working on. While I was there a woman sadly died. She collapsed and two men tried to resuscitate her."

Yates rubbed a hand over his jaw. "Collapsed?"

"Yes, collapsed."

The detective paced a few steps away then turned back. "Can you explain to me why, against all probability, your statement is the only one that made any sense?"

Elliot tensed. "How do you mean?"

"I mean the officers took statements from thirty people and they're all different." He held both hands out to the side. "Rambled nonsense about a performance gone wrong, some saying she *drowned*, others that she was attacked. One man claims she levitated two feet off the ground. Only yours and your friend's corroborate each other; according to you, the woman collapsed, you and two others tried to help, and that's it."

Elliot swallowed. "What can I say? Some people don't deal well with death."

Yates fixed him with a withering stare then stepped in closer. "What do you say to reports that you were spotted fleeing the scene?"

Elliot shifted away from him. "I didn't flee anything. I was there when the ambulance arrived and took her away. I gave a statement and then, like everyone else, went home."

The detective moved round to block Elliot from moving further towards the mouth of the alley. "You were snooping around at Whiteladies market. And Castle Park."

"Like I said, I'm a reporter." He wasn't sure what to say that wouldn't make Yates more suspicious. He tilted his head to one side. "You're working those cases too. What do you make of them?"

Yates ground his teeth. "I'm not here to answer *your* questions. Did you know she was going to die?"

"Did I...? No, of course not."

"But you knew something was going to happen there?"

The photograph from the market video still nestled in his inner coat pocket and, as he met Yates's stare, he toyed with the idea of showing it to him, but he just didn't trust the man to hear him out. If Yates really suspected the truth – and was at all ready to accept it – he'd be asking more pertinent questions.

"I'm sorry to disappoint you, Detective. I'm afraid it was just an unfortunate coincidence."

Yates held his gaze for a long few seconds and then leaned forwards, looking down at Elliot, who pressed his shoulder blades into the wall.

"I advise you to keep your nose clean, Cross. If I hear you're involved with anything suspicious, you'll be my first stop for answers. Understand?"

"Always happy to help." Elliot's words came out slightly more sarcastic than he intended.

Yates let out a frustrated growl and backed off. He started walking away. "You're a sad excuse for a human being, Cross."

"Uh huh." Elliot waited until Yates disappeared round the mouth of the alley and then sagged against the wall. He ran his hands through his hair, blew out a long breath and pushed off to walk up the alley.

He let himself in through the back door and walked through to the front office. When he saw Sam at her desk, he checked his watch.

"Very funny," she muttered, shoving a pile of post into her in-tray. "I know you said to come in late, but I just couldn't sit around at home doing nothing. I've cleared up everything urgent, so we should be able to work on the case with no distractions."

His lips twitched up into a smile, and the nauseating adrenaline churn in his gut from Yates's interrogation eased.

"Coffee?" she asked, gesturing with her mug.

"No, grab your stuff together. There's someone we need to see."

——•——

Sam suggested they walk the three-quarters of a mile from the office to the university. It was a nice day and there didn't seem any point in driving. They talked on the way, about the incident the day before and the man they were visiting. Sam had never met Geoff, but they'd exchanged a few emails and phone calls with him. He was... weird. But then, so were most of the people they worked with.

"He seems to get traded from department to department," Elliot said. "Last year it was English Literature, before that Ethnography."

"What does he actually study?"

"Demons, werewolves, vampires, that sort of thing. Classic myths and legends."

They picked up a footpath which led between the campus buildings and through a gap in a low wall signposted: Department of Humanities – Faculty Offices.

"Do you know if he actually, you know, *believes*?" Sam asked, wondering how much they should say. "I mean, are we asking him for real advice or hypothetical advice?"

The footpath cut through manicured lawn dotted with a few mature but slender trees, up to a door in a grand building with smooth stone walls and columns.

"I'm not entirely sure," Elliot said. "My impression has always been that he considers his subject real; it's everything else he struggles with. We'll play it by ear. Just... be nice to him. I don't think he has a lot of friends." He pressed the intercom button for office 1.4: Prof. Geoffrey Dorridge.

They waited. As Elliot reached out to press the button again, a shaky voice responded from the speaker. "Hello?"

"Geoff, it's Elliot Cross. Wondered if you could spare some time to assist us with something."

"You can't have my office."

Elliot glanced at Sam and raised an eyebrow. She covered her mouth, suppressing a snicker.

"Geoff, it's Elliot. From *Weird News*."

"Oh, right, right." The intercom buzzed and the door clicked open.

Elliot held it for Sam. "After you."

The layout inside the building still hinted that it had once been a house, or something similar, rather than a purpose-built facility. A staircase with a decorative balustrade rose from the hall, overlooked by gilt-framed oil portraits of former professors. A strip of thick, red carpet ran up the centre, held in place by brass batons, and rugs of the same carpet covered the varnished floorboards like stepping stones.

Geoff's office occupied one ground-floor corner. Papers drunkenly cluttered the tiny pinboard on the wall beside his door. Elliot knocked.

"Who is it?"

"It's Elliot. You just let me in."

There was the metal scrape of a chain lock being pulled back, then Geoff opened the door a crack and peered out. "Ah yes, right, right." He pulled the door wider. "Come in. Come in."

Inside the office the blinds were drawn, and the light from a desk lamp mingled with the blue glow from an old CRT monitor to illuminate amorphous mounds of clutter.

Elliot manoeuvred his way to the nearest window and raised the blind. As the daylight flooded in, Sam took in the state of the place; the large office was full, top to bottom, side to side, with stuff. A table – possibly a desk, but it was impossible to tell – filled most of the centre of the room and groaned under the weight of archive boxes and loose stacks of paper. Around the edges jumbled books clung resolutely to bowing shelves. She feared to touch anything in case it was load bearing.

"It's not healthy to sit in the dark like this," Elliot said. "You should get some fresh air once in a while."

Sam snorted; she'd lost count of how many times she'd said the exact same thing to him. He shot her a glare, but there was a touch of amusement in his eyes.

Professor Dorridge shuffled over to his desk by the far wall and sat in his creaking wooden office chair. The cushion exhaled a puff of dust into the sunlight.

"I know, my boy. Sometimes I just don't realise the time. So much to do!"

He wore a knitted V-neck sweater over beige trousers. Sam tried to guess his age; from the generous amount of grey in his scruffy beard and what remained of his hair, she'd have said at least sixty-five, but his face was round, even a little chubby, which made him look younger.

"I'd have thought you'd be taking it easy after exam season," she said. "The students don't start back until the end of September, right?"

Geoff spun round in his chair, eyes wide. "Students? Where?"

Elliot chuckled. "Don't worry, you're safe for now. Geoff, this is Sam, she works with me."

"Ah, right. Charming to meet you, my dear."

Elliot shifted a stack of papers off a second chair and handed them to Sam. She looked for a space on the swamped table in the middle of the room but there was too much risk of an avalanche. She settled for balancing them on top of a stack of archive boxes marked "Lycanthrope Sightings".

"Right, right. So, what was it you wanted, my boy?"

Elliot drew the chair up next to Geoff's desk. "Have you watched the news recently?"

"News? Oh no, never anything interesting there."

Elliot nodded patiently. "Well then, you probably won't have heard, but there have been several deaths in the city over the last week."

"Oh gosh. Here in Bristol?"

"Indeed. I need you to help me figure out how to stop it."

"Stop what?"

Elliot drew the photograph of the hooded figure from his coat pocket and set it in front of the professor. Geoff knuckled his eyes, then picked up and donned a pair of wire-rimmed reading glasses. He considered the photo, pushing his lower lip out.

"We're not sure yet whether this man is actively causing the deaths," Elliot said, "but I chased him from the scene of the last attack, so I'm definitely considering it."

Sam leaned on the table behind him and triggered a landslide of papers. "You can't see very well in that picture," she said, "but he looked like a regular guy to me, just wearing black clothes and makeup like a mime artist."

"Right." Elliot twisted round to look at her over his shoulder. "And did you see his hands?"

"No, I didn't get close enough."

"White gloves, again, like a mime artist." He turned back to Geoff. "The victims all died from seemingly invisible causes."

Geoff returned the photo. "And you suspect a supernatural element?"

"If you're willing to believe we saw a girl drown in an invisible tank of invisible water," Sam said, "then yeah, this gets a big tick in the not normal column."

"I see."

She wondered what was going through the professor's mind. Anyone sane should probably think she and Elliot were crazy, but Geoff seemed to be taking it all in his stride.

Elliot inched forwards. "So, what could it be?"

"Couldn't say, my boy. I've never heard of this mime character before."

Elliot's shoulders sagged. "Is there anything you can tell me? My first thought was that this could be demon related, but what *else* could it be? Is there such a thing as a magic user? Could a normal person be capable of this sort of influence?"

"Haven't a clue. Magic isn't really my area." Professor Dorridge scratched his beard. "But you may be right. Many demons supposedly have powers of telekinesis, mind control, and can affect the physical world. Perhaps this is a case of possession."

Even though Sam dealt with stories, even evidence, of the supernatural every day, it still felt surreal to be having such a matter-of-fact conversation with someone on the subject.

"Do you think that's the most likely explanation?" she asked. Maybe it was because her direct experience was limited to human spirits, but part of her was still struggling with the idea of demons.

"Could be, could be. Tell me what else you know."

"Well," Elliot began, "as far as we can tell, there's no connection between the victims – they didn't know each other and they were different genders and ethnicities. The attacks have mostly taken place once every two days. The last was yesterday."

Geoff nodded. "I see. What about a spatial pattern? Sometimes ritual killings are carried out in a symbolic alignment, to channel energy."

Elliot sat back in his seat, frowning in thought.

"The first was near the university," Sam said. "Then Castle Park. The farmers' market in Whiteladies Road; and then yesterday at—"

"Of course!" Elliot thumped his fist on the desk, making Sam jump. "I can't believe I didn't see it."

"What?" she asked.

"The cardinal points," Geoff supplied.

Elliot nodded emphatically. "Exactly! If the first attack at College Green is taken as a centre point," he pointed a finger on the desk, "then the subsequent attacks proceed anti-clockwise, east, then north, then west." He indicated the directions by pointing to the relative positions with his other hand.

"You think the next attack will happen somewhere to the south?" Sam asked.

"Possibly. Maybe. Geoff?"

"The cardinal points have many meanings in the occult world," the professor said, rubbing his palms on his thighs. "I would say a pattern of this sort is very likely to be significant."

The elation in Elliot's eyes faded and he sagged. "Of course, that still leaves us with a quarter of the city to search."

"Perhaps..." Geoff said. "You mentioned a park?"

"Castle Park," Sam said.

"Did all of the attacks take place outside?"

Elliot nodded. "Yes."

"Public spaces? Where you might find a lot of people?"

"What are you thinking?"

"Well, you see, it could be a matter of passing un-remarked, blending in and whatnot, but I think it more likely this entity is choosing hunting grounds which will provide a selection of victims. Yes, yes..."

Elliot's head snapped up. "You don't think they're just random?"

"Oh no. I highly doubt that. No, no, if this is a demon you face, they are usually highly selective. Chaos energies and all that." He waved a hand through the air.

Sam wondered what he meant by chaos energies, but Elliot ploughed on.

"And if it's a man using magic of some kind?"

"Well, I did say I could be wrong."

They were going round in circles of vagueness. Elliot's shoulders tensed and Sam could tell he was getting frustrated.

"You intend to confront this... mime?" Geoff asked.

"I really don't know." He adjusted his glasses and blew out a breath. "Yesterday, if I'd just known what to look for, I might have... I wasn't expecting him to be there."

"You think you could have prevented the death, had you intercepted him sooner?"

"Maybe. Will you help us figure out what we're dealing with?"

"Leave it with me, my boy, I'll see what I can dig up."

Elliot extracted himself from the chair. "You have my number?"

"Yes, yes."

"Thank you. And Geoff, lives may be resting on this, so..."

"Right, right, so you said. I'll make it my top priority." He rapped his knuckles on the desk for emphasis.

"Thank you, Professor," Sam added as they excused themselves and pulled the door closed behind them.

"Not what you were hoping for?" she asked as they exited the building into the late morning sun.

Elliot let out a sigh. "The optimist in me was hoping for an instant solution. A quick fix."

"I'm sure he'll come up with something."

He nodded. "Hmm."

8

When Elliot pulled up outside Sam's building the next morning, she was waiting by the side of the road with her camera and laptop bags slung over one shoulder, and two thermal mugs in her hands.

She climbed in and handed him his coffee.

"Do we have a plan this time? Like, a proper plan?"

He took a slurp of much needed caffeine. "Find the Mime before he chooses a victim."

"And then?"

He glanced warily at her.

"Right," she said, "then we make it up as we go along. Got it."

After visiting Geoff yesterday they'd returned to the office and spent the afternoon shortlisting possible targets, based on the professor's theory that the Mime would be attracted to places with lots of people. This meant either an event, which would draw a crowd, or a commonly busy space. The city centre and adjacent Broadmead shopping district were too central to fit the spatial pattern. The obvious choice in the south of the city was the football stadium, but a check of the calendar showed nothing scheduled. Meanwhile, Victoria Park, not far from Sam's home, was playing host to an aerial circus for the next ten days. It seemed a good option to start with.

There was no big top here. The spidery arms of the performance rigging stood proud of a collection of trucks, trailers and tents – naked and dizzyingly tall. The whole collection of vehicles stood within a fenced compound at least a hundred yards across.

"Looks like the fence goes all the way round," Sam said as they approached. The mesh fence – the type you saw around building sites – was mostly covered with white canvas, presumably so no one could watch the show without paying.

"Where's the entrance?" she asked. They circled at a distance. "Do you think he'd actually use the entrance?"

"Who knows? He could be capable of anything."

On the far side, a marquee interrupted the perimeter, with advertising banners pinned either side – obviously the box office.

Elliot glanced at his watch. His gut nagged that they'd used up their luck when they'd picked the music festival last time. "Alright. Let's assume he's not here yet. We'll watch the entrance from—"

"Over there?" Sam nodded towards a bench set back from the path, shaded by trees and partly concealed by shrubbery.

"Perfect. If we haven't seen him by the time they open, we'll go on in and check it out."

They sat, and Sam unpacked her camera. She took the cap off her telephoto lens and inspected the glass, then took a cloth from her bag and carefully polished away any smudges. She'd brought her older Nikon, Elliot noticed, probably worried about damaging her new one. He watched the way she handled it, careful but confident, like it was an old friend. Her experiments with photography had brought her into his life in the first place, not long after he'd left London. After what had happened to her back then, it was a wonder she'd ever touched a camera again.

He couldn't begin to understand where she found the courage to dive into the unknown the way he selfishly asked her to so often. He'd sent her off to the morgue the other day and hadn't even asked her whether she'd found it difficult.

She looked up with a start, suddenly aware of him watching her.

"I still owe you an apology," he said.

"What for?"

He leaned forwards with his elbows on his knees. "For the way I spoke to you the other day."

Sam returned her cleaning cloth to its pocket in her case. "Don't worry about it. We were both pretty stressed out."

"I know, but you were right. I was being stubborn, and what I said to you… I'm sorry."

Sam didn't say anything, but she twisted her camera strap around her hand.

"I need to feel like I'm winning." He shook his head. "No, I don't mean that. I need to feel like I'm making amends."

"For James?" she asked softly.

He glanced across.

"You are," she said. "You already have. Loads of times."

An uncomfortable lump lodged in his throat and he hung his head, eyes closed.

"You know I just worry about you, right?"

He let out a wry laugh. "Well, you don't have to. I don't pay you enough to worry." He turned to her, but her eyes were shuttered, the concern hidden away again.

"Yeah, well, that's not why I do it."

Elliot fixed his gaze on the entrance to the circus. Some apology.

For the next twenty minutes, he kept watch while Sam tinkered with her camera, then someone emerged from the marquee and began unzipping and rolling up the canvas.

"Looks like they're opening up," Sam said.

Elliot checked his watch – ten o'clock. The first show wasn't until midday. He still couldn't shake his suspicion that the odds were against them being in the right place.

"I think you should stay here," he said.

"What?"

"I doubt he's here. I'll just do a quick sweep and then we'll move on."

"No! What if he *is* here? You could get yourself killed. I'm coming with you." She tensed, staring towards the circus.

"I only meant—"

She elbowed him in the arm. "Shh. Look." She pointed and he followed her indication.

A black-clad person moved into view around the perimeter fence and crept with long, exaggerated steps towards the marquee. The man opening up was setting out some posts and ropes to give the punters somewhere to queue. Behind him, Elliot could see that barriers still blocked the way through.

Sam snapped off a couple of pictures with the full zoom of her telephoto lens, then showed him the display. The mystery man wore loose-fitting black clothes, including a sweatshirt with a wide hood. She'd only caught the side of his face, but the heavy black-painted outlines that framed his eyes over white cheeks and eyebrows were clear enough.

The Mime peered around the corner and then shrank back against the fence, like he was trying to avoid being seen.

"Come on," Elliot said. "Quietly." He rose slowly to his feet, making no sudden movements.

"How do you think he selects a victim?" Sam whispered. "How are we going to stop him?"

"I don't know. Like Geoff said, there must be something, otherwise why not kill the man there?" He pointed to where the

Mime was watching the man set out sandwich boards with the show times for the day.

"Do we go after him now?" Sam whispered.

"No, wait." Elliot laid a tense hand on her arm. The exposed space between where they watched, half-hidden by the dappled shade and plants, and the circus entrance, offered no way to sneak up. They'd have to wait until the Mime moved or they'd be seen.

The Mime stepped back from the fence, reached both hands out level with his shoulders and lifted one foot. Then he shifted his weight onto the raised foot and stepped up onto thin air.

"That's impossible," Elliot muttered, shaking his head.

The Mime climbed the invisible ladder to the top of the fence, then wrapped his hands around an invisible rope or pole and slid down out of sight behind the canvas and banners.

"Come on." Elliot nudged Sam's elbow and set off at a swift lope across the grass to where the killer had stood moments before. He felt for any trace of the ladder and found only a fading thickness to the air. It offered resistance but no solid shape.

"Can you feel that?"

Sam waved her hand through the space and shook her head.

"We need another way in," Elliot said.

"How about we just ask?"

She strode round to the man setting up the box office. Elliot hung back and let her do the talking.

"Morning," she said, brightly. "Do you think we could go in to take some pictures? We're press." She held her camera up in one hand.

The man checked his watch. "We don't actually open till eleven."

"I know. That's why we want to get some shots now, so we can show the circus setting up and do a piece on the people behind the scenes. Like, maybe we could ask you some questions after we're done?" She smiled sweetly and the young man mirrored her.

"Sure, I guess that'd be okay." He moved the barrier aside for them.

"Thank you so much." She glanced over her shoulder at Elliot and they hurried into the circus ground.

Behind the marquee, a wide route led straight towards the towering struts and ropes of the performance rig. Two narrower routes followed the fence line, clearly more for staff use, with the punters being funnelled forwards. Stalls and dormant burger vans cluttered the space between, restricting the view. A few people moved about their business, but there was no sign of the Mime.

Elliot nodded ahead. "Come on. He'll go where the most people will be, right?"

They made their way straight to the open field in the centre of the compound where the base of the huge circus structure was anchored into three flatbed trucks. They were parked, trailer ends together, in a triangle. Looking up to the top gave Elliot a disorientating sense of vertigo.

Off to one side two children – a boy and a girl – laughed and chased each other around a set of swings and a small climbing frame, but otherwise the enclosure was deserted. Elliot scanned the edges of the space. The Mime could be hiding anywhere, even under one of the trucks.

Sam grabbed his arm.

"What?"

She pointed to a tent just beyond the playground. "Look there. Do you see him?"

Almost concealed by the white canvas, lurking in the shadows, the Mime watched the children in the play area. Elliot and Sam darted to the nearest truck cab and peered around the grille.

The children's game brought them closer to the Mime's hiding place and, as they approached, he danced forward, as if he wanted to join in. The children slowed and stopped to watch as he put his hands out as if gripping a ladder, just as he had done by the fence. He ascended three steps and beckoned to the children to follow. The little girl shook her head, but her braver friend felt for the rungs and began to climb.

9

The Mime kept climbing until he reached the top of the invisible structure he had created, at least twenty feet up. There he stopped, stood up and beckoned to the child with a wide smile on his face. Lower down, the boy moved tentative feet up one invisible rung at a time. The little girl seemed to have more sense. She paced around on the ground, flapping her hands.

As the child neared the top, the Mime sat down, extended his legs away from the ladder and pushed himself forwards. He slid down to the ground in a graceful arc, bounced to his feet, turned a pirouette and bowed for the boy, who now clung fearfully to the top of the invisible slide.

As Elliot watched from beside the truck cab, the Mime returned to the bottom of the slide and gestured for the child to copy him. The boy, slowly, shakily, began to sit.

Abruptly, the Mime's happy-go-lucky grin turned sour, malevolent. He slid his hand down the edge of the invisible slide, then pretended to prick his finger on an invisible spike. He drew back and shook his hand, before doubling over in silent hysterics.

"If that kid slides down he's going to be impaled," Elliot muttered. He glanced over his shoulder at Sam. "Stay here."

He broke cover and ran towards the boy.

"Elliot, wait!"

He glanced back at where she crouched, hidden behind the cab, and flicked his hand, telling her to stay put.

The little girl was crying now. "Tommy, come down!" she kept shouting.

"Hey, kid, don't move," Elliot called as he raced towards them. "I'm going to get you down, alright?"

He glanced at where the Mime stood a few paces away. The moment he made eye contact, inhuman eyes flared with a fierce inner light. The Mime's grin widened, black painted lips splitting around white teeth. For a moment Elliot thought the man might attack him but then he retreated towards the swings, maybe curious to see what he would do.

"Kid, can you climb back down?" Elliot said, staring up at the boy, who shook his head. "Come on, you can do it. Try." The boy shifted to his knees and, gripping the invisible rails of the slide with both hands, tried to extend his leg back down, but his searching toes found no support.

Elliot felt for the steps he'd seen them both climb, but there was nothing but a faint trace of thickness in the air.

"Alright, don't panic," he called. "Here's what we're going to do. You're going to lower yourself over the edge, got it? Then you're going to let go, and I'm going to catch you. Can you do that?"

The boy huddled on the spot, sobbing quietly, but then he nodded. Agonisingly slowly he inched backwards on his knees, under the handrail, and lowered one leg over the side into thin air. A barely perceptible vibration passed up Elliot's legs from the ground and suddenly the boy began to rise higher, as if the invisible slide was growing taller.

———•———

Sam watched from her hiding space beside the lorry. The Mime stood watching the whole scene, silently chuckling at times like it was all one big game. A game he would change the rules for every time Elliot got close to winning. There had to be something she could do.

Maybe she could distract him somehow. But not from where she was. She'd have to get closer. If she circled around behind the tents and vehicles the Mime wouldn't see her, especially with his attention focused on Elliot.

She reluctantly tore her gaze away from the little boy and retreated along the line of the truck until she could safely cut across to the tents. As she squeezed through a gap to get to the space behind, she trod on some spare tent poles and nearly lost her footing. The poles were almost as thick as scaffolding poles but lighter and much shorter. She carefully picked one up, trying not to let it clang against the others in case any of the circus staff were nearby. Whacking the Mime in the head would certainly count as a distraction.

Moving from hiding spot to hiding spot she skirted the edge of the field with her makeshift weapon until she glimpsed the Mime's back between the edge of a marquee and a transit van parked to block up the adjacent space.

Elliot was still trying to coax the child into jumping down. The boy gripped the invisible handrails in tight fists and froze with one leg down, the other still kneeling on the edge of the slide. Elliot stood almost directly below him.

Sam took a few rapid breaths to psych herself up and crept towards the Mime, who stood beside the swing set with his back to her. She gripped one end of the metal pole in both hands, like a club. She'd never deliberately tried to hurt anyone before. What if she hit him too hard, or not hard enough?

She was close enough to hear Elliot now.

"Come on, kid. Tommy, right?" he called. "You can do this. Just dangle yourself over the edge, and when I count to three all you've got to do is let go." He glanced at her, very briefly, and she froze, waiting for the Mime to turn around.

As soon as it was clear Elliot hadn't given her away, she took another careful step forwards. A couple more and then she'd go for it.

"That's it, Tommy. Just a bit further," Elliot said.

She counted to three in her head, then rushed forwards and to the right of the Mime, raising the pole for a swing as she charged. She suddenly couldn't bring herself to aim for his head like she'd planned and instead she swung low, hitting him hard in the side. He doubled over silently. Not even a grunt of pain or a sharp breath. There was something frighteningly inhuman about that.

The moment the pole connected, the child on the invisible slide screamed. Sam spun to watch, transfixed, as he dropped, and her stomach dropped with him.

Then suddenly the Mime uncurled, back-handed her across the face so hard it felt like her jaw unhinged, and she fell to her knees.

———•———

Elliot's stomach lurched and he threw himself forwards, twisting to get under the kid and break his fall. The boy screamed, and a heartbeat later his small body hit Elliot's chest and Elliot hit the ground, hard. Pain shot through his left shoulder and his skull cracked against the ground.

Dazed, he rolled the kid off him. "Are you hurt?"

The boy answered with a scream but then the little girl ran up and threw her arms around him and he quietened down.

Elliot slowly sat up and waited a moment for the world to

stop spinning. He rolled his bruised shoulder, wincing, as the two children ran off.

He'd had his eyes on the kid when the Mime's invisible structure failed, and he had no idea whether the Mime did it on purpose or whether Sam had somehow caused the disruption. He searched for the Mime. There was no sign of the dark figure, but he did see Sam, picking herself up off the ground near where the Mime had been. That seemed to answer his question.

He gingerly pushed himself to his feet and jogged towards her.

———•———

Sam rubbed her cheek. Her legs shook as the adrenaline departed, leaving her feeling weak. The Mime had escaped, disappearing between the trailers and tents after he struck her. She hadn't realised attacking him would cause whatever was holding the boy up to dissolve. If she had, she would have thought twice about her distraction plan.

"Sam?" Elliot jogged up to her.

"Is the kid okay?"

"He's fine." Elliot rolled his shoulder and rubbed it with his other hand.

"Are *you* okay?"

He lifted his hand to the bruise on her jaw line. It stung and felt puffy.

She brushed him away. "It's nothing, just a little bruise."

"You shouldn't have gone near him." He massaged his shoulder again.

"What, you're the only one who's allowed to be a hero?"

A fleeting half smile crossed his lips. "I'm just glad the kid's alive. Come on, he's long gone now."

They sneaked back out the main entrance and returned to the car. By the time they got there, Elliot was still fussing with his shoulder.

"Let me have a look at it," Sam insisted.

"What?"

"Take your shirt off and let me see how bad it is."

Shifting awkwardly in the driver's seat, Elliot unbuttoned his shirt and slid it off his shoulder.

Sam ran her fingers over his skin, pressing gently to look for any swelling, but it seemed fine. A few lines of deep red-purple showed there would be some bruising to come out, but it probably didn't need a doctor.

"I think you'll live. Maybe we should put some ice on it later."

She glanced up and found Elliot watching her. The pause stretched out until she looked away, heart racing disconcertingly fast. She reminded herself that she was over her stupid crush, and when she looked back he was fastening his shirt buttons.

"I think you must have broken his concentration," he said. "Broken the link or disrupted his power so that his spell, or whatever it was, failed."

Right, evil mime artist, murders, work. "But we did it? We stopped him?"

"This time."

"Do you think he'll try again?"

Elliot closed his eyes and shook his head. He let out a long breath. "I don't think we can assume we've done anything but startle him."

She gingerly touched the bruise on her chin. "Do you think there's a chance he might go after the kid again?"

For a moment Elliot stared out the window and said nothing, then he turned to her. "I don't know, he might. But my gut says we scared him off. Maybe he'll try again somewhere else, but we have no way to know where."

"There's got to be something we can do."

"There is. Get more information." He slid his hands over the steering wheel and started the car.

———•———

Professor Dorridge sat at his cluttered desk.

"I haven't really made much progress yet, my boy."

Elliot stood next to him. He glanced over his shoulder to where Sam stood by the central table. "Sam? Can I borrow your camera?"

He waited while she switched the display on, selected one of the photographs of the Mime, and passed it to him. Then he held it while Geoff donned his reading glasses.

"Interesting looking fellow."

"Interesting is one word for it. This mime artist persona is more than just an appearance. It's the way he moves, and—"

"We saw him make an invisible ladder to climb over a fence," Sam added.

"There was something there." Elliot waved his hand, remembering the resistance where the Mime's ladder and the steps of the slide had been, the tingle it left in his fingertips.

Geoff reclined in his chair and stroked a thoughtful hand down his beard. "This ladder. It wasn't used to... to harm someone?"

Elliot shook his head. "Not the first one; he just used it to go over the fence, so he wouldn't be seen."

"Hmm. Interesting. Interesting." Geoff gathered a few scattered scraps of paper from across his desk, flipping each over to check both sides, but apparently he didn't find what he was looking for. He tossed them in a pile to one side and reached instead for a notebook lodged behind his keyboard and began flipping the pages.

"What are you thinking?" Elliot asked.

"Thinking, yes. It's about planning, you see, preparation. From what I've been reading, magic is strongly associated with ritual."

"So, you don't think something like this could be done with magic?" Until recently Elliot considered "magic" to be little more than an ignorant label for things people didn't understand, but he was willing to consider anything to explain what he'd witnessed over the last few days.

"No, no, quite the contrary, I think it *could*. But not without the proper preparation, you see. It's proportional. The more powerful the spell, or whatever you want to call it, the more preparation required. Manifesting invisible objects... Well, from what I've read that would take a few days of meditation, chanting, perhaps a blood sacrifice."

Elliot stepped away from the desk. "I see. So he'd be restricted to things he'd planned for, and we've clearly seen him adapt to the unexpected."

"Precisely."

"So we *are* dealing with a demon?"

"It seems most likely, yes."

"There was another thing," Elliot added, tabbing through more of the photos as he spoke. He didn't find any that showed what he wanted. "The intended victim today was a boy. This time the Mime didn't hide, he showed himself, and... it was like he was playing with the kid. He lured him into climbing up an invisible structure."

"A child?" The professor considered for a moment. "Well, children are much more susceptible to any illusion which relies upon the imagination. Could the child see what you couldn't?"

Elliot leaned on the back of the spare chair by the desk with both arms and flinched at the throb in his shoulder. "I don't think so. He was just more inclined to trust it, I suppose."

"Shame. Shame. A demon will always prefer a soul led to its own destruction over one taken." His voice took on a faraway tone and Elliot wondered what past experience he was reliving. The professor's eyes strayed to a framed wedding portrait at the rear of his desk, half hidden behind the clutter, faded with age.

"Do you have any idea how we can stop it?" Elliot asked.

Geoff scratched his cheek and stroked his beard. "Hmm. If we continue to assume that we are dealing with possession, the usual course of action would be an exorcism."

He made it sound simple enough, but a gut feeling told Elliot it wouldn't be so easy. "Well, I for one am no exorcist, and I'm not sure I'd know where to start looking for one."

"Leave that with me, dear boy. I'll see what I can dig up."

"Is it possible we're *not* dealing with possession?" Elliot asked.

"A manifestation? Pfft, highly unlikely. There's not been a genuine case of such a thing in a hundred years."

Right. Except for the story Elliot had published earlier that year, where a demon had bonded with its host to manifest physically. In that case the demon had killed and eaten at least thirty people before someone had stopped it.

He patted Geoff on the shoulder. "Keep looking."

He and Sam made their way out of the faculty building. They followed the footpath to the road, then took a shortcut through the park in the middle of the campus to where they'd parked the car. Elliot could feel his nerves fraying; he'd never felt so intensely vulnerable, like he'd strayed off the edge of the map into territory he wasn't equipped to navigate. Every shadow in the trees took on the form of the hooded mime artist.

In the centre of the park stood a sculpture of tall, narrow, mirrored panels arranged in concentric squares. As they neared it, a dark shape flitted past, and Elliot stopped in his tracks. He took a few steps closer, moving sideways, trying to see through the gaps, but all he could see was his own reflection, and Sam's.

"What is it?" Sam asked.

"I thought I saw something." He rotated on the spot, checking the surrounding park, but the trees and shrubs remained silent and devoid of dark figures. "Sorry, must have just been our reflection." He shook his head at how jumpy he felt.

"Don't worry, those mirror things are creepy weird at the best of times."

10

After they'd left Geoff's, Elliot drove Sam home and told her to take the afternoon off. She hadn't really wanted to be alone, but she wasn't sure how to explain that, and in the end she let him drive away without argument.

Though she tried to put the whole thing out of her mind, her thoughts kept drifting back to the hooded Mime, to the disconcerting way he'd moved and the chilling lack of any sound as she'd whacked him with the tent pole. She'd wanted him to grunt or go "oof" but there had been nothing. Eventually she gave up trying to concentrate on the TV and headed to bed.

When her alarm clock sounded the next morning, she rolled over and glared at it, then reluctantly sat up and rubbed her puffy eyes. Insomnia was a bitch.

Coffee, painkillers and a shower only took the edge off, and she still felt a bit delicate as she exited the cracked front door. At least it looked to be another nice day. She headed right, towards where she'd left her car.

Ahead of her, a ginger cat stood in the middle of the pavement facing away, tail fluffed, back arched. It hissed, but she couldn't see what it was reacting to.

"Hey, kitty," she called, approaching slowly.

The cat paced back and forth across the wide pavement. Sam felt her own hackles rise. The cat put both front paws up and jumped, scrabbling at nothing but air, before twisting to land where it started. It let out a low, warning moan.

Sam's stomach knotted. Traffic passed on the main road across the end of the street, and behind her a woman with a pushchair and a dog was walking away, but close by there was only the cat.

She took a few quick paces forwards. The cat flinched when it noticed her and ran away across the road, disappearing under a parked van. She reached her hand out and encountered something smooth and solid, like glass, or perhaps more like plastic since it wasn't cold. Invisible. Just like the box at the music festival that had trapped and drowned the girl.

Her heart hammered and she clenched her other fist. Adrenaline chased away any last trace of her insomnia headache.

"Where are you?" she hissed under her breath.

No figure appeared, but the lack of response felt chilling in its own right.

She ran her hand along the invisible wall. It continued, solid and uninterrupted, right the way across the street. Exploration up and down revealed no edges, top or bottom. She gazed longingly beyond it to where her car sat fifty feet away.

Behind her, the road entered an industrial estate. There was a cut-through she could take, but that sounded like the perfect spot for a demon mime artist to spring an ambush and leave her for dead.

Something hard pinged off her cheek and she flinched, spinning round. Another flicked her hair and she yelped.

"You don't scare me!" she said, wondering if she'd ever told a bigger lie. "If you're going to kill me, get on with it."

Another pea-sized pellet hit her forehead. She gritted her teeth. She could phone Elliot, or someone else, but by the time they got here she'd be dead, if that was what the Mime had planned.

"You're not even brave enough to show your face, are you?" she called to the empty street.

Another missile hit the back of her head and she spun to face the parked van where the cat had disappeared. Slowly she crept towards it, around the front and up onto the pavement. "Is that where you're hiding?"

At a tap on her shoulder she gasped, pivoted on the spot and found herself nose to nose with a black-and-white face.

She twisted away, colliding with the invisible wall, and pressed her shoulder blades against the hard surface, wishing it would dissolve.

The Mime considered her with stark eyes. Heavy makeup outlines accentuated the extreme contrast between the whites and the pure black pits at their centres. There was no humanity in them. The thing that stood in front of her was not a man, or at least it wasn't anymore.

His hood shaded his narrow, angular face. Around his throat, dirt crusted the black hoodie, and unwashed body odour rolled off him.

Barely as tall as her, he seemed smaller close up but no less threatening.

"What do you want if you're not here to kill me?" Sam forced out, trying to keep her voice level even though she was shaking all over.

He reached up with a white-gloved hand and stroked the back of his index finger down her cheek. Sam closed her eyes, holding her breath. He gripped her chin between his thumb and forefinger, pressing hard on the bruise he'd given her the day before.

Then, abruptly, he let her go. She opened her eyes. The Mime was looking over her shoulder, and she cautiously twisted to see what had distracted him. Beyond the invisible wall, a car approached. Sam's head snapped round. If the barrier remained, the car would hit it, but at barely thirty miles an hour the driver would probably survive with minimal injuries.

The Mime's eyes narrowed. Sam glanced from him to the approaching car. With only a few yards until impact, the wall melted away. Sam staggered backwards, darted between the parked cars and crossed to the other side of the road. She took off, sprinting as fast as she could, reached her car gasping for breath, and fumbled to get her key in the ignition. When she checked her rear-view mirror as she pulled away, there was no sign of the Mime.

———•———

Sam's key scratching against the front door lock lifted Elliot's mood. He'd hit a dead end trying to locate an exorcist. It wasn't as if priests offered such services in the Yellow Pages, and though he'd rung round a few churches none seemed inclined to take him the least bit seriously.

Sam clattered in and slammed the door behind her. He caught the sound of her sobbing and his heart skipped a beat. Jumping up from his desk he darted round to the door. "Sam?"

She covered her face with her hands and took a long, shaky breath.

"What happened?"

"He knows about us, Elliot. He was there, waiting for me. Outside my house."

He nodded slowly, trying to control the stab of panic that gripped him at the sight of the fear on her face. No, not panic. He wasn't sure what it was exactly, except it was intense and overwhelming. Panic and guilt and anger. No time to analyse it now, he needed to help her. "Did he hurt you?"

Sam wiped the few escaped tears from her cheeks then shook her head. "No, I'm okay," she said in a tiny voice.

"Come on," he said, nodding towards the office, "come and sit down. Tell me everything."

She followed him through, and he wheeled her chair over to his desk. For the next few minutes he listened quietly while she described her encounter, jotting down notes. She'd got closer than either of them had previously, and she described him like he wasn't a person at all but something alien, chilling, cold. He'd never considered that the Mime might go after her. There wasn't supposed to be an attack today, but they had no clue how strictly that pattern applied, if at all.

"So yeah, I ran as soon as the barrier came down," Sam finished with a shudder.

"Maybe he was just trying to figure you out," Elliot said. "I can't imagine many people have challenged him before."

"Yeah." Her wide eyes fixed on a spot of carpet beside the desk, and she knotted her pale hands in her lap like she'd lost something. He wasn't sure what to say to make her feel better. She'd been so brave, standing up to the Mime, but seemed so fragile now.

"Do you think the invisible things are real, or does he just make us *think* they are?" She looked up with pleading eyes. "What if it's all just in our heads?"

He realised she was connecting this to other traumatic experiences from her past, letting it grow into a nightmare she couldn't fight.

"No," he said. "Definitely not. Think about it, he might suffocate someone, or stop their heart through mind manipulation, but how could he burn them?" He tapped one of the photos pinned to the map behind him. "Alex Perry didn't imagine getting shot, did he?"

"You're right, you're right. I'm just twisting it all up in here." She tapped the side of her head.

"Listen," Elliot said, sitting forwards with his elbows on his knees. "We're going to figure out a way to stop him. I know you were scared, but at least we know more now, right?"

Her eyes slowly lifted towards him. "Yeah."

Elliot jotted a few notes down on his pad, partially to give himself a moment to control the anxiety roiling inside him. He scanned through the other notes on the page.

"You said you couldn't see him to start with?"

"No, but he was there. I think you were right; he has to be."

Elliot nodded. "And if his abilities are limited by range that gives us a certain advantage. At least we know that we're safe if we're away from him."

Sam hugged her arms around her middle. He had to agree; it wasn't much comfort after what had happened to her.

"I think we can assume, for now, that he can't influence what he can't see. He's had line of sight to all of the victims."

She nodded, staring into the distance again.

He wished there were some promise he could make so she didn't have to be scared, but they were in this now and there was no getting away from that.

She shuddered and rubbed her arms with her hands like she was cold.

"Sam?"

Her eyes fixed on him.

His lips parted, but he wasn't sure what he wanted to say. It was important to focus on the facts, things within their control. He consulted his notes. "He revealed himself after you called him out, correct?"

"Yes."

"That's interesting. That tells us something."

"It does?"

He tried to give her an encouraging smile. "Well, yes. If he's true to this mime artist persona, we probably can't expect him to speak, but it's clear that he does understand vocal communication, in English."

She blinked at him, then stood. "I need some water."

As she walked out, Elliot pushed his glasses up and rubbed his eyes. He wasn't handling this well. Maybe some time alone would help.

He picked up his mobile and dialled Geoff's number. It rang until the voicemail kicked in.

"Geoff, it's Elliot. Just checking in to see if you have anything yet. Call me."

He hung up and rolled his sprained left shoulder, wincing from the pain.

After a few minutes he followed Sam and found her sitting on the sofa in the back room. He watched her from the door as tears rolled down her cheeks. He should leave her alone, but he didn't want to; he wanted to put his arm round her and tell her he'd take care of everything. But that wouldn't exactly be appropriate.

She glanced up at him.

"Feeling any better?" he asked.

She nodded and wiped her cheeks. "So much for being brave."

"You did great." He perched on the arm of the sofa. "I'm sorry you had to face him – *it* – alone." He didn't want to risk it happening again. Right now he didn't want to let her out of his sight. He cleared his throat. "We should stay together. It'll be safer."

Sam looked up at him with a slight frown. "Okay."

"I don't think you should go home. I don't like that it knows so much about you."

Sam returned her gaze to her water glass and wiped her eyes with one sleeve.

"We can stay here tonight, or go to my place," Elliot said.

"You're right," she said. "That sounds like a good plan."

———•———

Elliot had to stop himself pacing for most of the day. Every time he felt the urge he sat down and wrote a list. The lists weren't much more use, but at least they didn't wear out the carpet.

Geoff would be the key, but he hated waiting. He called him again in the afternoon and again it rang out and went to voicemail. Geoff had better be working on the problem. The man had questionable priorities and attention span.

Sometime after six he ordered pizza and had it delivered so they wouldn't have to leave their safe little bubble. Sam curled up on the sofa with a slice of pepperoni while Elliot sat on the floor, knees drawn up. They left the news playing quietly on the television in case there had been any more incidents.

"Do you think he'll attack again tomorrow?" Sam asked.

"We can't assume he won't." Elliot jabbed his pizza crust into some dip. "I don't want to end up in a pattern where all we do is intervene. We need to make progress."

"We will." Sam placed her hand on his sore shoulder and he jumped, more from surprise than because it hurt. She snatched her hand back. "But we need to figure out a plan for tomorrow first."

The national news finished and handed over to the local news.

"One sec." She shoved the rest of her pizza slice in her mouth, slid off her seat and stepped over the pizza box. A moment later she returned with her laptop and climbed back onto the sofa.

Elliot waited while she clicked the mouse a few times.

"There's supposed to be a street theatre festival in the centre starting tomorrow."

As if to reinforce her point, the local news programme warned that the road through the Broadmead shopping district would be partially closed over the next few days.

"Looks like that's the biggest thing happening this week," Elliot said.

Sam relaxed on the sofa with her laptop on her knees. "What about the pattern though? It went south like we predicted but we stopped it. This festival's in the centre."

"Who knows? Maybe it did kill later that day, but we didn't hear about it. Plus, it approached you this morning. Maybe we're way off and these patterns we're seeing don't mean as much as we think they do." After all, what did they *really* know about this creature and how it worked?

Sam tapped a few keys on the keyboard. "I'll see what other options there are."

Elliot tilted his head against the sofa and looked up at her. "Thanks, Sam."

She smiled and he couldn't help smiling back.

"There's a couple of things I need to work on." He gathered up the empty pizza box and dirty plates to dump in the tiny kitchen and left Sam to her search.

In the main office he dialled Geoff's number. Voicemail, again.

"It's Elliot. Hope you're getting these messages. Where are you? Call when you get this. Please." Geoff better have a damn good reason for not answering.

At his desk, he pulled a book on demonic possession forwards from a small stack and tried to lose himself in its pages. But a few hours later when he set his books aside he still had no real idea how to stop the Mime. There were hints in the book about ways to track a demon using an object tethered to its energy signature, but he hadn't the faintest idea how to make such a thing work.

He hadn't heard Sam stir in a while.

In the back room she sat sideways on the sofa with her back to the armrest. Her head lolled, and her laptop gradually slipped sideways from its perch on her knees. Only the weight of her arm, resting across the keyboard, kept it from falling.

Elliot gently eased it out from under her hand, closed it and set it on the floor beside her. She pulled her arms in, curling into a tighter ball.

"I'm sorry I got you into this," he whispered.

He pulled the fleece blanket off the back of the sofa and draped it over her. Her breathing continued in the deep, even rhythm of sleep.

She'd tried to tell him, but the implications of tracking a murderer hadn't really sunk in before. He'd thought that if he could see it, or be there, he could stop it happening, and if there was any danger *he'd* be the one to face it. He certainly hadn't considered he'd be putting Sam at risk. Now the Mime had identified her, so there was no going back.

He squeezed onto the end of the sofa near her feet and turned the TV volume down to a whisper. She didn't stir. In the glow from the screen he watched her sleeping. She was a fighter, and she was smart. If they stuck together they'd be fine.

He wasn't quite sure when he drifted off, but he woke to the aroma of fresh coffee wafting up from a mug on the floor beside the sofa. He blinked and sat up from where he'd been slumped on the couch with the blanket over him. Sam was gone. He had no recollection of her moving, but hopefully she didn't feel he'd intruded on her personal space.

He rolled his stiff shoulders, the pain from his injury less this morning, then reached down for the mug. He took a long gulp; it had cooled enough to drink, but it couldn't have been there long.

Sam appeared at the door with her own mug clasped between her hands. "I was just about to come and wake you up."

Elliot bundled the blanket up into a ball and shoved it to one end of the couch. He cleared his throat. "I didn't disturb you, I hope?"

"No, it was fine. I was shattered, slept right through."

He checked his watch and gulped down another third of his coffee. "We should get a move on. The street theatre event starts at noon."

II

Cones lined the road through the centre of Bristol's Broadmead shopping district, to prevent people parking. Some performers took advantage of the empty Thursday morning to rehearse before it got busy, and Sam snapped a few nervous photos. A junior dance troupe in bright primary colours. Buskers competing for space and coins. An acrobat performing tricks with a pair of hoops. The only people wearing all black were the men with tool belts and "CREW" sweatshirts busy setting up a stage and lighting gantry in the middle of the pedestrianised zone.

There was no sign of any mime artists, demonic or otherwise.

After they'd completed a circuit of the quiet streets with no success, Elliot suggested they find a better vantage point. Sam followed him into a big department store where escalators criss-crossed up the front of the building behind a five-storey window. They rode up to the top floor where a balcony inside the store overlooked a panoramic view of the streets below.

Elliot leaned on the railing, an intense frown fixed in place.

Sam scanned the people outside through her telephoto lens. The view from the department store left many corners obscured, lots of places to hide, but at least the areas that were visible were all visible at the same time.

She paused on a man in dark trousers and a sweatshirt with the hood up, held her breath. Then another guy jogged up to him and clapped him on the shoulder. They both moved off and Sam exhaled. It was hard to make out faces and details at this distance. Even if they did spot the Mime, it could easily vanish by the time they descended to street level.

"Do you think we'll be able to stop him again?" she asked, her eye still glued to her viewfinder.

Elliot rubbed the back of his neck. "I don't know. It depends on what he tries, where and how."

Another person all in black caught her attention and she zoomed in.

"What if we're wrong?" Elliot muttered.

On the far side of the road from the department store, the man in black stood, completely motionless. Slowly, head leading and body following like a corkscrew, the figure rotated to face them. A hint of white face confirmed it was the Mime. Or *a* mime at least.

Sam gasped and pointed. "There."

"Where?"

She jabbed her finger. "Right there! By that phone booth."

The Mime's head panned smoothly, left then right.

"He's searching for a victim," Elliot said.

Then the Mime looked up, directly at their window, and Elliot shrank away from the railing.

"Or maybe not," he muttered. He grabbed Sam under the arm and tugged her towards the top of the escalator.

"Huh? Elliot, what are you doing?" She half tripped over her own feet trying to keep up.

"He's not looking for a victim. He's already got a couple picked out."

"What do you mean?"

"He's coming after us, Sam. We need to get out of here."

They made it down one floor, to the top of the next escalator. As Sam put her foot on the moving steps, Elliot pulled her back.

Someone shrieked lower down, and she spotted what Elliot had seen – the Mime, racing up the escalators on the opposite side. It reached the floor below them, and Sam saw its face for a fraction of a second before Elliot dragged her away.

"Stairs!" He pointed to a doorway to the left, further into the store.

Sam ran for it, Elliot right behind her.

As she reached the entrance to the stairwell, she smacked into something hard and staggered back. Elliot caught her before she fell, and she clutched her bruised wrist as he dragged her away from the stairwell. It suddenly clicked that what she'd collided with was invisible.

The Mime had blocked the way out.

"Get down," Elliot hissed as he shoved her behind a rack of coats. She dropped to her knees.

He ducked down behind her. "Keep going."

Of course, line of sight. If they could hide from the Mime, it couldn't hurt them. At least, that was the theory. They crawled through several displays towards a partition wall and took shelter behind it with their backs to the shelves.

Elliot glanced at her, his face pale.

"What do we do?" she asked.

He shook his head, which she took to mean less that he didn't know and more that he was still thinking. Well, it wasn't all on him. She crawled past him, stood cautiously and peered round the partition.

The Mime stood at the entrance to the stairwell with one hand to its forehead to shade its eyes, although the lights were hardly bright. It put one hand behind the small of its back and swept the room with its gaze. As it faced their hiding place, Sam ducked behind the partition and collided with Elliot standing behind her. He steadied her with a hand on her hip, which he immediately snatched away.

"I don't think it knows where we are," she whispered.

"Alright, think," he muttered. "If we can stay out of sight…"

"Back to the escalators?" Sam suggested, glancing towards the front of the store. She risked another peek at the Mime. It was moving away from them.

Elliot frowned. "We should split up. You go to the front, I'll—"

"No."

"But—"

She held up a hand. "Just no. We stick together."

The Mime reached the rear of the store and turned right. Sam and Elliot ducked low, making sure the rails of clothes covered them.

"Fine," Elliot said. He nodded towards the front. "Carefully. One rail at a time."

Sam nodded agreement.

Elliot parted the shirts on the rack they crouched behind, to check the Mime's position. Sam peered through the gap with him. The Mime tiptoed with long, exaggerated steps, arms held out to the side like a croquet hoop. Its attention was focused in front as it stalked through the rear of the store.

"Crawl to the next rail," Elliot said.

Sam led the way. At each rail they paused and took a peek. The Mime moved around the perimeter, away from them at first, but it would circle round to the front in time to head them off at this rate.

"Keep going," Elliot said.

The clothes rail cover ended where a wide walkway ran the width of the shop beside the rail across the window. Beyond this balcony the escalators offered escape. A couple of shoppers gave

Sam and Elliot puzzled looks as they peered out from between the clothes.

The Mime explored the right-hand half of the store. A few customers gave it wary looks too.

"Do we make a run for it?" Sam whispered, keeping her eyes on the Mime.

"I don't know."

"I think we should. Now."

She crawled out just as a rapidly striding woman using her pushchair as a battering ram rounded the corner. The woman swerved to avoid her.

"What the hell do you think you're doing?" she yelled. Her baby screamed in agreement and, with a muttered apology, Elliot dragged Sam out of sight. He glanced round the clothes. "It's coming, move!"

They crawled around and through the next fifty feet of displays before pausing near the centre, close to the partition where they'd originally hidden.

Crouched behind a shoe display, Sam caught her breath, staying low as the Mime stalked towards them through a sparsely forested casual wear section. She peered around the side of the Hush Puppies topped parapet.

The Mime was walking, slowly but directly, towards them. Then it paused. At the front of the store the indignant mother still bounced her baby, whose cries only escalated. The Mime fixed its stare on the woman, and Sam shrank back.

"What if it kills her?"

"I don't know how we can stop it without getting ourselves killed too." Elliot sucked his teeth, and his knuckles whitened where he gripped the shelf.

With her back to the shoe display, Sam faced the side of the store where the open doorway led to the stairwell. A couple walked through, unrestricted, and she grabbed Elliot's arm. He flinched as she touched him.

"The stairs," she said, pointing.

Elliot followed her indication. Another customer walked through. He nodded, checked the Mime's position. "Go, quietly."

Scrabbling across the scratchy store carpet, quick and quiet, they crossed to the stairwell. By the time they crouched at the edge of the displays, both Sam's knees and palms sported carpet burns and bruises from chrome rails.

The baby's cries abruptly ceased. They risked another quick glance. The Mime stood beside the woman, with its back to Elliot and Sam, and wiped its brow with a dramatic sweep of its hand. The mother hammered on an invisible, soundproof box.

"Go, now, I'll catch you up," Elliot said, giving Sam a gentle shove.

She waited a couple of seconds for a group to pass, heading towards the stairs, then broke cover and used them to shield her as she walked briskly across. She ducked out of sight as soon as the walls cinched in, and turned to watch Elliot.

He hadn't moved. He was still watching the Mime.

"Come on," she hissed, though she doubted he could hear her. He glanced at her and flicked his hand, urging her to go.

The woman in the invisible box had stopped trying to beat her way out and now rocked her baby quietly.

Elliot reached up and lifted a shirt down from the rail, his eyes fixed on the Mime. Sam wasn't sure what he planned on doing, but she suspected it was going to be something really stupid.

"Go," he mouthed, shooting her a glare.

She shook her head, but there was no chance to argue with him before he disappeared between the clothes rails. Sam thumped the wall with her fist and waited another two seconds before taking the stairs.

12

He should have followed Sam, but Elliot couldn't leave the woman and child trapped. Maybe it made no difference. Maybe the Mime would kill her anyway, or attack someone else. Chances were, he could do nothing more than delay the inevitable, but he didn't much fancy being the type of person who accepted that as a reason not to try.

Armed with nothing but a couple of slim theories about line of sight and distracted concentration, he crept between the shelves towards the Mime. If Sam was sensible, she'd get out while she could. He could find her later.

He crouched behind a partition wall, as close as he could safely approach without being seen, and peeked round the side. The Mime stood beside its unhappy victim. Its monochrome eyes scanned the room, searching. Elliot clutched the shirt in his fist.

When the Mime turned its back, he launched into a sprint across the ten-yard gap and wrapped the shirt around its head. He pulled tight, twisting the shirt in his hands. The Mime bristled in surprise, arms and legs shooting straight.

With an inrush of air like ears popping at altitude, the baby's cries exploded back into the room.

"Run!" Elliot snapped at the mother when she didn't move. Her eyes widened and she took off into the store.

Over the initial surprise, the Mime started to struggle. Elliot had the advantage of a good six inches in height, but the physical strength of the possessed man surprised him. The demon writhed and clawed at the shirt. Elliot couldn't hold on forever, and as soon as he let go it would attack.

With a wrench of his shoulders he swung the Mime round. It made no sound as he slammed it against the rail at the top of the escalator, but it went limp, winded. Elliot used the moment to tie the sleeves of the shirt together behind its head. He put both hands on its shoulders and hauled backwards as hard as he could. The dazed Mime crashed to the floor, shirt still obscuring its vision, and Elliot bolted for the escalator.

He raced down and vaulted the last five steps with his hands on the rails, landed hard, stumbled to his knee, then sprinted from the crouch towards the stairwell.

He nearly collided with Sam on the stairs as she returned from the lower floors.

"I told you to go," he snapped.

"I did. Where were you?"

He glanced over his shoulder. "Distracting it. Come on."

On the first floor, doors opened out to street level at the rear of the building. Outside, the lunchtime crowds had thickened into a welcoming throng of anonymity. Elliot urged Sam into the pedestrian current with a hand on her elbow.

"We're out of our depth here," he said. "This thing knows us, knows what we look like. It knew we'd come here."

Sam nodded. "What do we do now?"

"We can't go back to the office. It's too predictable."

"But we don't have any way to fight it."

"No. No, so we need to find one." He quickened his pace.

———•———

"Stop. He's not here." Sam prised Elliot's hand away from the intercom. He'd been holding the button down for a full twenty seconds.

"Where the hell is he?!" He backed away from Professor Dorridge's faculty building and looked up, as if expecting a sign on the wall.

"I'm sure he's just out."

Elliot huffed, then stalked away, peering through windows as he went. Sam stepped up to the intercom and pressed a different button.

This time someone answered. "Hello?"

"Hi," Sam said. "I'm a friend of Professor Dorridge. I was supposed to meet him here, but he's not answering. Could you let me in please? I'm worried about him."

After a brief pause the door buzzed, clicked, and Sam pulled it open. Elliot stomped back. She tried to suppress her smug grin as he marched through the open door, scowl still firmly in place.

There was no answer at Geoff's door either, but it wasn't locked. Elliot twisted the handle and pushed it open. "Geoff?"

Warm air escaped into the cool corridor, carrying with it the smell of warm dust and something sickly sweet and faintly nauseating.

Sam wrinkled her nose. "Hello?"

The lights were off, but the blinds were open. Sunlight slanted in through the windows, but the far corner was dimmer. Professor Dorridge sat at his desk, facing his computer screen as it showed a montage of family photographs.

Elliot stepped into the room and froze. Sam waited for him to say something, but he just stood there, so she squeezed past.

"Professor Dorridge? Is everything okay?" She reached to touch his shoulder.

"Wait!" Elliot grabbed her as she shook the older man.

The professor slid sideways, and the wheeled chair rotated out from the desk to display his bloated face. His eyes were open. Cloudy. Staring at nothing. A blue blush tinted his skin and lips.

Sam felt like she should scream, but all that came out was a whimper. A wave of needle prickles flushed over her skin and she tensed, but it passed.

Elliot moved her to one side, crouched down and touched the professor's forearm with the back of his knuckles.

"Cold." He rubbed a hand across his face. "Suffocated, I think. Shit, this wasn't supposed to happen." He stood, and kicked the nearest stack of papers into a fluttering cloud.

Sam flinched but she couldn't take her eyes off the corpse. It was like he hadn't moved since she'd stood in this very spot the day before yesterday, listening to him go on about demons and chaos energy like they were the most normal things in the world.

"I shouldn't have brought him into this," Elliot muttered. He leaned on the edge of the central table with both hands, shoulders hunched.

"It's not your fault." Sam turned to face him. "We didn't know it would follow us. Hell, we didn't know it was dangerous."

"It killed four people in broad daylight! That's a fucking neon light saying dangerous!"

"Elliot—"

"No. I'm just an idiot reporter who thinks he can poke his nose into things and hide behind a notepad when the blood starts flying. That's not how it works, and I should know that by now." He sent another sheaf of papers fluttering across the room and stormed towards the door.

"Wait, where are you going?"

"To call the police and report that my friend is dead."

Sam let him go. He needed time to cool off. He wasn't really snapping at her; he was just angry at the situation and blaming himself, like he did for most things. Of course, that left her alone with the body.

"Sorry," she murmured to dead Geoff.

Maybe the Mime had stopped by to kill him that morning, before it found them in town. Or maybe it had followed them on their last visit and he'd been dead all this time. It would explain the ripe odour to the room; he'd already begun to decompose. A half-drunk cup of tea on the desk had started to separate, and one of two biscuits on a plate had a single bite missing.

She glanced at the window, where the blind was still open. Where they'd opened it on their first visit.

He must have been sat at his desk when he was attacked. Researching something, with a nice cup of tea and a biscuit, then bam! Suffocated by some invisible thing. He probably didn't even see his killer.

Tears slipped down her cheek and she hastily wiped them away. No time now.

The pictures of Geoff's family continued to page across the screen. Proud children, now parents of happy grandchildren, all smiles and joy. She couldn't stand having them look so perky, so she nudged the mouse to banish the screen saver.

The screen cleared to show a website. *Myths of the Dagon Clan.*

She scanned some of the page, careful not to disturb the professor's body.

> *The possession of inanimate objects has long been associated with lesser demons of the Dagon clan. In many cases these possessions take the form of everyday objects such as vehicles, clocks, clothing or jewellery. More powerful members of the clan are said to be able to possess human hosts through contact with an inanimate vessel.*

He had made a start, then. She looked down at the desk, wondering what else he'd uncovered before the Mime had found him. The professor's keyboard rested at an angle, as if he'd flailed his arms across the desk when he was attacked. Covering her hand with the end of her sleeve, she reached to put it back in place – restore a little order, as pointless as that was – but a sharp pinch on the back of her hand made her flinch, and she knocked the keyboard further to the side. Rubbing the strange pain, she noticed the corner of a sheet of paper poking out from underneath the keyboard. She glanced briefly at the professor and then carefully pulled out the torn scrap of paper.

In Geoff's scratchy, old-fashioned handwriting was a name – *Gabriel Cushing*.

"Elliot!" she called as she rushed from the room.

13

Sam met Elliot returning along the corridor, head down, focused on his phone.

"Elliot, there's something you need to see." She beckoned with one hand.

He pocketed the phone and followed. The professor's body sat stiffly in the chair. It didn't seem like he was going to fall, but Sam felt his cloudy eyes follow her as she approached.

She pointed out the note and the web page.

Elliot glanced at his watch. "We've probably only got about five minutes until the police arrive. Grab any books or notes you can see."

She searched around the desk and found a couple of promising volumes which she squeezed into her bag. While she hunted, Elliot reached over the body to work on the computer.

"I'm going to email the browser history to myself," he said. "We can pick it up later."

"Mr Cross? Police," a voice called from the hall.

Elliot cursed under his breath and glanced at the body. "Stall them, one more minute," he hissed.

"How?"

"Anything. I need thirty seconds. Go!"

As she backed away, Sam spotted the professor's notebook lying open on the floor under the desk. It must have fallen when he was attacked.

"Elliot, look!" She pointed.

He nodded. "I'll get it. Go!"

She hurried out and met a uniformed police officer moments before he reached the door. Further down the corridor a younger police officer, a woman, spoke with a pale, trembling academic.

"Oh, thank God!" Sam threw herself at the older of the two officers, forcing him to take a step back. "I've never seen anything like it. Thank goodness you're here. We didn't know what to do."

She ticked off the seconds in her head. *Come on, Elliot.*

"Miss, you did the right thing. Now, let us take a look." He tried to move past her, but she pressed her hands to his chest, pushing him back further and keeping herself between him and the door.

"He was just sitting there," she said. "I didn't know what to do. I don't even know how long he's been there."

"I understand. It's alright. Jenny?"

The female officer glanced up.

"Please escort this young lady outside."

She smiled. "Sure. Come on, miss."

"No, wait… I need to tell you—"

"You need to let us through now," the older officer said, with a warning firmness that said she was trying his patience.

"What happens now? Will you take the body away or do we have to wait for—"

With a hand on her shoulder he pushed her to one side and stepped towards the door. She cringed. But then she heard Elliot's voice from inside the room. "Officers, thank you for being so prompt." He appeared by the doorframe and beckoned them through. Once they were past, he caught Sam's eye and nodded.

She waited in the corridor, twisting her hands together, while Elliot showed them in and then left them to examine the body. He joined her in the hall and they escaped, past the professor's ghost-pale colleague, to the fresh air outside.

"Did you get everything?" Sam whispered.

"I think so. Christ, that was close." He pinched the bridge of his nose, forcing his glasses up.

"Do you know that name? Gabriel Cushing?"

He nodded. "Yes. We're in more trouble than I realised."

A quiet ambulance arrived. Two beaten looking paramedics hurried past, there to confirm the death and pick up the body. Some people's jobs sucked every day.

"Do you have any idea where to find this Gabriel guy?"

"Vaguely," Elliot muttered. "Last I heard he was in Oxford." He rubbed his eyes again.

One of the police officers appeared at the door. "I'll need to take your statements," he called. "We can do it here, if you'd like to come through."

Elliot turned his back to the building as he moved away from Sam. "Don't lie, just omit, got it?"

She gave him a tiny nod.

For the next itchy half hour, Sam described exactly when they had arrived, how they had found the body, their movements for the last twenty-four hours. In minute, repetitive detail. As per Elliot's advice she tried to be completely truthful, bar of course the whole demonic psychopath dressed as a mime artist part.

The paramedics gave an initial cause of death as heart attack. Geoff had been a little overweight, fond of the odd cigarette. It was a logical conclusion.

She and Elliot were shooed out of the building with contact cards, in case they remembered anything else, and Sam got a stern glare from the older sergeant. Apparently he was still unimpressed by her hysterical woman performance.

———•———

"Oh great," Elliot muttered as they stepped into the daylight.

By the side of the road, DI Yates leaned on the hood of his unmarked car, smoking. He flicked his cigarette butt into the bushes and pushed off to meet them.

"Cross."

"Detective." Elliot put an arm out to usher Sam behind him. She didn't need any more interrogation today.

Yates glanced over Elliot's shoulder to where the paramedics were wheeling a black body bag out of the building. "You called this in?" he asked flatly.

"Yes, because I found him. I hadn't seen him in two days, couldn't contact him, so I stopped by and found him dead in his office." Elliot braced himself for an opening retaliation, but Yates stopped on the path a few steps in front of him, palms facing him, gesturing for him to calm down.

"A friend of yours?" the detective asked.

For a moment Elliot wasn't sure he'd heard him correctly. "I... Yes."

"I'm sorry to hear that. What was it?"

"A heart attack, maybe, but we don't know for certain yet." He felt Yates was lulling him into a false sense of security. "Was there something you wanted, Detective?"

"Look, everyone's telling me I'm wrong," Yates said. "That these deaths are all unrelated coincidences. But so far they all have one thing in common."

Elliot's shoulders tensed. "Oh, and what's that?"

The detective let out a wry chuckle. "You. You've taken an interest in every one."

He felt Sam move up beside him and touch his arm, just letting him know he wasn't alone. He clenched his fist behind his back, trying to keep calm, keep his tone in check. "Are you accusing me of something?"

For a long moment Yates said nothing. Elliot held his stare, unflinching.

"No," the detective eventually said. "I think you *know* something. Something you apparently don't want to share with me."

Elliot noticed a certain troubled look, a hint of vulnerability he'd not seen in Yates before, but he wasn't about to expose himself to the man's ridicule. Whatever further investigation Yates had done, maybe he was starting to see there was no rational explanation, but that didn't mean he could or would accept the truth. "What is it you think I know?"

"If I knew that, I wouldn't be here." He closed his eyes in a long blink, as if to hide an eye roll. "I want you to come down to the station, just for a little chat."

"A little chat? Does that mean you're arresting me?"

"No. I'm politely requesting your cooperation with an investigation."

Elliot weighed up the options. Best case scenario, Yates believed them and was willing to help stop the Mime. Worst case, Yates didn't believe him, detected something in their "little chat" which incriminated him, and he ended up in jail. The probability pointed to somewhere in the middle, where the whole exercise would just be a waste of both their time, but he couldn't take the chance and potentially leave Sam vulnerable to another attack. He took a half step sideways and ushered Sam in the same direction, skirting around Yates. "My apologies, Detective, I'm afraid I'm not available today."

Yates let out a frustrated growl. "Why do you insist on making this difficult?" He moved into their path. "I'm trying here, Cross. You have to give me something in return." Again, that flash of conflict in Yates's eyes made Elliot wonder what else the detective had seen or worked out.

"You see," Yates added, "I have a problem. I can put you at the scene of at least two deaths this week." He gestured to the faculty building behind them. "Your friend being the second. And while I don't think you're responsible, if you don't cooperate it forces my hand and I have to take the official line. Do you understand?"

Elliot drew himself up, but Yates had to be at least six two which gave him a height advantage of a few inches.

"So, this is how it's going to go," Yates continued. "I expect your cooperation at the station this afternoon. Understood?"

"Understood," Elliot said.

Yates nodded, regarded Elliot critically for a few more seconds, then headed for his car. Elliot physically sagged.

"Maybe this is a good thing," Sam said, making him jump. "I mean, it seems like he suspects something. Maybe he'll believe you, if you just talked to him."

"I don't think so. I think he's just hoping I can give him a way out. Make the anomalies go away." He shook his head wearily. "Besides, we have things to do."

"Aren't you going to the station?"

"No. We're going to Oxford."

OXFORD

14

Elliot pulled into a small car park outside a red-brick office building.

In the passenger seat, Sam stirred and stretched. "Did I sleep the whole way?"

"You needed it. Plus it gave me time to think."

She inclined her head expectantly, asking him to share his thoughts, but they weren't the kind of thoughts that would inspire confidence. Right now he needed confidence. He shook his head, and her eyes shuttered away the concern he'd seen there a moment ago.

She looked out the window. "Where are we?"

"A writer friend of mine works for the *Oxford Journal*."

"You think he might know where to find this Gabriel Cushing guy?"

Elliot shrugged. "It's a place to start." He doubted Julian would know anything, but he was the closest thing Elliot still had to a friend after cutting ties with everyone he knew in London four years ago.

"Should I come with you?"

"Actually, I wondered if you would start going through those notes we found. There's a coffee shop around the corner. Or at least there used to be."

"How come you know Oxford so well?"

He hesitated. "I grew up here. A lot has probably changed."

Sam stared at him. He avoided talking about his childhood because it inevitably led to thoughts of his brother's death, and of his parents whom he barely spoke to anymore. She'd never probed, for which he was grateful. On the odd occasions their conversations had strayed in that direction he'd kept it vague, let her assume his family was from London.

"Does that mean your parents still live—"

"Just outside town, yes. But I'm not—"

"I know. I'm sorry, I didn't mean… Will you meet me there? At the coffee shop?" She reached into the back seat for her bag and the books.

"Of course. I shouldn't be long."

He pointed her in the direction of the coffee shop and waited for her to walk away before he considered his next step.

A modest plaque on the wall by the door discreetly announced the *Oxford Journal's* presence in the inconspicuously drab, brick building – a former warehouse or factory on the bank of one of Oxford's canals – as if the humble local free sheet were embarrassed to be seen in such a notably academic city.

Elliot buzzed the intercom. "Elliot Cross to see Julian Walters."

Inside, he squeezed past a box containing three disused fax machines. Another security-controlled door barred further access into the offices, while an open door on the right led to a pokey reception room. A harassed young woman glanced up from behind her desk.

Elliot took a step towards her.

"I've already buzzed him," she said, shortly. "He didn't sound like he was expecting you."

"I'm sure he won't mind."

There were seats, but he was too nervous to sit. He and Julian had been best friends at school and college, but the last time they spoke they hadn't parted on the best of terms.

The door to the corridor opened and Julian emerged. He'd cut his blond hair short, and the neat goatee was new since Elliot last saw him. What was it, nearly two years now?

"Elliot? What the devil are you doing here?" He stuck out a hand and Elliot grasped it, thumbs hooked together like they had when they were younger. Julian clapped him on his shoulder – thankfully not the bruised one.

"It's something of an odd story."

"Good, I could do with some entertainment. Come on through, you can have some of our shit coffee."

Elliot followed his friend to the office staffroom where the avocado kitchen units and dull stainless-steel sink had seen a hard forty years. Julian offered him a seat at one of the chipped Formica tables and set a mug down in front of him.

"Sugar?"

Elliot sipped the coffee and grimaced. "Yes please."

Over their cups of sweet brown sludge, Elliot explained how he needed to find Gabriel Cushing and that his search was connected to the murders in Bristol. He didn't go into detail as to how.

"So, who are you with these days? Local? National?" Julian asked. "I didn't even realise the police were considering the deaths in Bristol as linked."

"They're not, but there is a link. One they aren't equipped to see."

Julian leaned back in his chair, as if Elliot had just told him he was carrying a bomb. "Don't tell me you're still doing that *National Enquirer* bollocks."

Elliot closed his eyes and pressed his lips into a thin line. "I am not getting into that with you again."

"Hey, if you want to piss your career up the wall, that's your choice, I guess." He said it offhand, but Elliot knew he at least half meant it.

He swallowed the comeback that sprang to mind, along with his pride. "Will you help me find this man or not?"

"You think he's in Oxford?"

"I did a couple of pieces on an incident he was involved in earlier in the year. I never met him, but one of my contacts told me he'd mentioned Oxford."

"I suppose I could make some calls. What does he do?"

"He's a... He's a demon hunter."

Julian scoffed. "A fellow nutcase, then. I'm sure you two will get on like a house on fire."

Comments like that from people like DI Yates rolled off like rain on a rubber sheet, but Julian used to respect him. His opinion mattered. Julian appreciated a good story as much as anyone, but, when Elliot had tried to convince him that some of the stories were true, he'd lost his support completely. Lost his oldest friend.

"Why is it so hard for you to believe? For Christ's sake, you write science fiction books."

All levity left Julian's features. "Yes, fiction. It's all fiction. Folk tales and stories, and false logic whipped up to explain weird coincidences. Not real. You need to start accepting that."

Elliot considered trying to argue, but they'd had this conversation before. Short of something miraculous happening directly in front of him, nothing would ever convince Julian the supernatural world existed. Instead, he rose to his feet and pulled a business card from his pocket.

"That's my mobile number. Call me if you... I could really use your help."

"You need help alright," Julian muttered, shaking his head. He stood and put a hand on Elliot's shoulder. "I'm worried about you,

Elliot. I know losing James was hard, but this has been going on for a long time now. Maybe you should stop and think. Is some self-professed demon hunter really the kind of help you need?"

Elliot shrugged off Julian's hand and stalked to the door. "A friend of mine died this morning," he said. "The police will record his death as a heart attack, or something, but I know he was murdered. Murdered by something that is trying to kill me. This man, Cushing, is the only lead I have."

Julian regarded him with a look of distressed pity that set Elliot's stomach churning. It didn't help that Julian's words echoed ones he'd used himself in the past – before he knew better – and the price had been his brother's life. He started down the corridor but stopped and returned to the staffroom doorway, bristling. Anger was easier than acknowledging how he *really* felt. "I wish to God it was all stories," he snapped. "But I lost the luxury of ignorance."

Julian's jaw dropped.

"Good luck with the fiction."

———•———

The coffee shop occupied the lower level of a narrow house at the end of a terrace. Two steps led down between iron railings to the door and, inside, windows to both the front and side let in plenty of light. Mismatched tables and chairs filled the cramped space, but, other than a couple of businessmen in suits, Sam had the place to herself. She treated herself to a large mocha and settled at a table with her back to the wall where she could watch the door. She felt nervous away from Elliot. They were both more vulnerable on their own.

The notebook from under Geoff's desk turned out to be a personal journal. Only a few entries post-dated the point when she and Elliot had asked him for help, but a quick flick through the rest gave her a better idea of how he used it. The journal was a place for him to think out loud, record his thoughts as they came to him. As such, the only organisation seemed to be a sort of linear progression – lines of enquiry followed then abandoned in favour of formerly sidelined ideas.

Sam found herself reading more because it gave insight into the man he had been. Thoughtful, empathetic, but often perplexed by the behaviour of other people. That this was all that remained of his mind, his personality, was deeply saddening.

After a while the businessmen finished their informal meeting and departed, leaving her alone. So when a dark shape moved across the window, it caught her eye. The back of a hooded head disappeared from view. The figure briefly reappeared in the side window, but she couldn't see their face.

The book slipped from her shaky hands and bounced off the edge of the table on its way to the floor. As she crawled under to pick it up, the door opened, making her jump, and she bashed her head on the underside of the table.

"Sam? Are you alright?"

She regained her seat, clutching her head. "Fine. Well, my head is fine, but we're not."

"Why, what have you found?" Elliot swivelled a seat around from the next table.

"It's not what I found, it's what found us. He's here."

"Where?"

"I saw him walk past the window. Just a few seconds ago."

"I came in that way. There were a couple of kids in hoodies. Was that who you saw?"

"I… I'm not sure. He went round that corner." She pointed to the side window.

Elliot rose and crossed to the window, peered out in both directions. "I can't see anything now."

"Ugh, it was probably nothing. Just my mind turning shadows into monsters." She tucked her hair behind her ears and took a sip of her mocha to calm herself down. "Did you have any luck with your friend?"

He rolled his eyes and approached the counter. "I thought Julian would come around to the idea of *Weird News* eventually, but he likes his other world neatly parcelled and separate from the real one. He still won't take me seriously."

"I'm sorry."

"I'm used to it."

Sam watched him order an Americano, no sugar; he was hurting more than he'd admit. She gingerly probed the new sore spot on the back of her head, then opened Geoff's journal to the penultimate entry.

"So, what do you have?" Elliot asked when he returned to his seat.

"Not all of it makes sense to me; I don't think he ever intended for it to be read by other people. Mostly it records ideas he's looked into and dismissed."

"Like what?"

"Well, look." She slid the journal towards him. "Here's where he says it's probably not magic. About the trend towards more powerful spells needing more preparation and, well, *stuff*. Like he explained the other day."

"Is there anything else?"

"He was fairly convinced there was some kind of demonic presence. But he says that demons cannot manifest physically. At least not for long. Especially in daylight."

"So, that body is human. Or at least it used to be."

"Right." Sam turned the page. "In the last entry he seemed to be working on possession versus some kind of willing collaboration."

Elliot took a deep gulp from his coffee. "Not sure which one I'd be rooting for, to be honest."

She had to agree. On the one hand, it meant there was another victim involved, one it may be impossible to save. On the other, it could mean they faced two opponents.

———•———

Elliot found them a budget hotel on the outskirts of the city, in a service area off the arterial road that connected Oxford to the nearest motorway. He detoured via a retail park after Sam insisted she really couldn't spend another day in the same clothes. They picked up a couple of changes and some other essentials.

By the time they'd checked in at the hotel it was close to eight o'clock, and after a bad night and a long day they were both flagging.

The hotel didn't serve food in the evening, so they sought out the service station food court. The food was as artificial as the white tables and paper-lined plastic trays, but they felt comfortably anonymous surrounded by lone businessmen tapping away on smart phones, and distracted families herding sleepy children on the way to somewhere else.

"So, where do you think we should start tomorrow?" Sam asked.

Elliot rubbed his eyes. "I don't know."

He'd never dreamed that Geoff would be in danger. Never even considered he could be putting himself and Sam in the crosshairs. Reporters operated with something approaching immunity in the human world. Or at least neutrality. He forced down some food, not even really tasting it.

"Do you think it'll find us here?" Sam asked.

Elliot glanced up. She held her box of noodles in front of her, shoulders hunched like she wanted to be small.

"I don't know. Maybe."

This wasn't how it was supposed to work. Reporters could stand on the front lines, microphone in hand as bombs fell, delve into criminal worlds, take on corrupt multinational companies, but they always remained a pace distant. External. It was the soldiers, moles and whistle-blowers who were targeted for retribution, not the reporter they confided in.

The human world understood the unspoken rule of "don't shoot the messenger". But the supernatural world didn't play by human rules.

Maybe it should have been a comfort, an excuse why he hadn't seen the attack and Geoff's death coming. Instead, he found himself wondering what the hell he'd been doing for three and a half years. What the hell was he doing now?

Darker and darker thoughts began to chase around his head. Thoughts of failure and worse, ones that said this was only what he deserved.

"Elliot?" Sam stood beside the table with her tray. "Are you going to finish that?"

He looked down at his half-eaten burger and pushed the tray away. He didn't feel like eating; his stomach was too unsettled. Sam cleared it away, and he sat forwards with his hands clasped on the table, head slumped.

When she returned, she sat opposite him. "It's okay, we'll figure it out." She reached across the table, but he snatched his hand away and pushed his chair back with a sharp squeal.

"Will we?" he said, the despair spilling out in his voice. She made it sound so easy. The trust in her eyes for him made him feel like a liar, a fraud. "I don't think you quite understand that right now my only plan involves running and staying alive."

"What about Gabriel Cushing?"

Elliot stood. He needed to clear his head. He needed a run. "You keep looking at me like I have answers. I don't know what to tell you. I wish I had some magical way to find one man in a whole city, but I don't, alright? I need some air." He left her sitting there and strode towards the exit.

NO ANSWERS

"Excuse me?" Elliot knocked quietly on the open door. In the room beyond, two women sat at a table, while a man stood beside them. They huddled round some paperwork and a tape recorder.

The man turned. "Can we help you?"

"I'm Elliot Cross. I was told to—"

"Ah yes, come in. Do have a seat."

The younger of the two women, an attractive Indian police constable, reached for a jug of water standing in the middle of the table with a stack of paper cups. She poured a cup and slid it across the table for him as he sat down.

He licked dry lips. "Could someone explain—"

"We need to ask a few questions. Regarding the death of your brother," the man said.

"Yes, I understand that. But could you please explain what happened first? We've been waiting for days and no one will tell us—"

"I'm sorry, Mr Cross," the constable said. "I'm afraid you may find the details distressing, but we will do our best."

She pressed a button on the tape recorder and the harsh click made Elliot jump.

"Interview with Elliot Cross. DC Jalela Gosh and DS Frank Cannock conducting. We are joined by Mrs Lyndsay Haskin of Her Majesty's coroners."

Elliot watched the spools of the tape rotate slowly as the room grew oppressively hot. He took a sip of water to cool his throat.

DC Gosh opened the file in front of her and slid it across to the coroner.

The older woman took a drink from her cup. "The post-mortem examination shows that Corporal James Cross died of…" She took a deep breath. "…severe crush injuries. The most likely scenario being that a large, heavy object hit him at moderate speed, crushing him against a wall or another large object." She met Elliot's eyes. "I'm so sorry."

Elliot rubbed the bridge of his nose and pressed his fingers into his eyes, feeling his contacts slide. "I don't understand. I was told he was found on the platform of Piccadilly tube station."

"That's correct," Cannock said from beside him. "Which leads us to believe he may not have died where he was found."

After his lenses settled, he regarded each of them in turn. They watched him expectantly. "Are you… are you saying he was mur… moved? You think someone—"

"We're not sure yet," Gosh said. "Which is why we are hoping you can help us."

Cannock drew up a chair beside his colleague. "We'll need a formal statement but, for the record, when did you last see your brother?"

Elliot swallowed hard. "He, umm, stopped by my place, that night. I-I told him…" He closed his eyes and took a breath. "I had somewhere to be. I didn't know – I thought he was—"

"What time was this?" Cannock asked.

"About six. He only stayed about ten minutes."

"And your whereabouts for the rest of the evening?"

Elliot blinked stinging eyes. "I was at the National Press Awards. I left home about twenty past six, got a cab to the convention centre. I went straight from there to The Dorchester, with colleagues. I was there until about midnight, I think. I was pretty drunk by then."

Gosh pointed to the report in front of her. Elliot couldn't read it from where he sat, but her superior nodded.

"And after that?" Cannock asked.

Elliot cringed. "I went back to my... well, she's not really my girlfriend as such, but... her place."

The two detectives nodded.

"Can you give us a name?" Gosh asked.

"Do I have to?" He didn't need them questioning Cat, not after he'd called it off with her yesterday.

"Our best estimate for time of death is between one and three a.m.," Gosh said. "So yes. We'll need her to confirm your alibi."

Alibi? That didn't sound good. "Alright. Catherine, Catherine Tanner. I was with her until about two thirty, then I took a cab home. Are you considering me a suspect?"

Gosh forced a smile. Cannock remained unreadably neutral. The coroner kept her eyes down.

Cannock broke the silence. "No, not at this time. Just eliminating possibilities. Can you think of anyone who might have wanted to harm your brother? Someone with a past grudge perhaps?"

Elliot shook his head. "No, I don't know. I don't..." He set his elbows on the table and sank his face into his hands. "I didn't believe him."

Cannock leaned forwards with his forearms on the table edge, hands clasped. "Mr Cross, it's important that you tell us everything. Was someone threatening your brother?"

"I'm not sure. H-He said *something* was after him, that it killed a woman from his unit. I'm sorry, he did tell me her name but I can't remember. He said it was coming for him."

The company around the table collectively leaned in.

"*It*, Mr Cross? What was *it*, exactly?"

Elliot raised his head, hands still pressed over his face. "I don't know. I thought he was being ridiculous." He rubbed his hands over his eyes and felt the sting of tears. "I don't know. I don't know."

15

Elliot bolted awake the next morning with the sun in his eyes and leaden guilt in his gut. He'd told Sam it was hopeless and left her sitting alone in the service station.

"Shit."

He'd only meant to take a few minutes, to grab his running shoes from the car and calm his mind down with a quick jog round the car park. But when that hadn't worked he'd found himself venturing further than intended, and by the time he returned Sam had retired to the hotel. She'd texted him to say she understood he needed some time and that she'd see him in the morning, so he hadn't disturbed her. Now that felt like the wrong decision.

He raked his hand through his hair, pulled on a clean pair of black chinos over the underwear and T-shirt he'd slept in, snagged his key card from the desk and darted out into the hall. He knocked softly on the next door along.

During the pause he listened for movement. He was about to knock again when Sam cracked open the door. She peered out with puffy, red-rimmed eyes and a thin set to her lips.

"I'm sorry," he said before she could speak.

For a long moment she glared at him in a way that made him feel small, then her eyes dropped. "Good," she said. "Give me a second, I'm not decent." She closed the door and he stood awkwardly in the corridor for a few minutes until she opened it again, wider this time.

He followed her in.

"I made a start," she said as she dropped into the chair beside the dressing table and opened her laptop. "I checked the electoral roll, but I couldn't find anything. I'm guessing Gabriel Cushing lives off grid, but that doesn't mean we won't be able to find someone to point us in the right direction. It took a little while to download the database, and it was a bit late to start making calls last night, but I have a list of names to start with. I found four of our contacts in the area, and some paranormal societies we could try. Do you want to see?"

Elliot sat on the edge of the bed behind her, speechless.

She twisted round in her seat. "Or do you want to carry on with the pity party from last night?" There was a touch of a smug grin lurking behind her mask of disapproval.

He closed his eyes and slowly shook his head, smiling. She was like a fountain of optimism sometimes. "No, I'm done with that. I am sorry for the way I spoke to you, and for walking out. I just needed to clear my head."

She slid off her chair and sat beside him. "And I'm sorry you felt like I was dumping all the responsibility on you. I didn't mean to. I just wanted to talk it through."

"I know."

"I'm scared too. But we can't give up."

He felt a strong compulsion to hug her. He settled for touching the back of her hand with his. "You're right. Thank you."

"Do you want to go through the contacts?" she asked, nodding towards the laptop.

"Absolutely. But how about we take a look over breakfast?"

"Okay, sounds good." She smiled, and more of the weariness left her eyes. "I might grab a shower first though. Meet you down there?"

"Sure."

He decided to take the opportunity for a shower too, and when he reached the hotel restaurant he found Sam already returning with a plate to an isolated table in the corner. Her laptop sat open beside her.

"I got you coffee." She pointed to a mug by the place opposite her.

"Thanks. Let me grab something to eat and then we'll see what you've got."

When he returned from the buffet, Sam angled the laptop towards him and shifted her seat round so they could both see the screen. The database contained contact details for everyone who'd ever done work for *Weird News*. While Elliot knew for a fact there were no members of the inner circle of serious, regular contributors based in Oxford, the outer circle network contained several hundred people. Sam's search had identified four names nearby.

"Kevin Matthews doesn't have a phone number, but I doubt he'll have information on anything at ground level," he said.

"Is he the UFO guy?"

"The same."

"Hmm."

Next on the list was an older lady who wrote a semi-regular recipe column for them including herb lore – a practising Wiccan and major gossip.

"I included her, but she's actually out in the sticks," Sam said, pointing to the address, which, while it contained Oxford, was actually a village several miles out.

"Okay, we'll put her on the back burner. That leaves Fiona Prince and Liam Townsend."

Sam wiped some crumbs off her fingers and pushed her empty plate to one side. "Fiona is going to be our best bet, don't you think?"

"Agreed."

An Oxford university professor of ancient civilisation, Fiona Prince had provided some excellent historical counterpoint pieces on cults and religions, especially when it came to demons and deities. From the one time he'd met her in person, Elliot suspected she knew more about the supernatural than she let on. If he was right, who better to help them find out if Gabriel Cushing, demon hunter, was in town?

Sam excused herself to fetch them each a second cup of coffee. It was half past nine already, so Elliot dialled Fiona's number. No answer, but he left a message.

Sam returned with their mugs as he was calling Liam.

"Liam? It's Elliot Cross, *Weird News*."

"Oh hey, how's it going?" Liam replied with a soft lilt of Irish accent.

"Not one of my best weeks, in truth." Elliot shared a look with Sam. "I'm looking for someone in Oxford. Reckon you might be able to help with that?"

"You're here now?"

"That's right."

"Who's this guy?"

Elliot quickly checked to make sure they were out of earshot of the other hotel guests. "A man named Gabriel Cushing. He's a… an expert on the occult." Liam's interest in the supernatural related to the afterlife and spirits, and Elliot wasn't sure where he might stand on demons and demon hunters.

"Huh. Doesn't ring any bells, but I could take you round a few places."

"Today?"

"Sure. You know where The Retreat is, yeah?"

"I know it. We'll be there in half an hour." He hung up and sat with his coffee cup clasped between his hands, plan forming.

Networking was what he did. He should have played to his strengths from the beginning. It was only his pride that made it a personal challenge. At least Sam had her head screwed on.

After breakfast they checked out, taking everything. If they kept moving, they could keep one step ahead of the Mime. In theory.

———•———

The Oxford Retreat occupied a beautiful old grey-stone building on the bank of the river, beside a bridge. There was a convenient car park on the opposite side. As they approached the pub over the bridge, Sam paused in the middle of the span and studied the building through her viewfinder. A lilac in full bloom at one corner offered a wonderful colour contrast with the grey masonry and the bright fresh green of a weeping willow trailing fronds in the dark water. She snapped off a couple of pictures. Gaggles of tourists loitered outside, but no one appeared to be waiting to meet them.

Inside, clean, modern fittings indicated the old building had undergone a recent re-fit. Sam scanned the few morning customers – a couple by the bar, a few singletons dotted around the tables at the edges.

"I don't think he's here yet," she said, nodding towards the bar. "Latte?"

Liam worked as a nurse, which gave him access to patients for his research subject – out-of-body and near-death experiences. He was working on a book. Sam might have worried he'd be a complete weirdo if she hadn't read the articles he'd done for *Weird News*. She'd found his one on "the bright light at the end of the tunnel" myth quite touching. He wrote like a sane person.

The bartender handed her two cups, and she took them over to where Elliot was sitting absently watching a group of aimless tourists, like his mind was elsewhere.

"Do you know what he looks like?" she asked.

"I've not actually met him before."

At that moment a man walked in, straight up to the bar, and hailed the bartender. Sam caught sight of tattooed words on his forearm as he held it up. He rubbed his hand over buzz-cut hair and then turned, scanned the room and homed in on them. A smile curved his wide, expressive mouth.

"Elliot?" Liam asked as he walked over.

Sam glanced at Elliot as he stood.

"Do we stand out that much?"

"Nah, saw your picture on the website. Park there a sec, I'm parched."

Liam returned to their table a moment later with a very pre-lunch pint. He set his drink down and held out his hand to Elliot. Both his arms were tattooed, but he didn't stay still long enough for Sam to read them.

Elliot grasped his hand and Liam jerked him forwards into a half hug, half back slap. "How's it going? It's good to finally meet you."

"Likewise." Elliot rolled his injured shoulder. "This is Sam, she works with me."

Liam flashed her a grin and a wink as he slid into the seat beside her. "So, what's the story?"

While they sipped their drinks, Elliot explained about the Mime, the Bristol murders and Gabriel Cushing. He kept to the skeleton facts, avoiding most of the more impossible supernatural details. Sam wondered whether he was still smarting from his friend's rejection yesterday, or just being cautious because of the public setting.

"You're having me on."

Elliot tensed.

"We're not," Sam said. "There's more to it. More you're probably best off not knowing. Right now, we just need you to trust us. And to find Gabriel."

"Right." His grin faded, suddenly serious. "Well, pub landlords'd be a good place to start. I know a few we can speak to. Can you describe this Cushing guy?"

"Only second hand," Elliot said. "I've heard he's in his mid-thirties, average height. Classically educated, I believe. Speaks with a Queen's English tone."

"Grand." Liam took a gulp from his drink. "Not like toffs are rare in these parts. But here, you can give 'em a demo."

Sam snorted into her coffee, spraying droplets, and Elliot glanced at her in alarm.

"Sorry," she muttered, reaching for a serviette.

"Are you saying I sound—"

"Like a fancy-pants Londoner?" Liam filled in with a smirk. "Only when you speak."

"Alright, alright, enough. This isn't helping."

Sam smiled at the indignation in his voice as she dabbed at the drops on the table. "So, where do we start?"

Liam downed the last of his pint and slammed the glass on the table. "The dog's bollocks."

"Excuse me?" Elliot said.

"The Dog and Ball? Everyone knows it as—"

"Right, I see. Let's get a move on, then."

Over the next few hours they toured pubs, hostels, shops and more. Liam introduced them to owners, landlords, friends, bartenders, regulars. It didn't seem there was anywhere in Oxford he wasn't familiar with.

"Cheers, mate," Liam said to the stocky, bald bartender at the Angel & Greyhound as he turned away from the bar. As he re-joined Elliot and Sam by the door, he shook his head. Still nothing.

"Where next?" Sam asked. "Does anyone else want to stop for lunch?" She rubbed her grumbling stomach.

"One more," he said, heading for the door. "It's just round the corner."

Outside, she fell into step beside him. Elliot followed a pace behind. Liam turned down a narrow alley. Set back from the main street stood a shop with a pentacle motif sign jutting out.

"This Gabriel guy has to get his supplies somewhere, right?" Liam said. "And Rosa's is legend."

They paused outside. Dreamcatchers, crystals, and other pseudo-occult frippery filled its bay window, all surrounding a large fantasy painting featuring a not-quite-naked elfin woman petting a dragon.

Fantasy girls could have big boobs *and* tiny waists. Sam crossed her arms. Real women had to choose one or the other. "Are we going in?"

Elliot snapped his attention away from the window display. "After you."

A bell above the door tinkled. Sandalwood and spices assailed her senses. In the front part of the shop the neat shelves of scented candles, pretty leather-bound stationery and silver jewellery looked fairly mundane, but, as she ventured further in, the atmosphere changed. Antique books and trinkets. Glass cases with unique amulets and jewelled knives. Beyond a worn, solid-wood counter at the rear, shelves extended back, full of glass jars with handwritten labels. The woman behind the counter tipped dried leaves from one of the jars into the bowl of a beautiful set of brass scales. When the scales balanced, she took the bowl off and tipped the contents into a paper bag, which she wrote on and sealed with a piece of tape.

Thin braids ran from her temples to a clasp at the back of her head, decorated with striped feathers from some bird of prey. Her makeup framed mature eyes with metallic copper and chocolate brown, which accentuated her Mediterranean complexion. With her flowing dress and shawl, she could have stepped out of one of those fantasy paintings.

She glanced up as the three of them approached. "Good afternoon," she said, with a warm smile and a hint of a European accent. "Liam! How are you?"

"Not too bad, Rosa, not too bad. How's business?"

"Oh, you know. Candles and love potions mostly." She air-quoted love potions, which Sam took to mean that the things she sold were about as potent as rose water. "But the New Age stuff pays the bills and means I can stay open for my regulars. Friends of yours?"

"Rosa, this is Elliot and Sam. They run *Weird News.*"

Rosa's face lit up. "Oh! You're one of my best sellers." She nodded towards a rack beside the counter where last month's issue took the prime spot. "Welcome." She reached across the counter to clasp both of their hands affectionately. Sam's cheeks heated with pride and she had to resist the urge to glance over at Elliot to see his reaction.

"What can I help you with?"

"We're looking for someone," Elliot said. "His name is Gabriel Cushing and he's—"

"*Oh mio.* I haven't seen him in months," Rosa said.

They'd been searching all morning and hadn't encountered a single trace of evidence that he even existed. Now suddenly they had someone who knew him standing right in front of them.

Elliot shot a quick glance at Sam and she nodded urgently.

"You know him?" he asked.

"Oh yes. He's… You know what he does?" She glanced warily between the three of them. "What he *really* does, I mean?"

Elliot nodded. "He's a demon hunter, we know. We need his help."

Rosa paled slightly. "He used to come in quite regularly. Two or three times a week. Then I might not see him for several weeks, but he'd always pop up again. But this time? This time it's been months."

"How many months?" Elliot asked.

"Oh, about three or four."

Four months ago they'd published their second article about a demon Gabriel reportedly hunted and killed. Elliot's research suggested Gabriel had walked away from the fight alive, but what if something had happened to him since?

"You don't happen to have contact details for him, do you?" Elliot asked.

"I might. Let me check." Rosa disappeared through a beaded curtain into a back room.

While they waited for her, Elliot's phone rang. He checked the screen. "It's Fiona." He accepted the call and started for the door. "Elliot Cross."

The bell tinkled as he went out. Sam stayed inside with Liam. She tried to catch a glimpse of the tattoos on his arms so she could read what they said, but he kept moving, picking items up off the counter. When she glanced at his face, she caught him smirking like he was trying not to laugh.

"You're doing that on purpose," she said.

He chuckled. "Guilty. D'you want to see?" He held both arms out, wrists together. Held like that Sam could see the way the words scrolled from one arm onto the other.

"There is rejoicing in the presence of the angels of God over one sinner who repents," she read.

"Luke, fifteen, ten."

"Are you a big fan of scripture?"

"I've read it, but I'm no bible thumper. The Lord and I have an agreement to stay out of each other's way."

She leaned on the counter. "So can I ask why you have a verse permanently inked into your skin?"

He grinned and joined her, standing close. "It's a reminder."

"Why, do you have sins to repent?"

He locked eyes with her. "What do you think?"

She suddenly felt uncomfortably warm. How many sins could he have accumulated? He couldn't be much older than Elliot, if he wasn't younger.

Elliot returned, pocketing his phone. He paused when he saw them, and Sam shifted further along the counter. Her stomach twisted like a nest of snakes.

"Fiona can meet us at two thirty," he said, with a slightly puzzled frown.

The beaded curtain behind the counter swished as Rosa re-emerged. "I'm sorry. The only address I have is a post office box, and the phone number I had has been disconnected." She held out a slip of paper. "Here."

Elliot took it. Sam sensed the frustration leaking out from behind his closed expression. The first hint of anything and it went nowhere.

"Thank you," she said.

"No problem." Rosa regarded Elliot with her head canted to one side. "Do you mind my asking why you're looking for him? I'm sensing it's not just an interview you're after."

Elliot lifted his gaze from the slip of paper. "What? Oh. No, we have a demon that needs killing."

She nodded softly. "And that's not something you've faced before?"

"No."

"Interesting. All paths start somewhere, I suppose."

Elliot frowned. "What do you mean?"

"Oh, nothing," Rosa said, smiling. "You just have something about you that reminds me of him. Gabriel, I mean."

"We best be making tracks," Liam said, putting a hand on Sam's arm. "Be seeing you, Rosa."

"Take care of yourselves." The three of them started for the door. "Oh, and Sam," Rosa called. "Whether something is a curse or a gift simply depends on your perspective."

Sam paused, staring at her. "What?"

Rosa smiled. "Just something to think on."

"I… Okay." She followed Elliot and Liam out into the street.

16

"I'm just saying, I thought it was a bit rude," Sam said sullenly. Elliot glanced across as they walked through the historic heart of Oxford towards Fiona's college. "What?"

"Just because we didn't find anything useful doesn't mean he wasn't trying to help. I don't see why he couldn't stay for lunch."

"Because." He wished he could think of a decent reason, but the truth was he simply hadn't wanted Liam there. Fiona had agreed to meet them, and he wanted to eat and move on, not indulge in a social outing.

They paused across the street from the grand façade of Wadham College. A regular-sized door set into the centre of a much larger slab of studded oak opened like a portal to another realm. Beyond, Elliot glimpsed sunlit, meticulously manicured lawn.

By the door, a sandwich-board sign prohibited access to the college quads, except for official business and organised tours.

"This is kind of cool," Sam said.

Elliot frowned. Something didn't sit right with the scene in front of them.

"You know, because we get to be official visitors." She grinned.

They crossed the road and walked up to the door. Elliot peered through into the shadowed tunnel.

"Why isn't there anyone here stopping people?" he muttered. Every other college entrance they'd passed was manned by a security guard to stop the throngs of tourists wandering about where they weren't allowed.

Sam poked her head inside. "Hello?" She stepped through. "Bathroom break, maybe?"

Elliot scanned the street one last time, then stepped into the passage through the building which led to the sunlit quad.

"So, how do we get to Fiona's office?" Sam asked.

Elliot checked the directions he'd taken down while talking to Fiona earlier. "Straight across and then—"

Something sharp jabbed the back of his hand and drew a spot of blood. He stopped short, looked up.

On the far side of the quad the Mime lounged against the wall. A couple of students walked by, deep in conversation. They only spared the black-clad man brief glances.

Elliot reached his hand out and flinched when he encountered a point. Invisible. He traced the spike to its base where it met thick bars of what felt like wrought iron. Carefully, he worked his way along the invisible barrier. More spikes jutted out in a regular grid pattern, barely six inches between them, like a portcullis. He followed it sideways until it met the wall. Sam, checking the extent of the barrier in the other direction, reached the side too.

"Go back!" He rushed to the door that led to the street, and hit another invisible obstacle, this one solid and smooth but for a ridged texture and the odd splinter. Wooden, like the huge oak door.

Across the lawn, the Mime extended both arms out to the side as if soliciting praise from some unseen audience as it advanced towards them.

Elliot sucked in a hard breath and surveyed the space they were trapped in. A side door led into the building and he darted towards it. He twisted the handle and tugged, but the door was locked.

"Elliot, it's moving!" Sam cried.

She stood, hands curled round the bars of the Mime's invisible metal grate as it slowly drove her backwards. The Mime now stood only a few paces away. It turned its arms in a circle, as if cranking a large wheel. Each turn wound the spiked barrier forwards by some mechanism, shrinking the space between it and the wooden door.

Elliot put one foot up on the wall and heaved on the handle, but the sturdy door wouldn't budge. "Come on!" He let go and staggered across the flagstones. "Look for anything we can use to brace the wall, or break through this door."

Sam hunted around the dim edges of the passageway, her phone pressed to her ear. "Damn, it's going straight to voicemail."

"Fiona?"

She nodded. "What do we do?"

Elliot glanced at the Mime. It continued to turn the wheel, cranking the spiked trap ever tighter, with a wide-eyed expression of mock terror etched on its face. There was no way to blind or distract it this time, and they knew of no other way to break the illusions it created. Nowhere to hide. He stepped on a drain cover and looked down. The spiked metal grill fitted the space they were in perfectly, from edge to edge and from floor to ceiling, but it was a *fixed* shape.

"Help me lift this."

Sam crouched opposite him and dug her fingers into the gaps in the steel cover. They forced it up enough to slide it sideways. Below, the recess descended maybe a metre to where it intersected several narrow drainage pipes. Not big enough for him, but Sam might fit.

"Get in," Elliot said.

"What?" Sam lost her balance as the creeping spikes jabbed her in the back.

"Get in and I'll move the cover back," he whispered, indicating the hole with a look. "It should pass right over you."

Her eyes filled with fear. "And if it doesn't?"

He swallowed hard. The advancing spikes prodded his shoulder, forcing him to step to the side. "There's no time to argue. Get in!"

"I'm not leaving you up here to die," she said, as if the idea were unthinkable.

He grabbed her arm and shoved her towards the hole. "You won't have to if you get past and distract it. Now move."

Her eyes widened as she grasped the plan, and she swung her legs into the drain.

He risked a glance past her shoulder at the Mime. It stood framed in the archway, its hands still gripping the wheel as it cranked the barrier forwards. Its eyes flashed, triumphant, malevolent. It seemed totally unconcerned by what they were doing.

"Hurry, Sam. I can't have your death on my conscience. I just can't." He'd rather die than live with that.

Her eyes filled with tears, but she squeezed into the hole. Elliot stood, gripped the advancing metal and strained against it, trying to buy her more time. Suddenly she yelped and scrambled out of the hole, clutching her ankle. She pulled her hand away. It was spotted with blood.

"I can't. There's something in there! Something big and moving…"

He glanced into the hole but couldn't see anything. If whatever was down there was invisible then it was the Mime's doing, like the animals at the market in Bristol.

"Shit. Not like this," Elliot growled. He braced his feet against the smooth flagstones, but the wall kept inching closer, driving him back. His heels met the wooden door behind them. Sam joined him, shoulder to shoulder, arms between the advancing spikes.

The Mime's eyes burned with hate as it jerked the wheel round. The spikes advanced in short jolts. Elliot held the grid at arm's length with his elbows locked for about ten seconds before the pressure became too much. His shoulders screamed as he fought against it, but his efforts did nothing to slow the creeping advance of death. It wouldn't be long. The first spike made contact with his chest and he tried to flatten himself against the door. He turned his head to the side and locked eyes with Sam. Silent determination shone through her tears.

"I'm sorry," he said.

"Don't be."

A crackle of sparks and smoke burst behind the Mime. Its black-framed eyes widened. It spun in a panic, tripped and sprawled on the ground. The metal grid with the spikes abruptly dissolved. Elliot and Sam slumped down with their backs to the door. The Mime scrambled to its feet, leapt over them and disappeared into the street.

When Elliot's heart rate had slowed a fraction, he looked up, to see someone walking towards them through the clearing smoke.

17

Sam moved onto her knees, hugging her middle with shaky arms. Elliot put a hand on her shoulder.

"Are you alright?"

She shook her head but then nodded. He knew what she meant: no, but we don't have time for that now.

Still trembling from the adrenaline and fear, Elliot forced himself to his feet. The man in front of him tucked a box of matches into a worn black satchel and straightened his tweed jacket.

"In anticipation of crossing paths with a demon foe, I find it wise to carry a supply of firecrackers," he said.

Elliot took in the man's round face and full, neat beard. Under the jacket he wore an olive shirt, cream tie and navy cords.

"Who are you?"

"Gabriel Cushing. I heard someone was looking for me."

Though his hair receded slightly at the front, he was younger than Elliot had expected. There were no hard lines around his eyes, but one look into their depths warned Elliot not to confuse youth with inexperience. He saw a controlled, calculating surety there.

"How did you know that would work? The firecrackers?" Elliot helped Sam stand.

"An elementary fact. Demons are frightened by the laughter of children, the sound of church bells, and firecrackers. I find the latter to be the most portable."

"Does it always work?"

"Alas, it often becomes less effective when employed repeatedly. Now, perhaps you could explain who *you* are?"

"Elliot Cross." He held his hand out and Gabriel shook it, briefly but firmly. "This is Samantha. We run a publication with an occult focus."

"*Weird News*? Yes, I am familiar with it." There was a scathing edge to his words. "Your first article on a certain homicidal coat provided minor aid in tracking the demon."

"Glad to be of assistance," Elliot muttered.

Gabriel moved past them towards the doorway to the street and paused. "As to the follow-up article." He let out an exasperated sigh. "A most *thorough* account." He stressed the word "thorough" as if it were a bad thing.

"I fact-checked every word in that article."

"No doubt." Gabriel levelled a cold stare at Elliot. Though the man was no taller than him the steel in his eyes made him feel small. "Personally I don't agree with exposing such matters to the harsh light of day. It encourages curiosity among foolish people ill-prepared for what they may encounter."

Elliot bristled. Gabriel's inflection blatantly suggested he was one of those foolish, ill-prepared people.

"People have a right to know. Perhaps if more people like us shed light on the supernatural, people would be better prepared."

Gabriel exited through the door towards the street. Elliot followed him. "Wait, where are you going? We're supposed to meet with Fiona Prince."

"Ms Prince doesn't need to be involved," Gabriel muttered.

Elliot quickened his pace until he was walking alongside him. "Excuse me?"

------·------

Sam followed a pace behind. Elliot usually shortened his naturally long stride when they walked together, but Gabriel stalked with fast, angry steps that forced Elliot to walk at pace to keep up, and this left Sam breaking into a jog every few yards.

Gabriel paused and Sam almost ran into his back.

"You have a vehicle, I presume?"

"We're parked on the far side of the centre," Elliot said.

"Very good. Lead the way."

As they crossed the city, Sam tried to listen to their conversation, but more was being said with icy looks than words. Every time Elliot tried to bring up the Mime, Gabriel glared pointedly at the throngs of tourists, shoppers and locals milling around. If she got too close she'd suffer frostbite, but Elliot wouldn't back down, and she felt proud of him for that.

The tension remained tangible until they reached the car. Elliot drove them south out of the city, to another hotel on the ring road. Gabriel calmly informed them he would wait in the hotel lounge while they checked in.

Sam followed Elliot to the reception desk. She caught up as the receptionist informed him they only had the one room left. His shoulders tensed.

"That'll be fine," Sam said to the receptionist. She glanced at Elliot and the wary expression on his face. "It's okay. I'd rather not be on my own anyway. No need to spend more than you have to, right?"

He wet his lips, frown deepening. "I'm not sure it would be… proper."

"Oh, screw proper. What is this, the nineteenth century? We're friends, aren't we?"

"Of course."

"Well, then."

The receptionist patiently waited for them to finish. Elliot closed his eyes for a moment. "Just the one twin, then."

She nodded and started tapping on the keyboard.

While Elliot paid, Sam watched Gabriel, who had settled on a leather sofa in the lounge with a book open on his knee.

"Do you think he knows what he's doing?" she asked. "That firecracker trick was pretty cool."

"I hope so. I know him by reputation. He comes from a line of demon hunters who dedicated their lives to eradicating the demon Ka."

"The possessed coat that ate people?"

"That's the one."

Of all the stories they'd dealt with, she'd really struggled to wrap her head around that one. How could a *coat* eat anything, let alone a whole person, or thirty? But that wasn't important right now.

"Okay, second question," she said. "Can we trust him? I don't think he likes you very much."

"Picked up on that, did you? Well, we'll just have to talk him round."

One of the hotel staff set a tray on the coffee table in front of Gabriel. Sam and Elliot joined him as he poured three cups of tea from a large pot.

"Now, Mr Cross, enlighten me about this demon."

Over the next half hour, Elliot explained every detail about the Mime and how they'd come to be involved. He described every attack they had researched or witnessed, especially the child at the aerial circus where they'd intervened and drawn the Mime's attention, and the encounter in the department store.

"And now you believe it's tracking you?"

"It followed us here from Bristol," Sam said.

For the first time Gabriel seemed to focus on her. He glanced between her and Elliot as if speculating how they fitted together. "Even the weakest of demons possess additional senses and certain powers of clairvoyance. I suspect it was able to divine a location where you would be present at a future moment, and thus intercept you."

She reached into her bag and drew out Geoff's diary.

"Our friend Geoff was helping us research. He thought the Mime might have some connection to Dagon. I think that's why he thought you could help."

"Thought?"

"It murdered him," Elliot said. "Executed, you might say, before he could explain his reasoning."

Gabriel set his teacup down. "Unfortunate. This friend of yours, did he have any other theories?"

Sam handed him the diary, open to the last entry. "I think he was working on something about the Mime's appearance. The dark clothes, the gloves, the makeup. But his notes are all disjointed."

Gabriel scanned Geoff's scratchy handwriting for a moment. "Interesting speculation, perhaps, but unusual and dark appearances are common among possessions. More likely it is merely a persona affected by the demon." He sat further forwards, returned the book and retrieved his tea. "Even if there is some truth to your friend's theories, I suspect it will be inconsequential. It will have no bearing on our course of action."

"What course of action?" Sam asked.

Gabriel took a long sip. "Exorcism, of course."

"And how exactly do you intend to get close enough to perform an exorcism?" Elliot asked.

"I have a number of wards, which should suffice to fend off any attacks. Also, if yourself and Samantha here are the primary targets, then the element of surprise will be on my side."

Sam slowly lowered her cup. "You want to use us as bait?"

"Quite the contrary. I shall be going alone."

She and Elliot exchanged a look of dismay.

"You can't!" Elliot said. "Gabriel, you haven't seen what this thing can do. We have."

Gabriel shook his head. "A demon's power is heightened by the fear felt by those around it. My lack of fear will diminish its influence."

From what they'd seen so far, the Mime didn't like being confronted by the unexpected, that was true. But it seemed to grow bolder every time. Who knew whether it was the firecrackers or the appearance of an unexpected new opponent that had chased it off. Either way, it wouldn't be so easily scared again.

"I really think you should consider taking me with you," Elliot said calmly. "To watch your back."

Sam's head snapped round and she glared at him. "Taking *you*? What about me?"

He held his hand out, a signal to keep out of it. She took that to mean he had a plan. He kept his eyes on Gabriel, and Sam shivered as the frosty atmosphere from earlier returned.

"I wouldn't be able to focus on the ritual if I had to defend you at the same time."

Elliot's jaw tightened. "You wouldn't need to defend me. I'd be there to protect you. I can take care of myself."

"As you aptly demonstrated this afternoon."

"It blindsided us, came out of nowhere! We had no reason to suspect it was even in the same city."

Gabriel set his cup down and stood. "As may be, but I will still be going alone."

Sam and Elliot stood too.

"Stay here." Gabriel shouldered his satchel. "I will return once the ritual is complete."

Sam glanced between the two men, waiting for Elliot to say something, but he didn't. "You—"

Elliot nudged her in the ribs, and she bit off the end of her words.

"Good luck," he said.

Gabriel nodded to them then strode towards the desk, where he waved the receptionist over.

Sam grasped Elliot's arm. "You can't just let him leave!"

"He won't listen to me."

"That's... So? We can't let him go after that thing on his own."

The receptionist made a phone call. When she hung up, Gabriel walked towards the bathrooms at the rear of the lounge.

"You're right." Elliot gestured to the double doors at the front of the foyer. "Which is why we're going to follow him."

18

They ran across the car park. Elliot slid into the driver's seat of the BMW and angled the rear-view mirror to watch the front of the hotel. Sam retrieved her camera from the boot. A few minutes passed before Gabriel emerged. He paced the short stretch of pavement outside the sliding doors until a taxi arrived. Elliot sat rigid, his hand poised over the key in the ignition. When the taxi moved off, he followed.

From the hotel the taxi took the ring road west, then diverted off into a series of narrow rural lanes. Elliot kept as much distance between them as he could without losing sight of it.

"Where's he going?" Sam asked, one hand clutching her camera tight.

Elliot didn't have an answer for her. Maybe Gabriel had spotted them following and was trying to throw them off by directing the taxi through the twisty lanes. But the route seemed too purposeful for that. Eventually, the taxi entered a hamlet and came to a stop outside a small chapel with a dilapidated graveyard squeezed in alongside. Elliot slowed, and parked down an adjacent lane where he hoped they wouldn't be noticed. He and Sam watched through the rear windscreen.

Gabriel emerged and headed inside. The taxi stayed.

"Should we follow him in?" Sam asked.

"No. He's stopped for supplies, I should think."

"We passed a whole bunch of churches on the way here. Why *this* one?"

"Good question, but I don't want to miss our chance to follow him when he leaves."

They waited for nearly ten minutes. Elliot drummed his fingers on the door handle, doubt beginning to creep in. He was about to give in when a flash of movement by the church stilled his hand. Gabriel trotted down the flagstone path and climbed into the taxi carrying nothing but the satchel he'd taken in, though it bulged more than before.

They tailed the taxi back to the south of the city, where it stopped outside a townhouse in the middle of a white terrace of three. Elliot pulled in behind a transit van parked further down the road and watched the front of the house in the wing mirror. Again, the taxi kept the meter running, but this time Gabriel was only a few minutes. He returned carrying a brown leather case with a traditional snap fastening.

"Next stop demon fun?" Sam asked, as the taxi crawled away once more.

"We'll see."

They soon recognised that the route the taxi now took would lead them back to Fiona's college.

The car rounded the last corner, left, past the square bastion of the Weston Library, opposite the college. It passed a police car and an ambulance, and indicated in on the left. Elliot snagged a space on the college side. They weren't exactly inconspicuous or quiet in the M5, but if Gabriel hadn't spotted them already he likely had no suspicions they would follow him.

Sam fitted her telephoto lens to use as a telescope. When Gabriel exited the taxi, they both scrunched down in their seats until he'd crossed the road, then Elliot cautiously peered over the steering wheel. Police tape fluttered across the doorway into the quad, and a uniformed officer stood watch.

"What do you think happened?" Sam asked.

"I don't know. Maybe the Mime dispatched whoever was watching the door before we arrived."

"I hope Fiona's okay."

That was the other possibility Elliot didn't want to consider.

Gabriel approached the building, about thirty yards away. Though Elliot couldn't see his face, the police officer shifted his feet, body language emanating suspicion.

Sam watched through her camera. "Gabriel's got something in his hand, like a weight on a chain, only it's flat. Like a coin with a hole in the middle." She clicked off a shot and showed him the display.

"A construct, maybe."

She inclined her head, asking him to explain.

"Something I read about. It's supposed to be possible to link a demon's energy signature to an object and then use it to track the demon." Sometimes he needed to remind himself that he wasn't a complete amateur, no matter what Gabriel might say.

Sam returned her eye to the viewfinder. "Cool. Oh, wait, he's on the move." She clipped her lens cap on.

Gabriel set off at a quick walk, heading towards them. Elliot ducked down, but the demon hunter crossed the street before he reached them.

"Come on," he said, reaching for the door handle. "Stay out of sight."

They slid out of the car and followed at a distance along the wide thoroughfare through the heart of Oxford until they reached a busy junction. Traffic and tourists dodged each other around an island where a medieval church and its grounds stood, defiant, seemingly frozen in time – a relic the city obligingly worked around. Gabriel paused, and Elliot pulled Sam down behind a railing crowded with bicycles. He peered between the handlebars.

Crouching beside him, Sam squinted through her camera. She twisted the zoom to maximum. "He's dangling that construct thing again. Whoa."

"What?"

"It moved. I mean, it was swinging one way and it changed direction, by itself."

Gabriel wound a halting path through the streets of Oxford, pausing at every junction to hold the construct at arm's length and watch the way it swung. The Gothic college architecture gave way to red brick and then a mismatched array of nineteen-thirties' semis and younger buildings. Watching the way Gabriel confidently consulted the device renewed Elliot's hope. Maybe the exorcism would work. Maybe he should have a little more faith.

Gabriel paused at a T-junction opposite a building with boarded windows. It looked like a disused community hall. Rampant weeds broke apart the patch of concrete car park in front. An open porch with moss-clogged gutters jutted out, from which a few roof tiles had let go and now littered the ground with smashed remnants.

Elliot ducked behind a parked car, Sam beside him.

The demon hunter walked from one corner of the building to the other, watching the construct intently, before returning to the centre. He pocketed the device and stepped under the porch.

"He's going in there?" Sam said.

"Looks like it. We'll follow as soon as he's out of sight."

Gabriel tested the door and found it locked. He cast a glance each way down the road, then stooped and picked up a chunk of broken tile. A short, sharp tap smashed one of the glass panels beside the door and he reached through to unlock it. Adjusting the strap of his satchel, he entered.

Elliot allowed a count of five to let Gabriel move further in, then gave Sam's elbow a gentle nudge. They broke cover, ran across the road, gingerly picked their way over the broken glass and tiles, and followed Gabriel into the dim interior.

They stepped into an asymmetric entrance hall. Drifts of rubbish in the corners and graffiti tags scrawled across the wall suggested squatters had made a home from the place. But they hadn't been there for a while, based on the overlying dust and mildew. A double set of mouldering wooden doors sat at an angle to the rest of the foyer, fractionally ajar.

Sam crept over and crouched by the crack. "It's dark but I can see him. He's standing in the middle of the room with the construct."

"Is this the only way in?"

To the left, corroded signs on two doors indicated ladies' and gents' toilets. A door to the right seemed a likely bet for a storage cupboard, and another to the right of that stood open. Elliot peered through the last door into a long thin room with a desk and some empty racking. Wires sprang from holes in the walls. A board had slipped from one broken window, allowing enough light in to see that it didn't connect to anywhere.

Sam shifted her head from side to side. "I think there's a door at the back, on the right," she whispered. "And there's a stage, so there must be a way round to there."

Elliot reconsidered the door he'd dismissed as a cupboard and tried the handle. It opened on stiff but silent hinges. Beyond, a long, narrow corridor ran the length of the building. Water-damaged noticeboards lined the walls, covered with old club schedules and children's paintings, overlaid by more spray-paint tags.

Sam appeared by his shoulder, camera clutched in front of her chest.

They crept the length of the corridor. At the far end, the door Sam had glimpsed separated them from the hall. But going through it would be just as obvious as using the main door. The other option was a short staircase which led up to the stage. Sam placed a cautious foot on the first step. Despite the drab and depressing appearance of the place, the damage and neglect was mainly cosmetic; the stairs didn't so much as creak. Elliot followed her up.

The stage was almost pitch black, the curtains drawn. Where a trickle of light filtered over the top from the hall beyond, Elliot could see they hung from a movable gantry held up by ropes. While Sam crossed to the other side of the stage, Elliot gently pulled the edge of the curtain aside and peered out. The hall was bigger than he'd imagined, big enough to double as a sports hall for five-a-side or basketball. Mounds of clutter – boxes, scattered chairs and other rubbish – lay in piles along the edges.

Gaps in the roof and several small, un-boarded windows high up let in some light, which pooled in the middle of the space, leaving the edges of the room in deeper shadow. The sun was already low. If they were there for any length of time, they'd soon find the place too dark to see, and Elliot doubted the building had power.

Gabriel stood in the brightest spot facing the stage, with his case and satchel by his feet. Elliot could just make out his features.

"Demon, show yourself!" Gabriel commanded. In the damp silence of the building his voice boomed.

A shadow at the side of the room, half hidden behind several boxes, shifted and stood. The Mime, hood drawn low over its white face, moved slowly around to face Gabriel. The demon hunter's expression set into a grim mask of determination.

"Unnatural thing, I command you to leave this realm and return to whatever hell you came from." His voice carried a fervour and strength of conviction that Elliot couldn't help but admire.

———•———

On the opposite side of the stage, Sam gripped the grimy curtain in one hand. The Mime's dark form was hard to focus on in the gloom, as if its edges were fuzzy. It folded its arms. She got the distinct impression it was saying, *Yeah? Make me.*

Gabriel widened his stance and lifted his chin. "I warn you not to trifle with me, demon." He stooped and withdrew a wooden cross from his satchel. In the other hand he clutched a glass bottle, open at the top. "This realm is the domain of man. You are not welcome here!"

He flicked the bottle and a few drops splashed across the floor by the Mime's feet. "*In nomine Patris et Filii et Spiritus Sancti…*"

The Mime looked down and back up, unflinching.

"… *Exorcizamus te, omnis immundus spiritus.*" Gabriel took a step forwards, brandishing the cross in one hand, and flicked another splash of what Sam guessed was holy water. This time it spattered across the Mime's face and it clamped both hands over its eyes and dropped to the floor, writhing. Sam bit her bottom lip to keep herself silent. He was going to do it!

"*Omnis satanica potestas, adjuramus te.*" Gabriel advanced with the cross, bearing down on the squirming demon.

Abruptly, it froze. Gabriel hesitated. The Mime clambered to its feet, mouth open, hands clutching its stomach in a silent belly laugh. Sam's blood ran cold.

Gabriel retreated to his bags. "Your tricks will not dampen my resolve. I will banish you, demon." He reached down. This time he withdrew a battered bible and thrust it towards the demon. "*Humiliare sub potenti manu dei, contremisce et effuge.*"

The Mime looked quizzically at the ceiling as if waiting for the hand of God to come reaching down. It shrugged.

"*Cessa decipere humanas creaturas.* You have no power here, demon. Be gone!"

The Mime clasped both hands to its left hip and then drew one up and away as if pulling a sword from a scabbard. Sam clamped her hand over her mouth before she cried out a warning. Elliot had a plan.

She hoped.

The Mime brought the invisible blade down in a steep slash and the bible in Gabriel's outstretched hand cleaved in two. He dropped the severed book, recoiling.

A hand grasped Sam's shoulder and she let out a squeak.

"Shh. It's me."

"Jesus, Elliot!" she hissed.

"We have to do something. He's losing."

"Like what?"

"What do we know about it? What's the one thing we've figured out so far?"

She peered past the curtain. The Mime stood with its legs apart, both hands resting on the hilt of the invisible blade in front of it, like a cane. Gabriel retreated to his supplies once more.

"Line of sight," Elliot said, answering his own question.

"Right, it can't influence what it can't see."

He tugged the curtain in front of her eyes. She glanced at him and then up at the massive fabric sheet. "Oh, okay. But how?"

"If we can lure it onto the stage, we can drop the whole thing over it."

"And how do we lure it?"

"I'm still working on that part."

She glanced into the hall. Gabriel stood firm with his cross. "Tell me your name, demon."

The Mime lunged. Gabriel stepped back.

"Reveal your name to me. I command you."

The Mime raised its clasped hands.

"Speak! By all that is just and right, give me your name."

The invisible blade cleaved down. Gabriel stumbled and fell in his haste to dodge the swing. The blade missed, but gouged a deep sliver from the floorboards, and the Mime raised it once more. Gabriel rolled to his knees, ducked. The blade slashed through the air above his head. He scrabbled inside his bag, glancing up at the Mime. As it advanced, he whipped out and brandished something that looked like a cross with a pair of old iron scissors attached.

The Mime froze.

Gabriel's jaw set hard as he narrowed his eyes. He slowly rose to his feet. "You know this?"

In the shadowy room, a flare of light from the Mime's eyes illuminated Gabriel's face. It flung one arm behind it, and Sam imagined she heard the blade clatter to the floor.

"It's giving up?" She glanced over her shoulder at Elliot.

"I don't think so. Get ready to drop the curtain on my call. That rope there." He pointed into the gloom to a rope hitched around a rail at the side, then moved towards the middle of the stage.

"Wait! Elliot, what are you going to do?"

"Distract it."

Apprehension fluttered in her stomach.

Gabriel's voice echoed beyond the curtain. "Look upon that which has drawn demon blood, and know you are no match. Reveal your name, demon."

The Mime crouched. It wrapped both hands around the handle of some invisible object. One hand slid down a stout pole shape towards the floor. It strained to lift a bulky weight loaded at one end of the shaft. Like some kind of mace.

With a rush of motion, the Mime hefted its weapon up above its head. As the weight dropped it slid both hands to the end of the handle and added to the momentum until the floorboards by Gabriel's feet exploded in a shower of splinters.

Gabriel jumped aside, but the Mime charged, barging with its shoulder to send him sprawling. It dragged the heavy mace – or whatever it was – along the floor, gouging a long furrow in the wood, and then swung it up into its hands for another blow. Gabriel scuttled backwards, but the Mime closed the gap in one stride. The weapon tipped forwards from the point of balance…

"Hey!" Elliot's voice rang out across the room.

The Mime twisted as the mace fell. It swept past Gabriel's shoulder and thudded into the floorboards.

"I thought you were after me."

Sam poked her head further through the curtain. Elliot stood in the centre of the stage, fists clenched, feet apart, knees loose, ready to move. The Mime's eyes flashed hot white. It took two small steps away from Gabriel, then broke into a run.

Elliot backed through the curtain as the Mime leapt onto the stage in one agile bound.

"Now, Sam!"

Her heart seized in her chest. She lunged on hands and knees for the rope. One sharp tug on the trailing end released the hitch. The falling curtain tore the rope through her hand, scorching the skin on her palm, and she yelped.

An instant later, Elliot gripped her by the arm and yanked her to her feet. He tugged her to the front of the stage, past where the Mime wrestled with the curtain. They jumped down.

Gabriel picked himself up. He stood with his scissor-crucifix in a white-knuckled grip.

"We need to leave," Elliot said, scooping up Gabriel's leather case in his free hand without breaking stride. After a moment's pause, Gabriel retrieved his other satchel, slung it over his shoulder, and hurried after them.

Outside, Sam started to cross the road to retrace their steps, back to the college where they'd abandoned the BMW, but Elliot tugged her in the opposite direction.

"This way."

"But, the car—"

"We'll go back for it later."

He shoved her ahead of him and closed the gaping bag in his hands before breaking into a run. Gabriel kept pace behind.

"I feel I may owe you an apology, Mr Cross," Gabriel said between gasps. "That thing recognised the ward that wounded Ka. There may be some connection after all."

Sam hadn't heard an actual apology in there, but she was too busy trying to gasp air down her dry throat. Running was Elliot's thing, not hers! A couple of hundred yards away, the far end of the street opened onto a busy main road humming with traffic. She gripped her camera to stop it bouncing against her chest, and clutched at the stitch in her side, dropping a few paces behind the two men. When she glanced over her shoulder, she saw a black flash duck between two cars.

"It's following us!" she gasped.

Elliot slowed a fraction, allowing her to catch up, then paused. "Cross over and keep going. Keep behind the cars." He pressed Gabriel's leather case into the other man's hands and looked pointedly at Sam. Gabriel nodded. Whatever that exchange meant, she wasn't following it.

"Go," he said, giving her a push.

She took the next gap between a van and a people carrier. Gabriel followed her and they ran flat out for the relative safety of the busy street. With barely twenty yards to go she glanced over her shoulder for Elliot, but he wasn't there. She slowed. Gabriel ran right past her.

A cold wave washed over her. "Elliot?"

Though she was panting hard from running, her chest tightened until she couldn't draw breath.

"Come on!" Gabriel called from the mouth of the street.

She took a step back down the road, eyes darting from side to side as she searched for him. It couldn't have him, it couldn't!

Gabriel's hand closed around her arm.

"We must keep going," he said.

"No, I'm not leaving him. Elliot!" She resisted Gabriel's grip as he urged her onwards.

19

Elliot stood his ground, waiting for the Mime to catch up, and giving Sam and Gabriel a chance to put some distance between them. The demon paused and they locked eyes along the road. Then Elliot took off. He shot across the road and ducked into the next side street on the left. The Mime followed.

Running parallel to the main road they were aiming for, he hunted for the next right turn that would allow him to reach it. Fifty yards ahead a car exited a junction. He glanced over his shoulder; the Mime was still behind him. Lengthening his stride a fraction, he opened the gap between them. He crossed the road in front of a delivery van, earning a sharp blast from the driver's horn. A few seconds later he reached the mouth of the side road. Up ahead, the shops, pubs and people beckoned. He let his mind find the groove where there was nothing but his feet and the pavement, and ran.

He burst onto the main road, clipped the shoulder of a pedestrian and carried on across to the far side. A car swerved to avoid him. Behind him, tyres screeched. A woman screamed. There was a meaty thud and a crunch of plastic bumper and headlight glass. Elliot spun round.

The Mime lay sprawled in the road. The driver of the car beside it leapt out and raked both hands down his face.

Elliot paused, gasping.

A bus passed on the near side of the road, between him and the Mime. Warm exhaust ruffled his hair. Away to his left, Gabriel tugged Sam across the road by her arm as she fought to go back. Gabriel, not looking where he was going, collided with a bus shelter.

The bus puffed out a gust of oily smoke as it accelerated, and the scene of the accident came back into view. Two drivers argued over the cracked bumper, but the body on the ground was gone. Elliot scanned the street but caught no glimpse of black and white.

He darted after the bus. Its brake lights flashed as it approached the stop. Gabriel still had hold of Sam, gesturing wildly, although Elliot couldn't hear what he was saying. The bus stopped and a single elderly woman boarded. Elliot pushed himself harder. As he closed the gap to a handful of yards Sam looked up.

"On the bus!" he shouted. She glanced at the waiting bus. Gabriel reacted faster, moving towards the doors. Elliot reached them and clattered aboard.

"I lost it," he said. "We should get away while we can."

Sam's face was pale, her eyes downcast. She clutched her camera in both shaking hands and followed Gabriel further down the bus while Elliot dug out some cash to pay for tickets to the end of the route.

The bus pulled out. Elliot held on as it bumped its way along the road. There were only a handful of passengers. Sam and Gabriel had taken seats across the aisle from each other.

"I think we'll be okay," he said as he joined them.

Sam fixed her gaze out the window, posture rigid. He slumped down in the seat in front of her, still trying to catch his breath. Without warning, she thumped her fist into his arm.

"Don't you ever do that again!" She glared at him and then returned her eyes to the window, lips pressed together in a thin line.

He stared at her for a moment, rubbing his arm where she'd hit him. She sucked in terse breaths.

"Sam?"

She refused to look at him. After a moment he twisted in his seat to face Gabriel. "Can we agree that this thing is dangerous now?" He raked his hair back and wiped the sweat from his temples.

"Certainly. I must confess I greatly underestimated our enemy, but we have learnt much from this encounter."

"You were nearly killed," Sam said, dragging her eyes away from the window.

"Indeed, and I must thank you for intervening in such a timely manner."

"What was that thing you showed it?" she asked. She spoke directly to Gabriel, not even sparing a glance for Elliot, which hardly seemed fair. It was Gabriel who'd got them into this mess.

The demon hunter unclipped his satchel and pulled out the strange crucifix with the scissors attached. He handed it to her. A stylised carving of flames curled up from a handle bound with cord.

"It's a ward created by my grandfather. Wards are used to repel demonic and other entities by channelling and focusing the energy of the bearer. Energy that comes primarily from belief, conviction."

"You mean it works because you believe it will?" Sam asked, turning the object in her hands.

"Yes. In part. This one was specifically attuned to the energies of the demon Ka. The symbolism of scissors and fire proved highly effective given the fabric nature of its manifestation. Plus, the pointed end makes a passable weapon, in a pinch."

A brief smile crossed Sam's lips but faded quickly. "It didn't repel the Mime."

"No. We are dealing with something different here. Different, but related in some way."

"So, I guess Professor Dorridge was on to something. The Mime is connected to Ka, and to Dagon, right?"

"It would seem so."

Elliot sat sideways and rested his arm across the back of his seat. "I wish we knew how far he got. At least maybe we'll get somewhere researching the connection ourselves now."

The bus wound its way into the leafy northeast suburbs of Oxford. When it began to circle back towards the city centre, Elliot pressed the bell. They alighted onto a wide, tree-lined avenue. The doors closed behind them and their getaway vehicle trundled off.

"So, what now?" Sam asked. Her words were still mostly directed at Gabriel, Elliot noted.

Wide streets branched off the trunk road they stood on, filled with SUVs, kids' bikes and capacious houses with well-kept gardens.

"Call a taxi, I suppose," Gabriel said. "We should recover your car, Mr Cross, and return to the hotel."

"Will you please stop calling me that?"

"Certainly. But my point stands."

Elliot shook his head. "The car is back at the college. We can't risk it."

"On the contrary, I believe we can. The journey out here has given me time to form something of a hypothesis."

Elliot glanced at Sam. After nearly getting her killed twice today he wasn't about to lead her straight back into trouble. The Mime hadn't made an appearance at their hotel, so that seemed like a safe bet. "Let's figure out where we are, call a taxi, and then you can explain your theory."

While he pinpointed their location with the GPS on his phone and then dialled a local firm to pick them up, Gabriel and Sam walked a few yards up the road to where a low garden wall offered a convenient seat.

Elliot joined them, once their ride was on its way, and sat on Gabriel's other side.

"Something troubled me about the way we escaped," Gabriel started. "When I first encountered the two of you engaged with the demon this afternoon, it had created those moving walls to trap you. So, why did it not simply impede our progress in a similar way?"

"It can," Sam said. "Back in Bristol it blocked off an entire road. But I think it was showing off or something, because when a car came it made the wall disappear. Well, you know what I mean, made the invisible wall be not solid anymore."

"And at the department store," Elliot added, "it sealed off the exit." He looked past Gabriel to Sam. She held her camera in her lap, tabbing through settings, and kept her eyes down.

Gabriel nodded. "Precisely. We know it is capable of such feats, so why not use them? What I believe we have observed today indicates that it does not have a boundless supply of energy. Its reserves can become depleted and it must spend time recuperating."

Elliot nodded. It made sense. In Bristol the Mime created grand, flamboyant means to dispatch its victims. A recovery period would explain the two-day gap between attacks. But he wasn't about to give Gabriel a free pass.

"What makes you so confident?"

"Consider the evidence," he said. "When I confronted it, the demon used only simple tricks. It manifested small, simple weapons, with no moving parts, and used its own physical strength to wield them." He counted the first point on a finger and then indicated the next. "Secondly, the location where we found it was isolated – a hiding place where it thought itself safe." He dropped his hand to his lap. "There is ample evidence in the lore that demons are creatures of energy. That they expend energy to influence the physical world."

Elliot nodded. "And science tells us that energy is finite. It cannot be created, only changed from one form to another."

"Precisely. Though there are many things science cannot explain, that principle largely holds true in the occult world. I believe our conclusion is logical."

"And it was slower," Sam said, lifting her head.

She looked at Elliot for the first time since they'd left the bus. "When we tried to follow it at the festival, after it drowned that girl, it outdistanced you easily. Today it was chasing us, but it couldn't catch up."

Elliot smiled. "Good point."

She dipped her chin and re-focused on her camera as if she'd suddenly remembered she wasn't talking to him.

While they waited for the taxi, Elliot and Gabriel went over the details of the Mime's previous attacks, in light of their new theory. Gabriel quickly alighted on the same thought Elliot had had about the two-day period between attacks. It all seemed to fit. Low on energy already, and having just been hit by a car, the Mime would be licking its wounds for a while. They agreed to go back to the college for the car.

20

They collected the car, then returned to the hotel. Sam and Elliot agreed to meet Gabriel in the pub next door after they'd taken a moment to freshen up in the room. But, as soon as Sam saw the inviting twin bed, she wanted nothing more than to sink into it and sleep for a week.

The night before, after Elliot broke down and left her sitting alone in the service station food court, she'd stayed up researching, and even when she had gone to bed she hadn't slept well. After a morning traipsing around Oxford with Liam, nearly getting impaled by their enemy, playing spies scurrying from doorway to doorway following Gabriel across town, and then running for her life until her legs liquefied, she was shattered.

But all that was nothing. The cold swoop in her stomach when she'd realised Elliot wasn't behind them had left her truly drained.

If Gabriel hadn't stopped her, she would have run back, regardless of the danger. In that moment she hadn't cared what could happen to her. She only knew she had to get to Elliot. She wished she could stay angry at him, because the anger was simpler than the dark knot of fear that twisted her gut at the thought of losing him and dealing with what that meant.

"Are you alright?" Elliot asked.

She sank down onto the foot of one of the beds. "Just tired."

He stood watching her, but she kept her eyes on her hands in her lap. What was she supposed to say?

"Alright, then."

"I thought you were dead," she muttered, voice hitching around a lump in her throat. She glanced up at him. He frowned, mouth working as if he couldn't find the words he wanted. Then he walked over and sat on the other bed, across the gap from her, his elbows on his knees.

"I'm sorry. I didn't mean to scare you."

She nodded softly. The apology helped, but she wished she could know what he'd been thinking when he'd sent her on ahead and drawn the Mime away. He seemed so quick to put himself in danger for her. What did that mean?

"Are you coming down to get something to eat?" he asked.

"I think I'll stay here. I just want to sleep."

"Alright. I'll bring you something back, yeah?"

"Sure."

Another long, tense pause. Sam's heart pounded. She felt raw and confused, running on empty, which was making her emotional, irrational. She didn't want to say something she'd regret later.

Elliot sighed and then stood. "I'm going to call Fiona," he said. "Then do you mind if I grab a quick shower?"

"Sure, go for it."

He nodded, slipping out of the room to make his call.

Sam kicked her shoes and jeans off and got under the covers. She couldn't deal with this right now. He'd never said anything to suggest he had feelings for her. She knew he cared about her as a friend, but she had no reason to believe it was more than that. But then, she'd never said anything either. Her feelings for Elliot were too tied up with what she'd been through at university. She couldn't trust them.

Better that they stayed friends, colleagues and nothing more. The immature, naive crush she'd developed was just some saviour complex she'd projected. It didn't mean anything. She'd moved on. Or at least that's what she'd told herself. She knew him, flaws and all, now, and her feelings had changed. But after today... maybe they hadn't changed in the way she thought they had.

He'd risked getting himself killed to keep her safe. Twice! What was that about? She flopped a pillow over her head, pressed it down over her face and let out a muffled groan. Elliot was so hard to get a read on, but then he viewed the world through some peculiar filters sometimes.

The important thing right now was dealing with the Mime. If they survived, *then* she could figure out what the hell this thing between her and Elliot was or wasn't.

———•———

By the time Elliot finished his shower, Sam was asleep, or dozing at least. He dumped his sweaty clothes in a heap on the armchair and walked round to the side of her bed. He crouched down, watching her for a moment, and then gently shook her shoulder. Her eyes flicked open and locked onto his.

"I'm going to meet Gabriel. I shouldn't be long."

"Okay," she said, closing her eyes again and smiling. She snuggled down into her pillow and the corner of his mouth quirked up. He gently rubbed her shoulder and got to his feet.

The midsummer evening sky hadn't quite lost its final trace of blue as he walked across the car park to the pub opposite the hotel. The day's heat lingered, and a few bats swooped in the fading twilight, catching insects on the wing.

Despite the warm weather, a fire crackled in a hearth at the pub, welcoming and homely. Elliot ordered a pint and took it over to where Gabriel was sitting at a table beside the open fireplace.

"Ah, Mr Cross." He looked past Elliot. "Samantha won't be joining us?"

"She's sleeping. And what did I say about calling me that?"

Gabriel chuckled. It was the first time Elliot had heard him laugh. There was a soft quality to it that peeked through the cracks of the hard veneer the man presented. They took a moment to place a food order before the kitchen closed. Elliot asked them to bag an extra sandwich for Sam.

"I wanted to thank you once more for your intervention this afternoon," Gabriel said as they returned to their seats.

"You didn't think I was going to sit back and let you take all the risks, did you?"

"I'd hoped so, but I'm glad you didn't."

Elliot took a sip of beer and reclined in his seat. "Hopefully we'll be safe tonight. Tomorrow we need to find a way to stop this thing."

"Agreed. There is a friend of my father's who lives near here. A man of the cloth who knows more about demons than most. He is a trained exorcist and agent for the Vatican in such matters."

Elliot nodded. "Sounds like the kind of man we need."

"Indeed. After our encounter with the demon today, I wish to seek his counsel."

"Alright. I called Fiona Prince. She's agreed to meet us at ten."

Gabriel huffed and took a long pull from his glass.

"You still don't want us to see her, do you?"

"Mr Cr–Elliot, Ms Prince is a colleague and, dare I say, friend of mine. She is not someone I would wish to see endangered."

While Elliot wanted to argue that a simple meeting could hardly put her in danger, Geoff's death provided ample evidence to the contrary. "How do you know her?" he asked, opting to steer the conversation in a different direction.

"I was briefly a student of hers, in my undergraduate days. We've kept in touch and she aids me in publishing my academic work."

"Does she know about—"

"She does not." Gabriel paused with his glass partway to his lips. "But she may suspect."

Elliot still had a feeling Fiona knew far more than she would openly admit to. "When I spoke to her earlier, she sounded eager to help, even after I explained that you'd found us."

"Hmm."

Elliot watched him. He'd never tried to hide what he did with *Weird News*. It hurt when people he'd counted as friends rejected him even though he'd been honest, but he couldn't begin to imagine how much harder it must be to maintain a lie to trusted friends. How exhausting that must be.

Gabriel's eyes turned distant. He took a deep breath. "The last decade of my father's life was devoted purely to the eradication of Ka. Our family... What had been a calling became an obsession that consumed him. We grew distant. When the demon took his life, I vowed to avenge him, but, with the demon vanquished..."

Gabriel fell silent. Elliot waited for him to go on.

"You might say I lost my faith."

"What do you mean?"

Gabriel sipped his drink and regarded Elliot over the rim of the glass. "I had thought instead to devote my time to more academic pursuits."

In other words, retire from demon hunting. "But, with your knowledge, you help people. You—"

"I have sacrificed a lot." His gaze fixed coldly on a point in the distance. He didn't say the rest, but the inference was there. He'd done his part, and he owed the world nothing more. A moment later he refocused on Elliot and blinked away the troubled look in his eyes. "Why do you feel so strongly about what you do, Elliot? Your mission to shed light, as you put it."

"It was a way I thought I could make a difference. People don't believe in monsters anymore. I should know. I lost my brother because of my ignorance. And arrogance."

"A self-imposed penance?"

Elliot frowned. Sam criticised him for punishing himself, but he didn't see it that way. He just wanted to make up for his past. "People shouldn't have to live with that."

"Hmm." Gabriel took another sip.

Elliot chuckled and shook his head. The man was incorrigible.

"I was raised into this life," Gabriel said. "It is a lonely one, most of the time. If not by circumstance, then by choice. One isolates oneself, to keep people safe." A wistful sadness hid behind his smile. "You are a lucky man to have a woman who understands you and the life you lead."

"What?"

"To have someone close. A confidant. Perhaps if I'd had that I would have seen my duty in a different light. The way my father did when he and my mother—"

"Are you talking about Sam?"

Gabriel nodded.

"I… She's not my girlfriend."

"Oh, I apologise, I assumed because—" He bit off his words and took a gulp from his beer.

"Because what?"

"Never mind. I was mistaken."

"She works for me." His mind raced, mentally replaying the last half a day, trying to figure out what could have given Gabriel that impression. Sam was someone he internally classified as out of bounds, like a sister – or, not quite, more like a friend's girlfriend. Gabriel's assumption had completely pulled the rug out from under him and he was suddenly worried he acted inappropriately towards her.

"Say no more," Gabriel said, waving a hand. "Perhaps you can answer another question for me instead. This life was my birthright. You chose it after a tragedy. What drew Samantha to it?"

"She… she stumbled upon something. Something that… She went through an ordeal, and she found me when she was looking for answers."

Gabriel nodded but didn't press for details. Elliot was glad he didn't, because Sam's past wasn't something she liked to talk about, and it wasn't his place to share what had happened to her.

Their meal arrived shortly after. Elliot couldn't remember the last time he'd had such an unguarded conversation about the supernatural with anyone but Sam. He was still wary about Gabriel's attitude to the way he worked, but he had no fear the man wouldn't *believe* him.

"How do you do it?" Elliot asked as he shook vinegar over his chips. "Deal with people who don't believe, I mean."

"Often it is a matter of offering an alternative they can latch on to," Gabriel said.

"A convincing lie?"

Gabriel paused while he chewed, then nodded. "Yes. I remember one time I'd tracked a mischief demon to a delicatessen. Incorporeal, you understand, so no one could see it…" He gestured with his fork as he spoke. "… but it was causing a rash of stomach upsets and minor psychoses among the customers. I could hardly walk in and perform a cleansing rite in front of everyone."

Elliot finished off his pint while he waited for Gabriel to continue.

"I didn't have much time, so I took a recent piece of correspondence from the university, marched in holding it up, and announced I was a health inspector and I was shutting the place down. The place cleared out and no one so much as looked at the piece of paper." He chuckled. "People see what they expect to see."

He supposed that was true, for the most part, but not for everyone. His list of contributors proved that. Gabriel's bluff could have unravelled too easily for his liking. He preferred to keep his lies more manageable, and he'd had plenty of experience of that back in London. Not that he was going to tell Gabriel that right now.

"That was pretty bold. Does it ever make you feel like a bit of a con man?"

Gabriel laughed. "Occasionally, yes."

"I've met some ballsy con men, I can tell you that. This one guy... Do you want another drink?"

They continued exchanging anecdotes and stories until, after one more pint than was probably sensible, Gabriel called himself a taxi. They agreed to meet at Fiona's college at nine fifty the next morning. Elliot waved him off, then returned to the hotel.

When he reached the room, he eased the door handle down, trying to be as quiet as possible. The light was still on and Sam lay curled up on her side, deeply asleep. He flicked the switch by the door to change the lighting over to the side lights rather than the bright overhead. The paper bag with the sandwich crinkled as he set it down on the desk. Sam stirred but didn't wake up. He quietly took his shoes and jeans off and washed up in the bathroom.

He wished Gabriel had explained why he'd jumped to the conclusion he had. Not that what Gabriel thought was important, but it had left Elliot wondering what he'd seen to give him that impression.

When he slid into bed he lay on his side and watched her for a while. It wasn't something he'd ever let himself consider before. It wouldn't have been fair to her. From the moment they'd met they'd been on an unequal footing. She was a scared, twenty-two-year-old student who'd just experienced something that would scar her for life. He'd just turned twenty-seven and was dealing with the fallout of walking away from his career, his life, and trying to get *Weird News* on its feet when few people would take him seriously. She was vulnerable, he was a wreck, but when she'd sought him out needing help he'd offered what he could.

In some ways, he still thought of her as that scared, vulnerable twenty-two-year-old. But that was nearly three years ago now. They'd both changed. She was smart, capable, considerate, and, despite the things that had happened to her, courageous and determined too.

She shifted in her sleep, tucking her chin in towards where her hands hugged the duvet tight. Her hair fell forwards across her forehead. She murmured, a wordless sound, and screwed her eyes tighter. Stuck in some bad dream.

He should probably admit to himself that he cared about her more than he should. A lot more than he should. But she was his employee. It wouldn't be right. It wouldn't be fair. He couldn't hurt her like that. And he would; he knew where that path led.

NO STRINGS

"Cross?"

Elliot lifted his eyes from his laptop. "What?"

Some guy whose name he couldn't remember nodded towards the glass partition at the end of the office. The blinds were drawn in Cat's room.

"*She* wants to see you." His lip curled.

Elliot glanced around. Several people in the office suddenly became intensely focused on their work. He swallowed against the sudden bitter taste in his mouth.

"Alright."

He closed the screen. The article wouldn't come together anyway. Three days' compassionate leave was a joke. No one got over losing a family member in three days. He couldn't focus, couldn't sleep.

He rubbed his eyes – his contacts were itchy – and scratched at the stubble on his cheeks. Would have been good if he'd made time for a shower and a shave that morning. He'd been avoiding Cat since he returned to work yesterday, but he should have known she wouldn't let him get away with ignoring her.

As he walked the length of the office, eyes followed him. They all knew. Catherine had made sure of that. She liked breaking the rules, but she liked getting away with it in plain sight more. Five days ago he wouldn't have cared, would have met every disdainful stare with a smug smirk. They were just jealous, after all, and the no-strings arrangement worked for him and Cat. But he could have done without the scrutiny and the judgement right now.

Actually, he could have done with someone to talk to, but Cat wasn't his girlfriend. Not like that. Over the last few days, as the missed calls racked up, he'd struggled to work out what label fitted their relationship.

He took a deep breath before he opened her office door.

She sat behind her desk, finishing up a call. The sharp lines of her bob matched the bold cut of her jacket and the dark eyeliner flicks around her cool eyes. She was all angles to the world, Cat. Sure, he got to see the physical curves underneath, but she'd yet to reveal any emotional softness.

"No. No extensions. I want it done." She held a finger up to Elliot and he closed the door behind him.

"So? Work late…" She sucked her teeth. "And why would I care about that…?" Her eyes flicked up to him. "Good to hear." She set the phone down in the cradle and fixed her full attention on Elliot. "You haven't been taking my calls."

"I know. I'm sorry, I've had a lot on my mind."

She rose from her desk. "I never had you figured for soft." Her eyes strayed down to his crotch; as if she needed to emphasise the double meaning in her words.

Elliot clasped his hands in front of himself. "My brother died. It's been a lot to process."

"I heard. You usually come knocking when you need to work out some stress." She moved round the desk and stepped close to him, forcing him to move his hands to avoid touching her. She put her arms on his shoulders, wrists crossed behind his neck.

"I haven't been ignoring you," he said.

"I should hope not."

He closed his eyes as she pressed a kiss to the corner of his mouth, then he took hold of her wrists and eased her back. "Cat, I'm... Not now."

She pursed her lips, the way she did when someone pitched her a moronic story idea.

"It's not you," Elliot said, cringing. "Look, I've been asking myself a lot of difficult questions these last few days, about who I am." He moved away from her. "And I'm not sure I like the answers."

"What do you mean? There's nothing wrong with you." She waved a dismissive hand. "You're tenacious, conveniently flexible. You're good at what you do. Don't go growing a conscience all of a sudden."

His stomach cramped. You were either a good person or you weren't, and he was rapidly reaching the conclusion that he fell on the wrong side of that line. This was a case in point. What the hell kind of person was he that she only admired him for his flexible morality and lack of conscience?

"Can you not? I don't need that from you right now."

She regarded him shrewdly, calculating, and then moved round in front of him, trapping him against the desk. She took hold of his belt in both hands. "You just need to work out some tension." She licked her lips as her hands worked the buckle.

"Please, that's not..." He squirmed out to the side, refastened his belt.

Cat's shoulders dropped, not sagging but tensing back as she held herself taller and folded her arms. She gave him an expectant look, like she was waiting for him to come to his senses.

He retreated towards the door. "I'm not sure we should do this anymore. It's not... What do we really get out of it anyway?"

She stood there for a moment, unreadable. He couldn't tell if she was upset, angry or what. Then she reached for the mug on her desk.

"Skimmed, no sugar," she said, holding the mug out to him.

"What?"

"Well, you must be good for something, since you won't be getting any page space any time soon."

She'd really do that? Sideline his work to retaliate? He locked eyes with her, but he couldn't bear the chill in her gaze for long. He snatched the mug out of her hand and wrenched the door open.

21

Elliot jerked awake when a pillow hit him in the head.

"What?" He clawed the attacking cushion off his face and sat up.

Sam giggled from the other side of the room. "Rise and shine," she said. "We've got work to do."

He groped for his glasses on the side table. He sensed payback for dragging her out of bed last Sunday, but the bright grin on her face instantly lifted his mood and he chuckled. He couldn't remember the last time he'd started a day with a smile. "Alright, alright." He untangled his legs from the duvet and sat on the edge of the bed.

Sam was already dressed, in jeans she'd brought from Bristol and a new short-sleeved checked shirt. Her hair was damp from an earlier shower, and she held a steaming paper cup of coffee.

"How long have you been up?" he asked.

"Couple of hours."

He glanced at his watch in alarm.

"Relax, it's not even eight o'clock yet. I crashed out last night and woke up at like half five."

She handed Elliot the coffee and he took a sip.

"So, what's the plan today?" she asked

"We're meeting Gabriel and Fiona first. Then he has someone else to see, a priest."

"Do we have time for breakfast?"

"We said ten, so yes, plenty."

"Great. I want to call Joyce Perry. She must be wondering why I never got back to her about Alex. And Marie. She's been texting me non-stop."

In the last couple of days he'd barely spared a thought for anything but the Mime. His emails would be piling up and they had a publication deadline looming in a little over a week.

He'd been so close to giving up the night they arrived in Oxford, but he felt far more optimistic now. Finding Gabriel had helped, but not as much as discovering that the Mime had limitations. Limitations they could take advantage of. They had proof Geoff was on the right track, and new sources to tap in Fiona and Gabriel's priest friend.

Sam stood texting as she finished her coffee. For the first time in days, Elliot felt he could spare a moment for the life that would be waiting for him in Bristol when all this was over.

"Oh." Sam looked up from her phone. "Liam says he's working today but to call if we need anything."

"You gave Liam your number?"

She shrugged. "Yeah?"

"Oh."

"Why?"

"Nothing. You go on down. I'll catch you up."

She flashed a smile and pocketed the phone before heading out.

He threw on his last fresh shirt and the same black chinos he'd worn the day before. When he headed down to the hotel restaurant, he took his laptop with him and, over eggs and toast, set about sorting through his emails and replying to the critical ones.

After breakfast they checked out and drove into the centre of the city. Elliot's nerves tightened as they drew closer to the college where they'd been attacked the day before. Every shadow caught his eye, but none of them materialised into the Mime.

They found the college entrance reassuringly back to normal; the lack of a continued police presence suggested that whatever the incident the day before, they'd dealt with it. A uniformed security guard now manned the portal door. As they approached, he was engaged in conversation with Gabriel.

Gabriel spotted them approaching and glanced at his watch. "Right on time, excellent."

He'd shunned the dowdy academic look today and dressed in a dark purple paisley-print casual shirt over the same navy cords. His top button was left casually undone and he carried his tweed jacket folded over his forearm. Though he barely knew the man, Elliot found it strangely unsettling, like seeing a warrior without his armour.

"We're free to go on in," Gabriel said, indicating the door. From the way he fiddled with his cuffs and re-settled the strap of his satchel, Elliot wondered whether Gabriel felt that same sense of exposure himself.

He took a deep breath and held it as he followed Gabriel through the archway where they'd nearly been impaled. Today they passed through unhindered and proceeded to follow the path around the edge of the quad to another door.

The dark oak panelling, brass trim and red carpets inside were so similar to Geoff's building in Bristol that it set Elliot's stomach churning. The Mime often seemed to get ahead of them. Could it have targeted Fiona?

After ascending two flights of stairs, they stopped by a heavy door with a brass nameplate: Prof. F. Prince.

Gabriel raised his hand to knock but hesitated. "I'm still not sure what you hope to achieve by involving Ms Prince," he muttered.

"Let's just see," Sam said brightly. "We don't know until we ask, right?"

Gabriel shook his head and knocked.

A moment later the door opened and a bespectacled face peered out. "Come in, come in," Fiona said, throwing the door wide.

Up on the top floor, the room nestled under sloped ceilings. A dormer window opposite the door let some light in, but the angles of the room kept the area around Fiona's workspace dim. To the left of her desk stood a whiteboard, while on the right, tucked under the eaves, was a spare chair. Bookshelves lined the shallower right-hand side of the room. Unlike Geoff, Fiona kept her things neatly ordered, and her office felt less cramped, even though it was much smaller.

"Fiona, it's good to see you." Gabriel pressed a kiss to both of Fiona's cheeks.

"How've you been, Gabriel? I haven't seen you for weeks. I really had been meaning to call before I heard Elliot was looking for you."

Gabriel beamed, a warm, genuine smile. "We've both been busy lately."

"So *you* contacted Gabriel, then?" Sam asked.

"Oh yes. When I got Elliot's message."

Elliot had met her once before, briefly, when he'd attended one of her public lectures a year ago. In her mid-forties, she brimmed with the self-confidence that came at the balance point between the energy of youth and the wisdom of maturity. She cut a striking figure in her cream satin blouse and grey pencil skirt and put Elliot in mind of one of his old university lecturers, a woman who'd made him feel every inch the awkward teenager whenever he was in her presence.

"Elliot, it's been too long."

He smiled and shook the hand she offered. "Definitely. This is Sam. She works with me."

Sam stepped forwards and shook Fiona's hand. "It's nice to meet you."

"Thank you for seeing us," Elliot said. "As I started to explain on the phone—"

"Ah yes." She turned to her desk and began rummaging through piles of books and papers. "The mime artist character you described didn't ring any ancient bells, so to speak, but strangely enough it was familiar. It took me a while to work out why, but then I found it."

Gabriel's eyes followed her as she moved, and Elliot wondered whether Fiona made *him* feel like an awkward teen. Gabriel had a few years on Elliot, granted, but surely he and Fiona weren't—

"Here!" She pulled a book from the pile entitled *20th Century Exorcism,* whose faded black dust jacket suggested it must have been printed in the middle of the century itself. She leafed through and opened it to a page with a full plate picture. Elliot took the book and held it so Sam and Gabriel could see.

In the foreground, a young woman in a white nightdress writhed on the ground outside the ornamental wrought-iron gates of a Gothic, institutional building. A priest crouched beside her with a comforting hand on her forehead.

"In the background," Fiona said, leaning on her desk with her arms folded and feet crossed at the ankles.

Some distance away from the main subjects of the photo, grainy and indistinct, stood a man in black garb. The face was clearly different, the features less angular, but the pattern of the makeup was familiar. Though the hooded coat and other clothes were a different cut, they created the same overall effect.

"It could be a coincidence," Elliot said. Barring the face shape, the resemblance was uncannily, specifically accurate.

"Perhaps, but it seems unlikely, don't you think? Now, normally I'd start looking for the earliest reference. Most demons are as old as time. But this case seemed so unusual, and when I remembered this image I began to wonder if we could track it backwards."

Gabriel cleared his throat and took a half step away from Sam and Elliot. "You believe this is a *real* demon?" he asked tentatively.

Fiona waved a dismissive hand. "Oh please, Gabriel. Let's not beat about the bush. I'm quite aware that there are real demons in the world, as are you."

Gabriel took another sidestep, then silently sagged down into the chair beside Fiona's desk with a frown.

Elliot took a closer look at the picture and noted the date. Nineteen seventy-eight. "If we're to accept that this is the same mime, we'd have to accept that he's at least fifty years old, and the man we saw wasn't in his fifties."

"Not necessarily," Fiona said. "Not if we're dealing with possession. Two different hosts inhabited by the same supernatural entity."

"True."

She took the book from his hands. "Maybe if you give me the rest of the story it'll jog something else loose."

"Right. Well, as far as we can tell the attacks started in Bristol, about ten days ago. Strange deaths with no visible cause. We began our investigation and first encountered the Mime when it attacked and killed a young woman by drowning her in mid-air."

Gabriel shifted uncomfortably in his seat. "I'm not sure we need to impart *all* the details."

Fiona pursed her lips and folded her arms again. "Go on, Elliot."

Elliot glanced at Gabriel, then proceeded to explain about contacting Geoff, finding him dead, and fleeing Bristol in search of Gabriel. He described their encounter at the college.

"Oh." Fiona put a hand up to her mouth. "Yesterday. They found that young security guard. Do you think that could have been—"

"It seems most likely," Gabriel said, rising to his feet. He seemed to have snapped out of his momentary catatonia and reached a grudging acceptance about including Fiona. "What did you hear about it?"

She shrugged. "Not much. There hasn't been any official word. Some rumours said it was a drug overdose."

"Interesting. There seem to be few materials this demon cannot manifest in invisible form. So far, we have witnessed both simple solid objects, or weapons, and those with complex moving parts."

"Like the gun used to kill Alex Perry," Elliot said.

"Precisely. The mauling in Bristol also shows it can manifest animals."

"There was something in the drain here yesterday too," Sam said with a shudder.

Gabriel nodded. "And furthermore, it can create substances and chemicals. Water and flammable accelerants, certainly. It would not be an illogical leap to suggest it could create and administer a toxin."

Elliot indicated the book that Fiona still held. "That picture, did it relate to a series of supernatural deaths?"

She nodded. "You're wondering whether we can identify a pattern?"

"If we could, it might help us predict what it'll do next."

"Which would be a substantial advantage, certainly," Gabriel added. "However, ultimately we may need to discover its origins in order to find a way to stop it. Your professor friend in Bristol suspected a link to Dagon, and from the way it reacted to the ward I used against Ka it would seem he was correct. If only we knew what led him to that conclusion."

"Connecting ancient names to modern events can be difficult," Fiona said, smoothing her skirt. "A lot gets lost in translation over time."

"Then let's attack it from both ends," Elliot said. "If you think you can trace it backwards, and Gabriel has ideas to find the origins, somewhere in the middle we'll find what we need. I'll forward you anything we uncover at our end."

"I'll get right on it."

"Thank you. Right now we have other leads to follow up."

Sam opened the door and she and Elliot stepped out into the corridor. Gabriel lingered with Fiona.

"Try to be careful," he said. "This entity has targeted individuals it perceived as threats before."

"I will, Gabriel."

Sam nudged Elliot and indicated the end of the corridor with a tilt of her head and a flick of her eyes. He followed her outside. Gabriel caught up as they exited the building into the quad, his expression dark and subdued.

———✦———

Sam sat in the back seat of the BMW while Gabriel directed Elliot out of the city. She recognised the winding country lanes from the day before when they'd followed Gabriel's taxi. Soon the tiny church with its decrepit little graveyard emerged from among the slate-roofed cottages. Elliot parked in the same lane he'd stopped in previously, and the three of them walked to the church.

As they approached, Sam took her camera from its case. She clicked off a wide shot of the church and pulled it up on the Nikon's display. Approaching midday, the light was flat. Flat light equalised, giving everything the same weight and attention, and didn't distort colours and shapes. It was truthful.

A low stone wall surrounded the churchyard, and a flag-stone path wound up to the entrance. As she crossed through the gap in the wall, a chill on the back of her neck raised goosebumps. Rosa had tried to tell her she had some kind of gift, but she wasn't gifted, there was something wrong with her. A flaw. A chink that made her vulnerable.

Raising her camera to her eye with shaky hands, she focused on the nearest cluster of historic graves and clicked off a shot.

Elliot put a hand on her shoulder and she jumped.

"Hey, sorry," he said. "I was just... Are you alright? Being here, I mean?"

She inspected the shot – mottled grey stone, a few patches of lichen, parched summer grass and weeds. Nothing out of the ordinary.

"I'm okay."

"Do you want to wait in the car?"

She stuffed the camera back in its case and rubbed the prickle on her arms. "I'm fine. Just, don't leave me on my own."

"I won't." He put his arm out, letting her go first.

Gabriel was already at the top of the path and Sam hurried to catch up.

The cool, dim church welcomed them in. Their footsteps echoed on stone slabs under the vaulted ceiling.

"Jack?" Gabriel called.

A man in black emerged from the shadows in the wings. Sam and Elliot both flinched, but the man who approached them was no skinny, hooded mime. He wore belted black jeans and a simple black shirt over his broad shoulders and chest, the collar interrupted by a block of white at the throat. His greying hair was so short as to barely leave a shadow across his scalp and didn't hide the hairless scar on the side of his head, or the nick out of his ear. He looked more like a retired boxer than a priest. Or a battle-scarred alley cat.

"Elliot, Sam, this is Father Jack Monroe," Gabriel said.

"Good to meet you." Elliot put his hand out and the priest shook it.

Sam shook his hand too; his wide palm and firm grip swamped hers.

"Gabriel explained over the phone that the demon you're facing is more powerful than he anticipated."

"Quite so," Gabriel said. "It now seems clear this creature shares an affiliation with Ka. It recognised my grandfather's ward and reacted with... hostility."

"No wonder you're concerned." He gestured towards a door at the side of the church. "Come, let's sit and see what's what."

He led them into a side room with mismatched chairs and a central table. Once a retiring room, it now seemed to function as combined office, meeting and storeroom. Boxes and bookshelves cluttered the edges.

Father Monroe indicated a tea urn on a trestle table off to one side. "We might as well make this civilised. One thing you can always count on: no demon can defy the sanctity of consecrated ground."

"You mean we're safe here?" Sam asked.

"Completely."

She dumped her camera and bag on one of the chairs and headed for the tea. Elliot started to follow her, but she waved him back. He took a seat with Gabriel and Father Monroe while she drew hot water into four mugs.

"It killed yesterday, at the college," Elliot said. "If it returns to the pattern it displayed in Bristol then we should have until tomorrow before it attacks again."

"What was this pattern?" Father Monroe asked.

"We have a theory that it depletes its energy when it attacks and must spend time replenishing itself," Gabriel said.

Sam fished the teabags out, listening with her head tilted to the side.

"A recovery period?"

Gabriel nodded uncertainly. "That was the theory, yes."

"I'm afraid your theory has a flaw, Gabriel. A death caused by demonic actions in this world can unleash a vast amount of potential energy. Demons are creatures of energy. They feed on it."

"So, you're saying it's more like it was sleeping off a big meal?" Sam asked as she set two cups of tea on the table for Gabriel and the priest.

"That's one way to put it."

Gabriel banged his fist on the table, slopping tea everywhere. "Of course! Only an unsuccessful attack drains it. Each time it failed to kill it became weaker and weaker." He blanched at his own implication that he'd faced it at its weakest and what that could mean.

"So it might be coming for us again now?" Sam locked eyes with Elliot across the table.

"Possibly," Gabriel said. "Or it may seek a new victim. Harvest more energy."

"How can we stop it, Father?" Elliot asked.

Father Monroe reclined in his chair and steepled his fingers. "It's hard to say. It is a demon, no doubt remains there, and exorcism is how you vanquish a demon. But as Gabriel has already tried a generic rite... well, it could mean it requires a specific ritual or conditions. And of course, a powerful demon must always be addressed by name."

"We don't know its name," Elliot said.

"There are ways to entreat a demon to divulge its name."

"I thought the very same thing," Gabriel said. "Unfortunately, it seems this demon has no voice with which to speak."

Father Monroe wet his lips. "Then you may be in a lot of trouble."

"Tell us something we don't know." Sam handed Elliot his tea and took the seat next to him.

The priest paused for a moment, then sat forwards with his elbows on the table. "It's said that for every demon, there is a demon hunter. I'll call my contact at the Vatican. They keep records of all the major demon hunting families; perhaps some-one has hunted this demon before."

Gabriel reached to the side and patted his shoulder. "My friend, we could ask no more. Thank you."

———•———

Over tea they repeated every detail of their encounters with the Mime, in case Father Monroe could shed new light on them. They'd told the story so many times now, Sam and Elliot were starting to finish each other's sentences as they handed off parts of the story to each other. As Gabriel and Father Monroe moved on to discussing the technical aspects of exorcism, Sam took her camera and excused herself to explore the church.

Out in the churchyard she'd felt a chill prickle her scalp, the tickle at the edge of her mind that haunted her dreams. But inside, the church held only peace and quiet. The only spirit in here was the holy one.

The sun caught one of the side windows and sent a shaft of coloured light down onto the altar. She crouched and framed the shot. With a shallow depth of field, she could focus on the crucifix standing on the altar, and the pattern of light across the wood, but the foreground and background would dissolve away.

As she clicked off a shot, she heard footsteps. Elliot, keeping an eye on her.

"When we write this up, we're going to want pictures," she said, with her eye to the viewfinder.

"I wouldn't know where to start," he said. He walked past her and took a seat on the end of the front pew. "I don't even know which bits we *should* tell anymore."

Sam re-capped her lens and joined him. "I know what you mean. I used to think that one day we'd find a big story like this and it would be our big break. And everyone would have to believe because we'd have proof."

"And no one would ever have to be afraid of the dark."

"Exactly. But we can't, can we? I mean we could, but no one is going to believe what really killed all those people. The police'd probably arrest us for mass murder!"

Elliot chuckled and shook his head. "Pretty sure Yates is going to do that anyway."

She twisted towards him until her knee brushed against his. "Maybe that's not the point. Maybe we can do more than just publish it. Like Gabriel."

For a moment he gazed up at the window above the altar. She uncapped her lens and captured a shallow focus shot of his face, as if it might reveal his thoughts.

He regarded her with a half-hearted scowl which softened almost immediately. "I've always seen myself as a pen-is-mightier-than-the-sword person."

"I don't know. I'm pretty sure there's more to you than that." She touched the back of his hand with hers and watched as he closed his eyes.

Gabriel and Father Monroe emerged from the retiring room, still in conversation.

"Jack, you know I can't do that," Gabriel said, on the edge of hearing. "The library… *The Collection* is only—"

"For those who have need of it. I know." The priest glanced over to where Elliot and Sam were sitting. "But not all of us grow up in this life. Not all of us choose it. Sometimes it chooses us."

Gabriel took a tense breath. "I'll wait for your call."

"It may take a day or two to get a response. In the meantime, if you need anything else call me."

Elliot stood, and Sam packed her camera away.

22

From the church, they returned to Oxford. Gabriel owned plenty of books on demons and was keen to get started on identifying the Mime. He gave Elliot directions and, as they turned onto Gabriel's road, Sam realised they'd also been here before. They parked on the street outside the townhouse Gabriel had visited briefly the day before. The front door of the impressive four-storey residence stood barely six feet from the road, under a shallow portico.

Sam and Elliot waited while Gabriel unlocked the door, then followed him into a square entrance hall, tiled with a mosaic of hexagonal black and white tiles. She'd expected the place to be subdivided into flats, but it wasn't. On the right, a staircase led up to the first-floor landing, and beneath it stood an antique dresser with a mirrored back. More stairs descended to basement level on the left, and beside the banister stood a rack and hat stand with a collection of shoes and coats. Only a pair of internal doors with frosted glass panels divided the hall from the rest of the ground floor.

"This is a somewhat temporary residence," Gabriel said.

He descended the stairs to the basement. Sam and Elliot followed. At the bottom, the tiled floor continued along a short hallway. Doors led off either side.

"I rent this room from the family who own the house. Acquaintances of my father. Antiquarians by trade. After their eldest two children left home, they had room to spare." He unlocked the door on the left, under the slope of the stair. "Do come in."

Gabriel flicked the light on as he entered, and they followed him into a spacious bedsit. Two slot-shaped windows, high up on the right-hand wall, allowed some daylight in. At the rear, a door stood ajar to an en-suite bathroom.

"I travel so much I've had no need for more substantial lodgings."

The room did indeed feel like a work in progress. Boxes and suitcases formed a stack between two disordered bookcases along the wall to the left of the door, as if still in transit – in or out wasn't clear. Also to the left of the door, jutting out from the opposite wall, stood a neatly made bed and, to its right, a wardrobe with drawers. A jacket wrapped in a dry cleaner's plastic cover hung from one handle.

Gabriel moved immediately to a desk set against the wall to the right of the door and began to collect strewn papers into a card wallet. "My apologies for the disorder. I was in the midst of drafting a paper when I received Fiona's call yesterday."

He stuffed the wallet into one of several wooden magazine files on the desk and closed the screen of a vintage laptop.

The remaining quarter of the room was set up as a sitting room, with two worn armchairs, a side table and a tall reading lamp. Sam moved further into the room and perched on the arm of one of the chairs. She ran her hand over a crocheted blanket draped over the back. Elliot hovered beside her as Gabriel bustled about collecting books from various shelves and boxes.

"That should get us started," he said. "With luck we will find further evidence of the connection your friend identified."

He handed a portion of the pile to Elliot.

Sam took a share too. She rotated the top book in her stack to read the title. "So, best case scenario, what are we hoping to find?"

"The demon's origins and history, for starters," Gabriel said. "Then allegiances, connections, any evidence that it has previously been thwarted and how. We must seek to understand it if we are to have any hope of overcoming it."

"So, life story, then. Gotcha."

"The owners of the house are away at present," Gabriel said as he exited into the hallway. "A research trip." He indicated the door opposite with a nod. "My fellow lodger is visiting family. As such, I propose we make full use of the communal facilities."

"Spread out and raid the fridge?" Sam asked.

"You could put it that way, I suppose."

He led the way upstairs and through the frosted double doors into the wide open-plan ground floor. Sam's eyes popped – this floor alone had to be bigger than her entire flat. Most of the dividing walls of the Georgian house had been stripped out, except for a few supportive sections which the owners had accentuated with contrasting deep red paint and mirrors. Thick rugs covered dark oak floorboards, and solid antique pieces combined with quality modern furnishings to give the place a timeless quality. The antiquarian business must bring in a few quid.

She took her pile of books and wove her way round two huge black leather sofas that dominated the left side of the room. A massive flat-screen TV hung on the wall. How nice it must be to curl up on one of those squishy sofas and watch a movie. She placed the books carefully on the glass-topped oak coffee table.

Elliot set his books down too and took a seat on one of the expansive sofas. He took the top book from the stack. Gabriel sat on the second sofa and withdrew a notebook from his satchel, ready to get started.

Sam watched the two of them. Talk about kindred spirits. She'd put money on Gabriel being as bad as Elliot when it came to making time to take care of himself. "I'll get coffee on."

A retro-styled kitchen shared the right half of the house with a dining area. French doors opened onto a garden where several planters held evergreen shrubs. She cracked the doors open to let in some fresh air. After checking a few cupboards – and confirming with Gabriel that they could take what they wanted – she found enough supplies for a picnic.

She returned to the lounge with a tray of mugs, cheese and pickle sandwiches, biscuits and fruit.

Gabriel peeked out from behind his book. "Thank you, Samantha, this looks... Ooh, custard creams. Delightful." He beamed like a happy child.

Sam took a book from the table and sank down into a cushy leather beanbag, with her feet stretched out in front of her, while the boys tucked in.

The three of them read in virtual silence for most of the afternoon. Her first book didn't offer anything useful, so she set it aside and took another from the stack. She leafed through it, trying to get a handle on what it was. Though physically the book was modern, the text inside talked about events she knew from history, like the assassination of Julius Caesar, as if they'd happened recently.

In a section about the Philistines she stumbled upon the name Dagon. She glanced up at the guys briefly, then read on.

Though togas were apparently still the height of fashion when the book was written, it talked about the ruined temples as if they were ancient. Dagon, it seemed, was worshipped as a god by the Philistines, the Amorites and others since well before the time of Jesus. A shiver ran up her spine at the thought of something so ancient and powerful being real. It also sounded like Dagon had been a big deal, with temples, statues and cities to his name, despite the fact that the people who worshipped him had a god for everything – hundreds, even. That made him, like, a boss god.

Or boss demon.

Gabriel had explained that while the various mythologies and theological canons of human civilisations were useful guides, even frameworks, for understanding otherworldly entities and their shifting hierarchical power structures, most got their interpretations very wrong. Dagon and the biblical demon Baal were, he explained, probably two different names for the same entity – worshipped by one culture, feared by another.

Since the Christians considered Baal to be essentially one of Satan's generals, it was a safe bet to say he was pretty high up the demonic food chain.

Did that make the Mime a lieutenant? Or was it lower down the pecking order? A corporal or a private, maybe? Somehow until this point, the concept of *demon* hadn't fully sunk in. She felt hugely underqualified to do battle against the legions of Hell. Or with "innumerable, diverse, multi-phasic beings from any of several hell-like dimensions whose energies resonate with our own," as Gabriel put it.

Among some descriptions of temple engravings, a paragraph stopped her in her tracks.

She inhaled sharply and Elliot glanced up. "Found something?"

"Listen to this." She scrambled out of the beanbag and sat on the end of the sofa. "'The honour guard of the Lord Dagon be thusly named. The master of thread, the shroud of the dead, the sibilant claimant, the darkest raiment, the cloak of the unclean, the wielder of the unseen.' The wielder of the unseen! That has to be the Mime."

"May I see that?" Gabriel took the book from her and set it on the coffee table before him. "I must have read this passage a hundred times. I had believed it referred to Ka by a multitude of names."

Elliot set his own book aside.

"The darkest raiment is most certainly Ka," Gabriel continued. "That name is used elsewhere most frequently."

"And the others?" Elliot asked.

"I find myself confronting the unsettling possibility that they in fact refer to other entities entirely."

Sam watched him as a deeply troubled look took hold in his eyes. "That's bad, right?"

He blinked and focused on her, the distress hidden away. "Perhaps, perhaps not. In all the years my family hunted Ka, nothing ever gave us reason to suspect other forces related to the demon were active in this world."

"Where does that passage come from?" Elliot asked.

"The writings of a first-century Jewish priest. It's a first-hand account, but it has been translated several times." He picked the book up again, holding it gingerly like it might burn him.

Elliot reclined in his seat. "So, this thing has been around a long time. That's not the best news."

"Let us not get disheartened. We now have an idea of what we are looking for."

Sam stood and stretched. "Well, before we crack on with that, I'm going to get us some dinner and drinks."

"Wait, you can't go out!" Elliot grabbed her wrist as she moved past.

She looked down at his hand and he let go.

"Sorry. I didn't mean—"

"Relax, I'm not going anywhere. There's stuff in the cupboards I can whip up. I mean, if we're okay to do that. Gabriel?"

Gabriel dragged his eyes from the passage in the book. "Oh yes. Yes, quite alright."

———•———

While Sam prepared dinner, Gabriel and Elliot re-sorted the books. In light of Sam's discovery, Gabriel wanted to review certain well-thumbed volumes himself. He piled less familiar ones for Elliot and Sam.

Elliot was glad of the break when Sam called them, and they joined her at the dining table to eat. Gabriel remained subdued. The revelation that his old enemy Ka was merely one of several demons with a common cause had clearly shaken him.

After the meal, they swiftly uncovered further references to the wielder of the unseen, but never with a true name attached. Gabriel began collating notes.

"I think I have something here," Elliot said, towards midnight. He shifted forwards on the sofa and rested his book on the edge of the coffee table. "'… the shaper of air, wielder of the unseen, bound by fealty to offer tribute within the first lunar cycle after the gods of love and war unite.'"

"An alignment of Venus and Mars? Now, that is intriguing," Gabriel said.

"I was more interested in the word 'tribute'. Could that be the reason for the murders?"

"Perhaps. Who is the fealty paid to?"

He scanned the page again. "It doesn't say. Dagon?"

"Hmm."

He pulled his phone from his pocket and loaded the calendar app. "The first attack that we know of took place on the twentieth of June. A waning crescent. Not a full moon or new moon."

"The sickle moon is also a powerful symbol in the occult world."

"It said within the lunar cycle, right?" Sam said. "Does that mean it'll stop after a month?"

Elliot rubbed his eyes under his glasses. "A time limit. Christ, that's all we need."

Sam glanced from him to Gabriel. "But, if it stops, isn't that a good thing?"

"It depends," Gabriel said. "If it means we lose track of the demon, or it retreats to the spirit world, we may not be able to stop it when it re-emerges."

"And in the meantime, who knows how many more people it might kill." Elliot reached for his laptop. "I'm going to forward this to Fiona. Maybe it'll help her pin down a pattern."

———•———

They continued with the research for another hour. Fear of the Mime catching up with them, the risk to more innocent victims and the newly added ticking clock of the moon phase made it hard to put the books down. But as they pushed into the early hours, the words began to blur together. Elliot felt his eyelids drooping. Sam sat at the other end of the sofa. Her head rested on her shoulder and the book in her relaxed hands sagged to one side.

Gabriel rubbed his eyes and stifled a yawn.

"Maybe we should call it a night," Elliot said quietly. When Gabriel looked across, he nodded towards Sam.

"Perhaps you're right," Gabriel said. "I fear we may have exhausted what we might learn here anyway." He set his book down and got to his feet. "I shall bid you good night. I trust you can make yourself comfortable here? There are blankets in the chest there." He indicated a blanket box tucked away in the corner of the room. As he left, he closed the frosted glass doors quietly behind him.

Elliot eased the book from Sam's grip and her head snapped up.

"I'm awake!"

"Shh, it's alright. Time to get some sleep now anyway." He shifted off the couch and flicked the main light off. A floor lamp still shed a warm glow.

Sam swung her legs up onto the sofa and curled up with her head on the wide, soft armrest. "Did you find anything else?" she asked.

"Nothing much." He took a cushion from the other sofa and Sam lifted her head so he could slide it under. Then he selected a blanket from the box, shook it out and draped it over her. He remembered the night she'd stopped by the office and made him sleep on the sofa after he'd nodded off at his desk. So much had changed since then.

"Comfy?"

"Mm hmm."

He found another blanket and cushion, took them over to the second sofa, switched off the lamp and settled down. In the light from the street, which spilled in through the bay windows, he watched Sam draw the blanket tighter around herself. What Gabriel had said the previous day about the two of them returned to the front of his mind. She was there for him, even at his lowest moments. Even when he was being his worst, irritable, unhelpful self. She didn't have to put up with him, she did it by choice. He really didn't understand why, but he was grateful.

———•———

The next morning Elliot's phone buzzed from the side table. He sat up, felt for his glasses and pushed a hand through his hair. Daylight streamed in through the French doors. He glanced at the time before he answered the call. Ten past eight.

"Elliot Cross."

"Elliot." The hint of Irish lilt gave the caller away.

"Liam? Everything alright?"

"I'm fine, but this bloke on the news ain't."

"What?"

"On the telly. Man, you need to see."

Elliot stifled a yawn. "Hang on, give me a sec and I'll call you back." There was no sign of Gabriel yet. Sam still slept, curled up facing away from him.

He hunted around until he found a TV remote, then clicked on the news with the volume low.

Police tape fluttered across the end of an alley behind a correspondent with a microphone. "… wallet and other possessions were found with the body. Police are considering that this could be a racially motivated attack."

Across the bottom of the screen the headline scrolled past: *OXFORD: Body of man, 34, found in alley with severe lacerations to chest and abdomen.*

"Police urge anyone who might have been in the area last night to please come forward with any information."

Elliot's phone buzzed again and he jumped.

"You seeing this?" Liam asked when he answered.

"Yeah, I see it."

"Crazy shite like that doesn't happen around here. The guy on the news said it was done with a fecking sword. Reckon it could be your man?"

He remembered the Mime's blade slicing into the floorboards at the abandoned hall. Simple tricks because it was low on energy.

"Demon. And yes, I think so." He pressed his thumb and forefinger to his eyes, trying to think clearly. "Look, can you do something for me?"

"Sure. Whatever you need."

"Find out everything you can about this murder. Where, when, and whether there's been any others in the last two days."

"Will do. What are you going to do?"

"Figure out a way to stop it."

He disconnected the call. On the other sofa, Sam sat up, her hair a tangled mess from restless sleep. She tried to finger comb it into order.

"Another death?" she asked quietly.

He nodded. "I'm going to wake Gabriel. We need to get a move on."

23

Sam set coffee brewing while Elliot went downstairs to wake Gabriel. When he returned, she handed him a mug.

"We're out of milk," she said. "But I put extra sugar in it."

"Thanks."

"Give me your keys. I need my toothbrush."

She fetched their toiletries and cleanest remaining clothes from the car. When she got back, she found Elliot still watching the news. The dead man hadn't been named yet. Had the Mime killed him as part of its tribute, or to harvest the energy of his death so it could come after them with all guns blazing?

She pushed down the rising fear. They were making progress and they were with Gabriel now; he'd figure it out.

"Dibs on the bathroom if you're just going to stand there."

Elliot dragged his attention away from the TV long enough to take his clothes, then Sam ventured upstairs to the main bathroom. She rushed through a shower and scraped her wet hair into a ponytail, looped back on itself in a messy twist to keep it off her neck.

When she came down, she found Elliot dressed, shaved and talking to Gabriel who, in full tweed suit, pale striped shirt and dark green tie, looked ready for action – in a kind of Sherlock-Holmes-Doctor-Van-Helsing kind of way.

"We must expand our research," he announced. "Samantha, you and I will be paying a visit to the Bodleian. I'm certain we will find what we need in The Collection."

She glanced at Elliot. "What about you?"

"I'm going to check in with Fiona," Elliot said.

"I should have liked to have accompanied you," Gabriel said, "but my skills will be better employed at the library. Best we get started as soon as possible."

"Split up?" Sam said, regarding both of them in turn. "That sounds like a stupid plan. We know it killed last night. Any of us could be targets now!"

Elliot extended a placating hand. "I know, which is why I want to stop by the college. It's two minutes from the library. I won't be long."

She nodded. "Okay. Do you think we should warn the others?"

Gabriel tensed. "Others? Do you mean to say there are yet more persons involved?"

Sam cringed. "Just Liam. He was helping us look for you. And... maybe Rosa."

"Not involved exactly," Elliot said, edging between them. "We visited Rosa's shop, and I've asked Liam to look into the death this morning, that's all."

"After everything that has happened, you thought that wise?" Gabriel asked coldly.

"We can't afford to be too cautious." Elliot's voice took on a hard edge.

"No, what we cannot afford is more callous risking of people's lives. We must be careful not to involve anyone else unless absolutely necessary."

Sam edged away from the two of them, trying to reach minimum safe distance. Elliot could be impressively stoic in the face of criticism, but if he had a list of trigger words then "callous" would definitely be on it. It was one of the words he used to describe himself when he talked about his brother.

"Why are you so dead set against enlisting help?" Elliot asked. "The longer we take, the more innocent people will die."

Gabriel's expression darkened. "And you would choose to sacrifice people you know instead? Friends?"

Sam realised this wasn't about Liam, it was still about Fiona.

Elliot sneered. "You don't even know me, Gabriel, so don't you dare tell me what I would or would not sacrifice and for what. This isn't about whose life is worth more. You know full well that it's in our interests to beat this thing as fast as possible."

Gabriel held Elliot's dark glare, unflinching. "Quite."

"You seemed comfortable enough bringing in Father Monroe yesterday. So tell me, is it that you don't want help, or just that you don't want *our* help?"

"Elliot…" Sam put a hand on his forearm but he shook it off.

"Jack is perfectly capable of defending himself. Unlike amateur—"

"You want to talk amateur?" Elliot stepped forwards, shoulders set back, and took full advantage of the scant inch he had in height over Gabriel. "Who saved your amateur backside when you blundered in to fight that thing unprepared?"

"I have already thanked you for your actions. But your insistence on involving people unnecessarily is reckless and ill conceived."

"This is how I work!" He threw both arms out to the side. "It's what I do. Network, build contacts, tap sources. The more people you have on the case, the more you can accomplish."

Gabriel tilted his chin up. "That may work for news stories and gossip, but this is about life and death."

"All the more reason to attack it from all angles. Surely an army is stronger than a single warrior?"

"In war there are always casualties. I risk only my own life."

"Oh yes? So everyone should just let you protect them, is that it? Have a little *faith*?" Elliot stressed the word faith like it had another meaning Sam wasn't privy to. From the way Gabriel stared at him, jaw set, eyes blazing, she suspected the barb had found its mark.

Elliot shook his head slowly at Gabriel. "What gives you the right to decide who gets to do their part?"

Sam pushed in between them. She put a hand on Elliot's chest and shoved him back a step. "You know what? Let's go do some research! Because this…" She indicated the space between them with a finger. "… is not helping."

Gabriel shook his head and pasted on a weak smile. "Quite right, Samantha." He walked away, towards the kitchen.

"And you," she hissed at Elliot. "Back the hell off, will you?! We need his help!"

Elliot blinked, took his glasses off and rubbed his eyes. "You're right. I'm sorry."

"The Bod is not far on foot," Gabriel called from the kitchen. "I suggest we walk, Samantha. I've called ahead. Hayward is expecting us."

Elliot took a few deep breaths, calming himself down. Sam knew the issue would surely resurface at some point. She touched his arm. "Be careful, okay?"

"I will. You too."

———•———

Sam walked with Gabriel through the streets of Oxford, past ancient college buildings and modern shops. They crossed onto a narrow, cobbled street between a Gothic church and another grand building, both carved out of the ubiquitous yellow sandstone of the city, and emerged into an open space.

The cobbled path ringed a green lawn, at the centre of which stood a magnificent, circular building. Chunky stone-block arches supported thick columns beneath a domed roof. Far from elegant, the building emanated strength and solidity. The morning sun bathed half of it in bright light, while the lower half remained in shadow.

Sam stopped and reached for her camera. She knelt to frame the shot upwards and capture the building's full imposing weight against the blue-sky backdrop.

Gabriel paused further ahead. "Samantha?"

"One second." She tilted the camera and took another shot with a different angle.

Gabriel's footsteps approached. "Ah, indeed. The Radcliffe Camera. A part of the library, but not the part we are visiting today."

She inspected the shot as she stood. Gabriel joined her and she showed him the display.

"You have quite the artist's eye," he said. "Did you know the word camera originally meant a room and had nothing to do with photography?"

Sam smiled. "I think that was part of my first ever lecture at university."

"You studied photography?"

"Yes."

"Do you have a particular interest in architecture?" He indicated the path with a wave of his hand, and they started walking.

"Yes and no. I like catching moments mainly. But with buildings, I like the ones that have identity. Personality. Do you know what I mean?"

"Most definitely. I think you will find our destination to be quite characterful."

They continued past the spectacular Radcliffe Camera towards the older building behind it. A passage led through to a courtyard, similar to the gate into Fiona's college, only much narrower. Sam itched with apprehension at entering the enclosed space; the Mime had trapped them so easily before. But people were passing through unhindered. A lot of people. Once they reached the threshold, they almost had to fight their way through.

Gabriel sighed as they emerged into an enclosed square, busy with tourists.

"The Schools Quadrangle," he said, wearily. "Once the heart of academia. Now a gathering place for Harry Potter fans."

Sam walked forwards and spun on the spot, gazing up. The beautiful building surrounded the flagstone quad on all four sides; three storeys of carved baroque detail and sparkling leaded windows, topped with crenellations.

At ground level, studded oak doors led into different parts of the library under blue plaques with Latin titles: *Naturalis philosophiae, Schola Metaphysicae, Schola Mvsicae*, and so on around the square. Despite the crowds, it felt like she'd stepped into some magical realm. She clutched her camera, too overwhelmed to know where to start.

They'd entered through one wing. To their left, the main entrance to the library was set into a solid, ribbed wall, interrupted by only one large window and a plaque above the door. The striking simplicity contrasted dramatically with the opposite end of the quad where a flamboyant tower rose above the main gate that led to the street. Pairs of columns on each floor drew the eye up another two storeys above the adjacent wings, to where pointed turrets reached skyward.

"This is amazing," she breathed.

"The Tower of the Five Orders. Quite the most ostentatious expression of academic hubris," Gabriel said. "The view from the top is quite spectacular."

Her head snapped round. "We're going up the tower?"

His mouth crinkled in a mischievous smirk and he inclined his head towards the imposing entrance to their left.

They passed a group of tourists taking pictures with the bronze statue that stood a few paces in front of the door, and entered a lobby of sorts. Directly in front of them several staff issued stickers to a tour group, beside doors signposted: Divinity School.

"That is one of the oldest purpose-built parts of the university. Dates to the fifteenth century," Gabriel said, indicating the doors. When the tour guide escorted their group in, Sam caught a glimpse of fine stonework and airy glass. But sight-seeing and pretty architecture weren't why they were there. Gabriel angled left towards a sweeping desk and glass barrier gate at one end of the lobby. The security guard behind the desk perked up as Gabriel approached.

"Good morning." Gabriel rooted around in his satchel. "Would you be so kind as to call Hayward Ross and ask him to meet me and my guest at the turret staircase?"

"Uh, sure. And you are?"

"Gabriel Cushing."

The man frowned but picked up the phone and dialled. He held a short, hushed conversation, then hung up.

Gabriel withdrew a plastic card from his wallet and swiped it over the access point. The glass gate swung open. Sam huddled close to follow him through.

"Oh, and I have another guest joining me. Please contact Hayward when he arrives."

Gabriel nodded to the man and passed through a doorway into a stairwell housed in one corner of the building. "I do wish there was some regularity to the staffing here. Used to be they all knew me and my father when we walked in." He trudged up the wide wooden staircase.

At the top, they emerged into a long room. For a moment Sam felt a little disorientated, then she realised they were on the top floor of one wing of the quad. It was warm and stuffy where the summer sun struck the windows.

She followed Gabriel along the aisle between rows of solid wood desks occupied by studying academics. She wanted them to be wearing robes, but they were just typical students – casual clothes, highlighters, iPods, headphones. Around the top of the wall a strip of small portraits gazed down from above the bookshelves and windows. Her hands tensed on her camera, but she wasn't sure if she was allowed to take pictures here and she didn't want to dawdle.

They traversed the full length of the floor and turned left at the end. Now that they were on the side of the quad with the tower, she could see how it intersected with the lower floors where the walls cinched in at the sides. Through an opening in one corner she glimpsed the worn stone steps of a spiral staircase. Beside it, a sign warned "Authorised access only".

At the foot of the staircase a man stood by the window, looking down into the quadrangle below. Sunlight highlighted his sharp cheekbones, sunken eyes and the lines across his brow. His crisp grey shirt accentuated the angles of his lean body. Sam's hands strayed to her camera, but she stopped herself when the man noticed them.

"Gabriel, I wondered when we might see you again." He held out a hand with enlarged knuckles.

His full head of wavy, greying chestnut hair seemed out of keeping with the rest of his sparse, undernourished frame, and Sam found herself speculating on whether he wore a wig.

Gabriel shook his hand. "It was only a matter of time. Hayward, this is Samantha. She and her friend will be assisting me."

The man eyed her warily, then pulled Gabriel to one side. He dropped his voice to a low whisper. "You mean to take her—"

"To The Collection, yes."

"Are you quite sure?"

"Yes, indeed. Samantha and her colleague are… I believe they will have need of it. Now and in the future."

The librarian's expression warmed. "Referrals don't come higher than those from the Cushing family. Let me show you up."

He stepped onto the spiral staircase. Gabriel gestured for Sam to go next. They passed one door which led into a wood-panelled room, but continued up. She caught a glimpse of the city from a tiny window in the turret wall. Seen from above, the library formed a gilded frame, with the quad a grey canvas dotted with colour where people stood.

Hayward glanced over his shoulder as they approached a second door. "The official story is that this room is used for university archives." He produced a key from his pocket. "The truth is a secret that men have died to protect. Only a select few have knowledge of The Collection, and fewer still have access."

Sam suddenly felt like she was under interview.

"You must never disclose what you see here," Hayward said. "Do you understand?"

She nodded.

He unlocked the door. "Welcome to the most important collection of occult literature in the world."

The room was almost pitch black. Sam breathed in the musty scent of leather and parchment, old wood and printers' ink. Hayward crossed to the window on the right, which overlooked the quad. He raised the blind a couple of inches. There were windows on all four walls, but the other three had thick blackout blinds pulled completely down.

Where the light spilled in from the window stood a walnut-veneered table, surrounded by wooden chairs with green leather seats and backs. Four long, brass reading lamps with green glass shades sat in the middle.

"We have nearly three thousand volumes here, all of them pertaining to the occult," Hayward said. "Of those, around two-thirds are believed to be the only copies in the world."

A tall bookcase divided the room in half. The books on it, and on the shelves below and around the window, appeared more modern than she'd expected. Some even had glossy jackets. Hayward gestured for her to follow him as he moved into the shadows at the rear of the room.

"The oldest physical books we have are a few handwritten monastic manuscripts from the fourth and fifth centuries, but there are transcriptions of pre-classical texts which date back thousands of years."

Like venturing into the past, the books on this side of the room were older. The librarian ran his hand along the black, aged wood of a long lectern, which stood behind the central bookcase, shielded from the light. On the lectern sat an enormous book with thick, crinkled pages, bound in cracked leather and brass. Sam reached to touch it but stopped – maybe she wasn't allowed.

"The original collection of the university held some two hundred and fifty chained books from the late thirteenth and fourteenth centuries," Hayward explained. "Before Duke Humphrey's library was built above the Divinity School in the fifteenth century, they were housed in a room at St Mary's Church."

Sam crouched to inspect a stack of five huge, archaic books on the shelf below the lectern. There were two other stacks, each arranged below a reading space. A second lectern held more, back to back with the first. Each of the thick leather covers included a brass clasp where a chain tethered the book to the wooden frame.

"During the reformation the Church ordered the destruction of all books of a superstitious nature. Of course, that included many of those held in the original collection."

"What happened?" Sam asked, standing.

"The most priceless and important books were hidden, packed into crates and buried until the danger passed. Afterwards, they were moved around many times, always kept secret except for a few trusted individuals, until one of my predecessors was able to relocate them here."

Gabriel joined them. "You will find history records a different fate for those books, which is for the best. The fewer who know about this collection, the safer it will be."

"Quite so," Hayward said. "Which is why I must insist that you never mention its existence. To anyone."

"I understand."

They returned to the table. Gabriel had already selected half a dozen volumes from the shelves. Hayward excused himself with a promise to check in on them and assist later.

Sam lowered herself into one of the seats around the table by the window and selected the top book from the stack. She ran her fingers over the leather cover, heavily embossed with images of devils and harpies.

Gabriel took his notebook from his satchel, uncapped a fountain pen and scratched a few words. "We should start by following the trail we began to uncover with my volumes. Focus on the lore surrounding Dagon and the period around the turn of the first millennium."

Sam cracked open the book and peered at the close, hand-written calligraphy.

"How's your Latin?" Gabriel asked.

"Er, non-existent?"

"Not to worry. I shall focus on the original texts, while you review later studies and translations."

"Sounds good."

She closed her book, handed it to him, and he swapped it for a faded cloth-bound one from the pile.

Elliot's phone rang as he approached Fiona's college. He assumed it would be Sam, but the display showed Liam's number. He must have found out something about this morning's victim. Elliot hit the answer button. "That was quick."

"Er yeah, I got your info. But look, man, I think this bloody thing's after me. What should I do?"

"Don't go near it. Stay out of sight." Elliot broke into a run, back towards his car. "Where are you?"

"At work. The hospital."

"Which one? Where can I pick you up?"

"John Radcliffe. Drive up to the ambulance bay. I'll meet you there."

He swung into the car and buckled up. "I'm ten minutes away. Hold on."

It entered his mind that this could be a trap set by the Mime, to lure him in by scaring Liam. But, despite what Gabriel had said earlier, he didn't want to be the kind of man who sacrificed friends. Trap or not, he had to do something. He drove through the city and soon pulled onto the road leading to the hospital. He spotted an ambulance and followed it into the complex. Tall, glass-and-steel hospital buildings lined the left side. At the top of the slope, the ambulance made a hard left into the covered bay.

Elliot continued past and pulled up in the drop-off zone. There was no sign of Liam. He took out his phone and dialled. Liam answered after a few rings.

"Shite. I can't get out! What do I do?"

Elliot climbed out of the car and walked towards where the ambulance crew were unloading an elderly patient into a wheel-chair. "Stay calm. Where are you now?"

Liam's voice dropped to a whisper. "Fourth floor, near radiology. Jaysus, I think it's here."

"What you can see?" The sound of a door banging open and a clatter came down the line. "Liam?"

"It came up the stairs," he whispered. "I ducked into a ward, but I think it knows I'm—"

A loud crack and a muffled cry drifted from the phone. Elliot broke into a run. "Liam!"

24

Elliot slowed to a walk as he approached the ambulance bay.

"Hey! Hey, you can't go in that way!" one of the paramedics called out to him.

He hesitated.

"Main entrance is that way." The paramedic pointed up the slope.

Elliot briefly considered making a run for it, but then a security guard stepped out and took up a spot by the door.

The walkie-talkie on the man's belt crackled. "Any available security personnel to the f-fourth floor. We have a... a... Just get up here!"

The guard didn't move. He eyeballed Elliot. Obviously he wasn't allowed to leave his post.

Stifling a growl of frustration, Elliot jogged towards the main entrance. He strode in, past the reception desk, and spotted a floor plan. Coloured lines marked the routes to various departments. He followed the one marked radiology through several corridors to a bank of lifts and a staircase. Bypassing the sparse crowd waiting by the lifts, he took the stairs, bounding up two at a time for the first two floors, then slowing to a jog.

He reached the fourth floor and took a moment to regulate his breathing before he opened the door. To the right of the wide corridor were workstations, a waiting area and doors to various treatment rooms and offices, but on the left a ward ran the entire length of the floor, separated from the corridor by a long, windowed partition.

Nurses and doctors huddled across the walkway from the ward. They talked in low whispers, slanting occasional glances towards the young security guard who stood with his back to the wall beside the only obvious door into the ward. Twenty paces away. He held a radio in a white-knuckled grip.

From inside came a man's scream.

Elliot balled his fists, crept up to the partition and peered through into the ward. A row of beds extended from each side, with a gangway down the centre. Cowering behind one of the beds at this end, a couple of children cried and clung to a young female nurse. Further back, a man held a trembling middle-aged woman sitting on a bed wearing a hospital gown. At the far end, near the door, was Liam. In pink scrubs. He floated three feet off the floor, arms and legs extended. Elliot caught a glimpse of the Mime's black hood and white face and ducked out of sight, heart pounding.

His knee clipped a fire extinguisher hanging from a hook on the wall. He lifted the canister down and tested the weight in his hands. One good blow to the head and the Mime would be… Well, it had to slow it down at least.

"Is anyone getting this?" the guard pleaded on the radio. "I need help here. This psycho is killing a guy." He glared at the cowering medical personnel. "Someone call the fucking police already!"

Elliot took a deep breath, pushed off the wall and strode down the corridor. Halfway to the door he changed his mind. The

Mime might not give him an opportunity to land one good blow, but if he could blind it first he might have a chance. Without breaking stride, he adjusted his grip on the extinguisher, pulled off the seal and tensed his hand around the trigger.

The security officer took one look at the expression on his face and retreated a step.

Elliot reached the door. Barely three paces in front of him, the Mime froze in the act of winding an invisible crank. Liam twisted his head to look, teeth gritted. The Mime's eyes narrowed, flaring white, black makeup creasing. It lunged, but before it could get close Elliot aimed the extinguisher at its face and squeezed the trigger.

White fog erupted from the nozzle and engulfed the Mime. Liam yelped as he dropped, then curled into a ball on the floor, groaning.

Elliot advanced on the Mime with the stream of gas, driving it back towards the far wall. His fingers ached holding the tight trigger, but he didn't dare let up. A white-gloved hand reached out of the cloud to swipe at him. Missed. His legs thrummed with adrenaline, like he wanted to run. The Mime charged. He leapt aside and swung the extinguisher upwards. The canister caught the demon on the chin and knocked it off its feet. It landed hard, sending curls of white smoke out to the sides.

Elliot rushed to Liam's side. "Can you walk?"

"If I have to," he said, struggling to stand. He clutched his shoulder.

The Mime burst out of the fog and grabbed for the extinguisher. Elliot shoved Liam towards the door and tightened his hold as the demon latched on. An unfamiliar urge to fight roared inside him. To smash that hideous grin until the light vanished from those inhuman monochrome eyes. He twisted the extinguisher left and right, trying to win back the weapon so he could end this. But there was no dislodging the demon's grip. His hands began to slip from the sweat on his palms. The Mime's mouth widened with silent, manic glee. Panic threatened, but the rage was hotter. It boiled out of Elliot in a wordless roar. He twisted the nozzle towards the Mime's face and squeezed. It released its grip and staggered back, but he caught a lungful of the gas that set him coughing, head whirling. He swung the canister wildly through the fog and nearly lost his balance when it didn't connect with anything.

With a crack of shattering glass, a rush of air sent the fog cascading towards the door. Elliot rushed forwards, brandishing the extinguisher. His shoes crunched on broken window glass. He looked out, sucking in fresh air. The Mime bounced down the side of the building like an abseiler. Running like a bloody coward so it could regroup. Elliot stuck one arm out and felt invisible rope straining from a point further up. He glanced around desperately for something, anything, to cut it loose, but there was nothing to hand. The Mime reached the ground and ran off into the complex, and Elliot thumped his fist against the wall.

"Elliot, man. You okay?" Liam asked.

With a sharp shake of his head, Elliot dragged himself away from the window. He set the extinguisher down and re-settled his glasses. The struggle had left his limbs tight, agitated. Liam leaned in the doorway, grimacing.

"Come on, we need to get out of here." He moved past Liam into the hall.

The young security guard stopped him with a hand on his shoulder. "Hey, you can't leave! You can't just do stuff like that!" His voice trembled as if he wasn't sure whether that was true.

"You need to let us go," Elliot said calmly. "Otherwise that thing may come back."

The man wet his lips. "But he just... Out the window? It's the fourth bloody floor!"

Elliot shrugged off the man's hand. "Believe me, it's alive. And we're leaving." He and Liam strode towards the stairwell, and the shell-shocked young man let them go.

———•———

They saw no trace of the Mime, and no invisible barriers stopped them, as Liam led the way through the hospital and out to the car. He groaned as he folded into the passenger seat but settled down once they got moving. He rubbed his shoulder absently as his eyes wandered appreciatively over the dashboard of the M5.

Elliot glanced across. "Are you going to be alright?"

"I'll survive. Just a few pulled muscles. And can I just say, I took what you were saying with a pinch of salt before, but now...? Yeah, wow." He rubbed his wrist with the other hand. Livid bruises ringed the joint.

Elliot checked the rear-view mirror again. Still no sign of the Mime. "I don't understand why it came after you."

"Who knows?"

"I thought it went after Geoff because he found something important."

"Well, speaking of finding things, I did that legwork you asked about."

Elliot glanced over. "Oh?"

"Yeah. Had a chat with a buddy of mine who works in the morgue. The initial report said, and I quote, 'wounds consistent with a large, non-serrated, bladed weapon'."

The Mime's sword, no doubt.

"And I, uh, I took a quick walk down to where it happened,

before my shift. Stealthy like. There's a shop with a camera across the road, so I asked the guy there if I could take a look."

"And?"

"And yeah. Black hood, white face, freaky eyes. Not too clear in the video, but definitely the same guy. No sword though, but then I guess there wouldn't be, would there?"

Elliot nodded, concentrating on driving as they approached the college. He parked in a street space across the road. They both climbed out and paused, waiting for a gap in the traffic.

"That doesn't really give us anything to use against it," he said, and stepped off the curb.

Liam hesitated before he followed. "Well, sorry! What else were you expecting?"

"Sorry, that's not what I meant. Of course I'm grateful you looked into it. It's just… I thought it killed Geoff to cover up what he'd found. What you were doing was no threat, so I thought we'd get away with it. I just assumed it wouldn't notice you." He wondered when it had identified Liam as a target. Had it been following them around the morning before it attacked them at Fiona's college? Then there was the fact it hadn't outright tried to kill Liam, only stalked him and inflicted pain, so maybe it had all been about luring Elliot out.

"Hey, I'm a little sore, but I'm still here," Liam said.

They approached the entrance to the college. The security guard nodded to Elliot, recognising him from the day before.

"That's not the point," Elliot said as they stepped through the inset door. "I brought you and Fiona in even after it killed Geoff. That was stupid."

"Don't beat yourself up. You couldn't know."

Elliot shook his head. That wasn't the point. Gabriel was right; involving people put them in danger. They couldn't know when they were being watched, or what the Mime might divine with whatever powers of clairvoyance it possessed, so simply contacting people drew attention to them.

They made their way up to Fiona's office. She met them at her door.

"Elliot, great—" Her eyes strayed past him and fixed on Liam. "Oh, hello?"

"Fiona, this is Liam. He works at the hospital. He's been helping us."

Fiona smiled. "Okay, then. Come on in." She let the door swing open and crossed to her desk. "It's been slow going, but that information you found about the planetary conjunctions certainly sped things up this morning." Her whiteboard showed a timeline, with a series of points branching off. "There's definitely something to it. I've found several that correlate with clusters of unnatural deaths."

While Liam took the seat to the side of the desk, Elliot studied the timeline. The first instance on Fiona's list – Hampshire, 1824 – was isolated from the rest of the evidence by over a century, but from the late nineteen fifties the timeline branched off at semi-regular intervals.

"Data is fairly hard to come by before the modern era, so I've focused on the post-war period. Only the incident I showed you yesterday, in nineteen seventy-eight, made any connection to a mime artist. But it all seems... plausible."

"Have you been able to figure out any kind of pattern?" He certainly couldn't spot one among the dates and locations on the board.

"I'd say. The conjunctions aren't at regular intervals. They might be as close together as six months or as far apart as three years. It ebbs and flows with the movement of the solar system, as you might imagine."

"Is every conjunction a candidate? Our source mentioned the—"

"The moon, yes. That's where it gets interesting. Every episode I've found started when the conjunction coincided with a crescent moon." She picked up a whiteboard pen and approached the board. "Now, you said 'one lunar cycle', which we thought meant one month, right? But I don't think that's correct. Whether it's a waxing or waning crescent doesn't seem to matter, but it does influence what comes next."

"What do you mean?"

She uncapped her pen and pointed to one of the dates on the board. "This one started under the waning crescent, and the last incident I can associate with it happened twenty-one days later." She wrote the number of days by the date. "But this one, which happened under the waxing crescent, petered out only nine days later."

Elliot pondered the implications for a moment. "You're saying the full moon marks the end point, no matter when it starts?"

"Exactly."

"So, when does that mean—"

"We have until the seventh."

Elliot blinked at her. The seventh of July was only three days away.

"What happens then?" Liam blurted from beside the desk.

Fiona shrugged. "I don't know."

"The demon will disappear until the next time it's due to emerge," Elliot said. "We'll lose track of it and be back to square one."

"So, you're saying we have to stop it before that happens? Oh man! How are we going to find a way to stop this thing in three days?"

They were looking to him for answers he didn't have and for a moment fear threatened to overwhelm him. He pinched the bridge of his nose, trying to marshal the rising panic. "Any way we can. I need to check in with Gabriel and Sam at the library. They may have made progress there."

"Should I come with you?" Fiona asked.

So far, the Mime hadn't targeted her, but there was no guarantee it wouldn't. It had gone after Liam, after all. "I think maybe you should, yes. We'll all be safer if we stick together."

"Alright. Let me get my things together."

While Fiona packed, Elliot studied the whiteboard. Half a dozen dates and locations were circled, and four more had big question marks next to them, including the most recent instance: Hackney/Islington, 2005.

"Everything okay?" Fiona asked.

He dimly realised he'd been standing there for a while. "Fine." He dragged his eyes away from the board. "Ready?"

She swung a heavily laden satchel onto one shoulder. "Lead the way."

25

"Staring at it won't help," Gabriel said.

Sam set her phone on the table and pushed it away. "I know. But what's taking so long? He was only going to see Fiona and then come straight here. And why didn't he reply to my text?"

"I'm sure he'll call to update us when he can."

"I know." She turned her attention to the book in front of her. The dated language was heavy going. They'd not found anything of use yet, but they'd only been working on it for an hour. She skimmed through another few paragraphs, then a phrase jumped out.

"Huh."

"You've found something?" Gabriel asked.

She worked backwards and read the page in detail. "Maybe."

Gabriel rose from his seat and moved round to her side.

"It says something about a pact – a deal – made with 'that which gives shape to air'." She scanned the next page. "There's nothing about who made the pact, or where, or when."

"May I see?"

She handed the book to Gabriel and waited while he scanned the page.

"What do you think?"

"An obscure reference indeed, but quite possibly significant." He opened the book to the inside cover. "This book is a travel journal of sorts. Written by a monk from the eighteenth century."

Sam twisted in her seat to watch him as he flipped between sections of the book. "It seems the part in question was written on a pilgrimage to Tintagel Castle in Cornwall."

"Well, that's something, right? Maybe we can at least narrow our search down to southern England, rather than, say, the world. That seems pretty significant to me."

Gabriel returned the book. "Provided this does refer to a geographically relevant event."

"Well, we can keep reading, maybe we'll find more about it." She soldiered on through a few more pages of dense eighteenth-century prose, then suddenly her phone vibrated across the table, making her jump. She grabbed it, fumbled for the answer button.

"Elliot?"

"We're on our way."

She let out a tense breath. "What happened? What took so long?"

"It's alright, we're fine. I just got sidetracked on my way to Fiona's, that's all. I'm bringing her and Liam with me."

"Liam? Wait, what do you mean, sidetracked?"

"I'll explain when I get there."

"You can't explain now?" She shifted nervously in her seat.

"I won't be long. I promise. Just stay safe, alright?"

"Okay. And you."

He hung up and Sam sagged in her seat. Her hands trembled. Gabriel watched from across the table with an inscrutable expression.

"They're on their way," she said.

"Something happened?"

"He wouldn't tell me. Fiona and Liam are coming too."

Gabriel nodded, left his seat and crossed the room to where Hayward Ross stood by the card catalogue making notes on a pad of paper. They held a whispered conversation, and the librarian departed.

Her racing pulse gradually normalised. She held her phone in her lap. Why did Elliot always have to be so evasive?

"You're very fond of him," Gabriel said as he returned to his seat.

Her head snapped up. "Of course. He's my friend."

"May I ask how you became involved with his… publication?"

Sam relaxed her grip on the phone, slid it into her pocket. "I met him online, through a forum. I was looking for answers after something happened to me. We emailed for a while and he really helped me through it. After that, I started taking pictures for *Weird News*."

"I see."

"After a while I started helping with stories, and eventually he asked if I'd work for him full-time."

"May I ask what happened to you? That originally set you on that path?"

She stared at her hands. So far, Elliot was the only one who knew the whole story. The only one who believed her. But maybe Gabriel was someone she could trust to understand. She stood and moved to the window. From the high vantage point she could see the whole quad laid out below, complete with ant-sized tour groups. The rest of Oxford sprawled into the distance.

"I apologise," Gabriel said. "I had no right to—"

"No, it's fine." She smiled, then returned her gaze to the window. It was easier if she didn't have to look at him. "I was working on a project for my uni course. Long-exposure night sky images." She traced her finger through the dust on the windowsill, forming a wonky five-point star. "I was twenty-one and big into gothic romance at the time. You know, sexy vampires and werewolves and stuff. So I thought, I know! I'll take my pictures in a graveyard."

Gabriel's seat creaked as he leaned forwards. "You found something, when you developed the images?"

She glanced at him. "Yes. Figures."

"Extraordinary. Nearly all examples of spirit photography have been proven hoaxes."

"I know. I researched into it after I saw the prints. I wanted to understand. In my stupid, naive way I thought they were trapped and needed my help."

"You tried to make contact?"

"I did. With this sketchy ritual I found online." She took a deep breath to steady herself. "One of the spirits took control of my body."

"That must have been very traumatic."

She nodded. "I was trapped inside my own head for three days while it…" Her chest tightened. "I think spirits must miss earthly pleasures. It took drugs, binged on food, stole things, got into fights. And at this one bar there was a guy and… well, you could say it indulged itself." She twisted her fingers into a knot.

"I'm so sorry."

She'd never treated her own body so callously and there were moments when she'd feared she might get stabbed to death, or die of an overdose.

"I fought back. I don't know how, exactly, but I found a way to take back control." Tears brimmed. "I was a mess afterwards. No one believed me. They all thought I'd done those things and I was making up some ridiculous story as an excuse." Many of the memories from her possession were blurry, distorted muddles of sensation and panic, but those from immediately after, the looks on her friends' faces, haunted her so clearly.

Gabriel watched her with an open expression of understanding and sympathy, which she hadn't expected. It forced a lump up into her throat. "My boyfriend dumped me. My friends all turned their backs on me. I even started to question myself, you know? Like, maybe I was losing my mind." She wiped her eyes on her sweatshirt sleeve. "That was worse, in a way. Like I'd survived one nightmare only to face another. My parents wanted me to see a therapist, but what was I supposed to say? That was when I met Elliot. He seemed different. He believed me, for one, and I felt like he understood."

Gabriel nodded softly. "Because of what happened to his brother?"

"I think so. He helped me draw a line and start fresh, like he had. You could say he inspired me." She smiled to herself. "He wasn't big on showing his face back then though, so when I actually met him in person for the first time I thought I'd made a mistake."

"Oh? How so?"

She wiped the last tears from her cheeks. "I imagined him older, more world-wise. More like you, actually. Then I met this lanky, flustered young guy, and I was like, there is no way that's the same Elliot Cross."

Down in the quad the tourist ants milled around, oblivious to the arcane knowledge stored above their heads. Ignorant, like she'd been. "If I'd known the risks, I could have kept myself safe." She turned to face Gabriel. "That's why Elliot and I believe people need to know the truth."

"I understand. It must have been very difficult for you. But, were information freely available, people would abuse it."

"Some abuse it now, but the rest of us blunder about in the dark, not even realising there are monsters just out of sight. It's all very well setting yourself up as a defender of the people, but how can you ask everyone to rely on you when you can't be everywhere at once? No one was there to protect me."

Gabriel dropped his eyes to his book and ran his fingers across the page. He blinked slowly, brow creased.

"What?" she asked, moving back to her seat.

"These past two days have thrown into sharp relief how much evil there still is in the world. You have to understand, I – my family – our focus had become very narrow."

Sam stared at him as she sat. They'd become dedicated to one purpose – a purpose he achieved – and then what? He looked up at her with sorrowful eyes, a hint of guilt in their depths, and she understood. "You were going to quit."

"I was, yes."

"So you'd not only keep people ignorant, you'd abandon them too?"

He shook his head. "I didn't see it that way."

"Didn't?"

He smiled uncertainly and closed his book. "I have revised my opinions of many things since I encountered the two of you."

"Oh?"

"Growing up in this life, I've always been aware of a divide between those like my father, his allies and myself, and those who were unaware of the things we fought. That divide seemed static, timeless, immutable."

"And what Elliot does threatens that divide?"

"Yes, but that's not… Having never done so myself, I'd never contemplated the idea that people can and do enter into what I arrogantly thought of as 'my world', at different times and for different reasons. To have witnessed that transition has been quite humbling." His soft smile held a strange mix of regret and wonder. "My father taught me that to need others was weakness, but seeing the two of you, the way you need each other, I see things I didn't expect."

Sam twisted her damp cuff in her fingers. "I don't know. I'm sure he'd be fine without me."

"I don't. I think he needs you more than you know, Samantha. Certainly more than he realises himself."

She puffed out a breath. "We should get on with the research."

A few moments later, voices and footsteps drifted up the spiral staircase. Sam closed her eyes as relief flooded through her.

"I thought it was a myth," Fiona said as she emerged into the room.

Gabriel chuckled and stood to greet them. "You'd heard about The Collection?"

"Only rumours," she said.

"Well, as you can see, it is quite real. And we must ensure it remains nothing more than a rumour beyond these walls."

She took a step towards the rear of the room where the antique lecterns stood, and gasped. "Oh, goodness, are they…?"

Gabriel followed. "Let me show you around."

While Fiona explored the dark recesses of The Collection with Gabriel, Hayward returned to the card catalogue by the window. Liam came in next. He wore pink scrubs over a navy long-sleeved top, and battered running shoes. He still had a fob watch clipped to his breast pocket. He must have come straight from work, which only raised more questions.

"Hey, Sammy," he said when he saw her. "So, this is the bat cave?"

"Looks like. What's with the pink?"

He glanced down at himself, then sat in the chair on her left. "Suits me, don't you think?" He shrugged, then winced.

Elliot took a seat next to Sam on the end of the table nearest the door, directly opposite where Gabriel had been working.

"How've you been getting on?" he asked.

She glared at each of them, settling on Elliot. "Really?"

"What?"

"What do you mean *what*? What happened to you two? Where have you been? I was worried sick!" She covered her face with both hands as tears prickled. After her emotional confession to Gabriel she still felt raw.

"Hey," Elliot said softly. He reached out, but stopped before he touched her. "We're fine. It was nothing. A little run-in with our black-and-white friend, but nothing I couldn't handle."

Liam cleared his throat, and Elliot shot him a murderous glare. Sam pursed her lips. "If you say so."

"Really. It had Liam trapped in the hospital, but we got past it and got away. Nothing to worry about."

She looked to Liam for confirmation, but he wouldn't make eye contact. This wasn't over. If Elliot insisted on being stubborn, maybe she could pry the full story out of Liam later. "Okay."

"Anyway, what have you been up to?"

Sam reached for the book she'd been reading earlier. "Well, we might have narrowed things down a bit." She opened to the page she'd marked with a slip of paper. "There's a reference to a pact made with the Mime in the late eighteenth century, probably in southern England."

"Does it say who—"

"Oh, we wish. No, that's about it."

Gabriel returned from the stacks with Fiona and they joined the group around the table. "If we can find further references, we might be able to pin it down to a specific geographical location," he said.

"You said eighteenth century," Elliot said. "Do you know when exactly?"

"Seventeen ninety-four or five, I believe. Why?"

"Fiona identified a possible period of activity in eighteen twenty-four."

"That's right," Fiona added. "It's the earliest evidence I've found so far."

Gabriel tapped his fingers on his bearded chin. "Could it be significant that the activity post-dates this pact? Or merely a gap in our knowledge?"

"More likely a gap," Fiona said, sliding into a seat with her back to the window, next to Gabriel. "The further back you go, the sparser and more inaccessible the records."

Sam closed the book. "What bugs me is that the stuff about the tribute we came across yesterday was way older than the seventeen nineties."

"Indeed," Gabriel said. "How the two fit together could be where we'll find our answers."

"Fiona, tell Gabriel what else you found," Elliot said.

Fiona outlined the theory she'd arrived at, that the Mime emerged sporadically when an alignment of Venus and Mars coincided with a crescent moon, then disappeared when the moon turned full.

She dropped the implication that they only had three days to defeat the demon, and it sat like an elephant in the room. From the ashen pallor of Gabriel's skin, Sam understood the scale of the task in front of them.

26

Elliot closed another book and tossed it onto the pile beside him. He took his glasses off and rubbed his eyes. He worried he'd miss something, but there was no time to read everything in detail.

Sam had sent out for lunch and coffee, and they'd all ploughed on, but the afternoon had already dragged past and they were pushing on into the evening. Outside, dark storm clouds had rolled in, and rain drummed on the windows of the tower.

Gabriel dropped into the seat beside him and jotted a few notes in his notebook.

"We may have filled one gap in our knowledge," he said.

Elliot re-settled his glasses. "Oh?"

"The mime artist appearance. I dismissed it as a fanciful affectation, but Fiona is working through some first-century BC texts from ancient Greece. The art form of mime originated there, with masked performers using mimicry and mimetic action. It's far older than I realised. Far more significant."

"Are you about to tell me that the Mime – our Mime – is the origin of all mime?"

Gabriel closed his notebook. "From what we've been reading… yes. The wielder of the unseen found a cult following in ancient Greece and Rome. The performances would often include real executions and acts of debauchery."

"The tribute."

"Precisely. But, critically, the performers were human. Followers. There is nothing to suggest the demon itself physically manifested or possessed human hosts at that time."

Elliot consulted his notes. "The pact. Something changed."

"I think so. Until this event in the eighteenth century it seems the demon was known as a deity or incorporeal spirit, and perhaps even influenced its followers, but only indirectly. After, it became something else."

Elliot glanced around the room. Sam and Liam sat together at the end of the table furthest from the door, working on texts from the local archive. They'd found one more reference to the pact made in southern England, but they still had no idea where exactly, or who was involved.

"Clock's ticking, Gabriel," he muttered.

"I know. But we are making progress."

Having Liam and Fiona to help was speeding things up, but the guilt of putting them in danger weighed on him.

A tinny, electronic ringtone sounded. For a moment, no one moved. The sound came from Gabriel's jacket where it hung on his chair. He suddenly opened his mouth.

"Ah. Yes, that's me." He fumbled a clamshell phone from his jacket pocket and flipped it open.

Sam caught Elliot's attention across the table, lips pursed, silent humour in her eyes. He struggled not to laugh. Gabriel and technology seemed completely at odds with each other.

"Jack, yes, we're fine. Progress is slow but steady."

Father Monroe, calling to check up on them. Gabriel stood up from his chair and reached for his notebook. There followed a long few seconds where he listened and made notes while everyone watched expectantly.

"And you're absolutely sure this is reliable?" A pause. "Excellent.

This could be exactly what we need." He disconnected the call. "Jack's contact at the Vatican has provided a lead for us."

Fiona and Hayward joined them from where they'd been working in the rear of The Collection. Elliot slid out of his seat to give Gabriel more space.

"The wielder of the unseen was linked to a family of demon hunters in the nineteenth century. The line died out around the time of the Great War and thus the demon slipped from knowledge."

"What family?" Elliot asked.

"Penrose was the family name. There were several individuals recorded, but the earliest was Giles. Giles Henry Penrose."

Sam drew in a sharp breath. "I've seen that name!" She jumped up from her seat and pulled her stack of books forwards. "Oh, oh, which one was it?" She sorted through them, muttering. Elliot moved round the table to her side.

"Ah, this one." She sat down and leafed through the book, scanning a few lines on each page until she found what she was looking for. "Here! Family name fell into disrepute, blah, blah, series of deaths, yada, yada, eldest son sentenced to death... 'estates passed down to the youngest of the three brothers, Giles Henry Penrose, who sold off much of the land to compensate the families of his brother's victims.'"

"Is there a date?" Elliot asked, tilting his head to read over her shoulder.

"Yeah, seventeen..." She glanced up. "... ninety-four."

"That's it!" Gabriel crowed. "The Penrose family must have been involved with the pact that brought forth the demon. They then hunted it for nigh on a century and must have discovered something of how to fight it."

Liam shifted in his seat and half raised a hand. "But you just said the line died out. It's not exactly like we can ask them, now, is it?" He looked to Elliot.

"No, but it's a fixed point to pick up the paper trail." Elliot put his hand on Sam's back. "See what else you can find out, about Giles and the brother it mentioned."

"Sure."

He turned to Fiona. "Keep trawling through the ancient records. See if you can find anything about how to communicate with the demon. This Penrose family must have found something in order to make the pact in the first place. Maybe we can find it too."

"Alright."

"What can I do?" Liam asked.

"You can help me," Sam said. "If Giles's brother committed some crime then we should be able to look that up. Maybe, whatever he did, it'll give us a clue."

"Good," Elliot said. "Hayward, can you help them find what they need? And then work with Fiona?"

Hayward nodded. "Certainly. There are archives in the lower reading rooms where we might find something."

Elliot turned to Gabriel. "See if you can find any evidence of the family among the books here. If they were demon hunters someone must have known about them."

For a tense moment the two of them locked eyes, and Elliot suddenly realised he'd been dishing out orders without even thinking about it.

"If you think that would be a good use of your time," he added quickly.

Gabriel patted him on the shoulder. "An excellent suggestion," he said, then more quietly he added, "time is of the essence and we must deploy our resources strategically. An army may indeed accomplish more than a single man, and you rally your troops admirably."

Elliot blinked, lost for words. Gabriel had just knocked the wind right out of him. He lifted his head. Gabriel gave him a shallow nod with the hint of a smile. Still stunned, Elliot glanced over at Sam. She bit her lip, as shocked as him.

He slid into his seat and set his laptop on the table.

"What are you going to do?" Sam asked.

"Death certificates, census data, Land Registry. I'm going to see if I can find out what happened to the Penroses."

———•———

The surge of hope that came from having a clear target brought renewed energy. Sam found watching Elliot take charge reassuring. Networking and building contacts was what he did, but it was more than that. He excelled at coordinating people. It was all part and parcel of that wide-angle lens he viewed the world through, and it was how he was able to single-handedly manage *Weird News*. Since they'd first encountered the Mime he'd been struggling. Now he had something he could get his teeth into, and she could see the confidence boost it gave him.

Hayward escorted her and Liam down to the main reading rooms. The library would be closing soon, so the students would be leaving and they'd have the whole place to themselves. He explained where to find the resources they needed.

Before they made a serious start on researching the Penrose family though, she took time out to order dinner. Hayward had grudgingly allowed them to take coffee and sandwiches up to the secret library, provided no one touched anything until they'd washed their hands, but he turned deathly pale and stiff when Sam suggested pizza, like he might have nightmares about greasy fingers. But a late night looked imminent, and if she'd learned anything from working with Elliot it was that you couldn't do your best work when you were running on empty. Luckily there was a meeting room they could use on the ground floor, safely away from the precious books. Elliot and Gabriel both rushed anxiously through the meal, keen to get back to the research, but at least she'd managed to get some fuel into them.

When they headed back up, she watched Liam climbing the stairs to the upper reading room. Earlier he'd been moving stiffly, like his joints were giving him trouble, but he seemed better now.

They emerged on the upper landing and picked a desk in the middle of the long room. The others continued to the tower. Sam gathered a few books to start with and they settled down to read. She watched Liam quietly flipping pages until he started fidgeting, obviously uncomfortable under her scrutiny.

"What?"

"What really happened this morning, at the hospital?"

He glanced past her towards the tower, even though they were completely alone in the deserted library. "I don't think your boyfriend wants me to tell you."

"He's not my boyfriend."

Liam chuckled, marked his page with a scrap of paper and put his feet up, crossed at the ankle. "Okay, then. If you promise I won't get hit."

"Elliot would never do that. He's not violent."

Liam laughed again.

"What?"

He tilted back in his chair and started to explain what had happened. How he'd done some investigating before his shift, and how he'd arrived at work to find the Mime waiting for him. He'd tried to lose it in the hospital complex, and called Elliot, but it cornered him.

"So, I'm hiding in the ward and it tiptoes in, like it's playing hide and seek or some shite. Suddenly it's like I can feel ropes round my wrists." He pushed his sleeve up to show dark bruises and rope burns, already turning yellow at the edges.

"Oh." Sam reached out to touch him but stopped herself.

"Round my ankles too. And it started moving like it was turning something. But there was nothing there. Or at least nothing you could see." He settled his chair back onto all four feet and rolled his shoulders. "Pulled me right up off the floor. Hurt like a son-of-a-bitch, I tell you."

The hastily scoffed pizza congealed into a greasy knot in her stomach. It wasn't just that the Mime could kill with its invisible tricks, or even the chilling thought of dying without ever seeing what was killing you. No, it was the demon's sick creativity that scared her. It seemed to have no end of ideas for how to cause pain.

"And yeah, then Elliot rocks up and beats seven bells out of it with a fire extinguisher. It was pretty awesome actually."

She froze, a cold wave radiating out from her gut. "He what?"

"It's true." Liam nodded. "Blasted it in the face with the CO_2, then whacked it with the bottle end." He mimicked the moves as he spoke. "I think he totally could have killed it if it hadn't jumped out the window."

His grin wilted as he took in her expression. She'd thought Elliot was only hiding how much danger they'd been in. Now she wasn't so sure. Did he not want her to know he was capable of such violence?

"Don't tell him I told you, yeah?"

She shook her head. There were too many confusing thoughts jumbling her mind. She trusted Elliot more than anyone else in the world. She just wished he trusted her the same way. That he could accept her concern without pushing her away as if it somehow made him weaker.

"You two really aren't together?" Liam asked.

Sam had been lost in thought and his voice made her jump. "No. I work for him."

"Huh. Well, his loss, no?" His lips curved and he winked. Her already unsettled stomach fluttered with a confusing mixture of excitement and panic, followed by a wave of unfounded guilt. She nervously tucked her hair behind her ears where a few strands had escaped her ponytail.

Liam took his feet down off the desk and leaned forwards. "Hey, sorry. That was… I didn't mean anything serious by that."

"It's okay. I'm just… Too much going on in here." She whirled a hand by her head. Crazy was the word of the day.

"Yeah, no kidding." He opened his book to the place he'd marked. "We should get to work."

They read side by side for the next few hours, while it grew darker outside. Elliot texted her for updates every twenty minutes or so, but they had nothing to report. The various travel journals, biographies and almanacs were stabs in the dark.

Liam closed a book and pushed it away. He slumped in his seat, frowning. "What about newspapers? Didn't Hayward say they had microfiche?"

"Right! We know the year at least."

They left their piles of research materials strewn about the desk and headed to a room at the far end of the building. A pair of microfiche readers stood on a desk in the centre, and banks of tiny drawers lined the walls, filled with film sheets. It took a little while to get orientated, but eventually they found three titles from the South West with issues covering the right year.

Sam showed Liam how to use the machine and they paged through the poor-quality scans.

"Jackpot!" Liam cried suddenly.

Sam jumped at the exclamation and took a breath before she inched her chair closer to see what he'd found. The page came from *The New Exeter Journal*. Fourth of February, seventeen ninety-four.

"'Twelve murdered in satanic ritual,'" Liam read out. He sucked his teeth as he read on. "Right, so a bunch of people go missing one night and the police go looking for them. They find them – all dead – in the ruins of this old chapel in the grounds of the Penrose estate. And there's this guy, Edward – Giles's brother, I guess – kneeling in the middle of it, covered in blood and guts and the like."

She grimaced at the image in her mind. "Nasty. Is there more?"

He spun on through the issues and they found another article a week later.

"This one talks about the trial. Sounds like something of a witch-hunt to me."

"What happened?" Sam asked, trying to read past his arm. The hooded microfiche reader was hard to see unless you were straight on to it.

"Looks like they tried to accuse him of Satan worship, or witchcraft or some shite. There was this big clash with the magistrates." He paused as he read and scrolled down. "Right. Looks like the local bylaws still allowed witchcraft as a charge, but the newer national laws didn't."

"Huh. There must have been some supernatural aspect to the murders to warrant people calling for a witchcraft trial."

Liam turned his head, and she realised how close she was to him when she felt his breath on her cheek. She hastily sat back, flustered.

She caught a hint of a crooked smile as he refocused on the reader, but it vanished suddenly.

"Oh, here we go!" He sat up straighter. "They sentenced Edward to death by hanging, but get this…" He glanced at her with an excited light in his eyes. "'During the hanging, witnesses claim he climbed an invisible ladder and freed himself from the rope.'"

"That's our Mime!" She grinned at him and her eyes connected with his in the shared moment of the breakthrough. "Okay, okay," she said. "What else does it say? Did he escape?"

Liam read a few more lines. "Nah, they just shot him in the back as he ran."

They both fell silent. The electric hum of the lights in the microfiche readers and the tap of rain on the windows became the only noises in the room. Liam reclined in his chair, which creaked.

He indicated the article with one hand. "Does this mean we can just shoot the thing and it'll die? Because that sounds like a pretty obvious thing to try, no?"

"If the host is possessed, that could mean ending an innocent human life." She shuffled in her seat. "Although, if Edward Penrose made a pact with the demon and became the Mime, that does sound like it was his choice. Maybe that means all the hosts are willing partners."

"Does that make it okay to kill the host?" Liam asked.

She shrugged. "I don't know. What if Edward was tricked? I mean, it's a demon, right? They're pretty much known for lying. Maybe he didn't know what he was doing."

They sat in silence for a moment, weighing up the alternatives.

Liam twisted his seat so he sat facing her. "Okay, I'm just putting this out there, not saying I agree with it, but... say we kill it, and kill the host, willing or not – doesn't that mean we save people? People it would have killed."

"Maybe."

"So? Greater good, and all that – do you think we should?"

Her fingers itched like she wanted to hold something. Her camera was upstairs with Elliot. "I don't know. If the host is trapped, he's suffering worse than anyone right now. He shouldn't have to die."

Liam frowned at her, but she couldn't tell him how she knew that. It had been hard enough opening up to Gabriel earlier.

27

Up in The Collection at the top of the tower, Elliot added a name to a sketchy family tree of the Penrose line. Giles had two brothers, Edward and Robert, who both died in seventeen ninety-four. One executed, the other murdered. Edward had made a victim of his own brother.

Giles went on to become a demon hunter, and his descendants after him, and Elliot wondered why. Had Giles felt responsible for what Edward had done? Maybe because he'd missed an opportunity to stop it happening. Did he ever forgive himself?

He looked up sharply as footsteps pounded up the stairs. Sam burst out at the top.

"We got it!" She held up several sheets of paper.

"Got what?"

"All of it," she said, grinning.

Her excitement banished his maudlin introspection like a light through darkness.

"Giles's brother, Edward? Definitely the original Mime," Liam said.

Sam squeezed in beside Elliot and spread out her pages. They had newspaper articles, photocopies from books and a few pages of handwritten notes. She tucked her hair back and started to talk him through everything they'd found.

"This is brilliant. Well done."

She beamed at him.

"We think the house was somewhere near Okehampton," she said. "It sounds like they were less big lords of the manor, more middle-class gentleman farmers. Especially after Giles sold most of their estate."

Elliot pulled his laptop forwards and clicked across to a browser window he already had open showing a satellite image of a sprawling, medieval farmhouse.

"Is that…?" She sucked her lower lip, peering closer.

"That's the Penrose house. It's still there."

Liam took a seat beside Sam and put his arm across the back of her chair. Elliot tensed as his eyes fixed on where Liam's hand curled towards her shoulder, but Sam drew his attention back to the screen.

"So, do we know who owns it now?"

"I'm not sure yet." He pulled his family tree notes forwards. "Here's what I've found so far. The last male heir in the Penrose line, Charles, died in the Great War. His assets transferred to his sister, Emily, who'd already married a Henry Carter. They inherited the house and it passed down to their daughter, Rosemary. So, while the direct male line of the Penrose family died out, the family did continue through the female side."

"So there may still be a chance of finding a descendant?" Gabriel asked from across the table.

"No, sadly not. Rosemary Carter – or Clary as she was after she married – died in nineteen ninety-four. The house was put up for auction and her assets revolved to the state."

"She had no children?" Sam asked.

Elliot tipped his head towards her. "She had a son, and a sister, but they both died in the Blitz."

"Oh."

"So, whoever owns it now, they're not going to know anything about the Penroses," Liam said.

Elliot shrugged. "Probably not."

"So we're screwed?"

"Not necessarily," Gabriel said. "We may find something at the house. Records, for instance. And local archives may hold more."

Elliot closed his laptop. "Right. We need to decide on our next step."

Fiona and Hayward joined the four of them around the table, and Elliot swiftly brought them up to speed on what Sam and Liam had discovered, and about the house in Devon. Once everyone was on the same page, he put the question to them.

"We have two choices," he said. "We stay here in the hope we can still find what we need in the library, or we head to Devon and take our chances following the Penrose lead there."

"Surely we have to go," Sam said. "Or at least someone has to. We don't have time to wait and see. Our three days is nearly down to two already."

Elliot nodded. That was his thought too. "Gabriel, you agree?"

Gabriel pondered his answer before he spoke. "Yes. As you say, we cannot afford to be too cautious."

"Does that mean we're going on a road trip?" Liam asked.

Elliot glanced at Gabriel nervously. A deep frown furrowed the demon hunter's brow. "We can't all go."

Liam's face fell. "What? No, come on! Don't bench me now."

"Elliot's right," Gabriel said tersely. "The two of us will go while the rest of you remain here."

"Oh no," Sam said. "No, no, no. You are not leaving me behind. No chance."

Elliot winced at the look she gave him. In his mind he'd imagined the three of them, and he didn't want to leave her behind either. He wasn't wholly sure he could do this without her, but that didn't sound like the kind of argument that would go down well with Gabriel.

He met Gabriel's eye. "Let her see it through. She's been in this from the start."

Gabriel considered each of them, a small, enigmatic smile behind his beard. "Very well."

"If she's going, I'm going," Liam said.

Elliot noticed again how close he was sitting to Sam. "No, it's—"

"He can help, Elliot," Sam said. "Please?"

The pleading tone in her voice sent an unfamiliar and disconcerting jolt of jealousy through him. He couldn't help but speculate on *why* she was so keen to bring Liam along, which naturally led him to analyse his own reasons for *not* wanting him there. Those were thoughts he wasn't ready to examine too closely.

"And me," Fiona said suddenly, drawing everyone's attention. "I can help too."

Gabriel twisted sharply in his seat. "Absolutely not!"

She pursed her lips and he shrank. "You think you can order me around now? Gabriel?"

"I apologise." He closed his eyes and took a breath. "But I would feel more comfortable if I knew you were safe." His eyes darted towards the others, and Elliot got the impression he would rather be having this conversation with Fiona in private.

"Wouldn't I be safer with you?" She reached across the table for his hand.

He tensed as she touched him, and shook his head. "No doubt the demon will follow us. There should be no threat to those who remain behind."

"And if it doesn't?"

He reached into his jacket pocket for his mobile. "I shall call Jack. While we make the trip to Devon, the rest of you should seek shelter on consecrated ground. The demon cannot reach you there. Once we confirm it has followed us south, you will be safe to return to the library."

"You have an answer for everything, don't you?" Fiona glared at him.

He closed his eyes. "Please, I... I need you to keep working here, in case we are unsuccessful."

It was the first time Elliot had seen him shaken, vulnerable. Even when the Mime had had him on the ropes at the abandoned hall, ready to bash his skull in with its mace, he'd remained unflappably calm.

Fiona's expression softened. "Alright. This time."

"I'll stay, of course," Hayward said. "These books are what I know. I'll be of more use here."

Gabriel gestured his agreement with a nod. "Thank you."

He and Elliot both regarded Liam.

"I'm still going," he said, folding his arms. The effect was somewhat ruined by the pink scrubs, but Elliot didn't think he was going to budge on the matter. He'd rather not argue further at this point anyway.

"Fine," he said, with a sigh. "Pack up anything we need."

"What, now?" Sam said. "But it's gone midnight!"

"I know, but we need to get moving."

"We need to sleep."

Elliot glanced over at Gabriel. "What do you think?"

Gabriel rubbed a contemplative hand across his beard. "Any delay gives the demon the opportunity to strike against us. We should leave immediately."

"It's alright," Elliot said to Sam. "You can sleep in the car."

"Yeah, but what about you?"

He tried for a smile. "Couple of double espressos and I'll be fine."

She scowled at him, and his grin wilted.

"Samantha has a point," Gabriel said. "However, I have a theory. If the demon is to follow us it will have to deplete its energy to do so. Therefore, if we can put some distance between us and Oxford, we might gain a brief respite."

"See?" Elliot said. "Let's hit the road and we'll stop when we get there."

"Okay. Can we see if we can find a twenty-four-hour supermarket on the way though? I don't know about you, but I'm out of clean clothes."

"Yeah, I wouldn't mind a chance to pick up something that isn't pink pyjamas and all," Liam added.

———•———

Outside, the rain had set in. It pummelled against the windows. The odd flicker of lightning lit the darkened library with an eerie glow, and low rumbles of thunder growled in the distance. Not the best weather for a long drive, late at night, but there was no getting around it.

The six of them descended from the tower, leaving the precious Collection locked up and safe. They made their way down through the reading rooms. Wind rattled the leaded glass. From the flagstone-paved lobby they could hear the rain beating against the windows in the ancient Divinity School opposite the exit. Hayward pulled open the heavy door to the quad and the noise grew tenfold.

"Anyone got an umbrella?" Liam asked.

Elliot huffed. He adjusted the strap of his laptop case across his shoulder, and he and Gabriel started across the quad, towards the main gate. Sam, Liam and Fiona followed, while Hayward locked the door behind them. They were passing the bronze statue near the door when Gabriel put a hand on Elliot's arm and brought him to a halt.

Rain speckled his glasses, but he could still make out the flash of white in the shadows on the far side of the quad. He tensed. Gabriel's grip tightened as the Mime emerged. It danced forwards in a series of bounds and pirouettes, and Elliot got the impression it was trying to add some presentation to whatever show it had prepared. It froze, facing them.

Elliot didn't move. "Gabriel? What's it doing?"

"I don't know."

The Mime stood between them and their chosen exit, but there were two smaller gates in the wings they could use instead. Both were closed for the night, but hopefully Hayward would have keys. Elliot risked taking his eyes off the Mime long enough to assess the distance – not far.

He caught Gabriel's eye and nodded to indicate the door to the right. Gabriel acknowledged. Keeping their motions slow, they edged towards the exit. Elliot glanced over his shoulder. Sam was already guiding Liam and Fiona that way. Further back, Hayward held his keys ready.

The Mime brought both hands up beside its cheek as if it were holding a flute and began to play the imaginary instrument, though it made no sound.

Elliot frowned. "It's never serenaded us before," he muttered. "What the hell is it up to?"

The heavy rain plastered his shirt to his chest and back. He raked a hand through his dripping hair to push it out of his eyes. The flagstones were awash, and fat raindrops splashed on the surface.

The others were nearly at the door, when Fiona yelped and Liam let out a surprised gasp.

Sam shrieked and hopped forwards, staring down at her feet. "What the hell was that?"

The Mime still played its invisible flute. It danced from one foot to the other like a court jester, then lowered the instrument from its mouth. Its grin was full of malevolent glee. All around them the standing water began to splash up, as if disturbed by a thousand tiny feet.

Sam screamed, and Elliot whirled round to see her trying to brush something off her hip. Whatever it was pulled at her jeans and sweatshirt with sharp, invisible claws.

"Back inside!" he yelled. "Now!"

28

The sensation of hundreds of small furry bodies running past his ankles sent a violent shiver up Elliot's spine. Claws hooked into his trouser leg. He shook his foot to throw the creature off and ran to Sam. Unable to see which end was which, he grasped the invisible squirming rat where it clung to her hip. Before he could fling it away it sank its teeth into his finger.

"Little bastard!" He pitched the rat across the quad.

More claws pinched and snagged his clothes. Liam untangled a rat from his scrubs – the pink fabric now stained red from bites and scratches – and threw it into the swarm. Hayward was ahead of them, making his way back to the library entrance.

Gabriel huddled close to Fiona, kicking the rats away from her. He swept his leg left and right, connecting with anything that got in the way. With only tights on under her skirt the rats had free access to her skin, and her legs ran red.

The Mime pranced about with its invisible pipe. Elliot glared, and swiped another rat off his clothes.

"Ow!" Sam shrieked. Her hands grasped something in her hair at the side of her head. A deep, scarlet scratch opened across her cheek.

"I've got it." Elliot grabbed the rat, felt his way to its face and clamped his hand round its jaw. Clawed feet scrabbled against

Sam's scalp, opening more scratches. He pulled and the rat came free, dragging chunks of hair with it.

The rain washed the blood down her face, where it flowed freely, making the scratches look worse than they were. Or at least he hoped that was the case.

He stayed close to Sam as they retreated to the door. Liam and Hayward were already there, but Gabriel and Fiona had fallen behind.

The Mime barged into Gabriel and knocked him down. He cried out, covering his face with his arms. Scratches appeared on the backs of his hands, but the thick tweed of his suit offered effective protection.

Before Gabriel could regain his feet, the Mime advanced on Fiona, hands extended as if it were carrying something, like a sack or a sheet. It tested the weight in its hands, judging for a throw.

Elliot unslung his laptop bag and thrust it at Sam. "Get inside. Go!"

Fiona backed away from the Mime, kicking out at the rats around her. She put her foot down on one of the small bodies and her ankle twisted. Elliot launched into a sprint as she fell. The Mime tossed the object in its hands and Fiona flinched as the weight hit her.

"Gabriel!" Elliot ran to his side, dragged him up, and they both darted towards Fiona. She screamed and writhed, jerking from side to side as the swarm of rats overwhelmed her.

Whatever held her down was heavy. Elliot felt strands of thick rope – a net – the fibres soggy. Invisible or not, it still interacted with the real world, soaking up the rainwater.

"Find the edge."

A motion out of the corner of his eye made him turn. The Mime lunged for him, hands gripping the handle of some weapon. The sword again – its go-to favourite when it was running low on energy. Manifesting so many rats must have drained it. Elliot rolled aside. The demon tripped, and sprawled onto the flagstones.

He threw himself on top of it, pinning it down. "Get her out!" Clawed feet snagged at his shirt and scratched his exposed forearms. He ignored the pain and kept his grip, trying to buy more time.

Gabriel found the edge of the net and hauled it off Fiona. She lay dazed on the wet ground in a spreading crimson puddle, her blouse stained deep red, cuffs and collar shredded to ribbons from a thousand tiny claws.

"No," Gabriel breathed.

"Get her out of here!" Elliot yelled.

Gabriel scooped Fiona into his arms, struggled to his feet and rushed for the door.

———◆———

Hayward had the door open by the time Sam got there. Liam reached for her hand and pulled her inside. She dumped her bags and Elliot's on the floor and turned back in time to see Gabriel pick up Fiona.

Behind him, Elliot struggled to hold the Mime on the ground. He cried out as the rats continued to attack.

She started for the door, but Liam grabbed her wrist. "Don't."

"He needs help!"

"He's got this," Liam said, dragging her back inside.

The Mime bucked under Elliot and threw him aside. Sam held her breath. As the Mime tried to get up, Elliot kept hold of its filthy black hoodie, and wrenched it sideways. It hit the iron railings around the statue, headfirst, and sagged down.

The standing water abruptly stilled. The rats ceased to exist the moment the Mime lost consciousness.

Elliot pushed himself to his feet and jogged to the door. He reached it just as Gabriel staggered inside with Fiona. Liam and Hayward pulled the door shut, sealing out the noise of the storm, then Hayward flicked on the lights. They weren't bright, but were enough to see by.

Elliot swiped his hair back with both hands. His soaked, shredded shirt clung to him, and blood-tinted rainwater ran down his forearms below where his sleeves were rolled up. He looked over at Sam. "You alright?"

She nodded, pressing her sweatshirt cuff to her stinging cheek.

Fiona let out a moan as Gabriel set her down on the floor.

"Fiona?" He knelt beside her. His hand hovered by her bloody cheek, close but not touching.

Liam dropped down beside them. "Raise her feet," he said, lifting Fiona's bleeding legs into Gabriel's lap. "Bit higher. That's good."

While the cuts on her legs looked bad, they weren't bleeding freely. The worst of the blood loss came from deep, ragged holes in her wrists and neck, as if the rats had chewed in search of her veins. But then, they weren't just rats, they were the Mime's creations. Part of its will.

Liam pulled his pink top and the shirt underneath over his head. He wrapped one round each of Fiona's wrists.

Sam's lips parted. Arcing from each shoulder blade and trailing down to his waist were angel wings. Tattoos, for sure, but as another flash of lightning flickered through the windows and changed the slant of the light she could almost believe she saw the feathers move.

He glanced over his shoulder. "I need something else for her neck. Anything you have, to stop the bleeding."

Sam took her sweatshirt off, then lifted her T-shirt. Elliot averted his eyes, head tipped up like he was suddenly very interested in the ceiling. She re-donned her hoodie and handed the shirt to Liam, who pressed it to the raw wound on Fiona's neck.

"Help me put pressure on it," he said.

She knelt beside him and took over squeezing one of Fiona's wrists.

Liam pressed his fingers to the crook of Fiona's elbow, searching for a pulse where there was less damage.

"She's lost a lot of blood and she's going into shock." He glanced at Elliot. "We need to get her to a hospital. Like, now."

Sam focused on holding Fiona's wrist tight in her grip. She watched Liam. It was like he'd switched into a different mode. Serious, intensely focused.

"Hayward, is there another way out?" Elliot asked. "One that doesn't lead straight back to our friend out there?"

"Yes. There's a tunnel. It connects to the Radcliffe Camera. If we go that way, we can gain a little distance before we venture out."

"Can you carry her, Gabriel?"

Gabriel nodded. The colour had drained from his face and his hands trembled.

"She's going to be fine," Sam said. "Right, Liam?"

He locked eyes with her. "Yeah."

Fiona moaned again, head lolling to the side. She was either semi-conscious or simply delirious with pain.

"Lead the way, Hayward," Elliot said.

Hayward started towards the corner stairwell. Gabriel picked Fiona up, and Liam followed close beside him, continuing to press the makeshift bandages to the worst bleeding. Sam dropped back; there wasn't room for both of them.

She pressed her sleeve to the deep scratch on her cheek. As the adrenaline deserted her, her eyes stung, and she was glad her wet hair dripped down her face to hide her tears.

Elliot put his hand on the small of her back and she jumped. She wanted to fall into him, wanted him to hold her, but he took his hand away almost immediately.

"Come on," he said.

She collected her bags and hurried after the others, down a staircase to basement level. Hayward had to find the right key and unlock the door, but then they were through, into a dimly lit corridor, which doubled back on itself to take them under the Schools Quad. Cables and pneumatic tubes lined the wall, like they were delving into some Cold War bunker. Hayward moved briskly ahead.

There was enough room for two people to comfortably walk side by side, but Elliot stayed behind her, bringing up the rear. She could sense his presence like the tingle in her neck she felt when spirits were near. Or maybe it was the tunnel giving her the creeps.

About fifty yards along they emerged through a door into a wide, subterranean room packed solid with metal racking. The shelves hung from movable rails, so close together there was no room to pass between them. Floor to ceiling, wall to wall, books. Only the dim green glow of two fire escape signs lit the way. Hayward led them past the long, silent stacks, turned left, and continued to the far corner where a set of stairs led up.

They ascended into the circular reading room on the ground floor of the Radcliffe Camera. Gabriel set Fiona down on a desk. Liam checked her pulse again and she mumbled something.

Gabriel's electronic ringtone made everyone jump. He reached into his pocket for the phone. "Jack? Yes, we're in the Radcliffe Camera." He paused. "Be careful, the demon is close by."

A few minutes ticked past. Outside, the rain seemed to have eased, or else the thick walls and windows of the round building muffled the noise. A loud knock sounded on the door. Hayward opened it and let Father Monroe in. He shook the rain off his long coat and wiped a hand over his scalp.

"Did you see it?" Elliot asked.

The priest shook his head. "No. You might have scared it off, for now." His eyes fixed on Fiona and widened at the sight of the blood-soaked clothes tied around her wrists.

"We need to get moving," Elliot said. "Can you take her to the hospital?"

"No problem."

"I will accompany you," Gabriel said.

Fiona stirred and lifted her hand weakly. "No, Gabriel."

He crouched beside the desk and gingerly took her hand. "It's alright. We need to get you help."

She tried to shake her head. Liam still held Sam's shirt to the mushy wound on her neck.

"No. Go with Elliot." She swallowed, grimacing.

Gabriel glanced at Elliot. "We can't leave her now. The church. Consecrated ground. Without it—"

"No," she whispered.

Father Monroe put his hand on Gabriel's shoulder. "I'll stay with her at the hospital, consecrate the room. I can keep her safe there."

Gabriel fixed pained eyes on Fiona. Sam could see the conflict raging inside him. She was sure he knew that heading to Devon with them, to find a way to defeat the Mime, was the right thing to do, but that hardly mattered. She wasn't clear what kind of relationship Gabriel and Fiona had, but he clearly cared about her. Deeply. If it were Elliot lying there, maybe dying, nothing could make her leave, no matter what the right thing to do might be.

She edged closer to Elliot and glanced at his face. He watched Gabriel with a tense set to his jaw and a dark cast to his eyes. She wondered what he was thinking.

He stepped towards Gabriel. "We should move now, before it comes back. She'll be safe. You know it's going to follow us."

Gabriel nodded, not taking his eyes off Fiona.

That was it, decided.

Elliot and Liam checked the coast was clear, then the two parties set off from the library in different directions. Father Monroe carried Fiona, accompanied by Hayward, towards his vehicle, while Elliot led Sam, Gabriel and Liam to where he'd parked that morning.

There was no sign of the Mime. Maybe Father Monroe was right and Elliot had injured it, or scared it off. They could hope that meant it would take a while to catch up. It also meant it would likely find another victim to replace the energy it had used attacking them. Someone out there, right now, could be dying.

She caught a hint of a grimace on Elliot's face as she and Liam, bloody and wet, climbed into the rear leather seats of the BMW, but he didn't say anything. Gabriel took the front passenger seat.

As Elliot started the car and pulled away, his mood darkened further, until he had a permanent scowl etched on his face. When they reached the junction at the end of the road, he turned to Gabriel.

"We're going to kill it."

"Yes," Gabriel replied, his voice low and full of dark intention.

DEVON

29

Sam's wet clothes left her shivering at first, and the windows fogged with condensation, but the BMW's heated seats and climate control soon took care of that. Elliot hit the main road southwest, away from Oxford, and kept driving. She was glad he did. Though it was nearly one in the morning, and they were all soaked through and scratched up from the rats, she wanted to put a good few miles behind them before they paused for breath.

A tense silence filled the car, broken only by the rapid beat of the windscreen wipers on full tilt. Oncoming headlights sparkled through the rain. Elliot and Gabriel radiated tension from the front. Sam guessed Gabriel was preoccupied with thoughts of Fiona. Elliot was probably finding ways to make the whole incident his fault, like he always did. Beside her, Liam fidgeted in his seat, clearly uncomfortable, and occasionally slanted glances her way like he wanted to talk. She wondered how he was coping with his first encounters with a demon.

She wanted to talk too. Share how terrified she'd felt watching Elliot struggle with the Mime, and tell him how amazing he'd been. Reassure Gabriel that Fiona would be okay, not because she knew that to be true but because it felt like saying it might *make* it true. She wanted to moan about how much the scratch on her cheek stung, and laugh at how silly that was just to lighten the mood. But she couldn't find the strength.

The route to Devon skirted the edge of Bristol. As the lights of the city neared, Sam spared a thought for her home and the *Weird News* office, and wondered what chance she had of seeing them again.

A little after two in the morning, Elliot pulled off the motorway into a retail park to the northwest of Bristol, where a massive supermarket still glowed green and open. He parked up and stretched.

"Half an hour, then we hit the road again," he said.

They bailed out and hurried across the rain-lashed car park. A security guard eyed them warily as they approached, which was hardly surprising. Elliot with his ripped, bloodstained shirt, Sam with cuts across her face and blood matted in her hair. Liam, shirtless, his tattoos and short hair making him look like a gangster, despite the pink elasticated trousers. And Gabriel, who by comparison could have stepped out of an H. G. Wells novel.

While Liam gathered first aid supplies, Elliot, Gabriel and Sam picked out fresh clothes. Sam found some blue jeans, a T-shirt and a cream zip-up hoodie. After they'd paid, she followed the boys into the men's loos; there was no one else around in the middle of the night to care and she didn't want to be on her own.

Gabriel had made it through relatively unscathed, apart from a few bloodstains on his clothes. The supermarket didn't carry much in the way of tweed, but he found some dark trousers and a pale striped shirt that vaguely suited him. He washed the small cuts on his hands, stuck a couple of plasters over the worst of them, and excused himself to keep watch from the deserted supermarket café just outside.

Elliot stripped off his shirt and binned it, then stood at the sink to clean the scratches and bites on his forearms with disinfectant. There were shadows of older bruising around his shoulder, where he'd injured it in Bristol. He seemed vulnerable, raw, and he was holding himself rigid as if trying to hide it. She wanted to touch him. Take the cotton wool from his hand and clean his cuts, so he'd know she was there, that she cared, and that none of them blamed him for what had happened.

He kept glancing up to the mirror, watching her while Liam inspected the scratch on her cheek. She tried to catch his eye, offer a smile, but he averted his eyes like he was embarrassed or ashamed. It made her ache inside.

"I don't think this needs stitches," Liam said, startling her.

He used butterfly plasters to pull the edges of the cut together. It stung like crazy, and when she drew in a sharp breath he winced in sympathy. "Sorry." He gently teased her hair from the scratches on the side of her head. "Not much I can do about these except clean them."

"Okay."

He swabbed away the matted blood. Though his fingers barely whispered against her skin, they felt warm, soft, and comforting. She closed her eyes as the pain melted away. When she opened them, she caught Elliot still watching her in the mirror. He was leaning on the counter with both hands, jaw clenched.

She dropped her gaze and pushed Liam's hand away. "That'll do."

"I'm not done."

She glanced at Elliot, but he was focused on dressing the worst of the scratches on his arms now.

"Okay, fine."

She kept her eyes open as Liam finished cleaning her cuts. He sucked on his teeth while he was concentrating, which made her awkwardly aware of his lips. She tried not to think about how close he was, or the glimpses of the tattoos on his arms as he worked. The ones with the verse about repentant sinners. He didn't seem to have many scratches, and even the bruises round his wrists from the Mime's ropes looked better than she remembered.

Once they'd finished patching up their wounds and changed into clean clothes, they looked far more respectable. Elliot had found some black jeans and a dark blue shirt, and immediately rolled the sleeves up. Liam swapped his pink scrubs for navy combats, a T-shirt and hoodie.

Before they left, Sam headed back into the supermarket and gathered some food and drinks to take with them. As she put them through the checkout, Elliot joined her. He slurped from a vending machine coffee and silently helped her bag up the supplies.

She was sure his tense expression in the bathroom was his way of covering up other things he didn't want to show, but it seemed to have ebbed away, replaced by a downcast sag. Did that mean he'd buried his thoughts deeper, where they would fester? She could ask him what was on his mind, but she'd learned years ago that his maudlin moods usually passed if she didn't draw attention to them. Maybe the caffeine fix would lift his spirits.

"I'm going to need a pay rise after this," she said as she handed over her debit card.

A half smile tugged at his lips, then faded. "Yeah, we'll sort something out."

"I was joking. I don't care about—"

"I know."

He didn't say anything else, just gathered up the bags and started walking. She pocketed her purse and hurried after him.

———•———

Heading south on the motorway, Elliot let the six-speed BMW cruise at nearly a hundred miles an hour. Except for a few lorries hauling night-time freight, the road was his – empty and eerie in the murky yellow-grey streetlight. The rain eased to a steady drizzle, which left the road surface slick. He rested one hand on the top of the steering wheel, dropped the other into his lap.

His M5 didn't have the softest suspension, but driving long distance it was a dream. Like when he ran, it was simple. Just him and the road. He could let his mind chew through problems while the car chewed through miles without effort.

Dry now, and warm, the tension eased. By the time they passed Taunton, Sam and Liam were both asleep.

Elliot watched them in the rear-view mirror. Liam slumped back in his seat with his chin tucked down and his arms folded, softly snoring. Sam curled sideways and her head dipped towards Liam's shoulder.

Gabriel twisted in his seat to look behind them. "Still no sign of our friend," he said quietly.

"I'm sure it's back there somewhere." Elliot glanced sideways at him. "Are you still worried it'll go after Fiona?"

"No. I suspect it's following us at a distance." His voice sounded clipped, strained.

"But you're still worried about her."

Gabriel said nothing.

Part of him wished he'd listened to Gabriel's protests about involving Fiona in the first place, but he couldn't help but wonder where they'd be without the information she'd found. That sounded like the kind of cold logic someone with flexible morals would use to justify hurting someone. Selfish.

"I'm sorry I dragged her into this," he said, rubbing his eyes. "It was my fault." He glanced at Sam in the mirror. With the way her head was angled, he could see the angry scratch across her cheek. "All of this is my fault."

"Don't blame yourself. I don't blame you," Gabriel said. "I could have insisted. The demon could have targeted her anyway if it identified a connection. There's no way to know."

"Alright, but—"

"At my home this morning, you asked me what gave me the right to decide who could do their part."

Elliot took his eyes off the road. "I know, I'm sorr—"

"No. You were right. Fiona chose to contribute, as did Samantha and Mr Townsend back there. Neither you nor I get to make that choice for them. To do so would be disrespectful of their efforts."

A slow-moving lorry forced Elliot to change lanes and gave him a moment to digest Gabriel's words. Was it about respect, or was that just a way to abdicate responsibility? The line didn't seem clear anymore, if it ever had. "You wouldn't have said that a few days ago," he said.

"No."

In the long silence that followed, Elliot glanced at Sam again. She flinched in her sleep, murmuring wordlessly. More bad dreams.

"May I ask you something personal?"

"You may ask," Gabriel said.

Elliot smiled at the implication that there was no promise of an answer. "You and Fiona. Why aren't you... You care about each other, but you're not..." He tailed off as Gabriel glared at him. "Forget it. None of my business."

Gabriel's expression softened and he relaxed in his seat with a sigh. "I shouldn't think I'd need to explain it to you."

When Elliot looked across, Gabriel indicated the rear seat with a tilt of his head and a flick of his eyes.

"That's different."

"Is it? Ms Prince is a number of years my senior and our relationship has always been professional. It wouldn't be… proper."

"So, it wasn't just about hiding what you do? About keeping people at a distance?"

Gabriel shook his head. "That has a lot to do with it, but no. It is complicated for multiple reasons. I value her friendship and support with my work too much to jeopardise it. I'm sure you understand."

Elliot nodded, and glanced in the mirror again. Sam twisted round until she had her back to the side door and her head tucked under the bottom edge of the headrest. She clasped her hands close to her chest.

———•———

When they hit Exeter, they ran out of motorway. Elliot took the A30 towards the north of Dartmoor and Okehampton. The clock ticked past three forty-five and he struggled to keep his focus on the road. They'd outdistanced the storm as they drove south and west; the roads were still wet, but the skies were clearing.

The car strayed towards the verge and the tyres scuffed over a patch of loose grit, which clattered under the wheel arch. Elliot sat up straighter as a spike of adrenaline chased away his drowsiness. He rubbed his eyes, slapped his cheek, then cracked the window down to feel the fresh air on his face.

"Perhaps we should find somewhere to stop soon," Gabriel said.

"I'm aiming for a hotel a bit further along this road."

In the back, Sam stirred, woken by the noise and the draught. She yawned and stretched, then reached forwards and touched Elliot's shoulder.

"Where are we?" she asked.

"Nearly there."

In another fifteen minutes he picked up signs for the local service area and turned off the main road. They pulled into the hotel car park and he killed the engine. A thick silence descended. It was so quiet here on the edge of Dartmoor that it made his ears ring. The four of them gathered what they needed from the boot and headed in as the first threads of dawn lightened the sky.

Their arrival flustered the lad manning the front desk, doubly so when they asked for rooms. "Check-in doesn't start until midday," he said, flapping.

Elliot was too tired for any of the guy's shit. He leaned forwards over the counter. "We're not checking in for Monday night, we're checking in for tonight, now. Just charge me another day and give us some sodding keys."

Eventually the receptionist managed to find the right buttons to press on the computer and found them two twin rooms.

Elliot handed one key card to Gabriel. He paused, then handed the other to Sam. As Gabriel and Liam set off along the corridor, he snagged her elbow.

"I can share with Gabriel, if you want," he said, keeping his eyes down.

She folded her arms and scowled at him like he'd insulted her. "I'm going to forget you said that."

He glanced at Liam, down the corridor. "I just meant, if you wanted—"

"I know what you meant," she snapped. "And you don't… Just no, okay?" Her voice cracked as she tried to inject force into it without raising above a hissed whisper. She stalked away from him.

For a moment, he stood there, afraid to follow in case she slapped him, then caught up with the three of them outside the adjacent rooms.

"I think we should set a watch," Gabriel said. "With so little time until the full moon our black-and-white friend might act unpredictably."

"I'll do it," Liam said. "I slept in the car anyway."

"Excellent. Wake me at seven and I'll take over."

"Did you sleep in the car?" Sam asked Gabriel.

"No, but—"

"Then you sleep. I can get up at seven."

Gabriel hesitated, then smiled. "Thank you, Samantha, that's most kind."

"What time do we want to hit the road tomorrow?" she asked.

"We all need some sleep," Elliot said. "Let's take it easy, get breakfast and head off late morning."

Liam headed out to the foyer to keep watch, while Gabriel disappeared into his room. Sam swiped her key card.

"You don't have to get up at seven. I'll do it," Elliot said as the door closed behind them.

She sighed with frustration. "You drove us here. Just get some sleep, will you? I don't know what's going on with you right now, but I am perfectly capable of getting up at seven and keeping an eye out for trouble for a few hours."

She stared at him, expectantly, but he didn't know how to respond to what she was really asking. "Alright."

With a long blink, lips pressed together, she sat on one of the beds.

He sat on the other and kicked off his shoes. He'd upset her when he'd suggested she go with Liam. And why? It was like Gabriel said in the car; he valued her friendship and support too much to risk losing her from his life. He needed her, for so many reasons.

She flopped back onto the bed with a groan, wriggled up until her head met the pillow, closed her eyes and stretched with a lazy smile. For a moment he yearned to lie with her, smile with her, bask in the joy she poured into his life, and the thought made him cringe with guilt.

He didn't know how to deal with this.

Since leaving Bristol he'd reluctantly accepted that his feelings for her ran a lot deeper than he'd realised, far deeper than they should. The way Liam looked at her made his insides cramp, but if she went with him it made things simpler. Easier. It took the problem away so he didn't have to face it. Wasn't that just him all over? Selfish. He didn't get to make decisions for her just because it was easier for him. Not ever.

He should apologise. Explain. "Sam?"

She opened her eyes, lips parted. "Yeah?"

The words stuck in his throat before he could even figure out what they should be. Too many thoughts about responsibility and respect were still churning around his head. He was exhausted, scared, and they still had a demon to fight. "Goodnight."

He stood and headed for the bathroom. When he emerged, she'd stripped off and cocooned herself under the covers.

30

The long day and tiring drive left Elliot so drained he crashed out immediately. He drifted awake briefly when Liam knocked on the door to wake Sam for her watch. Enough to hear there'd been no sign of the Mime.

The next thing he knew, Sam was shaking his shoulder, telling him it was half nine. Still no move from the demon. Not that he expected their luck to hold for long. It was surely waiting for a good opportunity.

An hour later, after breakfast, they headed out to the car. Gabriel had spot-cleaned and dried his tweed jacket overnight, and he once more wore it like armour.

The final leg of the journey took them further through Devon. Sam navigated from the back seat, using an OS map she'd bought at a petrol station along the way. The isolated Penrose farmhouse awaited, a mile or so outside a small village west of Okehampton. Elliot felt itchy with apprehension. Impatient. If there was nothing relevant at the house this would be a wasted trip.

Eventually, a narrow gravel lane turned off between stone gateposts, with Hunter's Haven chiselled into the masonry. The whitewashed two-storey farmhouse rose up on the crest of a shallow hill. Asymmetric wings and extensions stretched out from the sides, as if the house had been added to in different phases. As the approach swung round through wild, overgrown gardens, they caught a glimpse of a large stone barn at the rear. Elliot parked beside a muddy Land Rover.

Liam agreed to wait with the car, to keep an eye out for trouble, while the three of them approached the house. Their footsteps crunched on the gravel.

"Perhaps you should let me do the talking," Gabriel said.

Elliot cast him a withering look. "What exactly are you going to tell them?"

"We need access to the roof space to search for possible evidence, so I intend to inform them we are building inspectors checking for asbestos."

With a roll of his eyes, Elliot pushed past him. "A house this age isn't going to have asbestos, and we don't have protective gear. Don't overcomplicate it. Lies are easier to manage if you keep them small." He wasn't proud of it, but he could be a damn good liar when the occasion called for it. Skills he'd picked up in London.

He rang the bell and rolled his shoulders, ready to use whatever assertive, coercive techniques he needed to get them inside.

A few moments later the door cracked open and a very elderly face with lank grey hair peeked out. "Yes?" She pulled a threadbare cardigan closed at the front.

He downshifted to disarming and respectful. If he scared her they'd get nowhere. He'd have to play this carefully, maybe take a bit of time. "Good morning, ma'am," he said brightly. "My name is Elliot Cross, I'm a reporter. My colleagues and I are researching the Penrose family who once owned this house. Would you have a few minutes to talk to us?"

The old woman opened the door a little wider. "Work for one of those websites, do you?" she asked.

"Something like that," he said, smiling wide. "Say, you don't think there might be anything still in the house, do you? From the previous owners? Maybe tucked away somewhere?"

She narrowed her eyes. "Rosie said you'd come looking, one day." She looked him up and down, appraising. She didn't seem impressed. "Never reckoned you'd be so skinny though."

Elliot opened his mouth, but no words came out.

"You knew Rosemary Clary?" Sam asked.

"Oh yes. She was a Penrose, you know, not by name but by blood, and blood is what really matters." She slanted a look at Elliot. "I'm Irene. Come on in, come on in." She retreated inside.

Elliot glanced over his shoulder. Sam shrugged and Gabriel flicked a hand to encourage him to follow the old woman.

The ceilings hung low, but not so much that Elliot had to duck. Uneven floorboards rippled the worn rugs. He glanced into an expansive, dust-covered sitting room to one side, before following their host towards the rear of the house. They entered a long, rustic kitchen. Windows looked out into a farmyard, with outbuildings on either side and a gated stone wall at the far end. Beyond, pasture extended to meet woodland maybe a quarter of a mile away. A pair of high-seated armchairs, one draped with a blanket of mismatched knitted squares, stood in front of an open fireplace. It was laid but not lit. It appeared Irene mostly lived in this one room, which was no surprise. She had to be over eighty. There was no way someone her age would be able to maintain a house this big on her own.

"What did you mean when you said someone would come?" Elliot asked as Irene filled the kettle and set it shakily onto its stand to boil.

"Rosie told me the secret had to be protected but that some-one would come looking eventually, someone who was... who'd know what to do with it."

"But Rosemary died without a will. How did you end up living here?"

"Ah, well… Rosie and I agreed that it would be better if people thought the secret had died with her. She knew she wouldn't live forever, so she gave everything to me, over her last decade or so. When it happened, I bought the house at the auction and the little that was left went to the government." She wobbled over to the kitchen table and pulled out a chair.

Sam took the one next to her.

"My name's Sam," she said. "Elliot you met. And this is Gabriel."

Elliot stayed standing, watching her as she put her hand on the table, reaching towards the old woman with open warmth. She was such a natural when it came to winning people over. Maybe because she was always so sincere.

"What is the secret, Irene?" she asked.

"The journals. And the keys, of course." She glanced up at Elliot and Gabriel. "It's all up in the attic. You'll have to fetch it yourselves though."

"Would you mind if we took a look now?" Elliot asked.

"No time like the present. Tea has to brew anyways."

"I'll stay here with her," Sam said, meeting his eyes.

Gabriel led the way along the hall to the foot of the staircase and up. Seven doors branched off the wide landing. Dust lay thick on the moth-eaten carpet, and a quick glance into the rooms revealed furniture covered with sheets and further doors into other rooms deeper in the house. Elliot wondered how long it had been since Irene had ventured upstairs.

"Here," Gabriel said, pointing to a hatch above. A small brass ring hung at one end.

Reaching up on tiptoes, Elliot snagged the ring and released the hatch. The ladder squealed on stiff hinges. Once he had it partway down, Gabriel helped pull it the rest of the way. Cascades of dust followed it.

"Should have brought a torch," Elliot muttered.

Gabriel rummaged around in his satchel for a moment, and produced a small metal penlight.

"You must have been in the Scouts." Elliot took the torch and put his foot on the bottom rung of the ladder.

The light penetrated the thick blackness of the attic. Solid floorboards covered the rafters, so at least they didn't have to worry about falling through the ceiling. But that was where the good news ended. Boxes, piles of clothes, furniture – the space was crammed full.

"Let's start at one end and work our way across," Elliot said.

They cleared a space to work in and systematically moved things into the space to check underneath before moving on. In a chest of drawers Elliot found a collection of jewellery. Some of the stones sparkled like real diamonds, and there was enough gold to make a small ingot.

"Do you think she has any idea what's up here?" He held up a brooch. The cluster of precious stones glittered in the torchlight.

"I couldn't say. Much of this had probably been here for many years before she acquired the house."

Elliot lifted a newspaper off the top of a crumbling stack. December 12th, 1932. "Indeed."

"Shine the light over here."

Elliot swung the torch around. Gabriel lifted a stack of curtains off a leather trunk and dumped them in a pile behind it. The fabric threw up a cloud of dust and they both coughed.

Gabriel wiped his eyes. He unfastened the trunk's buckles and raised the lid, revealing a collection of leather-bound books. Selecting one at random, he opened it. Elliot angled the torch over his shoulder so they could read the neat but old-fashioned handwriting.

"'March fifth, eighteen sixty-two,'" Gabriel read. "'I have tracked the demon to the southern island of Japan where several victims were found decapitated. It has never ranged so far before. Our worst fears are realised – its growing power will soon enable it to manifest anywhere in the world. With only a few days until the full moon, I fear there is little I can do but stem the tide.'"

"I think we found the journals," Elliot said.

Gabriel returned the book to the chest and closed the lid.

———•———

Down in the kitchen, Sam had fetched Liam in. Between the two of them and Irene, they drank their way through a pot of tea while Elliot and Gabriel rummaged around upstairs.

"Did Rosie ever say *why* she was so sure someone would come?" Sam asked.

Irene rose slowly from her seat and shuffled over to a dresser at the side of the long kitchen. She pulled one drawer open, closed it and tried the next. Sam exchanged a look with Liam. He shrugged.

From a third drawer, Irene lifted a photo album. The leather cover flaked in places and the gilding was tarnished. She set the album on the table.

"Rosie's sister died in the war, you know." She opened to a page in the middle and pointed to a black-and-white photo of two pretty teenage girls in culottes and summer blouses, leaning against the side of a vintage car. "That's Rosie." She indicated the elder sister. "That's Elizabeth."

Sam wasn't sure how that answered her question, but she was fascinated by the pictures. "Who's that?" she asked, pointing to another picture on the same page where the two girls sat with a woman on a tartan blanket, taken on a picnic somewhere.

"That's their ma. Emily. She was born a Penrose, you know. Of course, she were brought up that girls don't do the fighting, after what happened to her aunt Jezebel, but it weren't always that way. Rosie and I used to read the stories. They're all true, you know. Those Penrose boys always married women with fire in their hearts, they used to say." She chuckled.

Sam traced her fingers over the picture. "She was Charles's sister."

Irene looked at her sharply. "That's right."

"Do you have any pictures of him?"

Irene turned to a page earlier in the album. In a two-inch portrait photograph, a young man in First World War military uniform gazed proudly at the camera. A chill ran up Sam's neck. His eyes held a kind of troubled determination she recognised. And the hair, with the unruly curl just behind his ear…

She closed her eyes and shook her head. *No way.*

"You were going to tell us about Rosemary's sister?" Liam prompted.

"Oh yes," Irene said. "Poor girl. Got herself in a mite of trouble back in the thirties."

"Oh?"

"Their ma didn't know, of course. Elizabeth made Rosie promise not to tell their parents. And by the time Emily told Rosie the family secret, well, it was too late. Elizabeth was already gone, and there was no way to find little Sarah."

Sam frowned, trying to decode Irene's rambling story. "Who's Sarah?"

"Elizabeth's little girl. Got herself knocked up when she was only fifteen, you see, and back then it weren't proper for a young girl to raise a child on her own, so they—"

"Put the baby up for adoption," Sam breathed.

"That's right."

She glanced at Liam, who shrugged as if to say anything was possible.

"So, did Rosie think Sarah would come back, when she looked into who her birth parents were?"

Irene sighed. "She never did though."

"And you think Elliot—"

There was a loud clatter as Elliot and Gabriel lugged a heavy leather trunk into the room and dropped it on the tiled floor.

"Yes, that's it," Irene said. She closed the photo album and pushed it to one side.

Elliot crouched beside the trunk and swiped his hand over the dusty leather, revealing an emblem – a crest – on the top: a shield-shaped border of roses surrounding a crossed quill pen and sword. Beneath, in Gothic lettering, was the name – *Penrose*. Sam's stomach fluttered with excitement.

Gabriel wiped sweat from his forehead. His eyes fixed on Sam's teacup. "I don't suppose there's any more tea?"

"We drank the first pot." She got up to put the kettle on. "What took you so long?"

"There were a lot of items to sort through. It took some time to locate what we were looking for." He crouched, opened the trunk and lifted out a book. "We will need to set these in order, to fully understand the chronology."

Over the next half hour they organised the journals into the different writers. It was somewhat confusing, because at any one time there was usually more than one member of the Penrose family actively crusading. Sam used her laptop to create a visual representation of how each member of the family overlapped, and for how long they were active.

There were eight names in total, one hundred and forty-two volumes, the earliest being those of Giles Penrose and the most recent those of Charles. Over time the handwriting evolved, and the writing implements changed from scratchy dip pen and ink to smoother cartridge pen. The earlier books included beautifully inked sketches and watercolours, the later ones, newspaper clippings and photographs, held in with rusted pins and decayed paste.

Elliot opened the final journal to the last entry. "Listen. 'Tomorrow they are sending us across no-man's-land to attack the German trenches. I am under no delusion that I will survive, and so I send this journal home to my sister. My father and uncle are dead. I am the last of House Penrose. The demon still roams, and none now are left to fight it. I pray that God has mercy on the world. My great-great-grandfather believed in the power of blood. If he is right, there may be hope. But the family name dies with me. I was so close, and I do so hate to leave unfinished business.'"

An envelope fluttered to the floor from between the final pages. Sam slid off her chair and stooped to pick it up. "It's a letter." She unfolded it. "'My dearest Emily. I doubt that we will see each other again, lest it be in paradise. Such a place is hard to imagine here, in this Hell on Earth. I pray God will forgive us for the sins we commit here.

'Know that I love you, and that the spirit of our family lives on, through you and your girls. Put this journal with the others and keep it safe. The secrets within must be preserved.

'Live well, dearest sister. My heart is with you. Charlie.'"

He'd known he was going to die, known with almost complete certainty. It must have been so hard to write that letter from a place at the end of all hope. It brought a sting to her eyes and she blinked a few times before setting the letter down on the table.

"There is much to do," Gabriel said. "We must study these journals and learn all we can. Somewhere within lies the key to defeating our foe."

31

With so much material to review they decided to attack from multiple angles. They each picked up the story at different points through the one-and-a-bit centuries the journals covered. Elliot took one near the middle, the first volume by Mordecai Penrose, Giles's grandson. The man had an entertaining turn of phrase that tended towards the sarcastic and Elliot imagined he would have liked him. He sat across the table from Sam, who was reading some of Charlie's diaries and chatting with Irene about what she could remember from reading the journals with Rosemary decades ago.

They didn't get far before Gabriel drew their attention.

"Extraordinary." He set the oldest volume reverentially on the table.

Elliot looked up. "What is it?"

"This journal starts out as a personal diary, with no mention of the demon or the murders. It seems Giles Penrose was a keen journal writer before he ever became a demon hunter. I will read you some of his writing."

He flicked to a page near the beginning. "'October twenty-eighth. Edward has been acting strangely these past few weeks. He has taken to purchasing a great many pairs of gloves, though the weather is still quite mild. He keeps them in his bedroom and wears a different pair each day, and yet always seems unsatisfied. Today a messenger came from the post office to say a new order had arrived. I intercepted the message before Edward could see and travelled to the post office myself, where I was surprised to find that what awaited collection was not more gloves but a crate of fabrics, in different shades and textures of white. When I returned to the house with the crate, Edward flew into a rage at my interference and has not emerged from his room in several hours. His behaviour is quite perplexing.'"

Gabriel flicked on a few more pages. "'Several times this week I have caught Edward talking to himself. His fingers bleed from hours of sewing. I am quite at a loss as to what to do. Father is still away in London and Mother refuses to believe anything is the matter. I am considering calling for a physician to examine him.'"

He turned another two pages. "Young Giles does call for a physician," he said, summarising, "but Edward conceals his odd behaviour. It continues some two weeks later thus: 'I was mistaken in thinking Edward was talking with himself. He is talking to the gloves, the ones he made from the white fabric. There are dozens of discarded, unfinished pairs littering his bedroom floor, but for this one pair he has carved two wooden hands, upon which they now rest atop his desk. They quite unsettle me when I am near them.'"

Gabriel lifted his eyes from the page. "The similarities to Ka run deeper than I ever imagined. It seems Edward Penrose created a vessel for the demon. A physical object for it to inhabit in this world. As the vessel for Ka took the form of a coat, so this demon—"

"Is the gloves?" Elliot stared at him. "You're saying the demon is in the Mime's gloves?"

"That is precisely what I am saying, yes."

"Is that the pact, then?" Sam asked. "The one we found mention of?"

"Oh yes," Irene said. "That's where it all started. Terrible business."

Gabriel nodded. "It seems Edward held trysts with the demon and performed this task for it. What the demon promised in return it is hard to say, but since his life ended quite abruptly it seems he was ultimately betrayed."

"Never trust a demon," Irene said.

"Quite right. Now, we must read on and see what else we can discover."

———•———

It quickly became clear that the Penrose family hunted more than just the Mime. While they always returned to how they might rid the world of their family's curse, the myriad unrelated quests and adventures chronicled by the demon hunters muddied the waters.

Sam fetched their remaining food supplies from the car, and they shared an indoor picnic at Irene's kitchen table. After lunch, they spread out to keep reading. Elliot took the second armchair, to give Sam more space at the table.

Through the rest of the afternoon he trawled through several journals, sharing passages of interest and listening to what the others had found. Irene shared what she could remember of the stories, but her memory was patchy. After a while she grew tired and settled in her armchair for a nap.

Giles recorded an in-depth account of his brother's crimes. The details of the deaths suggested they were the work of Edward, not the demon. A blood sacrifice to imbue the gloves with their powers. Only after the bodies were found, collected together in the ruins of the old chapel, did Edward start exhibiting the appearance and abilities of the Mime.

After his death, the gloves went missing, and Giles's journal returned to dealing with more mundane topics. His father fell ill and died soon after, and his mother developed severe depression, to the point where she went to live with her sister in Cornwall, leaving Giles alone to manage the repercussions of his brother's actions.

Despite the turmoil in his life, the young man married a local girl and had a son, Ethan, two years after the tragedy. A year after that, the demon returned, and Giles realised his brother had unleashed a monster into the world. From the volume of evidence in front of them, he must have seen it as his duty to right his brother's wrongs. Elliot wondered how he felt. Guilty, ashamed, resentful? Perhaps all of those things.

His descendants seemed to have mixed views about their duty. Mordecai, for instance, clearly enjoyed the life he led, styling himself as a kind of vigilante hero in his youth. Meanwhile his younger brother disowned the family and immigrated to America.

"Each time the Mime appears, it has a different host," Gabriel said, pulling Elliot's thoughts back into the room. "But even the Penroses seemed unclear as to how the host was selected and possessed."

Elliot glanced up from the volume in his hands to where Gabriel and Sam sat at the kitchen table, various piles of journals spread before them.

"What happens to the hosts when… at the end of the cycle?" Sam asked.

Liam, perched on a low stool in front of the fireplace at Irene's feet, stuck his hand up. "Here, this guy, William, witnessed it one time." He read: "'Amidst a great rumbling and shaking of the earth, a dark rupture in reality opened and the demon stepped out of this realm. Daniel and I watched as the host body was immediately consumed by fire. The stench of burning flesh permeated the air of the barn for some time after the void sealed shut.'"

"Doesn't sound like much of a reward," Sam said.

"Genuine collaboration is very rare," Gabriel said. "More often the human is tricked, and the demon never has any intention of fulfilling any promises it might make." He clasped his hands on the table. "We must also consider the possibility that the current host is already deceased. In mind, if not in body. Many victims possessed by a powerful entity suffer a kind of brain death, especially when the possession lasts for some time, leaving what is effectively an empty shell."

Sam rubbed her arms, drawing herself in small. "But what if he's not though? What if he was strong? There could still be someone inside, right?"

Elliot knew she'd be equating the host's experience with her own, so of course she wouldn't want to give up hope he could be saved.

Gabriel offered a sympathetic smile. "There's always a chance. But we may be forced to accept that rescuing the host comes second to preventing the demon from taking more lives."

Elliot could see where this conversation was going. "We can't just kill it," he said.

Everyone looked at him.

"Forget for one moment that the host may or may not be an innocent victim; if we kill the host, the gloves…" He could hardly believe what he was saying. "… the gloves, and the demon with them, simply flee back to Hell, or wherever it is they go." He tapped the journal in his hand, one of Mordecai's. "The Penroses tried it, many times. It doesn't work. The demon still reappears at the next conjunction."

"Agreed," Gabriel said. "But perhaps we simply require the correct weapon. There is mention here of a dagger, forged by Giles's son, Ethan. Although as yet I have found no mention of how it might be used against the demon."

"Well, by the end of the nineteenth century, William and his two sons, Daniel and Ezequiel, were putting all their efforts into finding the demon's name," Sam said. "They must have figured something out and knew that that was what they needed."

Gabriel's head snapped towards her. "Did they find it?"

"Not that I've found so far. There is mention of an oath, or something, that should the name ever be found it should be concealed, but it doesn't say where."

"So, where does this leave us?" Elliot asked. Some of what they'd uncovered they had suspected already and, while it had the outward appearance of progress, they still had no clear plan.

"We should keep going," Gabriel said. "We've barely scratched the surface and there is still a chance the remaining volumes hold what we need."

"And there's these," Liam said. He held up an iron ring from which hung several keys. The largest was chunky and ancient-looking, and the handle formed the Penrose family crest. "They were in the bottom of the trunk. There's a mention in this one." He held up one of William Penrose's early diaries. "Here: 'Over the last few appearances, the demon has grown less wary of us. It attacked us as we tracked it, and Joshua was badly wounded. Father and I agreed that the knowledge may be unsafe at the house, despite Ethan's charms. While I pursue our research here, Joshua and Father are to return to The Haven with the key and move the most precious items to the church. The demon cannot defile holy ground; they will be safe there until such time as we need them.'"

"Does it say which church?" Elliot asked.

"Oh, that'll be St Michael's," Irene said suddenly, making Liam jump. Elliot had thought she was asleep, but she must have been listening with her eyes closed.

"That'll be our next stop," he said. "But for now, let's keep going while we have the time." He stood, to stretch his legs and swap out the journal he was reading for another.

Sam crouched in front of the old woman. "Irene? Are you happy for us to stay a little longer?"

Irene stirred in her chair. "Oh certainly. Make yourselves at home. It's nice to have a bit of company." She winked at Liam, her smile devious. "You're welcome to stay, but you'll have to make up the beds. I'm not too good with the stairs no more."

"That's very kind." Sam moved aside as Irene unwrapped herself from layers of blanket and rose shakily to her feet.

"I've got a nice bit of rabbit in the fridge, fresh caught yesterday, if you're hungry?"

"Sure. I can give you a hand if you like?"

"Oh lovely, dear, thank you."

Liam stood and edged closer to Elliot. "Did she just wink at me?"

———·———

Two hours later, the aroma of stewing rabbit wafted through the kitchen and the clock on the wall ticked over the occasional rustle of pages. Gabriel stiffened in his chair, and Elliot raised his eyes from the journal in front of him. "Found something?"

"Earlier, Liam mentioned something about charms. I am reading some of Ethan's writings. A quite singular man, I must say. He harnessed the power of the occult to protect this house. Listen. 'Uncle Edward's blood called the demon forth. Mine will be the key to repelling it from this house. I will create a sanctuary, a haven, a stronghold from which we wage war. The ritual binds the house to the family bloodline. While a Penrose dwells within these walls, the demon will not be able to set foot within a mile.'"

"Well, that explains why the demon never tried to destroy the journals," Elliot said. "It must not have known the house was unprotected after Rosemary died."

A shadow flashed across the window. Elliot exchanged a look with Sam, before crossing to peer out into the farmyard behind the house.

"Could have been a cloud," Sam said.

He shook his head. "Too fast and too solid. Too big to be a bird." His heart pounded. With no sign of the demon on the road, he'd grown complacent, but of course it had followed them. And when it reached the house it had discovered the old defence gone. The fortress of its long-time enemy, vulnerable.

"It was probably nothing," Sam said.

Elliot locked eyes with her. "That's what I said when you thought you saw it in Oxford."

"Good point."

Gabriel joined him by the window. "Can you see it?"

"No. It must have gone round the side." He pulled the curtains across so the demon wouldn't have line of sight into the room.

"I think perhaps we should collect the journals together," Gabriel said. "In case we need to leave."

Elliot dropped his voice to a whisper. "It has us trapped in here. If we go outside we'll be sitting ducks."

Gabriel nodded. "I'll take Liam and see if we can find a vantage point from a window upstairs."

"Alright. We'll pack everything up down here."

Gabriel and Liam disappeared upstairs, and Elliot began gathering the books together. He slid the keys into his trouser pocket.

Irene was dozing in her armchair in front of the fireplace. Sam gently shook her shoulder. "Irene?" Elliot paused to watch them.

"Do you know how to make dumplings, dear?" she said.

Sam crouched down. "I don't think we're going to get to have that stew," she said softly. "Don't be scared, but we may be in a bit of trouble. We might have to leave quickly, but we'll take you with us."

"I see. Had a feeling it might go that way." She chuckled. "I used to wish I'd been born in their time – the Penroses – so I could have seen it all for myself. Maybe I'll get my wish, after all." Sam glanced at Elliot and he could see the anguish in her eyes.

———•———

Sam helped Elliot drag the full chest into the hallway. Irene sank her feet into a pair of wellingtons and collected a muddy walking stick from a bucket by the back door. She pulled on a wax jacket and clomped her way across the kitchen.

"Ready?" Sam asked.

"As I'll ever be. I'm tougher than I look, dear. Don't you worry about me."

Sam managed a smile through the fear gripping her insides like a fist.

"What are they doing up there?" Elliot said, standing at the bottom of the stairs, looking up.

The house abruptly darkened as the lights went out. The hum of the fridge faded, the whir of the electric oven died. Silence fell like a blanket. Sam held her breath.

"It cut the power," Elliot said.

She moved up close to his side. "What do we do?"

"I'm going up to see what's going on."

He put one foot on the creaking bottom step and Sam grabbed his wrist. "Wait, I'll go. If the coast is clear, you have a better chance of getting Irene and the trunk away from here than I do."

"Sam—"

She didn't let him finish before she darted up the stairs.

"Gabriel?" she hissed. Low sunlight slanted in through the windows, catching dust motes in the air.

"In here," he called.

She followed the sound of his voice to one of the bedrooms and found him plastered against the wall beside the window.

"Can you see it?" she asked.

"Yes. It has been moving around the house for some time."

She pressed herself up to the curtain on the opposite side of the window and peered out. The Mime scurried across the gravel driveway outside, running in a crouch.

"What's it doing?"

"I don't know. It runs to the house, pauses by the wall, then runs back to that spot on the lawn. There, see?"

The Mime reached the spot on the grass. It picked up something invisible off the ground and held it in one hand. The bulk of the object filled its grip, but it gave no indication it was heavy. It pinched the fingers of the other hand together and applied them to the end of whatever it was holding. Then, hand still grasping the short, fat log shape, it paid out a length of invisible cord or rope. A moment later it scurried to a new spot beside the house.

"Gabriel? Do you ever watch cartoons?"

"Excuse me?"

"Ever seen Wile E. Coyote and the Road Runner?" She could sense his frown without even looking at him. "We need to go. Now."

She hurried to the landing. "Liam!"

He appeared at the door to a room at the rear of the house. She raced past him, down the stairs. "We need to get out, right now!"

"Samantha, what is going on?" Gabriel called after her.

"It's laying explosives!"

At the bottom of the stairs she grabbed one end of the chest. Elliot stooped to take the other end, but she shook her head. "Get the car going. I'll bring this with Liam."

Elliot paused for a second but then nodded and headed for the door.

Liam took the other end of the chest and they slid it along the hall. Behind them, Gabriel took Irene's arm.

Elliot ran out onto the gravel. The BMW beeped and the lights flashed as he unlocked it with the remote, but then he froze, halfway between the house and the car, staring towards the lawn.

"Keep going," Sam said to Liam. They dragged the chest out of the door and a few feet across the gravel.

Gabriel and Irene stood on the threshold.

On the grass before them the Mime paused, crouching. Slowly, deliberately, it shifted position and put both hands out as if holding the handlebars of a bicycle low to the ground.

"Move!" Sam screamed. She gripped the handle of the chest with both hands and strained to lift it. With Liam's help she heaved the chest off the gravel and staggered a few paces towards the car.

Gabriel extended a hand to help Irene down the step at the front of the house.

The Mime lifted its hands to chest height.

Elliot still stood facing the Mime as Sam and Liam struggled past him to the car. He glanced from Gabriel to Sam, then back to the Mime.

The whole world seemed to inhale a breath, and everything slowed down.

Irene turned to see where her jacket was caught on the door.

Elliot launched into a run towards the house as a slow smile spread across the Mime's lips. Its hands descended, depressing the plunger.

NO WORDS

Elliot breathed in the steam rising from his coffee on the ride up to the office. Way too hungover for the stairs today. The rest of the team seemed equally subdued, starting their days with their heads down, trying to be invisible. No surprise, after last night's award ceremony, not to mention the after-party. Even Cat had the door and blinds closed in her corner office. Well, he'd only left her apartment at two thirty a.m., so...

The paper cup continued to steam gently on his desk while he numbed his brain deleting spam emails. His mind kept wandering back to his brother's unexpected visit the evening before – just as he was getting ready to leave – with some nonsense story. Something about a friend from his unit who'd committed suicide. He ought to make some time for him today, time he couldn't spare last night. He dialled James's mobile. Voicemail. Never mind, he'd try again later.

Mid-morning, Cat emerged. She looked way too put together, considering. She spotted him at his desk and walked over, expression neutral.

With a hand on his shoulder, she set a small glass block in front of him. The engraving read "Young Journalist of the Year", with his name below. "You left this at my place."

He flicked his eyes up to hers. A rebel smirk crept across his face. Next year he planned on losing the word "young". One step at a time. Everything would come together, and he'd be taking Cat's office by the time he was thirty. Editor-in-chief somewhere by forty. Then? Well, there were options. Politics, maybe, to prove to his father that firstborn wasn't everything.

Cat trailed her hand across his shoulders as she headed off for her meeting. He watched her, convinced she added an extra sway in her step just to tease him.

"Mr Cross?" said a voice directly behind him.

Elliot swung his chair round sharply. He took in the uniforms of the pair standing beside his desk and drew his shoulders back a touch.

The middle-aged female sergeant who'd spoken stood a pace in front of her partner, who held his hat in the crook of one arm, next to his body. Elliot's stomach churned.

"Is this about the Westminster exposé? Because everything in my article was freely available, public information."

"I'm afraid this is a personal matter. Would you like to go somewhere more private?"

The noises around the office surged in volume. Tapping fingers on keyboards, squeaky chair wheels, chattering voices, all bearing down on him. A thick, droning swarm that made it hard to think.

"No. What is it? Tell me."

"Your brother's body was found early this morning. I'm afraid we've had trouble contacting your parents."

Her lips continued to move but the words never reached Elliot's ears. A wall of sound – footsteps on carpet, the snap of a blind next to an open window, a ringing phone, and a million other tiny noises – pressed in on him and joined the overwhelming cacophony of thoughts inside his head. The air thickened and he clutched at his chest.

This wasn't right. He'd promised James that nothing would happen.

32

The explosion threw a shockwave out from the house that knocked Elliot off his feet. He hit the gravel on his back, quickly rolling onto his front and covering his head with his hands as masonry and glass rained down around him.

He clutched at his chest as he pushed to his knees, coughing, and wiped stinging eyes.

"Elliot!" Sam called through the thick dust that clogged the air.

"Here!"

She stumbled towards him and dropped to a crouch, one hand on his shoulder. "Are you okay?"

He nodded, clutching his throat, then shook his head to clear the ringing in his ears. Dust and glass shards flew from his hair. "Gabriel?"

The dust was beginning to settle, and he caught a glimpse of damaged walls and a sagging roof above. A moan reached them from where Irene's Land Rover lay, blasted onto its side.

Elliot stood and put his hand on the small of Sam's back. "Go back to the car," he said. He rolled his shoulders, grimacing, and walked towards the house. The extent of the destruction stunned him. Even though he'd witnessed what the Mime could do, this was on a completely different scale.

Gabriel had dragged himself up to sit with his back against the underside of the Land Rover. He panted, quick, sharp breaths.

Elliot dropped down beside him. "Are you hurt?"

Gabriel swallowed and winced. He reached one hand up to the back of his head and inspected his fingers, but there was no blood.

"Not badly." He stared towards the house. "There was no time…"

A gust of wind dragged the settling dust away from the house. The doorframe listed at a drunken angle, and the panel of the door lay in the hallway. From beneath the rubble emerged the bottom of Irene's wellington boot.

"Get to the car," Elliot said as he rose and broke into a run across the short stretch of gravel. "Irene?" The walls groaned ominously as he approached. He stepped over her booted foot, ducked under the slanted doorframe and crouched to lift a few chunks of plaster off the door. He tipped the heavy oak board up against the wall. Irene's head rolled to the side.

"Irene? Can you hear me?" As he pressed two fingers to her neck, her eyes fluttered open. "Don't worry, we're going to get you out of here."

She lifted one hand and grasped his wrist. "No, you're not," she said faintly.

"It's alright. You're going to be fine."

She shook her head. "Something's broken, lad, inside," she said. "I can feel it. Not much time."

The strength in her grip surprised him and she pulled him down. He leaned closer. "You have to kill it," she whispered. "Rosie always knew one of you would find your way home."

"Irene, please. If we can get you to a hospital…"

She took a laboured breath. "You won't see what you don't believe. Remember that, lad."

Her grip around his wrist loosened and her hand dropped onto her chest. Elliot closed his eyes. What had he done, bringing it here?

Behind him, Sam clattered up to the doorway. "Is she…"

He checked Irene's pulse once more. "She's gone."

"No. That's not fair!" Sam cried. "She was—"

"I know. We led it right here." He stood, and viciously kicked a lump of plaster onto the gravel.

"Elliot!" Gabriel called.

There was no time. They would have to leave her where she'd died and, damn it, she deserved better! She wasn't even part of the Penrose family, but she'd protected their secrets for nearly fifteen years. What reward was this for her?

The bastion of the Penrose family for over two hundred years, and he'd brought the enemy right to it.

"Come on!" Gabriel called as he and Liam lifted the trunk into the boot of Elliot's car.

Sam put her hand on his elbow. "We have to go."

He nodded and they ran for the car.

The crunch of footsteps on gravel announced the Mime's return. With one regretful look back at Irene's body and the house, Elliot leapt in and jammed the key in the ignition. Sam scrambled into the front. Gabriel and Liam closed the boot and threw themselves into the rear seats.

Elliot thrust the car into reverse and stamped on the accelerator. The car thudded into the demon, sending a satisfying shudder through Elliot's body. That might wipe the sick grin off its face. Gravel sprayed from the tyres as he launched the car down the driveway. In the rear-view mirror, he thought he saw the Mime put a hand up to shield its eyes.

He drove as fast as he dared along the narrow, unpaved road. It seemed longer than when they'd driven up.

The BMW jarred over a pothole, and Elliot gripped the steering wheel hard.

"Elliot, man, you'd better step on it," Liam said.

He glanced up at the vibrating rear-view mirror. "I don't see it."

"Oh, trust me, it's there."

"Got it!" Sam said. "Take a right at the end of the driveway."

Elliot took his eyes off the road for a fraction of a second. "Got what?"

"St Michael's Church." She waved the map.

As they hit a slight bend in the track, the back end of the BMW went light. Elliot struggled to rescue it before they spun out, and somehow managed to regain control.

"Is it still there?" he asked.

"Yeah, but it's not gaining on us," Liam said.

He strained for a glimpse in the mirror, but the hard suspension on the rough road surface meant everything was shaking. It was hard to see anything, especially with the evening sun at a low angle behind them.

"Watch out!" Sam braced her hand on the dashboard. The T-junction raced towards them and Elliot slammed on the brakes. The car skidded forwards. He wasn't going to stop in time. Praying they didn't hit the junction at the same time as any other traffic, he dropped the clutch, shifted down to second and steered with the skid. The car spun out onto the road. Clutch up. Accelerator down hard. For a heart-stopping moment the rear-wheel drive struggled for grip, then the tyres got hold and forced the car forwards.

As they shot down the wider country road Sam stared at him. "Wow. That was cool."

If he'd planned it, maybe. His heart was pounding so hard it felt like it might explode.

She consulted the map. "We need to follow this for about two miles, until we hit the village. The church is down a side road. It should be easy to spot."

Now on smoother tarmac, Elliot risked another glance in the rear-view mirror. Some two hundred yards behind them the Mime hovered, its feet around a foot off the ground, legs apart, crunched up, with its arms outstretched towards handlebars. As the road curved it banked around the turn.

Elliot wiped his forehead with the back of his hand and shifted into fifth. The speedometer crept up to sixty-five. The road wasn't straight enough to go much faster. Sam gripped the edge of her seat. Behind them, the Mime dropped back. He lost sight of it as they followed another bend in the road.

Signs at the side of the road welcomed them to the village, and a few cottages poked through trees and hedgerows.

"Slow down a bit or we'll miss it," Sam said. They whipped past a brown heritage sign. "There, take the next left."

The entrance to the side road was too narrow to take at speed. He braked hard. As they entered the turning, he pulled past a parked van and tucked the BMW out of sight, keeping the engine running, eyes on the side mirror, hand poised on the steering wheel. The Mime tore past the turning and kept going.

Elliot sagged in his seat, took a few hard breaths and pulled away, to continue to the church.

———•———

St Michael's Church stood at the end of the lane, with a wide turning area out front. Sam eyed the graves in the churchyard warily as Elliot pulled into a walled car park to one side. She retrieved her camera from the boot, then joined him to walk the short distance along the path towards the entrance. Her scalp itched and a tense knot formed between her shoulder blades. She wanted to take Elliot's hand, but she settled for clutching her camera tight against her chest.

Low evening sun warmed the rustic, granite walls of the church with yellow light and picked up every detail in the relief. She snapped off a quick photo. St Michael's seemed quite big for a parish church. It followed the traditional cross layout. A stubby bell tower rose from the centre. On their right as they approached, a modern red-brick extension jutted out.

A wide set of semi-circular steps led up from the pathway to an open porch on the side of the church. Gabriel hammered on the doors, waited for a moment, then knocked again.

"I don't think anyone's in," Liam said.

Gabriel took a step back and threw his shoulder into the doors. They shuddered, but the heavy wood and iron hinges weren't going to give in easily.

"Guys, you're not going to get in there without a battering ram or a key." Sam turned sharply to Elliot. "The keys!"

Elliot produced the Penrose keys from his pocket. "Probably a long shot, but we have to try something." He selected the most likely candidate and tried it. The key rotated with a satisfying clunk, and he pushed the door open.

"Perhaps we should bring the journals inside where we can be sure they will be safe," Gabriel said.

While Elliot and Liam fetched the trunk, Gabriel headed inside. Sam followed him. The stained-glass windows only let light in high up. Down among the pews the shadows lay thick and sinister.

She shuddered. "It's cold in here."

"Do you think?" Gabriel asked, as if he wasn't feeling it.

She rubbed her arms and helped him hunt for a light switch. It wouldn't look so spooky with the lights on.

By the time Elliot and Liam struggled in with the heavy trunk, warm lights brightened the interior of the church, and she'd found and flicked on several electric heaters to offset the chill. They set the trunk down. Elliot returned to the front door to lock it, then the four of them gathered in the central aisle.

Sam knew the demon couldn't get them here. There was no way it could enter consecrated ground. So why did she feel more vulnerable in here than outside? She pushed the feeling aside. The others obviously weren't creeped out by the place.

"We should split up and search," Gabriel said.

"Yes, but I also think someone should keep watch," Elliot added.

Liam stuck his hand up. "I'll take sentry duty."

"Excellent." Gabriel surveyed the church. "I'll take the left side. Perhaps you two can split the rest between you?"

While Liam hunted for a vantage point to keep an eye out for the Mime, Gabriel disappeared off to explore. Elliot walked towards the altar at the far end. Sam stuck close behind him. Gabriel could go exploring on his own if he wanted, but there was no way she was going to. Not here.

Thankfully Elliot seemed too absorbed to question why she was following him. On the left side of the chancel the pipes of an organ clustered against the wall and soared up towards the vaulted ceiling. Beside them, in the corner where the walls met, was an unassuming door, barely five foot tall. Elliot walked up to it, twirling and twisting the keyring in his fingers.

As they drew closer, a cool draft tickled Sam's neck. She pulled her zip higher and hunched her shoulders.

Elliot crouched beside the door. The brass lock plate bore the Penrose family crest, with the keyhole in the centre. Sam hovered beside him, biting her lip, while he compared the handle of the largest key to the engraving and then tried the key in the lock. It turned with a rusty scrape, and the door opened towards them.

The air inside the wall recess tumbled out, colder than the air in the room. Sam grasped her camera tight as the hair on her arms stood up. A fresh tingle in the back of her neck and head made her twitch.

Elliot's breath was shallow and rapid, and she caught a slight tremor in his hand as he released the doorknob. The door concealed a tight spiral staircase, encased within the wall. Dim light from the church only illuminated the first few steps, and shadows in the stairwell pooled like liquid darkness, flooding the lowest recesses of the crypt.

Elliot's quick search revealed no light switch in the stairwell. "Would you go and find Gabriel?" he asked.

"Sure. But don't you go down there without me and hog all the adventure."

He chuckled. It sounded forced. Sam trotted off. She found Gabriel leafing through some ledgers in a cupboard at the side of the nave, and told him what they'd found. He produced a torch from his satchel and followed her to the door.

Elliot took the light and shone it down the staircase. The twist of the spiral hid the bottom from view. Smooth patches in the middle of each step showed where feet had polished the stone over many years.

Sam took a photo of the stairs as Elliot was about to step down.

He flinched at the shutter click, and frowned. "You alright?"
She nodded. "Fine."

The frown deepened but he returned his attention to the stairs and stepped through the doorway. The underside of the spiral above forced him to duck as he lowered himself down each step, but Sam could just about stand straight.

One and a half turns down, the steps ended where they met an uneven stone floor. Four thick pillars supported the vaulted ceiling, and a sarcophagus sat squarely in the middle of the far end of the chamber, supported on granite blocks.

Elliot approached the tomb. His breath formed clouds. The air down here was unnaturally cold, and it wasn't just Sam's imagination this time. Her own breath misted in front of her. Gabriel's too.

Reaching the tomb, Elliot ran his hand over the stone slab. "Giles Penrose."

Gabriel inspected a shelf in the side wall, which housed another coffin. "And here, another grave."

Elliot panned the torch around the sides of the room, revealing the half-dozen occupied recesses in the rough stone walls.

"It's a family crypt," Sam said in hushed tones. She shivered as a soft pressure slid up her back, like a hand touching her.

"Almost," Gabriel said. "Only those who carried the mantle of demon hunter are entombed here. Their souls are unquiet. They will not rest until the demon is slain."

Sam's teeth chattered. She rubbed her arm with her other hand. "Is that why it's so cold?"

"Perhaps, yes."

She flinched at the sensation of fingertips brushing her cheek. Every time Elliot moved the torch, the shadows changed, like figures moving out of the corner of her eye. On the edge of her mind she sensed a presence, curious and calculating, taking an interest. In her.

She closed her eyes and silently repeated her mantras. *My mind is closed. I am impenetrable.*

"Sam?"

She jumped at the sound of Elliot's voice and her eyes snapped open.

"Are you sure you're alright? You can go back up, if you want to."

She shook her head. "I'm fine. Let's see what we can find."

She stayed close to him, and to the pool of light from the torch, while Gabriel investigated the far side of the chamber. There were seven members of the Penrose family here, from Giles down to the brothers, Ezequiel and Daniel, but not Charlie. Sam assumed his body was in a war grave in France somewhere. That seemed so wrong. He should be here, with his family.

Her neck and scalp tingled. She was intensely aware of the presence, watching her from the shadows. She rubbed at the sensation and tried to stay focused on what they were doing.

"I'm not looking in the coffins," she said.

Elliot panned the torch over the sarcophagus in the centre of the room as if he were contemplating doing exactly that. Now that they stood to the side, it became clear the supporting blocks weren't one solid slab. A gap remained between the footings at either end. He moved closer, and the light glinted off something metallic.

"That must be it," Sam said, kneeling for a closer look. Elliot joined her and they pulled a small wooden chest out from under the coffin. He dusted off the curved top, to reveal the Penrose crest burned into the wood.

Gabriel stood at the foot of the sarcophagus, and Elliot glanced up at him before pulling the keys from his pocket once more.

As Elliot worked out which key fitted the heavy padlock on the chest, the presence touched the edge of Sam's mind. Testing. Probing. Trying to find a way in. She tensed. *I am impenetrable. You are not invited.*

She repeated the words in her head, over and over.

Unlike the door, the neglected padlock squealed in protest as Elliot unlocked it.

With a sharp pinch at the base of her skull, Sam's grip on reality loosened. She tried to resist but the presence slipped past her like an eel, fluid and determined. The world receded as it effortlessly wormed its way through the cracks in her consciousness. She shuddered, but her body remained motionless.

"Do excuse me," a deep male voice said in her mind. "I require your services."

"Who are you?" she tried to say, but her lips didn't move.

She felt the horrible, gut-wrenchingly familiar sensation of her body moving without her command. Whoever or whatever was in her head put her hands out, palm up, then flipped them over, inspecting. Then it focused on Elliot.

Trapped inside, Sam screamed.

33

Elliot glanced at Sam. She knelt stiffly beside him, watching him with a strange intensity, head tilted to one side.

"Sam?"

She flashed a quick, tense smile, set her camera on the floor and indicated the box with a flick of her eyes. "Do proceed."

Elliot frowned at her, uneasy, but passed the torch to Gabriel and lifted the lid of the chest. The frozen hinges cracked and creaked as he raised the top with both hands.

A pale cloth covered the contents. He pulled it up and laid it back into the lid. At the top sat a stack of letters tied with string. He lifted the bundle out and handed it to Sam. Below, a slim, leather-bound book nestled next to a long, narrow object, wrapped in a suede cloth, secured with waxed cord. He took out the book.

"Another journal?" He flicked through several pages of strange diagrams, symbols, and blocks of dense, neat handwriting. "I think… There's no dates like the others."

Gabriel peered down. "That's Ethan's handwriting. It matches his other volumes. May I see?" He took the book and directed the light of his torch onto the pages.

Elliot lifted the remaining item. The weight of the package in his hand felt reassuring for some reason.

Sam set the letters down and leaned closer.

A gentle tug on the trailing end of the cord released the knot. He unwound the binding, unrolled the wrapping. The silence and cold in the room pressed in on him. With a final turn, a sleek wooden dagger hilt rolled into his palm. The package had been much longer, the blade part solid, but now there was nothing there. Elliot dropped the wrapping into the empty chest. The handle felt heavy at one end, as if it really did have a blade attached below the tarnished brass guard. He slowly brought his fingers up to the place where the blade should be.

The air resisted, but his fingers passed through. He rubbed them together against a gentle tingle.

You won't see what you don't believe.

He closed his eyes, felt the balance of the handle, the weight at one end trying to drag it from his hand. He pictured what the blade might look like and once more brought his thumb up to touch it.

A sharp edge bit into his skin, and he gasped. Gabriel shone the torch on his hand. Blood welled up in the tiny cut.

Suddenly, Sam seized his arm with one hand, her grasp so strong the bones in his wrist ground together, and her fingernails dug into his skin.

"Hey!"

The dagger clattered to the floor. She reached for it.

"My apologies," she said. "There is no time to explain."

Cupping the hilt in her palm she twisted Elliot's hand to bring his bleeding thumb towards it. She wiped the cut across the polished wood, leaving a smear of red, then slapped the hilt into his palm. Immediately the blade solidified. Elliot recoiled, and dropped the dagger into the chest.

Sam sat back on her heels, posture rigid. "The power comes from the strength of your conviction," she said in a low voice, patient but commanding. "Believe and you will see."

Then she slumped sideways, like a puppet with cut strings, and lay still.

Elliot's chest heaved with nervous breaths. "Sam?" He put his hand out to touch hers.

She stirred briefly, then bolted upright and scuttled back until she hit one of the pillars. Her wide eyes darted from side to side and her mouth hung open, jaw trembling.

"It's alright," Elliot said, reaching for her.

She flinched as he touched her ankle, but it focused her attention. She looked him in the eye for a second, then let out an anguished whimper, scrambled to her feet and ran for the stairs.

"Sam!" Elliot kicked the bundle of letters as he got up. He grabbed her camera and ran after her.

Up in the church he found her in the middle of the aisle, her back to him as if she'd been running for the door to escape. Liam stood in front of her with his hands on her shoulders, his eyes full of concern as he said something Elliot couldn't hear. Sam covered her nose and mouth with both hands and shook her head.

Elliot was glad Liam hadn't let her leave. The Mime was still out there somewhere.

His chest tightened and he hesitated. He wanted to comfort her, but maybe she needed space, or maybe talking to Liam would be better. He should never have dragged her down there, but she'd said she was fine, and he had no right to contradict her. But maybe he should have anyway? He could second guess himself in circles all day, but it had happened, and now he didn't know how to help.

Sam turned her head as he approached. Her eyes were full of tears. He hung back, afraid to crowd her.

She pulled away from Liam and walked towards him, her head down. One hand clutched her sweatshirt below her throat. She kept going until her forehead butted against his shoulder.

He set her camera down on the end of a pew and put his arms round her, one hand on the back of her head. He held her close, and she tucked her face in against his neck. Her hair was soft against his cheek. Warm. He closed his eyes.

"Shh, it's alright," he whispered. "I'm so sorry."

She shook with suppressed sobs, and his heart ached for her.

"I won't let it hurt you," he said softly, although it was hardly a promise he could make. He had no idea how to keep her safe. But Gabriel might. And if he didn't, they'd find someone who did. He could promise he'd never give up, never abandon her.

He glanced up. Liam had gone.

"Do you want to sit down?"

She nodded, and he released her but kept one hand on her back as she slid down onto a pew. He sat beside her with his arm across her shoulders and she leaned into him.

"Talk to me."

She glanced up into his eyes and he reached and wiped a tear off her cheek with his thumb. Her lips parted and she looked away. He suddenly realised how invasive he was being and withdrew his hand. He moved the arm across her shoulders onto the back of the pew, still there but not holding her.

"I think it was one of them. One of the demon hunters." She wiped her eyes with her sleeve, then twisted her fingers together in her lap.

Elliot passed her the camera and she wrapped the strap around her fist.

"I couldn't do anything to stop it."

There was nothing he could say to make it better, so he quietly waited for her to say more.

"I don't like it," she said, shuddering. "I hate the way it feels."

"I know. It's awful. I'm so sorry." He felt like he was just stringing meaningless words together, but he couldn't find a way to phrase the thoughts clamouring inside his head without sounding patronising. She had every right to feel angry and upset after being violated like that, and he didn't want her to think it made her weak, or that she had to hide her emotions.

"I felt your wrist crunch in my hand."

He tensed. "You could *feel* that?"

She nodded.

He let out a long slow breath as the weight of what she was saying sank in. When she'd been trapped the first time, before they met, the spirit had used her in dreadful ways, but he'd always imagined she'd been detached from it. A spectator. That would have been bad enough. He hadn't truly appreciated that she'd physically experienced everything. No wonder it still haunted her so deeply.

"It didn't hurt this time." She picked at a knot in the woodgrain on the pew in front. "He was... He spoke to me."

"Did that happen before?"

She shook her head and glanced at him, frowning. "No. The first time it was like it wanted me out so it could have my body for itself. This... He was gentle. He told me not to be scared. Maybe he didn't want to, but he had no choice."

Elliot rubbed the cut on his thumb and the dried blood around it. Maybe the spirit had only used her out of necessity, to convey its cryptic message, but it had still used her. "That doesn't make it alright, and you don't have to pretend it does."

He raised his head at the sound of Gabriel's footsteps. The demon hunter approached, carrying the chest.

"Are you alright, Samantha?" he asked, genuine concern in his voice.

"I'm okay." She sat up a little straighter, still holding her camera in her lap. Elliot hoped she wasn't just putting on a brave face to conceal her pain.

They shifted along to make room for Gabriel at the end of the row, with the chest between them. Before any of them could open it, Liam returned with four mugs held by the handles, two in each hand.

He set two of the mugs down on the shelf at the back of the pew. "Ow, hot." He sucked his knuckles.

Elliot looked up at him.

"Hey, I may not be English, but I know when a situation calls for tea." He shrugged and hiked a thumb over his shoulder. "Found a kitchen back there."

Sam reached forwards and took her mug. She sipped gingerly, and a little colour returned to her cheeks. Liam handed another mug to Gabriel and sat on the pew in front. "So, did we find treasure?" He nodded towards the chest.

"Of a kind," Gabriel said. He lifted the lid. Inside, the dagger still rested in the bottom, the blade now solid, grey metal. Sam watched with quiet interest and seemed to welcome the distraction.

Gabriel picked up the slim book. "I believe this is – for want of better phrasing – a spell book." He flicked through a few pages. "As I mentioned before, Giles's son, Ethan, became quite the master of the occult, harnessing blood magic and ritual binding to combat the demon. This is where he recorded his experiments and the details of his enchantments."

Elliot picked up the dagger and inspected the blade. "Ethan made this, didn't he?" He ran his fingers along an inscription engraved into the metal. "Forged in the fire of the heart…" He flipped it over to where the words continued on the other side. "… keen as the mind that wields it."

No one spoke. He looked up to find all three of his companions staring at him. "What?"

"What are you doing?" Sam asked.

"Reading the inscription."

"Mate, there's nothing there," Liam said.

Elliot frowned. "What do you mean? You can't see it?"

"See what?"

"The blade. Downstairs, it was invisible, then it became solid."

"It doesn't look any different to me," Sam said. "It's just a handle."

She took it from him and passed her fingers through the blade. Elliot cringed, afraid it would hurt her, and a sudden sharp pain stabbed his temple as his brain recoiled at the contradiction in what his eyes were seeing. "Please don't do that," he said through gritted teeth.

She hastily handed it back. "How come you can see it?"

"Blood." Gabriel looked directly at Elliot as he spoke. "The spirit that possessed Samantha did so to ensure your blood anointed the weapon, Elliot. Blood is a powerful bond."

"You're saying I'm bonded to this thing?"

"I don't know. I'll need to find out more. Perhaps Ethan Penrose recorded the details of its creation in this." He held up the small book.

Elliot retrieved the suede cloth, wrapped the dagger and returned it to the chest.

Gabriel set the book alongside it. "We cannot allow the demon to retreat into the spirit world. We may never have another opportunity. We must stop it, here and now."

Elliot closed the lid. "Alright, then. Let's figure out how to do that."

34

The kitchen Liam had mentioned was in the modern extension, part of a simple community hall furnished with mismatched sofas and folding tables. Before they started, Sam took their tea mugs through for a re-fill.

The buzzing florescent tube lighting, scratchy carpet, and cheap melamine worktops were altogether too human to be creepy. Plus, in here she was further away from the crypt and the spirits there.

She drew some hot water from the urn in the corner to make coffee. Tea was great for relaxation, but now they needed to focus. The church kitchen was surprisingly well stocked, with milk and fruit juice in the fridge, and cupboards full of biscuits, crisps and other snacks. Not the healthiest meal, but the sugar and carbs would keep them going.

She still hesitated before she took some chocolate bars from a cupboard shelf marked "Bumps and Babies".

"Ahh, go for it. They can buy more," Liam said as he came in.

"That's not the point." She puffed out her cheeks. "I'll write them a note and leave some money. Do you have any cash?"

Liam crossed his arms. "I'm okay with stealing."

She glared at him.

"Fine." He pulled his wallet from his pocket and handed over a twenty. "Happy now?"

She grinned at his grumpy face. "Thank you. That'll be one less sin for you to repent."

"Oh? So you're watching out for my immortal soul now?"

She opened one of the chocolate bars and poked the unwrapped end into his mouth. "What are friends for?"

He chuckled and took a bite. "Feeling better, then?"

Her grin faded. "Yes and no."

He didn't ask the question she was sure he was dying to ask, but he did keep glancing at her while she made the drinks.

"Why can ghosts do that to me?" she asked in a murmur. "Do you think there's something wrong with me?"

"Do what exactly?"

She tapped the side of her head. "Get inside." She rolled her eyes. "What am I saying? You probably think I'm nuts."

"No. Not at all."

"Most people don't even believe in ghosts."

Liam picked up one of the mugs and took a sip, his expression suddenly serious. "Every culture in the world has ghosts. And some kind of afterlife. That's no coincidence."

He nodded towards one of the sofas at the side of the room and Sam followed him over with her mug.

"We go somewhere when we die," he said as he sat down. "I'm sure of that. I don't know where, but every near-death survivor I've ever spoken to has told me some variant on the same story."

Of course, the articles he'd written for *Weird News* and the book he was working on. The whole reason they'd contacted him in the first place.

"I thought I knew something about life after death," he continued. "But meeting someone like you, who can actually talk to people who've died?" He shook his head. "It's... humbling."

Sam dipped her head, unable to meet his eyes. It didn't feel that way to her. "Why are you so interested in it anyway?"

He shrugged. "I don't know. I guess… you get close enough to death you start to wonder. It's a comfort to know it's not the end."

Sam supposed that working in the hospital he saw a lot of death. "Is that why you believe in angels too?" She sipped her coffee, glancing at him sideways over the rim of her mug.

He smirked and slouched back. "What makes you think I believe in angels?"

"Oh, I don't know, maybe the giant wing tattoos."

He laughed, then turned serious again. "Yes and no. That's always been there, right from when I was small. My mum used to say angels were all around us and, okay, that might have been the drugs talking, but it stuck with me for some reason." He put a hand over his heart. "In here. Like it feels right."

"Can I see them?"

"The angels?"

She giggled. "No, silly, the tattoos. Your wings."

"What? Now?"

She nodded.

"If you insist." He let out a melodramatic sigh, set his mug down and reached over his head to pull his sweatshirt and T-shirt off.

He turned his back and Sam gazed at the intricate pattern. When he moved his shoulders, it was like the feathers shifted. She reached for her camera, then remembered she'd left it in the church.

"Hey, I have an idea," she said.

"What?"

"Come with me."

He went to put his top on.

"No, leave that off. I want to take your picture." She grabbed his hand and dragged him off the couch.

"Err, Sammy. Do we really have time for this? And, uh…"

"What?"

"Nothing."

She led him through into the church and scanned the room for a good backdrop. The last rays of the setting sun lit up the windows above the altar with warm colours.

"Here." She dragged Liam up towards the altar and stood him in front of it, facing the windows. Then she hurried down the aisle to grab her camera.

At the far end of the nave, Elliot and Gabriel sat sorting through the Penrose journals.

She scurried back. Liam had moved. She shooed him back into position.

"Are you sure this is a good idea?" he asked, glancing down the central aisle.

"It'll only take a minute." She wrestled his shirt out of his hand and chucked it to one side, then framed the shot.

The windows filled the background with colourful imagery, and Liam's black-line tattoos contrasted beautifully. He twisted his head to the side to speak to her but didn't move his body. She pressed the shutter button just as he turned, and caught the line of his jaw in profile.

"Wow," she breathed, eye still fixed to the viewfinder.

"Are you done?" he asked.

"A couple more, please. Just a couple."

"Okay, fine."

She studied him and the shot through the lens, captured a few different angles. On the altar in front of him stood a large gold crucifix.

"Put your arms out," she said.

He scowled over his shoulder. "Really?"

"Just do it."

"Fine."

He put both arms out to the side, which flexed his muscles in a way that made the wings change shape. He let his fingers curl loosely but kept his wrists straight. Sam fancied she could hear the rustle of feathers. She shifted a little closer so she could fill the shot with him.

"Tip your chin down and to the left."

He did as he was told, and she snapped the shot.

"Can I move now?"

She lowered the camera and inspected the image on the screen. Perfect. "Yeah."

Liam snagged his top from the floor and pulled it on while she tabbed through the shots. He peered over her shoulder.

"Huh. Not bad," he muttered. "I look dead hot."

"Well, duh."

He laughed.

Sam turned to head back to the kitchen, and froze.

Elliot stood watching her from beside the front pew, his expression so conflicted she couldn't read it. Mostly he looked confused, but there was pain there too, and indecision.

"And I'm gone," Liam said. He jogged down the altar steps and off towards the kitchen.

Elliot cleared his throat. "We could use your help, if you're feeling up to it."

She clutched her camera tight. "Sure. I'll just finish getting the coffee."

He nodded and set off back down the aisle. Her stomach fluttered with nerves. Was he jealous? Taking Liam's picture didn't mean anything, but maybe Elliot thought it did. Thought she was flirting. She stared at him as he walked away. At the hotel he'd tried to push her towards Liam, but after the crypt he'd held her so close, and it felt so right.

She looked down at her camera and tabbed through to the picture she'd taken of Elliot at Father Monroe's church in Oxford, the one with his head tilted back, as if he were contemplating the destiny of the universe. Why did he have to make things so complicated? She took a deep breath and headed to the kitchen to fetch the drinks and food.

———⋅———

Elliot returned to where he and Gabriel were working on the journals and picked up a book at random. He slumped onto a pew, ignoring the fact that Gabriel was watching him. The pages blurred. None of the words went in.

He didn't know what he was feeling anymore. Seeing Sam with Liam had hit him with an intense surge of jealousy he hadn't expected, followed instantly by shame. He didn't want to be jealous, certainly not of something as silly as his photographer friend taking photographs. That wasn't who he wanted to be. But it wasn't really about the photographs.

Last night he'd half wanted her and Liam to take the decision out of his hands, so he didn't have to make it. He couldn't be with her, so why did he care whether she and Liam connected? Logically he shouldn't care, but something deeper than logic was at work. Something he couldn't control, ignore or will away. He probably needed to start accepting that.

He shook his head and re-focused on the book in his hands.

The neatness of the handwriting at the beginning seemed almost too careful, like someone taking their time. Later it became more fluid. The diary belonged to Ezequiel Penrose, Charlie's uncle, and the entries began in eighteen seventy-seven. Elliot scanned a few pages where Ezequiel talked about school and how his father encouraged him to write in his diary at least once a week, to get into the habit of it. He must have been quite young when he started. As time passed, he described learning more about demons, monsters, and how to fight them. In particular, *The Demon* – the family curse.

Then Elliot alighted upon an entry dated eighteen eighty that caught his attention and drew him in.

While he was reading, Sam and Liam returned from the kitchen. Sam set a mug and a chocolate bar in front of him. He kept his head down, afraid all his raw thoughts might show. He wasn't ready to have that conversation yet. Instead he let his eyes follow Ezequiel's handwriting.

Today is my sixteenth birthday. Since I turned twelve, I have learnt all about our family's duty but today I take it into my own hands. After dinner, Father and Grandfather took me to the drawing room where they poured me a measure of brandy and showed me something magical – a knife – or dagger, if I am to be accurate – created by my great-grandfather.

Initially, I did not understand what it was. Father unwrapped a velvet cloth on the side table, revealing a wooden dagger hilt with no blade. He instructed me to close my eyes and picture a blade, then he nicked my palm with the point and pressed the hilt into my hand. From that moment the blade became solid and real, as if it had been there all along. Father explained that the dagger recognises Penrose blood. Now I am a demon hunter as each of my family before me.

We toasted my birthday with the brandy (which did not taste as I expected, if I be truthful). I have promised not to tell my brother Daniel about the dagger; he is only fourteen and not ready to learn this secret yet.

Elliot rubbed the tiny cut on his thumb.

"What is it?" Sam asked quietly. She shifted across to the pew in front of him. When he glanced up, she smiled, warm and patient, but with a hint of concern in her eyes.

She could clearly tell something was up, and now he was making her worry. She didn't need his issues on top of everything she'd been through tonight. He just needed to focus on what they were here to do and deal with the rest later. He held the diary out.

"Here."

He waited while she read the passage. He knew when she read the part about Penrose blood because she gasped.

"Irene was right."

"What?"

"While you and Gabriel were in the attic, she showed us pictures. Of Charlie and his sister and her two daughters. I didn't think it could be possible. I mean, I saw the resemblance but it just seemed so—"

"Slow down. What are you talking about?"

"Elizabeth's little girl."

Elliot still wasn't following. Gabriel and Liam both stopped reading to listen. Elliot felt their eyes on him.

"Emily Penrose had two daughters, Rosemary and Elizabeth," Sam explained. "Rosemary and her son died, but that wasn't the end of the line. Elizabeth had a daughter, but she was only fifteen when she got pregnant so they put the baby up for adoption."

The breath froze in Elliot's throat. He gripped the back of the pew for the feel of something solid as his world tilted. "What was… What was her name?"

"Sarah."

He clutched at his chest, suddenly unable to breathe.

"What? Do you know who she is?" Sam asked.

"My grandmother was adopted, but it can't be—"

"My goodness," Gabriel said.

Elliot shook his head. "No. It's impossible. Just a coincidence."

"But your blood, on the dagger handle," Sam said.

He shook his head again. It was too much, too big. He was no demon hunter. He was just some self-centred journalist with a modicum of talent for organising people. He needed a drink, preferably a stiff one, but since that wasn't an option he settled for wetting his throat with scalding hot coffee. This must have been how Giles felt when the demon returned after his brother had died and he realised it was his responsibility to kill it. His family's responsibility. Elliot's responsibility.

Sam put her hand on his where it rested on the back of the pew. He closed his eyes and for once let himself focus on the comfort in her touch.

35

E lliot wanted nothing more than to hide with his thoughts
somewhere, so he could process the implications. But they
were running dangerously short of time. The full moon would
rise tomorrow night. At the very most they had until the moon
set sometime early Wednesday morning.

He compromised by reading a few more pages of Ezequiel's
first diary. He found following the young man's early initi-
ation into the world of his demon hunting family somewhat
comforting. Ezequiel's struggles to keep his own fear in check,
and expand his mind around repeated impossible revelations,
mirrored Elliot's own journey, and he was refreshingly honest in
his writings. A few pages were smudged with tears on the days
he recorded the horrors he'd seen.

Ezequiel, his father William, and his younger brother Daniel
were all active at the same time, towards the end of the nineteenth
century. Somewhere in the journals of the three men there must be
evidence of the discovery which led them to search for the name so
obsessively. And that, surely, would reveal more about how to use it.

"Ah!" Gabriel exclaimed. He continued reading the small
book of Ethan's notes in his hands until it apparently dawned
on him that they were all watching. "My apologies. I have both
good news and bad news, as the saying goes."

"Come on, then," Elliot said. "What's the good news?"

"I believe I know where the Penroses would have concealed the name of the demon. There is mention of a disused tin mine that belonged to the family."

"That's great. So, what's the bad news?"

"There is no record of its location."

Elliot set his book down and gave Gabriel his full attention. "Are you sure? Maybe it's somewhere—"

"Ethan documents an enchantment, to conceal the mine from the demon. Provided the location is never physically recorded the demon cannot divine its whereabouts. The only way would be to follow someone who knew where to go."

"So the Penroses really won't have recorded it anywhere. Great."

"Precisely."

"Well, that's helpful," Liam said. "What's the point of putting the name somewhere no one can find! Why not just write it in as many places as possible?"

"The true record of a demon's name is more than just information," Gabriel said. "It will be a relic of some kind. If the demon is powerful enough, no mere paper and pen could capture it for long, the ink would char or fade. Which would explain why we haven't found it elsewhere." Gabriel consulted the book again. "Ethan records his thoughts on the matter. He believed, should they find the name, that neither the house nor the church would be safe enough. The demon cannot enter or extend its abilities into the consecration, but were it determined enough it might find a way to destroy the church by more mundane methods. By starting a fire from a distance, for example. The only way to guarantee the safety of the name would be to keep its location secret."

"But how did *they* know where it was? Generation to generation, I mean." Liam asked.

Gabriel rubbed his beard. "It seems likely the location was passed down verbally. Memorised."

"Then we have no way to find it," Elliot said. "That's—"

"That's not true," Sam said in a small voice.

He twisted to face her. "What do you mean?"

"I mean we could ask them. Ask the spirit in the crypt. I could…"

He stared at her, appalled at the suggestion. "No. You can't possibly… You don't have to put yourself through that."

"But it's the only way."

He took his glasses off and rubbed his eyes. "We don't even know if they ever found the name."

"Actually…" Liam raised his hand. "… Charlie had it." He held up one of the books. "Says something here about waiting for an opportunity. Sounds like he had it all planned out. What to do. Doesn't say what exactly, but he seemed pretty psyched about it."

Elliot re-donned his glasses and glared at him. Liam cringed.

"It's okay. I think I can do it," Sam said. "He didn't hurt me last time. I think… I think I can trust him."

"That's not the point, he still—"

"I know. I don't like it either, but what choice do we have? Let me try."

Elliot shook his head, but she was right. It was the only option, and it was her decision.

———•———

Despite her offer, Sam was in no rush to head down to the crypt and invite the spirit in. She excused herself to get a glass of water and headed to the kitchen. A few minutes later, Elliot appeared in the doorway, hovering as if he was afraid to come closer. Sam wondered whether he was as mixed up about the whole situation as she was, with the revelation that the spirits in the crypt were very likely his ancestors.

"Hey," she said.

A weak smile appeared briefly. "Are you sure you're up for this? You know I'd never ask you to – not for me."

"I know. It's okay. It's not for you. And it's not just about the demon either. I think… I don't know. What I went through before was awful, but maybe there's more to it. It's still there, still a part of me, and I can't ignore that forever. I think I need to do this, for me."

He stepped into the kitchen and came towards her. For a moment she hoped he might hug her. She wanted him to, desperately, but he stopped short.

"Is there anything I can do?" he asked.

She gave it some thought while she sipped her water. "I don't know. I just wish I wasn't so tired. You know, because tiredness is great for mental agility and endurance."

"Get some sleep if you want." He nodded towards the sofas in the community room. "It's not like we can go anywhere until morning anyway. Gabriel and I can keep working the books."

The sofas were awfully tempting. "No. I won't be able to sleep if I'm worrying about it." She sighed. "Better to get it over with."

"Alright. So, how do you want to do this?"

Leaving her glass on the kitchen counter, she walked through to the church with him.

"I guess we go down there and I'll just, I don't know, tell him to take me over?"

"And then?"

"And then you talk to him."

His head snapped towards her. "Me?"

"Well, yeah. I can't do it, and he's your ancestor."

"Might be my ancestor," he muttered.

Still in denial.

Gabriel joined them beneath the church tower, in front of the small door to the crypt. "Are you quite certain about this, Samantha? We can explore other options."

"Thank you, but yes. I'm sure." She looked him in the eye. "Got any advice?"

He considered for a moment. "Most mediums have to train themselves to open their minds. You seem to have a natural aptitude for it, so that part shouldn't present a problem." He rubbed a hand across his beard. "Should you need to control or expel the spirit… Well, I believe the theory is one of mindfulness. Focus on a physical sensation that connects your mind and body, and it should act as an anchor."

"Like what?"

"It could be anything. Holding a treasured object, or listening to familiar music that evokes an emotional response."

Elliot walked away down the nave. For a moment she wondered where he was going, then he stopped and picked something up from one of the pews. He jogged back down the aisle and held out her camera.

Her fingers brushed his as she took it. "Thanks."

He nodded, eyes connecting with hers in a moment that made her stomach flutter.

"I would relish the opportunity to observe," Gabriel said, stepping back. "But I think in this instance it might be best not to overwhelm the spirits. I will continue with the books."

Sam glanced towards the crypt door, her camera clutched in one hand in front of her.

"Ready?" Elliot asked.

She nodded. "I think so."

He went first down the stairs, holding Gabriel's torch. As she followed him, the familiar tingle took hold in the back of her neck, spreading across her scalp. The air cooled until it bit at her cheeks and her breath puffed out in small clouds. She zipped her hoodie up tight. Her hand brushed Elliot's in the darkness and she slid her fingers into his. He drew in a tense breath, then squeezed her hand.

"Should we sit?" he whispered.

"Er, yeah, I think so."

They moved to the foot of Giles Penrose's tomb, between the four pillars. Sam kept a tight hold of Elliot's hand. She was afraid that if she let go he wouldn't touch her again. Right now she needed the contact and the strength she felt from it. The camera in her left hand was a poor anchor in comparison.

She awkwardly lowered herself to the cold floor and sat cross-legged. Elliot sat facing her. He set the torch on top of the tomb beside them, and it shed enough light for her to see his face clearly.

She took a deep breath and concentrated on the sensation of the spirit's presence, like a tingle or a tickle, fingers stroking her hair. It felt so alien to be seeking out that sensation, and she had to fight the instinctive urge to flee. The fresh memories of the spirit taking control earlier had dredged up her worst nightmares.

"Hello?" she whispered. A strong shudder passed through her and she squeezed Elliot's hand. She tried to remind herself that this was her choice and she was in control, but it didn't feel that way. Her mouth was dry and her hands trembled. "I-I'm here. If you want to talk."

There was a kind of empowerment in giving the spirit permission, instead of having power taken from her like before. She tried to focus on that, to help her relax. The presence on the edge of her mind stayed distant, hesitant.

"Look," she said. "It wasn't okay, what you did before, no matter how important you thought it was. But we need to ask some questions, so this is me giving you my permission to speak through me. Okay?"

A whisper touch brushed her cheek and she flinched. Then another on her neck. She sucked in rapid breaths as needle-sharp pinpricks tingled across her skin.

Relax, she told herself. She had to let it in. *Don't resist.*

She gripped Elliot's hand harder. "Don't let go," she begged.

With a pinch at the base of her skull, the eel-like presence slipped into her mind. She gave herself up to it and let her connection to her body dwindle to the single point where Elliot held her hand.

"I thank you, my dear. You are most accommodating," said the deep voice in her head. It settled in and she focused on controlling the rising panic. It was okay, he wasn't going to hurt her.

Sam's chin dipped, and her grip on Elliot's hand slackened.

"Sam?"

Her breathing slowed, from rapid, shallow gasps to deep, even breaths.

"Sam?"

Slowly, her head lifted. "Quite an extraordinary young woman." She looked Elliot in the eye, and her gaze was utterly disconcerting. They were still Sam's eyes, but somehow this was no longer Sam.

"Is she alright?"

The spirit nodded Sam's head. "Oh yes, she's quite safe. Provided I don't stay too long."

Elliot kept hold of Sam's hand, as much to boost his own courage as to help keep her grounded. He was genuinely talking to a ghost, a dead person, an incorporeal consciousness.

"Are you Giles?"

"No, my father's spirit is too weak."

Ethan, then. Charlie's great-great-grandfather and the master of the occult who created the dagger and the wards that protected the Penrose house.

"I was born after my uncle's time, so I had the luxury of approaching the task as a righteous calling, and not the penance my father suffered."

"He blamed himself?"

"Unfortunately. He shouldn't have. There was nothing he could have done."

Elliot nodded. He could all too clearly understand why Giles felt that way.

"So, come now, lad, what's your name?"

"Elliot. Elliot Cross."

"And you're, what? Grandson to Emily?"

"I'm not sure. If it's true, I'm her great-great-grandson."

Ethan smirked, a wholly unfamiliar expression on Sam's face. "My, how time flies. What year is it?"

"Two thousand nine."

Ethan blinked Sam's eyes several times. "Nearly a hundred years since young Charles's time." He shook her head slowly. "It must have taken so many lives."

"But we can stop it. If you can help us."

Ethan focused on him. "Yes, yes it must be you."

"We know we need the demon's name. Do you know it?"

The spirit shook Sam's head. "I know only what the spirits trapped here know. Daniel was the last to be interred. When he passed, he and his son were still searching."

"And Charlie's not here." Elliot breathed. That meant the spirits didn't know! "He found it. We know he did."

"If that's so, he would have concealed it to keep it safe."

"The mine. We know. Can you tell us where it is?"

Ethan nodded. "You understand you must not write it down, anywhere?"

"I do."

"The place is a mile southwest of Devil's Tor, on a bearing of two hundred and forty degrees. Take a bearing from the Beardown Tors of three hundred and ten degrees, and where the two intersect you will find the entrance. Can you remember that?"

Elliot repeated the instructions.

"I'm afraid I must depart now," Ethan said. "Else your young lady may suffer unwanted side effects."

"Wait. Once we have the name, how do we use it?"

Sam's body shuddered. "You have everything you need," Ethan said stiffly. "Make your family proud."

Sam slumped forwards, and Elliot reached out to steady her with a hand on her shoulder. She gradually sat up straight and took several deep breaths.

"Sam?"

Her eyes flicked up to his. "Wow."

"Are you alright?"

She nodded, eyes wide with wonder. "I'm fine," she said, like it came as a surprise.

"What did it feel like?"

She inched closer to him, still holding his hand. "Scary. Like standing on the edge of a cliff, or swimming out of your depth, maybe? You know you can swim, but you still feel all that water under you and it's hard not to panic. You know? But it was okay. All I had to do was hold on and it got easier and easier. He was so gentle. Did it sound like me? In my head I hear his voice, how he hears himself. It was... different. More so than I expected."

The breathless excitement in her voice, the light in her eyes, the tremor in her jaw as she caught her bottom lip between her teeth; she was so pretty when she was excited. Her whole being lit up.

"You're incredible," he said. He reached up, touched her cheek, and she tilted her head against his hand.

Suddenly she pulled away. "We have to tell Gabriel about the directions! Come on!"

She scrambled to her feet and pulled him after her.

The moment they emerged from the crypt, Liam raced towards them down the central aisle. "It's here," he said. "And it looks pissed."

36

They followed Liam to the porch, where Gabriel stood by the door, peering out.

Elliot squeezed past Liam. "Can you see it?"

Gabriel opened the door a little wider. Outside, a streetlamp mingled with light from the nearly full moon, bright enough to cast shadows. The Mime paced, like a caged tiger. It skirted the church at a distance, its motions jerky, agitated.

"Liam's right, it's angry. It's usually so controlled."

Gabriel indicated the line the Mime remained behind. "That must be the limit of the consecration."

Not that it offered much comfort, given the predatory glint in the demon's dead eyes. "Yes, but, like you said, that wouldn't necessarily stop it attacking the building from a distance."

"Did you get what we need?"

Elliot nodded.

"It will be low on energy." Gabriel drummed his fingers on the doorframe. "The act of following us here at pace must have drained a considerable amount, not to mention having to divine our location after it lost track."

"We don't know it hasn't killed in the meantime," Elliot pointed out.

"True."

Sam pushed in between the two of them. "You can't seriously be thinking about leaving while it's out there!"

Elliot dragged his eyes away from the door. "Well, we—"

"Where are we going to go? It's the middle of the night. We can't hike across Dartmoor to find a hole in the ground in the dark!"

She had a point. "I know. But we'll have to leave eventually." He checked his watch, then turned to Gabriel. "It's nearly midnight. Sunrise is what? Five, six hours away? We need to get supplies, drive onto the moor. We could park up, then set out as soon as it's light enough. What do you think?"

Gabriel glanced out through the door to where the Mime still lurked on the edge of the churchyard. "It will try to attack as we leave."

"Right. And we can hope that doing so leaves it too drained to follow us."

Gabriel nodded. "We may be able to bluff our way out. The items we found – the demon need not know we do not fully understand them yet."

"You and me, then, we stay apart, keep its attention divided."

"Agreed."

Elliot left Gabriel by the door and walked over to the chest they'd found in the crypt.

Sam hurried after him. "Umm, can I just point out that this plan is insane?"

"It's alright, all you and Liam have to do is get to the car."

"What, while you and Gabriel play piggy in the middle with the demon?"

His lips quirked. He couldn't help it.

She scowled. "That wasn't supposed to be funny."

He retrieved the book and the dagger. Sam trotted along beside him as he strode back to the door. "Elliot, please!"

"We have to leave at some point," he said. "Better not to give it time to plan, don't you think?"

She let out a frustrated growl.

Elliot unwrapped the dagger. The blade glinted in the shadows around the porch. He rubbed his thumb across the wood of the handle, polished smooth by the hands of successive generations of demon hunters, anointed with the blood of his ancestors. It felt like validation. Belonging.

He handed Ethan's book to Gabriel. "Someone get the lights."

Liam scurried off, and a moment later they were plunged into darkness. He re-joined them by the door.

Elliot handed Sam his car keys. "If this goes wrong, promise me you'll just drive."

She shook her head, glaring at him, and he pulled the keys out of her hand.

"Hey!"

He handed them to Liam instead. "Just in case. You two get away if you can."

Liam looked him in the eye and nodded. "Okay, mate."

Gabriel paused by the door and tucked the book into his inside jacket pocket. "I'll go first."

"No, I'll—"

"You must to get to the car. If I can distract it, you must make use of the opportunity."

Elliot moved up beside him, dagger in hand. "I'm not going to leave you out there to die, if that's what you're suggesting."

Gabriel grunted, wordlessly expressing disapproval, but didn't argue. He pulled the door wide open and stepped out.

The Mime ceased its pacing and stormed towards the church, fists balled at its side. It came to an abrupt stop at the edge of the grass, ten yards away, straining forwards as if the air had thickened around it to provide resistance. Elliot's eyes fixed on the white gloves it wore. The vessel. Surely part of the key to destroying it.

Gabriel slowly moved to the right, across the top step, keeping the Mime in front of him. Elliot stepped out behind him, but the Mime's eyes stayed locked on the demon hunter.

"I underestimated you before," Gabriel said, voice level. He reached into his jacket pocket and drew out the slim book from the crypt. "But not so again. Now we have the keys to your destruction." He stepped gradually sideways, ever further from the safety of the door.

The Mime watched Gabriel with a calculating stare, calmer now. The demon hunter reached the top step and descended one, then another. The Mime tensed.

"Demon," Elliot called, taking a step forwards. The Mime's head snapped towards him and its eyes flared with white-hot hatred. For his defiance, and the fact he wouldn't die? Or was it more than that? "You already know," he whispered under his breath as his stomach took a leaden swoop. "You already know I'm one of them, don't you?" Had it known all along, even back in Bristol? Before that? Had it come there to find him?

The Mime flexed its gloved hands into claws, then clenched its fists again.

Elliot edged left, away from Gabriel, and started down the steps. He held up the dagger. The Mime backed up a pace, and the furious light in its eyes dimmed. It certainly recognised the weapon. Sam and Liam exited the church and closed the door behind them.

"Charlie Penrose was all set to destroy you," Gabriel called, drawing its attention. "He knew how, but fate took him from the world before he had a chance, and for nearly a hundred years you've done as you pleased, with nothing to fear from anyone." He circled further around the Mime, until the demon stood between him and the car.

As the Mime turned its back, tracking Gabriel, Elliot gestured to Sam and Liam to get behind him. He inched closer to the border of the consecration, keeping himself between them and the Mime as they headed for the BMW.

The demon tensed in a half crouch, hands bunching and flexing as it moved further from the church trying to keep them both in view. Its head twitched from side to side, teeth bared in a snarl.

"You cannot hope to defeat us now," Gabriel called.

"It's only a matter of time," Elliot added. "And you know that, don't you?" The demon spun to face him, groping for its hip to draw the invisible sword. Gabriel was right; it was tired. Conserving energy. The air by its thigh glittered and Elliot's head spun. He shook it clear and risked a glance over his shoulder. Liam and Sam had edged along the church wall to the spot closest to the car park. Liam kept himself in front of Sam, shielding her – or perhaps holding her back.

"Demon!" called Gabriel.

When the Mime spun to face the other way, Liam and Sam made a dash for the car. The demon whirled back to face Elliot, sword held out in front of it in a fencing stance. The blade glittered like dust motes in the yellow light from the streetlamp. Elliot blinked hard and rubbed his eyes.

The BMW flashed orange as Liam unlocked it.

With a lightning twist, the Mime darted along the edge of the churchyard towards the car. As it ran, it stretched out an arm to snatch something invisible as it passed. A pole of some kind, by the shape, which took on the same glittering quality as the sword. He bolted to intercept it. The Mime hefted the weapon with its free hand. The pole ended in a wicked point and the Mime drew its arm back like a javelin thrower.

"No!" Elliot lunged as the demon's arm sailed forwards, launching the spear at Sam and Liam. He thrust out his hand.

His palm smacked into the shaft, and the spear thudded into the front of the car beside Sam, leaving a puncture in the middle of a deep dent. It clattered to the ground and collapsed into a mass of fading sparks.

The Mime shook its head, retreated a few steps, then ran. It disappeared around the bend in the lane, and Elliot stared at his own hand in shock.

Gabriel rushed towards him. "What happened?"

"It was a spear," he said.

"You hit it mid-flight?"

To that he simply nodded.

"How?"

"I could see it." He swallowed hard.

"Extraordinary. It looks like you've given our friend cause for concern. We should make the most of it; I doubt it will last long."

They drove in the direction of their hotel near Okehampton where, if they survived that long, Elliot planned to sleep for most of Wednesday. At the first petrol station they found open, Elliot topped up the BMW while Sam and Liam went in for supplies – water, food, another torch, a first aid kit, and a rucksack to carry what they needed on their trek. There were no compasses to be seen, but Gabriel's ever-helpful satchel of occult supplies came to the rescue.

After the pit stop, they drove up onto the edge of the moor and found an isolated car park beside a looming granite tor. Gabriel agreed to stay on guard while the rest of them snatched a couple of hours of sleep as best they could, sat in the car. A thick mist descended, obscuring the moon and stars, and slowly drew the darkness down upon them while they waited for the dawn.

When the sky began to lighten, Gabriel woke them.

Elliot took a moment to stretch his legs and let the cool, moist air on his cheeks chase his exhaustion away. Up on the high ground the balmy summer nights seemed a long way off.

"Girls on the left, boys on the right," Liam called over his shoulder as he strode towards the rocks of the tor, barely visible through the thick fog.

Gabriel shifted his feet. "As Mr Townsend colourfully puts it—" He bit the end off his words and headed for the rocks.

Sam spread their map out on the bonnet of the car. Elliot joined her as she traced her finger along the road they were currently on and stopped by the outline of the rocks. "We're here."

"Ethan said a mile southwest of Devil's Tor, which is…" He scanned the map until he spotted it. "There."

Elliot watched as Sam confidently used Gabriel's compass to work out the angles from the two tors Ethan had mentioned. He wondered when and where she'd learnt to map-read; a sharp reminder that there were many things he still didn't know about her. She pointed to the spot where the two lines would cross. "So, we need to get to somewhere around there, which is… smack in the middle of nothing. No roads. Should be a fun hike."

Elliot pointed to a label on the map that read "Merrivale Range". The mine was square in the middle of a military firing range. "Guess we better hope they're not training today."

Sam puffed out her cheeks and stared at the map again. "S'a long way. But, if we drive round and come at it from the south, there's a bridle path that heads in the right direction from here." She pointed to a green dashed line extending north from a road near Princetown. "At least we'll have a clear route to follow. We might even be able to drive partway along it."

"Sounds like a plan. What's that, about ten miles?"

"More or less."

By the time they'd all forced down something to eat, the horizon glowed a hazy, sickly yellow. Elliot pulled out of the car park onto the road and followed it southwest as it twisted across the moor. The thick fog limited visibility to only a few yards, and the verges faded away at the side of the road.

"It will likely have found a victim to replenish itself," Gabriel said as they drove.

Elliot flicked the radio on and tabbed through a few stations with the controls on the steering wheel until he found one covering the news.

Sam wrestled with the map in the back seat.

"... identities of the victims have not yet been released..."

"Turn that up," Gabriel said urgently.

Elliot tabbed the volume controls.

"... police are still trying to contact the parents of..."

"Parents? Does that mean kids?" Sam asked, squashing the map down in front of her.

"Shh!"

The four of them fell silent as they listened to the report. Details were sparse, but it was nearby. Nine teenagers on a residential school trip. A tearful teacher mentioned screams.

Elliot caught Sam's eye in the rear-view mirror. They'd seen it target a child before, but this was an order of magnitude more horrifying.

"... not ruling out a connection to the similar attack in Oxford, just three days ago."

If they were linking it to the man found in the alley that meant sword wounds. He glanced sideways at Gabriel. The demon hunter's stony expression said everything. Nine kids brutally hacked to death. A violent reminder that the creature they hunted was pure evil. Only a demon could wreak so much pain and suffering without a trace of compassion or mercy. What was more, the amount of energy released from those young lives cut short would have been enormous. The Mime would be fully charged, and it was only a matter of time before it came after them.

The road continued through bleak, desolate moorland. In a few places the fog thinned enough to glimpse hardy sheep, scruffy cattle and rugged Dartmoor ponies huddled together on the leeward sides of scrawny trees. After several miles they dipped down. The verges closed in as they passed by several houses and over a small stone bridge, then the road began to climb back out of the valley.

A thick patch of woodland ran along their left side. On the right, a ditch and a dry-stone wall separated the road from open fields.

"Sam, how much further along—" Elliot's head snapped back as the car lurched forwards.

Liam and Sam both yelped and twisted in their seats to look behind. Elliot squinted at the rear-view mirror and a fuzzy headache took hold between his eyes. Behind them, the mist parted and swirled around a void filled with glittering particles. When he tried to focus on what he could actually see, his eyes watered and his head swam, but when he relaxed and instead tried to picture what it was that followed them, the specks coalesced, like a dusting of golden snow, into the outline of a lorry.

"Jaysus," Liam muttered, craning his neck to see out through the boot window.

Elliot tilted the side mirror. Behind them, above the height of the car, the Mime floated in a seated position, with both arms extended holding a broad steering wheel, and its feet outstretched to pedals. As he watched, it pressed its accelerator foot down and lurched forwards, but there was no roar of engine noise.

With a crunch, the BMW jerked, snapping Elliot's teeth together.

"I suggest additional speed," Gabriel said, bracing himself against the dashboard.

"Yeah, put your foot down!" Liam cried.

Elliot pressed his shoulders into the seat, downshifted to fourth and accelerated hard. The BMW's engine growled and they surged into the fog. Ghostly trees whipped by on the left, while the mist hid the opposite side of the road. The frosted shape of the invisible lorry lost ground, but not much. Not enough.

He shifted back up to fifth. Sweat broke out on his palms and he gripped the steering wheel tight. He could feel every dip and lump in the road vibrating up through the chassis. The woodland receded from the side of the road, and the fog rushed in as the moors opened out on both sides. Unable to see, he instinctively eased off.

The Mime clipped the rear bumper again and Elliot growled his frustration. Then the solid stone wall of a narrow bridge raced towards them and his heart leapt into his throat. He braked hard and swerved, but the lorry – still right behind them – piled into the rear of the car. Tyres squealed as they skidded. Elliot wrestled with the steering wheel. The front wing scraped the wall, screeching, grinding, but they made it over the bridge and round the bend.

Elliot caught Sam's wide, terrified eyes in the rear-view mirror. The road straightened out and he gritted his teeth. The M5 would easily outdistance a lorry if only he could see where he was going! He'd have to chance it and hope his reflexes were fast enough. He shifted up into sixth and tried to put some distance between the car and the lorry.

A small but solid shape hurtled towards them and he swerved round it. A sheep. Sam spun in her seat and let out a horrified yelp. When he risked a glance in the mirror, he saw blood and matted gore clinging to the grille of the invisible lorry.

The next bend forced him to slow down. The ephemeral shape ploughed through the mist behind them. Elliot tried not to look; the headache it gave him made it harder to concentrate. All he could do was keep driving. They'd need to stop eventually, but surely the demon couldn't sustain this for long. How much chaotic energy did a lorry consume? And why chase them at all? Unless… Was the fog limiting the demon's range?

The Mime rapidly closed the gap. It rammed them again, off centre, sending the car careering towards the verge. The front left tyre dipped off the road and rumbled along uneven grass. Elliot fought to regain the tarmac, but he lost speed and the Mime pulled alongside them on the inside of the wide bend.

His hands shook. "Hold on!"

He braced himself as the Mime wrenched its steering wheel to the left and sent the lorry crashing into them.

Sam shrieked as the side of the car buckled and crunched. Liam threw his arm across her and braced himself against Gabriel's seat in front. Both passenger side wheels dipped into the verge and the low clearance BMW bottomed out with a harsh grating.

Elliot tried to accelerate as the road straightened out again, but the lorry stayed with him. In the hope it would continue straight past, he stamped hard on the brake, but the twisted metal locked the two vehicles together. The truck dragged them forwards. Tyres screeched across the tarmac.

Then the ditch on the left dropped deeper, the road narrowed, and all of a sudden there was nothing under the passenger side but empty air.

The lorry catapulted the car forwards and it rolled lazily through the air, the landscape whirling around them almost a complete revolution. They hung, weightless, for a heart-stopping moment. Elliot's whole body tensed even though he knew he should try to relax. He wasn't even sure how he had time for a thought like that to pass through his mind.

And then the BMW crashed down into the ditch. Elliot smacked into the side door, body compressed by the inertia, his head colliding with the glass. A blinding moment of agony. Sam screamed, more fear than pain in her voice.

The airbags in the front deployed, smothering Elliot in white. For a moment he had no concept of direction, which way was up, down, which way they were moving. Then the momentum ran out and the car rocked back onto its roof.

37

Sam hung upside down, held up by her seat belt, her legs jammed against the rear of Elliot's seat.

"We must keep moving," Gabriel said. He released his seat belt and dropped in an undignified heap into the roof of the car.

Sam and Liam followed suit. Broken glass from the side windows littered the underside of the roof and crunched under them. Her door was jammed shut by the bank. Liam tried his, but it wouldn't open either.

"Shift back there, Sammy." A cut on his left temple seeped blood where he'd struck the side of the car, but he seemed otherwise unhurt. She squeezed out of the way. Lying on his back, he kicked until his door gave in, then crawled out. Gabriel squirmed out through the shattered passenger window.

Sam stayed in the car. Elliot was still stuck behind the steering wheel, panting hard, staring dead ahead. Maybe badly hurt. She reached past the seats to touch him. As her fingers brushed his shoulder he swallowed and twisted his head to look back at her.

"Are you okay?" he asked.

"I'm fine. Can you move?"

He released his belt, twisted his way free and flopped onto his back. He stared up, eyes vacant, and his chest rose and fell with sharp breaths.

Sam knelt beside him. She couldn't see any blood, but he could have internal injuries. Her eyes burned with tears. "Are you hurt?"

His eyes locked onto hers, pleading, and she realised he was just in shock. He held out one violently shaking hand. It must have been ten times more terrifying for him behind the wheel.

She grasped his hand. "You did great."

He closed his eyes, took a deep breath, then they crawled out together.

Gabriel and Liam crouched behind the wreckage of the car, watching the road.

"You see anything?" Liam asked Elliot.

He scanned the road. "No, not anymore." His legs gave way and he slumped heavily against the car. Sam ached for him.

"We may not have long," Gabriel said.

She gestured to a dry-stone wall that topped the far bank of the ditch, parallel to the road. "Let's get out of sight."

She fetched the map while Liam prised the boot open to retrieve their supplies. Then they climbed over and sat with their backs to the wall. She spread the map out. The section of woodland they'd passed, and the bridge, were clearly marked, as was the bend where the Mime had drawn level before it ran them off the road. She pointed to the adjacent straight section.

"We're here. We need to get to here." She placed the finger of her other hand by their destination. There was still a good distance in between. Where she'd suggested they circle round there was now no point. Walking, it would be quicker to take the straight-line route.

"If we strike out this way, we'll hit this river or stream, or whatever it is. We can follow that up for a bit till we can find a place to cross and, on the other side, those are the Beardown

Tors Ethan mentioned. We can follow his bearing from there."

"How far is it?" Liam asked.

Sam used her hand span to measure the distance against the map's scale. "Three and a bit miles, give or take."

Elliot checked his watch. "That'll take at least an hour, maybe more like two over rough ground." He glanced up, squinting. "It'd be good if this held, but I doubt our luck will run that way."

For a moment she wasn't sure what he meant, but then she twigged. The fog acted like a smokescreen. Once it lifted, they'd be more vulnerable.

"Then let's get moving." She folded the map so it showed only the section they needed.

They climbed over the wall. She caught Elliot looking back at his car as they crossed the road, his face a careful blank.

"Your insurance cover act of demon?" Liam chuckled.

Elliot didn't even smile.

Sam wondered if the reality had sunk in yet. The car meant more to him than he'd ever admit, otherwise he wouldn't have kept it.

———•———

With the fog still so dense, it would be too easy to lose their bearings on open ground, so Sam elected to skirt the edge of the stone-walled field. As they trudged through thick, damp grass, trying to avoid prickly gorse bushes, she considered trying to talk to Elliot, but he had a dark, closed expression on his face and she really wasn't sure where to start. He seemed content to follow at the rear.

Instead she let Gabriel take the lead and fell into step beside Liam.

"Bet you're wishing you'd stayed at home now, huh?"

"Nah, I'm grand. If it weren't for the constant threat of death, I'd be totally into this whole treasure hunt deal."

Sam laughed. It was like following breadcrumbs. One clue to the next.

"Okay, but nearly dying in a car crash?"

He flashed a crooked grin. "Nearly dying? That? Nah, not even close. Trust me."

She waited to see if he'd elaborate.

"Remind me to tell you the story of my Millennium Eve sometime." He scanned the mist-shrouded moors around them. "I don't know. Something tells me I'm right where I should be." He shook off whatever was going through his mind and focused on her. "So, tell me, you going pro now? With the whole 'I talk to dead people' thing?"

She shrugged. "Oh no, I don't think so. Once was enough."

"But what if it's your calling?"

"I don't know. Maybe. I guess I need some time to process." She stumbled over a particularly dense clump of sedge grass and grabbed Liam's arm.

He steadied her. "I get that."

"It's just, what is it we talked to? It's too weird to think of some person's consciousness floating around with no body." She shivered and rubbed her arms.

"Better that than nothing though, right?"

"I suppose." She regarded him out of the corner of her eye. "Do you think it makes death less scary? Like, would you ever think about…" She gestured with a finger across her throat. "… to see what's out there for yourself?"

"Oh hell no. I've seen enough to last a lifetime and I am in no rush to leave this world, let me tell you!"

Again, she found herself waiting to see if he'd tell her more about whatever it was that had happened to him.

"There's something out there, but what if there's no beer, cheeseburgers... sex. Know what I'm saying? Nah, I'd rather keep my feet on the ground."

She glanced over her shoulder at Elliot. He looked away, as if she'd caught him watching them, his face tense.

They fell silent as they progressed onto the moor. Little in the way of bird song or insect noise broke through the dampening fog, lending the wide-open space an oddly claustrophobic quality. The ground beneath the dewy grass was relatively firm after the dry summer; they might have had a tougher time of it in winter. Sam's work shoes were sensible enough, but as her toes grew wetter and colder she thought wistfully of her walking boots, warm and dry and unhelpfully sitting in the bottom of her wardrobe at home.

The wall they were following met another at right angles and they scrambled over into another enclosure. They'd been walking for about half an hour when the wall angled abruptly left. She heard the trickle of running water, just ahead but out of sight.

She paused to spread the map out on top of the wall and re-fold it to show the next part of their trek. They weren't even halfway yet, and the fog was beginning to lift as the sun climbed higher.

Gabriel drew Elliot to one side. "I believe our respite is over."

Sam followed his gaze. Back along the wall, a dark shape darted through the thinning mist.

"Keep an eye on it," Elliot said to Gabriel.

"Why's it not attacking?" Liam asked.

"It's waiting for the right moment," Elliot said. "Out here in the middle of nowhere, it has no access to easy victims to recharge. It's going to bide its time."

"It may also be curious as to where we are going," Gabriel added.

Ethan's enchantment prevented the Mime from finding the mine using its powers of divination, but not from following them. They'd destroyed or given away every advantage the Penroses had hidden to keep them safe. When they reached the mine and found the name, they had to use it and succeed, or else it was all for nothing.

Elliot moved close to Sam's side and put his hand on the small of her back. She closed her eyes at the brief touch.

"How are we looking?" he asked.

"We should follow the river up. These trees might give us some cover. But we'll have to cross at some point."

The moorland sloped down into a valley littered with granite boulders. As they descended, the scale of the river emerged. Sam eyed the wide, fast-flowing water anxiously. She didn't fancy trying to cross that without a bridge or a ford.

They picked up a well-worn trail through the scratchy grass, running parallel to the river on their left. The demon seemed content to follow at a distance for a while, but when they approached the forest it vanished.

"I don't like it," Liam said, walking backwards. "I prefer having the fucker where I can see him."

Gabriel nodded his agreement. "Stay vigilant. It may be setting some kind of trap."

Elliot took the lead, in case the Mime had prepared any surprises for them. Sam followed close behind him.

They drew level with the patch of gnarled, stunted oak trees which clung to the slope on their right. Massive chunks of moss-covered granite broke up the ground in between, rendering the forest completely impassable. So much for her cover theory.

On the left, a stone wall separated them from the river, interrupted by the occasional stile.

As they tramped through the boulder-strewn grass, Elliot flinched as if something had buzzed past his ear. He spun, to look back the way they'd come.

Sam caught a glimpse of black behind them. The Mime crouched behind a boulder, aiming something in its hands. Suddenly Elliot grabbed her and jerked her sideways. An invisible object pinged off a rock behind where she'd been standing.

Elliot dragged her along as he ran. "Arrows! Move!"

Another invisible projectile swished through the grass along the line of the wall.

"Spread out," Gabriel said. "Don't give it a group to aim for."

Elliot released Sam's arm and she focused on scrambling over the uneven ground as fast as she could. The thick sedge – more reeds than grass – reached up to her knees and hid lumps and holes in the ground, ready and waiting to break any careless ankles. Her feet slipped inside her shoes and again she wished for proper boots. Elliot pulled ahead of her, dodging around and vaulting over boulders like he did it every day. Him and his stupid runner's legs. She tried not to follow the exact same route, and to move from side to side as she went. She didn't want to give the demon a clear shot.

She risked a quick glance over her shoulder as Gabriel jogged past her along the clearest part of the trail. Liam wasn't far behind. He picked his way over the boulders, keeping low to the ground like a cat burglar. Further back, the Mime raced along the line of the wall. It sprang onto the piled stone slabs and paused, one arm thrust forwards. The other drew the invisible string of its bow. It wasn't pointed at her, and as she dropped behind a rock she tried to work out where it was aiming.

Up ahead, where the woods spread further down the slope, Elliot paused with his back to one of the trees. He glared at the

Mime and ducked as it released its projectile. The bark splintered, right behind where his head had been.

Sam broke cover and ran towards him as he drew the dagger they'd found at the church. He gripped hold of the Mime's arrow and sawed at it with the invisible blade. With a few cuts he sliced through, and the arrow became solid in his grip. Sam could see the thick wooden shaft and grubby, greasy feather flights. Somehow the dagger had made it visible.

"How did you…?"

Down the path, the Mime staggered to the side and dropped to its knees. It glared at Elliot, eyes flashing hate, then pushed back up and darted into the trees.

He held up the arrow. It looked fully real and showed no sign of disappearing. If manifesting invisible objects drained the Mime's energy, how much more would it take to make them permanent and visible?

Gabriel caught up with them. "Is that…?"

Elliot threw the shaft to the ground and wiped his hand on his jeans. "One of the Mime's arrows. It's not happy."

Liam joined them, keeping a wary eye down the path. "Yeah, good plan. Piss it off more."

They used the moment to regroup. Further in the direction they'd been heading, the path petered out and the vegetation grew denser, so they took the next stile over the wall towards the river. Ten feet of fast-flowing water separated them from the direction they needed to go.

"I thought there'd be some kind of crossing," Sam said as she checked the map again. "I'm sorry."

"Afraid to get your feet wet?" Liam said. "Come on, it's not that deep." He paced along the edge for a moment, then stepped off with a splash. Water swirled above his knees as he waded upstream to where the others still hesitated. He offered his hand to Sam.

Gabriel adjusted his satchel strap and searched for a spot to climb down. Elliot kept watch for the Mime.

"Come on," Liam urged.

Sam reached for his hand. As she stepped close to the edge, he pulled her forwards, caught her over his shoulder and lifted her off her feet.

"Hey!" she shrieked, nearly dropping the map. She grabbed tight hold of his hips, though it didn't make her feel more secure. Her hair dangled into the surging water.

Liam chuckled as he waded across. "Hold still or I'm going to drop you."

"Don't you dare!"

She lifted her head as Elliot and Gabriel waded into the flow behind them. Elliot had a carefully neutral expression pasted on his face, but at least he wasn't laughing at her.

Liam set her down on the far bank. "Right, now help me up."

She grasped his hand, braced, and he heaved himself out of the water.

"You could have warned me," she hissed under her breath.

He shrugged, grinning. "Where'd the fun be in that?"

While Liam helped Gabriel out of the river, Sam moved to meet Elliot, but he found a spot where he could step out without assistance.

"Where next?" he asked.

"Straight up there." She nodded towards the steeply sloping moorland where it faded into the dissipating fog.

The first minute of the climb wasn't too bad, but it rapidly became a slog. Sam trudged up the slope, concentrating on keeping air going into her lungs through her dry, closed throat and putting one foot in front of the other. Elliot pulled a few paces ahead of her and she struggled to keep up. Gabriel plodded along behind, his breath laboured.

Liam stayed with them, less out of breath. "It's back," he called. "Still following us."

Elliot paused, squinting down the slope. "And it still has the bow. Keep moving."

At the top of the slope they ran for the relative shelter of a weathered granite outcrop – one half of the Beardown Tors. Panting, sweating like crazy, Sam crouched, spread the map out and tried to get her bearings.

Elliot cracked open a bottle of water from Gabriel's satchel and took a long gulp. "We can't stop for long," he said.

"I know. I just need a minute." She rotated the map, using Gabriel's compass to set it. They'd been relying on landmarks, but from here on the terrain would be fairly featureless, especially with the remnants of the morning mist still hiding the contours of the land. If they set off in the wrong direction, they would completely miss the Penrose mine. She orientated the compass to the bearing Ethan had given them.

Elliot handed his bottle to Liam and scanned the hilltop. Sam watched him, distracted from the map. "Do you see it?"

He shook his head, frowning.

"Maybe it gave up," Liam said. "Went to recharge." He raised the bottle to his lips.

Suddenly he jerked forwards, as if he'd been shoved. Water dribbled down his chin and his eyes unfocused.

Sam rose from her crouch. "Liam?"

"Little shite!" he croaked. "Shot me in the back." Blood spotted his lips.

Elliot caught him as he slumped. "Find something to stop the bleeding. Quickly!"

Sam was one step ahead of him. She dug through her pack for the first aid kit, tipped the contents out and grabbed a triangular bandage. Her hands shook as she tore open the plastic wrapping.

Liam drew shallow, shaky breaths through teeth gritted against the pain. Blood soaked through his sweatshirt around the invisible arrow. Elliot lowered him from standing to kneeling and braced to take his weight.

Sam moved to put the bandage over the hole in his clothes at the centre of the spreading stain, but her hand hit the shaft of the arrow. Liam gasped.

"Where is it? Elliot, I can't see it." Why was it even still there? Usually the Mime's weapons ceased to exist after it was done with them, so it must be close enough to be watching what was happening. She glanced at Gabriel, who stood alert with his back to them, gripping his scissor-crucifix in one hand.

"Don't pull," Liam hissed. "Leave it." He trembled in Elliot's arms, and his skin greyed. He was going into shock. "Pressure," he mumbled.

She wrapped the bandage around the invisible shaft and pressed. Liam groaned. His blood soaked through the fabric in seconds.

"I can't stop it," she gasped. "Why is it bleeding so much? Liam? What do I do? Come on, tell me."

He didn't respond.

She looked desperately at Elliot. Sweat dampened his forehead and he clenched his jaw.

Liam sagged, all the tension leaving him as he lost consciousness.

"Liam?" Sam pressed her fingers to the side of his neck. His pulse wavered, weak and fluttering. "Oh God. What do we do?" He couldn't die, not when they were so close.

"Take him," Elliot said.

Sam took Liam's weight and hugged him close to her chest. His head lolled against her shoulder.

Elliot pulled out the Penrose dagger and cut Liam's clothes away from the arrow. Blood flowed from the hole in his back, a steady stream. Where it smeared across his tattoos, it blurred the black feathers as if they were soaking it up.

"I think the arrow is holding the wound open. It's keeping the edges apart but letting the blood flow out."

The Mime, ensuring the wound would be fatal.

Elliot swiped his hair back. "Hold him tight." With the dagger, he cut the arrow shaft a little over an inch away from Liam's body. As the last fibres parted, both parts of the arrow solidified, and the bleeding slowed.

Elliot took Liam's weight again, and Sam checked for a pulse.

"I can't feel anything." Tears flooded her eyes and she swiped them away, trying to keep her vision clear. Had he lost too much blood? If they'd thought to cut the arrow sooner… She put her cheek to Liam's mouth. "He's not breathing."

Elliot closed his eyes, lips pressed in a thin line. "It's too late."

"No!" She dashed her eyes again, smearing Liam's blood across her face. "What about CPR?"

"The arrow is embedded in his back. We can't lie him down and we can't do chest compressions. It'd tear him up inside." He shook his head. "He's already gone."

"Don't say that!" She thumped her fist into his shoulder. "We have to try!"

She gripped the stubby end of the arrow with both hands and pulled, but her fingers slipped on the blood-slicked surface.

"Sam. Don't."

"Stop it! Stop giving up!"

She wiped the end of the arrow with the bandage, tried again, letting out a harsh cry as another three inches pulled free, tipped with a wicked barbed point. The wound ripped open, an ugly, mangled gash, and she pressed the blood-soaked bandage to it.

"Alright," Elliot said. "Let's turn him over."

They shifted Liam to the closest bit of flat ground and Sam set her clasped hands on his sternum. His skin was ashy pale, his lips blue. Fifteen compressions, then she pinched his nose, sealed her mouth across his and blew into his lungs. The salty, iron tang of his blood tainted her lips. Another fifteen, another breath. Compressions, breath. Again. When her arms started to go numb, she paused.

"Anything?"

Elliot checked for a pulse and shook his head.

A thin trickle of blood ran from the corner of Liam's lips. She leaned over him to start another round and Elliot put his hand on her shoulder. "There's nothing you can do. He's gone."

She collapsed away from the body and pushed her hair out of her face with a bloody hand. "But it was so fast." Her vision blurred, eyes swimming, and a tight knot lodged in her throat.

"I know. I'm so sorry."

"It wasn't your fault. It was my fault for stopping. We should've—"

"No, don't say that. Don't blame yourself. If it's anyone's fault it's mine. I should never have let him come." He pushed wearily to his feet.

Sam looked up at him. "You didn't know. The Mime could have shot any one of us."

If it was possible, he seemed to blanch even more as she said that.

Gabriel appeared by Elliot's shoulder, his expression distraught. "It's holding its distance. I'm not sure why. Now would be the perfect time to press the advantage."

"It's picking us off, but it must still want to know where we're going."

Sam stayed slumped beside Liam's body. Even though she'd only known him for a few days she'd let him in, talked to him about secrets she'd not even shared with her best friend. She put her ear to his chest – still warm, smelling of mellow spice, sweat and blood – praying she'd hear his heartbeat, but there was nothing. She hugged him and sobbed tears into his clothes.

Elliot crouched beside her. "We'll have to leave him here for now." His voice sounded hollow. "We can come back for him when it's over."

If they survived. He didn't need to say it; she was already thinking it.

They dragged Liam to a recess at the base of the rocks, where his body would be out of easy sight. As they set off along the ridge, Sam glanced back at his pale face, chin tucked down. She didn't want to do this anymore.

38

They followed the ridge north, then picked up a clearly defined footpath headed in the right direction.

Elliot stayed close beside Sam as they walked, as if being near her could counteract the emptiness inside. Liam's death weighed heavy on his shoulders. Another person he'd let down in the worst way. The girl at the music festival who drowned six inches in front of him. Irene, who slipped away holding his hand. Geoff, dying alone and afraid after they'd dragged him into this mess. Geoff's family hadn't even known he was dead until Elliot and Sam discovered his body and called the police. His little grandchildren...

Did Liam have family? Elliot felt like he should know the answer to that. He wasn't married, didn't have kids, but parents? Brothers and sisters? Maybe a little niece or nephew whose favourite uncle wouldn't—

He *should* know.

He would have, if he'd taken a few minutes to talk to him like a human being. But then, he was so good at putting himself first. He'd kept his distance because that made it easier to cast Liam in whatever hypothetical role his own selfish purposes required – informant, sidekick, dead weight, rival. Because that's what he always did. Made everything about himself.

Why not *friend?*

He rubbed his palms on his jeans. It was like the demon knew just how to get to him. Did it enjoy hammering home the point?

He glanced over at Sam.

Though she'd tried to wipe it off, Liam's blood stained her cuffs. As they'd set off from the tor, she'd taken her camera from her backpack, and now she hugged it close. Every now and then she held it up and studied the misty landscape through the view-finder, quiet tears leaking down her cheeks behind her shield.

Geoff, Irene, Liam. They all felt like reliving James's death all over again. Why couldn't he stop being so fucking self-centred? Stop and think about what really mattered for once.

Sam huddled close to his side, her shoulder brushing his. He slipped his arm around her and she drew in a tense breath. He didn't care if he was crossing a line. He needed her safe, protected. He needed her. If he couldn't get her through this alive, what point was there to any of it?

The demon followed at a distance, appearing at intervals but making no move to attack as they followed the path west. Liam's death would have given it a boost in energy. It could probably take them out whenever it wanted, but if it didn't follow them all the way to the mine it wouldn't be able to destroy the one weapon in the world that could kill it. The original record of its own name.

Gabriel walked beside them, glancing back every few paces to keep an eye on the demon. He held the crucifix with the scissors attached in one hand, and gripped the strap of his satchel in the other. If Elliot had to guess, he'd say the demon hunter was frightened.

The path descended on the far side of the ridge into another valley where several streams met. Exposed stone broke through the thin, boggy layer of soil on the surface, and clumps of stiff grass filled the cracks. The closer they drew to the streams, the more uneven it became. Some of the rocks outlined squares or rectangles, too regular to be natural.

Elliot squeezed Sam's shoulder. "How about we take another look at the map?"

She nodded, mute, and wiped a hand across her reddened eyes and tear-streaked cheeks.

He released her so she could put her camera away and get the map out of her pack, but he stayed close. He wasn't going to allow the Mime a clear shot at her. They stepped off the path and crouched down behind a boulder. Gabriel stood beside them, peering over the top of their cover.

Sam consulted the compass-bearing directions and pointed to a blue line on the map. She sniffed and rubbed her nose. "We need to follow this stream to where it starts. The mine should be close."

"Looks like there's a path that follows the same route, so we can stay on it until we reach the spring."

"Yeah. Then, who knows? The bearings only give us a rough idea where to look."

He touched her shoulder and she glanced up at him. "We'll find it," he said.

She gave him a courageous nod.

They crossed one of the smaller streams that met in the valley and climbed up the far slope. With the well-trodden footpath to guide them they upped their pace over the final half mile. They passed more boulders in the grass, and again many were too ordered to be accidental. More likely the remains of houses or huts. Very old.

The stream narrowed to a trickle.

"I believe we are close," Gabriel said, inspecting a short stone post beside the edge of the path.

Elliot joined him and crouched beside the square marker. Engraved into its surface, weathered almost smooth but still recognisable, was the Penrose family crest.

He stood and scanned their surroundings. The demon had either fallen behind, or it was stalking them with more caution. It would be wishful thinking of the most dangerous kind to assume they'd given it the slip. He'd underestimated it from the very beginning, but now he felt truly hunted.

They eventually found the source of the stream. Standing beside it he could see the way the watercourse cut a steep-sided V-shape into the land.

"Look." Sam pointed.

Some distance along the nascent valley, maybe twenty feet below where they stood, the land dropped down at an unnatural angle, steeper than the surrounding bank. Regular lumps in the edge of the valley beside it looked like stairs leading up to the footpath not far from where Gabriel had shown him the stone marker. He'd walked right past the top step.

They backtracked, and Elliot scrambled down the buried steps with Sam. Gabriel brought up the rear, keeping an eye out behind them.

At the bottom the ground levelled out. A thin layer of grass and weeds covered granite paving slabs, beyond which the stream trickled past. The soil and rock had been excavated away to create a flat shelf and a vertical face against the hillside.

Gabriel crouched to inspect a dark void under an overhang of earth only a foot or so high. "There is a gate of some sort behind here." He stood and dusted off his hands. "The bank has slumped down, obscuring the entrance, but I am quite certain this is it."

Elliot helped him pull the earth away from the opening while Sam kept watch. Behind the overhang, they exposed a rusted iron gate with a circular crest at its centre. Once again, it bore the Penrose family emblem. A flat lock plate bolted the gate directly into the stone around it.

"Sam, do you still have the keys?" Elliot called.

She scooted down from her vantage point and passed him the ring of keys. The largest one fitted, but the lock plate was rusted almost solid, and at first it wouldn't turn. He twisted it back and forth a couple of times and eventually it grated round.

Gabriel helped wrench the gate open and shone his torch into the gloom. The passage sloped steeply down into the rock, only wide enough to admit one person at a time. On either side, ridged granite walls showed that the tin miners had cut the tunnel into the rock by hand, with nothing more than hammer and chisel. Gabriel stooped and stepped inside.

The light of his torch delved deeper, and the darkness closed in behind him.

Elliot gestured for Sam to go next with her own torch.

Before he followed, he took one last look around for the Mime, but there was no flash of black and white. No movement. He was beginning to suspect they only ever saw it when it wanted to be seen.

In the mine, the air cooled rapidly. Elliot's footsteps scraped on damp, gritty ground, echoing off the rock. His feet were still soaked from the river crossing and his toes were numb.

Twenty or thirty yards in, they reached a split. To the right, the passage levelled out and continued, but on the left a shaft dropped down. Sam and Gabriel shone their torches down the hole, highlighting a level floor and an opening off to the side, twelve feet down.

Gabriel's torch beam settled on an engraving of the Penrose crest in the lip of the shaft opening. "I believe this indicates that we should go down." He pointed to several notches in the stone. "These serve as a ladder of sorts."

He placed the penlight between his teeth to free up his hands, adjusted his satchel, then set his toe into the first foothold and lowered himself down the shaft.

Sam kept her torch on Gabriel, but she stood stiffly, hugging her free hand around her stomach. Elliot watched her cautiously. Mines were dangerous places and there was every possibility some of the miners had died underground. The moist, chilly air penetrated into him, uncannily like the crypt at St Michael's. Deeply unsettling.

"Sam? Is there something here?"

She jumped at the sound of his voice. "No. At least, I don't think so. Just a bad vibe."

Did she experience the disquieting atmosphere the same way he did, or was she picking up more? "Promise me you'll say something if that changes."

She nodded.

Gabriel reached the bottom.

"Hey, give me your pack and the torch," Elliot said to Sam. She handed them over and he dropped both down to Gabriel. Sam climbed down next, then he followed.

The tunnel at the base of the shaft wound away into complete darkness. The last daylight from the entrance vanished as they followed a bend and then descended along a shallow slope. Elliot had to stoop to avoid hitting his head. The claustrophobic tunnel pressed down with the weight of all the rock above. His hands were restless, twitchy, and he repeatedly touched the dagger hilt where he'd tucked it through his belt. The fact he wasn't holding one of the lights left him anxious, a deep instinctive sense of vulnerability, and he kept close behind Sam. Close enough he caught traces of her warm scent against the cool, earthy background. The rock seemed stable, in no danger of collapsing, but he wondered what the quality of the air might be down here.

Their tunnel intersected another shaft, and again they found the crest guiding them down. Just for an excuse to take Gabriel's torch for a while, he offered to go first. At the bottom he splashed into a foot of freezing cold water and gasped at the shock.

Gabriel joined him, wading away from the base of the shaft to give Sam space.

"Let us hope that what we seek has not been damaged by water ingress."

Drips from the ceiling hit the standing water at irregular intervals. Plink, plop. Each droplet tightened his chest with tiny darts of panic as he imagined being trapped down here with the water rising.

They passed another shaft at the side of the tunnel. Sam shone her torch up. It extended as far as the torch beam penetrated. They were further underground than Elliot had realised. A slight updraft sucked air towards the surface and tugged his hair, tickling the nape of his neck.

Gabriel inspected the walls of the shaft, which seemed barely wide enough to accommodate a person. "A sump, perhaps? A pump house to remove the water may have sat above us."

The base of the shaft dipped lower, but the water level remained the same. If there were lower levels to the mine they were completely flooded. Elliot had to rationalise with himself that they must have been below the water table all along. There was no reason for the water to rise now. No reason at all.

They waded further along the tunnel and the slope rose. The water receded and left them walking on damp stone once more. The cold persisted, stealing away warmth with ruthless efficiency. Elliot shoved his fidgety hands in his pockets. Sam rubbed her arms and stamped her feet every few paces.

After another ten yards, they hit a dead end.

"This can't be right," Elliot said, peering past Sam and Gabriel at the bare rock face in front of them. He stood close behind Sam, and she leaned into him, creating a brief pocket of warmth where they touched.

Gabriel crouched. "The way continues."

Sam crouched down too, and in the light of her torch Elliot saw a small opening at their feet, no higher than their knees. The air in the tunnel flowed towards the hole. A subtle draft but enough to make him feel like it wanted to suck him in. Swallow him.

Gabriel set his satchel to one side. Taking the torch in his mouth, he lay down and wriggled into the gap. His legs disappeared, and for a moment Elliot found himself holding his breath, until the torch beam shone out of the hole.

"It's not far," Gabriel called. "It widens out on this side."

He wasn't going in there, into that *mouth*, without a light, he just couldn't. Even with Gabriel on the other side. He exchanged a glance with Sam.

She pressed her torch into his hands as if she could read his thoughts. "It's okay. I'll go next."

Leaving her pack with Gabriel's, she squeezed into the narrow opening. Elliot's hand clenched around the dagger handle and he pulled it from his belt. He suddenly felt very alone, his breath harsh in his ears. If they died down here, no one would ever find them.

It was fine. If Gabriel could fit through, he could. He knelt beside the opening. A light flickered on the far side.

"Sam?"

"I'm through."

It was fine. Easy. Taking a deep breath, he went for it. The rock pressed against his stomach, knees, hips, chest. It felt like being buried. He kept his eyes on the next inch of rock in front of his nose, concentrated on moving forwards. The air tasted like soda water and green tea. Every time his chest expanded his back touched rock points above. Teeth, clamping down. It was going to eat him alive. He clenched his jaw, sucking rapid breaths through his teeth. Too hard, too fast. Dizzy.

For a second he battled the urge to go back, but then there was a hand in front of his face. Sam's. He reached for her, still holding the torch, and she grasped his wrist. It quietened the rising panic and he shifted more easily through the last part.

On the far side the darkness gained an indescribable sense of space. The quality of the sound, the eddies in the air, the reflections of the torchlight, all expanded, like a release of pressure. He took a few deep breaths. Sam slipped an arm around his waist and rubbed his back in slow circles. He leaned on her. He didn't care how weak it made him, or what lines he was crossing. He'd been a hair's breadth from completely freaking out and he needed her.

She didn't say anything, but he got the impression she understood.

Gabriel panned his light around the new chamber, which was squarish, much wider than the tunnels they'd been following. To the right and left, passages led off into the blackness, and above them a shaft rose up.

"Is there light coming from up there?" Sam angled her torch up the shaft.

"It likely reaches to the surface," Gabriel said. "Whether it was deliberately capped or silted up naturally, the obstruction could easily shift over time."

Opposite the opening they'd crawled through, Gabriel's light settled on a shelf carved into the rock, on which sat a wooden chest. Thick layers of rust and limescale welded the padlock on the front into a solid lump.

Sam took a step towards it. "That must be—"

Her words cut off with a strangled yelp as she flew upwards. She grasped Elliot's arm for a fraction of a second before sailing off her feet into the darkness. Her torch clattered to the ground and rolled away.

"No! Gabriel, light!"

Gabriel swept his torch beam up into the shaft above them. The light clipped Sam's foot ten feet up, where she kicked, straining to reach the wall of the shaft.

"Higher!"

He panned the torch up. Sam clawed at something around her neck, face reddening. A rope of glittering motes extended up, and above it, staring down at them, framed by the trace of daylight at the top, was the white face of the demon.

NO TIME

The front door to Elliot's apartment shuddered under a violent impact and he jumped. The cufflink slipped from his fingers and, as he tried to catch it, the stack of index cards in his other hand went flying.

Another resounding thump on the door.

"I'm coming, I'm coming," he muttered as he trotted down the hall. He peeked through the spy hole before opening it, and flinched as his brother pounded the door again.

Taking a quick step back, he snatched the door open. James tried to knock on thin air.

"I'm not deaf!"

Despite hunching as if he were trying to make himself smaller, James filled the doorway with his big frame. He rubbed the fuzzy hair on the back of his head and glanced down the corridor. "Hey."

"Yeah, great to see you too." Elliot folded his arms, pulling his jacket tight across his shoulders. "Why are you here exactly?"

"Sorry, I didn't know where else to go. You're pretty much the only person I know in London."

"I'm not lending you money. You can ask Dad."

"I don't need money." He looked down the corridor again. "There's something, I dunno, I just need help."

Watching his brother's eyes dart about like a cornered animal unnerved Elliot. He waved James into the flat. Before he closed the door, he checked the corridor, but there was no one there.

James walked through to the living room and picked up *The Tribute* from the coffee table. Elliot had the front page today – an exposé he'd been building up to for weeks.

"Please don't tell me you came here to read my newspaper," Elliot said, leaning in the doorway.

James dropped the paper and finally seemed to focus on him. "What's with the tux?"

"Award ceremony in…" He glanced at his watch. "… thirty-five minutes."

James perched on the side of the couch, then stood up again. He wiped his palms on his combats. "I'm sorry, I know you're a busy guy. But there's something, someone, after me."

Elliot snorted.

"No, I'm serious. Something weird is going on."

"Weird isn't my area. Try the police."

James sat down again, his shoulders slumping. "I did. They didn't believe me."

"I don't have time for twenty questions. What exactly do you want?"

"Alright, alright." James took a deep breath. "I'm not sure what it is exactly, but it already killed someone." He slid off the arm of the sofa and onto the seat, resting his head in his hands. "The police say she hanged herself – that it was suicide – but Chelsea was a friend, in my unit. She wasn't unhappy or anything."

Elliot paced across the living room rug. "Alright, I'm sorry about your friend. But can't this wait till tomorrow? I really need to be—"

"But I saw!"

Elliot closed his eyes and pressed his lips together. "You found her? That's pretty fucked up, I'm sorry."

"No, but it's… There was no rope! She was floating there in mid-air. I know it sounds impossible, but that's what I saw."

Elliot perched on the edge of the coffee table. "I'm sure you thought you saw—"

"I'm not making it up," James snapped, thumping the armrest.

"Alright, alright. No rope." Elliot put both hands up, palms out. He waited for James to continue, and when he didn't he stood. "I'm still not clear what you want me to do about it."

"Well, you know… You know people. Police-type people. Can't you talk to someone? Back me up? Tell them to believe me?"

Elliot cast a longing glance down the hallway, through the open bedroom door at the cards and cufflink lying on the floor. "The police tolerate the press, they don't encourage it. If I start asking for favours all the time, I'll get a bad rep."

"Who said anything about all the time? It's just this one thing."

Elliot pinched the bridge of his nose and rubbed his eyes, the elbow of his right arm cradled in his left hand.

"I think the thing that killed her is after me," James added.

"What, the phantom rope monster?"

James inhaled sharply. "Could you at least try to take me seriously?"

"I would, if you'd start acting like a rational human being."

"Come on, you're my brother!"

Elliot crossed to the door into the hall. "Look, I get that you're upset about your friend. It's awful that she died. But that doesn't mean the bogeyman is after you. Just go home and get some rest." He nodded towards the front door.

James glanced at the door with wide eyes, like a child afraid of what lurked in the closet.

"Oh, for fuck's sake, James!"

"But—"

Elliot folded his arms again. "Go home. I have to get ready and this will wait till tomorrow."

James reluctantly stood. He wiped his palms on his combats again. "No, but... Can I stay with you at least? I don't want to be on my own."

Elliot clenched his jaw. "I can't. I have to be at this award ceremony. It's important."

"More important than family?"

"I've had enough of this." He walked to the front door and held it open. "Yes, the National Press Awards are more important than holding your hand because you're upset about your dead friend. There is nothing after you." He ground the words out through his teeth.

James stalked into the corridor outside. He turned as he crossed the threshold. "I know what I saw. If... I won't blame you. I love you, little brother."

Elliot suddenly couldn't meet his gaze. "Nothing's going to happen," he muttered. "I'll call after work tomorrow. We'll get a drink and we can talk about it then. Alright?"

James nodded. "Sure."

He walked away down the corridor. Elliot closed the door. After a couple of deep breaths, he returned to the bedroom and set his speech in order.

39

"Chelsea," Elliot murmured as the revelation slammed into him. How had he not seen it before? His own guilt had made one fact indisputable in his mind, so cast-iron certain that he'd blinded himself to the connection. He was wrong and James was right, and James had said there was no rope. But there was, he just couldn't *see* it. The Mime's creations were real in every way that mattered.

The glittering specks coalesced, thickening and darkening until Elliot could clearly see the twist in the hemp.

"Keep the light on her," he called to Gabriel as he started climbing. The rough surface of the shaft offered plenty of handholds.

Sam's feet swung as she struggled, and she clipped his shoulder as he climbed past her. As the shaft closed in around him, it became easier to find places to grip, and he moved faster. He risked a quick glance up at the demon, braced in the narrower section above.

Not this time. Not again. Not Sam.

Her back was to him, so he couldn't see her face and the fear that must be written there. He drew level with her and climbed higher, towards the twin points of white light above him. The demon's eyes.

"Gabriel! Open the chest!"

The Mime moved suddenly, scrambled past him, nearly knocking him from his precarious grip. It dropped into the chamber below.

The light from Gabriel's torch wavered, but Elliot could still see where the rope was. Sam's struggles were slowing, and he prayed it was because she realised what he was doing, not because she was losing consciousness. Once he was clear of her head, he took a deep breath and jumped. His hands grasped the coarse hemp, and he locked his ankles and knees around it to keep from slipping down. He let go with one hand, pulled the dagger from his belt and brought it to the rope below his handhold.

He focused every ounce of willpower he had into the cut. The blade sliced through the fibres like a razor. The rope parted. Sam dropped. Dangling from one arm, he swung his legs and dropped down beside her. Pain jolted up his shins as he hit the hard surface, and the dagger clattered to the ground.

His head snapped up, but the demon remained hidden in the shadows. Gabriel's torch, propped against a rock while he worked on the chest, still highlighted the trailing rope above them.

Behind him, Sam coughed and gasped. He crawled to her side, reaching for her in the darkness. Her arms locked around his neck.

"It's alright, I've got you." His arms closed around her. Her gasping breath warmed his neck, a tangible signal that she was still alive. He'd come so close to losing her that his whole being shivered with the thought. He sucked in the scent of her hair where his cheek pressed against her, then turned her head and found her lips with his. He needed to taste that breath that said she was still whole, still Sam, still with him.

She tensed for a fraction of a second, then tightened her hold around his neck and parted her lips against his, deepening the kiss.

"Elliot!" Gabriel's shout from across the chamber pulled them apart. He'd recovered Sam's torch and picked up the locked chest, but the Mime advanced on him, katana raised to the hip. Elliot could see it clearly now, the bright metal reflecting the torchlight.

"Help Gabriel open the chest," he said to Sam. He collected the dagger and rose to his feet. "Demon!"

The Mime's head swung round and it trained burning white eyes on him.

"I know who you are. You're the one who murdered my brother."

Its mouth curved into a malevolent grin and it pivoted to face him fully, sword held loosely at its side. Elliot tightened his grip on the dagger and stepped cautiously around the chamber, positioning himself between the Mime and his friends.

"You killed the girl, Chelsea, and then you went after him."

Still holding the sword, the demon brought its gloved hands together, clapping slowly, silently.

"I'm not letting you take any more lives. This ends here."

The Mime held up its free hand like a sock puppet and moved its fingers and thumb, a mouth mocking his words. Then it charged. Elliot twisted sharply out of the way before he was run through. The Mime wheeled on him. He grabbed its sword arm in his left hand, fighting to hold it back as he jabbed the dagger up towards its ribs.

"Don't kill him!" Gabriel yelled.

A last-minute twist of his wrist angled the blade into the Mime's side, carving a shallow, bloody line. It staggered back and clutched at the wound, eyes burning brighter still. Blood stained the gloves for an instant, then disappeared, absorbed into the fabric as if it was being devoured.

The Mime charged again, sword held level with its shoulder like a lance. Elliot ducked, and swept his leg out. The Mime tripped, sprawling across the slippery stone floor.

He glanced over his shoulder to where Gabriel and Sam huddled in the entrance to one of the tunnels, working on the chest. "I don't know how long I can hold it!" he yelled.

"We nearly have it," Gabriel replied.

A solid ball of rock, the size of a cricket ball, slammed into his chest and sent him reeling. His foot slipped and he crashed onto his backside. The dagger fell from his hand and skittered across the chamber floor. He looked up as the rock faded into glittering specks beside him. Across the chamber, the Mime drew back the pocket of a comically over-sized slingshot. A second stone bullet rocketed towards him and he threw his hand up to shield his face. The missile glanced off his forearm with a jagged stab of pain.

This time, before the rock dissipated, he grabbed it and flung it back at the Mime. It faded in mid-air, showering the demon with bright dust. The Mime flinched, and Elliot used the moment of distraction to scramble to his feet and cover the few paces between them. He ducked a third rock as it flew towards him, knocked the slingshot from the Mime's hand, and grabbed it by the front of its filthy black sweatshirt, trying not to gag at the foul stench that rolled off the host body.

"Not so easy when we can see it coming, huh?"

The Mime sneered at him and threw a punch that connected squarely with his chin, snapping his jaw shut and leaving a faint iron tang in his mouth. He growled through his aching teeth and drove the Mime backwards. They ducked out of the pool of torchlight and thumped hard against the side of the chamber.

Elliot braced one forearm across the demon's neck while it writhed, silently snarling. "Gabriel?"

"Almost there!"

The Mime's booted foot connected painfully with his shin. He cursed. When a second blow landed on his knee his leg buckled and he lost his grip. The Mime slithered out of his grasp and vanished down the tunnel, lost in the pitch darkness.

Elliot retreated towards Gabriel and Sam, straining for a glimpse of white eyes from the tunnel mouth. A glint of steel caught his eye and he recovered the dropped dagger from where it lay.

A crunch of rotten wood echoed through the chamber, followed by the tortured squeal of rusty metal hinges. Gabriel lifted a slim metal box from inside the chest. It was tarnished and pitted with black corrosion. He opened the lid. Inside, a small clay tablet nestled in a lining of decayed velvet. Elliot moved closer to see. A series of symbols impressed into the clay were clearly a language of some sort, but not one he recognised. Gabriel mouthed silent syllables as he studied them, then snapped the metal case shut.

"We have it."

"Then let's get out of here," Sam said, her voice croaky. She locked eyes with Elliot and rubbed her bruised neck.

He gathered her torch, his mind half on the demon and half on the fact he was going to have to crawl back through that tight passage. He pointed the torch at the tunnel mouth. As he took a first step towards it, the Mime materialised from the shadows and barred the way.

Gabriel ushered Elliot to one side and stepped forwards, drawing himself up. "I command you leave this place, demon. You who reside on this Earthly plane in the vessel created by Edward Penrose. You who are known as the wielder of the unseen, the shaper of air. Whose true name I now hold in my hand." He held the metal case level with his head.

The Mime froze.

"Hear your name and quit this realm forever... Mastho."

A thick silence descended over them. The demon stood utterly frozen, captured in the torch beams as if they chained it in place. Elliot stared, unblinking, afraid to miss the demon's final moment. Gabriel's silhouetted shoulders rose and fell with tense breaths.

Then the Mime spun, squeezed into the narrow passageway and fled.

Gabriel's shoulders sagged and he glanced back at Elliot. "Interesting."

"What do you mean, interesting? I thought the name was supposed to kill it," Elliot said. It was the *only* thing able to kill it. The Penroses had spent decades looking for it for precisely that reason. How could it not work?

"Apparently not."

"But it did leave," Sam added.

Elliot and Gabriel both stared at her.

"I'm just saying."

40

Elliot took Sam's torch and shone it through the narrow opening.

"I can't see anything," he said. There was a tremor to his voice which Sam thought was nothing to do with the demon. Had he known he was claustrophobic before they came down here? It wasn't something she'd ever seen in him before but then maybe this was the first time he'd ever done anything like this.

"I'll go first," she said. The cramped tunnel didn't bother her and she was the least likely to get stuck.

He shot a pained expression her way then closed his eyes. "No. I have to. In case it's waiting with any traps. I'll be able to see them." He squeezed into the tunnel on his belly and crawled through. Sam caught a few muttered curses. He was probably trying to get angry at it on purpose.

She followed and then Gabriel. They recovered their bags and began to trudge through the mine tunnels to the surface.

When the Mime's rope had yanked her off her feet, she'd thought that was it – her turn not to make it through this. She'd barely been able to think past the pain in her neck, and then only because of the numbing terror. Even though she'd been dimly aware of Elliot climbing up, and then the jolt up her legs as she hit the ground, she'd still thought she was dying. Until the electric jolt from that kiss convinced her she was still alive.

She rubbed her neck as Elliot helped Gabriel over the lip of the first vertical shaft. Immediately after, as she'd helped Gabriel with the chest, she'd been able to ignore the pain. Now it was getting worse again.

"What do we do now, Gabriel? I thought the name was all we needed," Elliot asked.

"As with all weapons, one must know how to wield it." Gabriel adjusted his satchel strap and directed the light of his torch down the next section. "I tried only a simple command. I suspect we need a different approach."

"Like what?" Sam asked. She'd been so focused on getting here, acquiring the name, that she hadn't even *thought* beyond that point.

"A full exorcism."

"Didn't we try that already?"

"Yes, but with the name the result should be quite different."

They followed the tunnel towards the second shaft, single file – Elliot at the front, Gabriel at the rear.

"Are you sure it's going to be that simple?" Elliot asked.

Gabriel didn't answer for a few paces. Sam twisted to look over her shoulder, instantly regretting it as pain flared in her bruised neck.

"The Penroses would not have dedicated so much energy to finding the name without the knowledge of how to use it," Gabriel said. "If there is more to it, the journals will hold the information we need." A waver in his voice belied his certainty. Sam suspected he was trying to convince himself as much as them. It was supposed to be over. Now instead they were virtually back to square one. No clear plan. It was exhausting, and that was surely affecting Elliot and Gabriel just as much as it was her. She tried not to think too far ahead. Focus on the first task.

Reach the surface.

"Do you really think the demon is going to grant us the luxury of time to research?" Elliot asked, as he walked stooped in the low passage.

"It's hard to say. Now we possess the name it may try to eliminate us before we can strike, or it may retreat. Remember, we have only until the full moon tonight before our window of opportunity closes."

"You think it might just try to wait us out?"

"That is a distinct possibility, yes."

If the demon went into hiding, it didn't bode well for their chances of stopping it. Even if they could figure out how to use the name, they'd have to find the Mime first. But they had to try. From the description in William Penrose's journal, when the demon crossed through a portal, the host body was consumed by fire. It wasn't wholly clear what happened to the vessel – the gloves – or how they returned, but that wasn't the point. Whether the host was a willing partner or a victim, either way he was a human being. If they didn't stop the demon, the host would die.

At the base of the second shaft, the first reassuring fingers of daylight filtered down. Elliot offered Sam a hand up at the top. He kept hold of her fingers for slightly longer than necessary, but she tried not to attach too much meaning to it. In the darkness it was hard to read his expression.

The air grew fresher as they neared the entrance. Eventually, Sam emerged cautiously into the open, blinking in the bright daylight. Elliot kept glancing at her, a wary look in his eyes. She wondered where they stood now, after that kiss. It had happened in a moment of desperation, but she desperately needed it to mean more. All her doubts and indecision had vanished. It felt right.

She rubbed her stiff, bruised neck.

"Do you still have the map?" Elliot asked, moving up close

beside her.

She nodded, unfolding the map on top of her pack. "The shortest way to the road is the route we were originally going to use to get here."

Elliot crouched beside her and flashed a brief, tense smile. She pushed her hair behind her ears, then traced the line with her finger. "We need to go just over a mile south, and then we should be able to find this track which leads to the road. Maybe we can hitch a ride, or at least get a phone signal from there."

"Alright. Are you ready?"

She nodded, stowed the map and swung her pack onto her shoulders.

Back the way they'd come, the Beardown Tors were visible in the distance where the fog had lifted. Somewhere over there, Liam's body lay in a dirty crevice, half hidden under the rocks, exposed and alone. His blood still stained her sleeves and lingered in her throat, metallic, earthy.

"What are we going to do about Liam? We can't just leave him up there."

"We have to," Elliot said. "I'll make the call later, tell the police where to find the body." His face was pale and pained, highlighting the bruise darkening on his jawline.

"But he's... It just doesn't seem right, leaving him out in the open."

"I know. But right now we need to get somewhere safe."

Their eyes met for a moment, then he laid his hand on her shoulder and dropped his gaze. She knew he was right. The important thing right now was staying alive long enough to reach the church, where they could catch their breath and plan their next steps in safety.

———•———

The mist had burned off while they were underground and, as they traipsed across the rough terrain, the lonely landscape rolled away for miles around them, basking under the July sun. Bees foraged the gorse bushes, crickets chirped in the grass. Sam clicked off a few photos, as a way to occupy her mind. They walked in virtual silence, concentrating on overcoming exhaustion for the forty-five minutes it took to reach the start of the track.

Elliot and Gabriel seemed to relax once they felt hard-packed gravel under their feet leading them back to civilisation. The lane sloped down past a plantation of conifers behind a low, grass-topped stone wall on the right. The going was easy, but Sam's neck throbbed with every step, growing stiffer and more painful. She didn't want to complain, but she desperately hoped there would be time to stop for an ice pack and some painkillers later.

In the distance, behind them, came the sound of running footsteps.

Without turning, she glanced at Elliot to check he'd heard it too. He tilted his head, listening, and one hand reached for the dagger tucked through his belt.

Gabriel drew his scissor-crucifix from his satchel.

The footsteps were gaining on them.

"Head for the trees," Elliot whispered to Sam, nodding towards the dense pines and the wall.

"What are you going to do?"

He gripped the dagger in front of him. "Try to slow it down."

She could hear the skid of each step behind them now. Any second it would be on them. She tensed, ready to run.

"Go!" Elliot barked, shoving her to the side in front of him. He wheeled with the dagger raised as she darted for the wall and vaulted over.

"Whoa! Jaysus! Mind where you're waving that fecking thing!"

Her heart stuttered and she fell in a heap on the far side of the wall. Ignoring the searing pain in her neck, she scrambled to her knees to peer over the top.

Gabriel stood behind Elliot, holding him up as he staggered backwards. The dagger clattered to the ground as he stared, wide-eyed, gaping, speechless.

Liam stood on the path, his hands held up in an attitude of surrender. His clothes hung ragged at the back, still soaked with blood. He held up one finger, then bent over. His shoulders heaved with deep, racking coughs, and he spat off to the side.

Sam climbed over the wall and approached him, her legs shaking so much she thought she might collapse. She'd never *seen* a spirit before, but with everything else she could do maybe it was possible. But then, Gabriel and Elliot could see him too. And his feet made noise on the ground. Ghosts didn't have footsteps, did they?

"You were dead," she said. "You were definitely dead. I checked. Twice." She'd *felt* the life leave him.

He put his hands out to the side. "And I feel dead and all. But don't worry, I'm not getting any human flesh cravings, so I'm not going with zombie."

"What?"

"My thoughts exactly."

Elliot seemed to regain a little composure, enough to stand up without Gabriel's support. He picked up the dagger, frowning at it like the world had lost all reason.

Sam walked up to Liam and poked him.

He jerked away. "Hey!"

"Just checking."

"Checking what?"

"That you're not a ghost."

He batted her hand away as she tried to poke him again. "Hey, still flesh and blood here. Literally."

He twisted to show her his back and she gasped. Though it had seemed far worse up on the moor, the ragged wound still oozed blood. She reached to touch it and he spun around, glowering at her. "Quit poking me, woman!"

"Does it hurt?"

"Of course it feckin' hurts!"

She took in his pale skin, the dark circles under his eyes and the sweat on his temples, and something in her mind finally clicked. He was alive.

He was *alive*.

She threw her arms around his neck and he stumbled backwards.

"Hey, hey, easy!" he cried, catching hold of her around her waist.

She buried her face against his neck where his skin was warm. His pulse quivered against her lips and cheek. Regular and strong and wonderful and alive. Tears pricked her eyes.

"It's okay. I'm okay," Liam murmured.

Her stomach cramped painfully with the terrible realisation that she'd made a mistake. She'd left him for dead, when he wasn't, and he'd been forced to find his way off the moor alone. Alone and badly injured.

"I'm sorry. I'm sorry we left you. I thought… I thought…"

"Hey, it's okay. I'm here, aren't I?" He gently pushed her back, and she wiped her eyes on her sleeve. Then he doubled over as another coughing fit racked his body.

Sam dug out a bottle of water to hand him. She glanced at Elliot and saw the same guilt that churned in her gut reflected in his face.

Gabriel replaced the ward in his satchel. "This is most… unusual."

Liam braced himself on his knees and coughed again. "Don't go reaching for any fancy words there, Gabe."

Sam found a bandage and a dressing in the bottom of her pack and nodded towards the wall. Liam walked over and sat down.

"Do you remember what happened?" Gabriel asked.

"I remember getting shot in the back and passing out," Liam said. "Then I came to, alone. I don't remember much in between, except that I know there's something I can't remember, know what I mean?"

He must have figured out how to get here somehow, and by sheer luck they'd chosen the same route and hadn't missed each other. She gestured for him to take his top off and climbed over to the other side of the wall so she could bandage the wound.

"No, no, hang on. You were definitely dead," Elliot finally said, as if only just catching up with the conversation. "I wouldn't have… We did check." He looked Liam straight in the eye, begging forgiveness.

"I know," Liam said simply. "Don't ask me to explain it. I don't know. Maybe someone up there likes me." He shrugged and winced, then pulled his shredded hoodie and T-shirt off.

Clotted blood clung to his skin, thick and sticky. Sam touched her fingers to his tattoos. Someone?

The gaping hole in him made her want to retch. It was so raw. Even so, she tried to examine it before she applied the dressing. The edges had the appearance of a wound several days old, not something that had happened only a few hours ago. Impossible, but there it was. She cleaned off the worst of the blood and bandaged him up.

He put his bloody clothes back on. "So, did you get it?" he asked. "The name?"

"We did," Gabriel said. "And we must waste no time." He began to lead the way down the slope. Elliot helped Sam over the wall to the path.

As they started to follow, a black shape darted from between the trees at the side of the track and vaulted the wall. Gabriel backpedalled, but the Mime landed cat-like in front of him, its hands clasped around the handle of something by its waist.

"No!" Elliot yelled. He launched into a sprint as the Mime thrust its blade deep into Gabriel's stomach.

Gabriel gasped, doubled over in pain. Elliot threw himself at the Mime and tackled it to the ground. Sam and Liam rushed forwards, catching Gabriel between them as he fell.

Sam stripped off her T-shirt from under her hoodie and handed it to Liam to staunch the flow of blood. She couldn't feel the sword. It must have pulled free or dissolved.

Elliot pinned the demon and grabbed its wrist. He smashed its hand on the ground repeatedly and shifted his weight so he could restrain its whole body with one hand and his knees. He drew the dagger.

"I can't kill you yet, but I bet you won't find things so easy if I cut your eyes out."

Sam's gut seized as Elliot lowered the point of the dagger towards the demon's face. All she could think about was what it would be like trapped inside, unable to fight or even scream.

"Elliot, don't! The host! Please!"

He hesitated. The demon wriggled and pulled one hand free. It struck him across the face, throwing him off balance, enough to squirm out from under him. Then it took off down the slope. With a few ungainly hops, it threw its leg over an invisible shape and began to pedal, hovering off the ground.

Elliot rose to a runner's crouch. He tensed, and for a moment Sam thought he might do something stupid like give chase.

"Elliot!"

His head snapped round to her, then his gaze settled on Gabriel, sagging in her arms. He closed his eyes and then, with a sharp shake of his head, stood and strode over. For a moment he'd seemed like a completely different person, cold and violent in a way she didn't know he had in him.

Gabriel gripped Sam's arm and sucked in tight breaths through clenched teeth.

"He's bleeding heavily," Liam said. "But it went in off to one side. If we can get him to a hospital…"

He left the rest unsaid; *if* they could get him there, then *maybe* he had a chance.

Elliot nudged Sam out of the way and pulled Gabriel's arm over his shoulder. "Come on, you're not allowed to die. We need you, damn it."

41

Liam took Gabriel's other arm, keeping Sam's balled up T-shirt pressed to the wound. He stumbled every few paces, still clearly in a lot of pain himself, and Elliot had to take most of Gabriel's weight.

Scurrying along behind them, Sam slung Gabriel's bag over her shoulder. The pain in her neck flared where it pulled against her bruises, but she needed her hands free to root in the pocket of her own pack for her mobile. She held the phone up, searching for a signal, but they were still too far from civilisation.

She kept checking as they went. It was slow going; Gabriel moaned in pain, struggling to put pressure on his right leg. They'd been hiking all morning, on barely any sleep and not much to eat, and they were all exhausted. Elliot might have been hiding it better until then, but, after practically carrying Gabriel for the fifteen minutes it took to reach the road, sweat dripped down the side of his face and soaked his shirt between his shoulder blades.

Thirty yards or so from the road, Sam finally had one bar of signal. She dialled the emergency services. They kept moving while she explained to the call handler that Gabriel was conscious but bleeding, and they had no idea how bad it really was. The woman instructed her to do all the things they were already doing and told her an ambulance was on its way. It would be with them in forty minutes.

"Forty minutes? Are you crazy?" she shouted to the phone.

Elliot set Gabriel down on part of the wall that had crumbled beside the road. Liam sagged against the stone, on the verge of collapse, but stayed with Gabriel while Elliot walked out into the middle of the road. He waved his arms at an approaching car.

"Yes, I'm aware we're a long way from the hospital," Sam said. "Don't you have, like, a helicopter or something?"

The silver people carrier skidded to a halt and the driver leapt out. A middle-aged man wearing a polo shirt and tan trousers. He looked like he'd been on the way to the golf course.

"Are you fucking mad?" he yelled, storming up to Elliot.

"Never mind," Sam said to the dispatcher. "We'll hitch a ride." She hung up, ran to Gabriel's side and helped him stand. He leaned heavily on her shoulder and she gritted her teeth. Liam, pale and sweating, coughed and spat, then dug up some inner strength to help lift Gabriel.

"I'm very sorry," Elliot said, approaching the driver, "but we really need your help."

The driver glanced at Gabriel and took in the blood-soaked bundle in Liam's hand, wadded against his side. "Jesus Christ!" He backed away, glancing at the open driver's door like he was judging the distance to make a run for it.

Elliot tensed and Sam wondered what he'd do if the man tried to leave.

"As you can see, we need assistance," he said. "You're taking us to the nearest hospital, now." He opened the rear door for Sam. His tone left no room for argument. The driver gave it his best shot anyway.

"Are you nuts? That man needs an ambulance!"

"Ambulance is half an hour away. We can be at the hospital by then if we move now."

Sam crawled in and scooched across to the far side.

"Fuck!" the driver cursed. "Why me?"

"Must be your lucky day, mate," Liam said. He turned his back to the man as he helped Gabriel to climb in. The man's face blanched at the sight of Liam's shredded, blood-soaked clothes. He must have been wondering what kind of lunatics he'd encountered.

Sam crunched up against the far door and twisted sideways so she could hold Gabriel's head in her lap. Liam squeezed in by his feet, hunched over, keeping pressure on the wound.

Elliot slammed the door, then jogged round to the front. Sam watched him through the side window. Before he climbed into the front passenger seat, he paused and scanned their surroundings – checking for any sign of the demon.

He swung into the seat and buckled up. "Drive fast, but if I say stop, do it, even if you can't see anything to stop for."

"Why?"

"The thing that did that…" He nodded over his shoulder. "… is still out there."

The man's sideways glance suggested he was having serious second thoughts about leaving the house that morning.

"Drive!" Elliot snapped.

The man flinched and started the car.

The nearest hospital with an emergency department was Plymouth, half an hour away. Sam hugged Gabriel where he lay on her. "Don't worry, you're going to be fine."

"Thank you, Samantha."

"You know you really can just call me Sam. No one calls me Samantha. Not even my parents."

He chuckled softly, then winced.

"Shh. Don't try to talk."

Liam focused intently on the wound in Gabriel's side, as if trying to will it closed. Sam narrowed her eyes. Was that what he was actually doing?

He coughed harshly and grimaced. He seemed to lose more colour as they drove, but he kept one hand on the compress and the other wrapped around Gabriel's wrist, monitoring his pulse.

Gabriel fell unconscious as they hit the outskirts of Plymouth, but his breathing and pulse stayed steady.

When they reached the hospital, Elliot jumped out and raced into the building. He returned with an orderly and a nurse, who between them pulled Gabriel's limp form from the vehicle and loaded him onto a stretcher. Though Liam looked ready to drop dead – again – he went with them, reeling off a string of information until the building swallowed them up.

Sam climbed out while Elliot strode off into the hospital. The driver stood by the front of the car with one hand on his head. She approached cautiously.

"Thank you," she said. "You probably saved his life."

He blinked, as if he didn't understand the words she was saying.

"I'm sorry about the blood," she added. "And for ruining whatever you were on your way to do."

"Oh, er…"

She took her purse from her pack and fished out a business card for *Weird News*. "We'll pay for the cleaning."

He glanced past her into the rear of the car, then took the card and studied it for a second. Sam was about to walk away when he raised his gaze.

"I know this," he said, vaguely. "My daughter reads this."

"Well, there you go," Sam said. "You can tell her you met the editor."

At that moment Elliot came striding out, searching for her.

"I have to go. Call us."

He nodded, still pale with shock.

She joined Elliot by the door.

"They've taken him straight to resus," he said.

That didn't sound good. She rubbed her bruised neck as the last of her energy ebbed away, leaving her raw and tearful. She wanted to curl up and hide.

Elliot lifted his hand as if he was going to touch her, but stopped and drew back.

She couldn't stand not knowing what the deal was now, since he'd kissed her. "We should—"

"You should get that checked," he said, indicating her neck.

She stared at him for a moment. Was he really going to deflect her like that? Change the subject? Tears pricked her eyes, but she blinked them away. Exhaustion always made her irrational and emotional, and she was probably reading too much into it. She rubbed her stiff neck again. It was agonisingly sore. Maybe she *should* deal with that first.

She eyed Elliot and the tension in the way he held himself, like he was ready to bolt. No, he was definitely avoiding the subject.

"Okay, fine. But when I get back, we are having a conversation."

42

Elliot sat in the waiting room while the doctors treated his friends. A dozen other people occupied the plastic seats, all keeping their heads down, minds on their own pain and worries.

After the doctors checked Sam over, they sent her for X-rays to make sure there was no damage to her vertebrae. The last he'd heard they were prepping Gabriel for surgery. Liam hadn't returned yet.

Physically, Elliot had made it through relatively unscathed. The few bumps and scrapes he'd gathered didn't require attention, but the feel of Liam and Gabriel's blood on his hands wouldn't fade, even though he'd washed them several times. Worse, every time he closed his eyes, he saw Sam dying with that rope around her neck.

He didn't know how much more he could take. When the Mime attacked Gabriel, it was like he'd watched the scene unfold from a distance, while some animal took him over. If the man in the car hadn't agreed to drive them, he'd been ready to knock him out and take the keys.

That wasn't him.

Then there was the fact he'd kissed Sam. While they'd still been escaping, he'd avoided analysing it, but now he had nothing to do but sit and think. He'd crossed a major line and he couldn't pin down exactly how he felt about it. No, that was a lie. He knew exactly how he felt. He'd known the moment she kissed him back, arms tight around his neck like that was where she belonged. He wanted that line to stay crossed. It was time he stopped lying to himself.

He was staring into space when Liam dropped into the seat beside him and handed him a can of Coke. He took it but didn't open it.

"Do you want to see something weird?" Liam asked.

"What?"

Liam turned his back and lifted his blood-stained top. The bandages Sam had applied were gone, and, where the Mime's arrow had pierced his flesh, there was now nothing more than a big, angry scab, two inches to the left of his spine. It looked awful. It also looked at least a week old.

"Weird," was all Elliot could come up with.

Liam pulled his top down and slouched in the seat with his knees out so only the tops of his shoulders pressed against the back rest. "So, you're the lost heir of some bad-ass family of demon hunters, Sammy's a ghost whisperer, and apparently I can't die. And, believe me, I have no idea what the hell's up with that."

Elliot nodded. That about summed it up.

"This a normal week for you?" Liam asked.

"Not as such."

Liam slurped from his can and let out a shuddering sigh. "Do you reckon Gabriel might know anything about…?" He indicated himself with a wave of his hand. "I mean *once* was… I'm telling you, I'm freaking out here."

"He might," Elliot said absently, watching a young man in paint-smeared tradesman's overalls, bloody cloth bound round his left thumb, try to open a bag of crisps one-handed.

"You know, I don't think it's just me and all," Liam continued.

"Hmm?"

"I've had patients of mine pull through when they shouldn't." You know, more than I can chalk up to luck." He took a deep breath and rubbed a hand over his short hair. "Like, back in Oxford? I'd have bet money on Fiona bleeding out. I thought she had no chance. Then suddenly it seemed like it wasn't as bad as I'd thought. Looking back, I think maybe it was me. I did something."

"Huh."

"Well, you're Mr Chatty right now, aren't you?"

Elliot shook his head and forced a smile. "Sorry. Just worried."

Liam's eyes narrowed. "She's fine. They're just being thorough."

Elliot sat forwards with his elbows on his knees and pinched the bridge of his nose under his glasses. It wasn't just Sam's injuries he was worried about. She deserved an explanation about that kiss, and he didn't know what to say to her.

"Feel free to tell me to feck off, but what the hell is it with you two?"

"Excuse me?"

Liam sat forwards with him. "You're both into each other, but you dance around it for some reason I can't figure out."

Elliot fixed his eyes on the empty chair opposite. "Why do you care? I'd have thought you'd be happy we aren't together."

"Whoa, whoa." Liam put both hands up. "I've got no agenda with Sammy. She's a nice girl and, okay, there might have been some flirting, but I never meant to… If you think I crossed a line then I'm sorry."

Elliot frowned, trying to pin down what Liam had actually done to make him suspicious. Maybe he'd only ever been reading meaning into the way he and Sam acted together.

"So?" Liam prompted.

"It's complicated."

"That's not a reason. Just uncomplicate it."

Elliot blinked at him. "What?"

Liam glanced across the waiting room, then clapped Elliot on the shoulder. "That's my cue. I'm going to go find some clothes."

At the far end of the waiting room, Sam emerged from the pharmacy clutching a paper bag. She scanned the room. When her eyes settled on him she smiled and walked over.

He stood as she reached him. "Hey. What's the damage?"

"Nothing serious. Just deep bruising. They said it'll probably be stiff for weeks though."

"Did they ask how it happened?"

"Yeah. I said it was a climbing accident. I don't think they believed me, but they can't stop me leaving. Is there any news?"

She took the seat Liam had vacated and Elliot sat back down.

"About Gabriel? Nothing more yet. They're trying to stabilise him before surgery." They shared a look that summed up the situation. If Gabriel died, they were in serious trouble.

Sam rubbed her neck and winced.

"I'll get us some coffee," Elliot said, shifting out of his seat.

She smiled. "Thanks."

There was a vending machine at the side of the room and he fished a few coins from his pocket. While the machine whirred, he watched Sam from a distance – bruised and exhausted, filthy, and covered in blood. She tucked her hair behind her ear as she read the notes on her medication with her nose wrinkled. For once he tried not to suppress the flush of affection that warmed him, or the paralysing jolt that followed. She meant more to him than anyone, and he did want to be with her, but if he fucked it up he might lose her from his life completely. He had to face the truth – he'd been hiding behind technicalities because that possibility terrified the shit out of him.

Closing his eyes, he took a calming breath. He didn't have to have all the answers right now. He only needed to make a choice to give it a chance. The technicalities he could deal with – uncomplicate them, as Liam had put it – if he wanted to.

He returned to their spot with two cups and held one out. She took it gingerly.

"We should talk," he said at the same time as she looked up and said, "We need to talk."

She smiled and some of his apprehension melted away. He sat beside her and took a sip of scalding hot coffee, noting the way she twined her fingers together around her cup and held it up like a shield, the same way she held her camera when she was scared.

He hated that he made her feel that way. "I'm sorry——"

"Don't take it back," she whispered.

"What?"

She glanced up, eyes moist. "Please, don't say it didn't mean anything."

"I wasn't going to say that." He wasn't sure where he'd planned to start, but it definitely hadn't been with that.

He set his cup down on the floor, took hers and did the same. Then he slipped his hand into hers and rubbed his thumb across her knuckles. She kept her head down, eyes on their hands.

"I was scared I'd lost you," he said quietly. "I've always had it in my mind that you were... that we're colleagues and that's the end of it. It wouldn't be appropriate so you're... off limits. I never allowed myself consider that we could be... more." He swallowed hard. "But we already are, aren't we?"

She lifted her eyes to his. "You are to me."

The way the light caught her damp lashes added a sparkle to her eyes. He took a deep breath. "I'm not supposed to... to feel the way I do about you. I'm supposed to be your employer."

"Do you think I care about that?"

"No, I know. But I do. I don't want to be that person. I don't *like* that person. I can't – it wouldn't be fair on either of us. You understand, right? I can't have that kind of control over you. I'd be too scared I might use it."

Her eyes filled with tears and her breath caught as the first of them dropped down her cheeks. "Please don't say that. It doesn't matter—"

"Hey, hey, let me finish." He brushed a tear off her cheek with his other hand. The feel of her jaw cupped in his palm and the hot flush to her face reassured him he was doing the right thing. "I just mean that if we do this, we have to go into it as equals. So, when we get home, I'm going to sign half my stake in the company over to you."

She blinked and wiped her eyes with her sleeve.

"*Weird News* is as much yours as it is mine now anyway," he added.

She frowned, then her eyes widened. "Wait, are you being serious?"

"Equal stake, equal salary. Partners. I mean it. If you want it, it's yours."

"You can't do that!"

He smiled at the incredulity in her voice. "Of course I can."

"But... But... isn't that a bit extreme? Are you sure you don't want to think about it?"

He looked her square in the eye. "I don't need to think about it. I know this is what I want. You and me, doing this..." He waved his hand as if he could encapsulate everything from the last two weeks with a gesture. "... together."

"You mean, *together*, together?"

"Yes." He tilted his head forwards until his forehead touched hers and closed his eyes. "If it's what you want too." He held his breath, waiting for her to say something.

"You know I do," she whispered. She dipped her head and brushed her lips against his, soft and sweet.

When she pulled back, she gazed into his eyes and, with a slow curve of her lips, her smile brightened into something mischievous and excited. He couldn't remember the last time he'd seen her express such joy. It lit up her face, brought a shine to her eyes.

An approaching figure dragged his attention away. He glanced up as a shadow fell over them.

"You brought Mr Cushing in?" the doctor asked. The woman's expression gave very little away, and Elliot braced himself for bad news.

"That's right," he said as he stood. "How is he?"

"He's not in any immediate danger. We're taking him into surgery now to repair some damage to his bowel, but it looks like he's been remarkably lucky."

"That's good to hear."

Sam stood and slipped her hand into Elliot's. "Thank you, doctor."

The doctor nodded. "It'll be a couple of hours. If you leave a number, we can call you when he's in recovery." She indicated the reception desk, then departed.

Sam still held Elliot's hand. "See, he's going to be fine."

"I know." He put his arms round her, and she rested her head on his shoulder. "And so are we."

43

There was little to do but wait. When Liam returned, freshly dressed in a new grey T-shirt and black joggers from a shop in the hospital foyer, he mentioned there was also a coffee shop with a lounge. Sam suggested they relocate, rest and recharge.

Elliot sent them on ahead. He still had Gabriel's satchel. Standing outside the glass entrance doors, he fished out the demon hunter's clamshell phone and dialled Father Monroe's number from the contacts list.

"Gabriel! I was getting worried," the priest said when he answered.

"Actually, it's Elliot. Gabriel is… Can you get to Plymouth?"

"No problem. Where are you?"

"We're at the hospital. Gabriel's been badly hurt. He's going to be alright, but… You said something before about some kind of sanctuary ritual?" It wasn't just *their* safety he was worried about. Gabriel's satchel still held the stone tablet bearing the demon's name, and carrying it around made him nervous. Earlier, he'd tried to take a picture on his phone, but after a few minutes the file corrupted. If the tablet was destroyed, the last remaining record would be their memory of the word, Mastho.

"What happened?" Father Monroe asked. "Gabriel called yesterday to say you'd seen the demon and found some information, but…"

Elliot pinched the bridge of his nose. "It's a long story. I can explain everything when you get here."

"But, Gabriel?"

"He's in surgery at the moment but there's nothing to worry about."

"Alright, I'll be there in an hour or so."

Elliot frowned. "You're not in Oxford?"

"No, Okehampton. I followed you down this morning."

Finally, a little luck going their way. "Okay, good. We could use your help. How's Fiona?"

"Stable, but she'll have a long recovery. Sit tight."

Father Monroe signed off, and Elliot relaxed against the wall, trying to quieten his mind for a few minutes.

Liam emerged from inside, holding a paper cup and a sandwich pack. "There you are. Hope this is okay. Sammy picked yours." He'd regained more colour. Only a trace of a graze remained on his temple from the car crash. The older bruising around his wrists had faded completely.

Elliot took the coffee.

"Sammy said you only have sugar when you're in a good mood, so I left it plain."

"Thanks." He eyed the coffee cup. Was that true?

"So, er, did you call in the cavalry?" He nodded towards Gabriel's phone.

"Something like that."

He followed Liam into the coffee shop, to a quiet corner where Sam lay curled up on a sofa with her hands hugged tight under her chin, eyes closed. She couldn't be asleep yet, but he didn't disturb her all the same. The bruises on her neck had darkened, and he could make out the twist pattern of the thick rope on her skin. The demon was going to pay for that.

He and Liam took chairs either side of the low table. Liam cracked open a can of Coke and slouched with his feet out. He glanced at Sam. "So, er, I guess it's down to us two for now. Do we have a plan?"

Elliot slurped bitter but creamy latte. "Get the journals, that's as far as I've got. I'll ask Jack to drive me up to the church."

"You're going to leave us here?"

Elliot hesitated. "I… Well, I have to—"

"Nah, let me go."

"What?"

Liam shrugged. "You're the one who can see the demon's whatsits; you should be here, keeping an eye on Gabriel and…" He nodded towards Sam. "Besides. I don't think it can kill me."

"You don't know that for certain."

"No? You've said all along, when it kills, it gets super charged, or some shite. It must have known I wasn't dead, but it didn't come back to finish the job, did it? Even though you left me up there."

Elliot twisted in his seat to face him. "About that…"

He waved a hand. "Ahh, don't worry about it. My point is, it would have been easy."

"So why didn't it kill you?"

"Bingo."

It made sense. Either the demon *couldn't* kill Liam, or there was something about him that meant it *chose* not to finish him off. But still. "That's a pretty flimsy theory to stake your life on."

"What can I say? I used to be a dab hand at the blackjack tables."

"Used to?"

Liam grinned at him. "We've all got past shite to deal with, right?"

Elliot let out a wry laugh. "That's true. Alright, you go. Maybe when Gabriel's awake we can start work on a plan here too."

Liam's phone buzzed. Elliot watched him as he texted one-handed, holding his can in the other. Up on the moors, when he'd believed Liam was dead, he'd regretted not taking time to get to know him. He'd treated Liam badly, projecting his own insecurity about Sam when there'd been no real reason to. For once though, he had a chance to make it right.

"Someone missing you, back in Oxford?" he asked.

Liam did a bit of a double take, then pocketed his phone. "Just workmates, asking why I'm not in."

"Is it causing problems?"

"Nah, I called round a couple of people last night and swapped a few shifts. It's cool. They're just being nosey."

Elliot smiled as he unwrapped his sandwich, and they slipped into chatting about life beyond the insanity of the last few days. He hadn't sat and talked, simply talked – except maybe with Sam – since before he left London. Maybe not even then. London had been… Everyone had an agenda; you were never not playing the game.

Chatting with Liam now felt comfortingly human. Normal.

When Jack Monroe arrived, Elliot handed Liam the Penrose keys. He stood beside the table to see them off, but didn't walk them out. He didn't want to leave Sam alone. After Liam and the priest departed, he squeezed onto the sofa by her feet, pulled her legs into his lap and tried to rest his eyes with his head tipped back against the cushions.

Too many thoughts chased around his head. He was past exhausted, to the point where the caffeine hit his body like a panic attack: itchy and irritable. Another uncomfortable hour and a half passed before his phone finally rang with the call to say Gabriel was ready for visitors.

He gently shook Sam's shoulder. "He's awake," he said softly.

She sat up, groggy from her nap, combed her fingers through her hair and rubbed her neck with a wince.

———•———

Dressed in a shapeless hospital gown, his legs tucked under the white sheets, Gabriel barely resembled his usual self. He'd been given a bed in a room of two, but the other side was unoccupied, the dividing curtains drawn back.

"How are you feeling?" Sam asked as they entered. She leaned over the bed and gave Gabriel a hug, which Elliot noted he genuinely accepted.

"As well as might be expected. A sword through the torso is certainly a unique experience. One I hope never to repeat."

"I'm glad you're okay," Sam said.

"As am I! Indeed, the doctor I spoke to stressed that I was lucky to be alive. He commended your actions in getting me here so promptly." He glanced at Elliot. "I believe I owe you my life. Again."

"I'm not keeping count," Elliot said, stepping closer. "And I think the one you should really be thanking is Liam."

"Ah yes. Our Mr Townsend has more to him than meets the eye, it seems."

"That mystery may have to wait. We need to talk about the demon and how we're going to stop it."

Gabriel's face dropped. "Indeed."

It was a little past two in the afternoon, which meant they had somewhere in the region of eight hours until moonrise, maybe less. After that, the demon could escape back to its hell dimension at any time, and they may never get another opportunity.

"We contacted Father Monroe. He and Liam are fetching the journals as we speak," Elliot said. "Once they get back, I'm guessing we'll have to plan for him to carry out the exorcism."

Gabriel put a hand over his stitched side. "Perhaps. I fear I am going to be somewhat stuck here." He glanced at Sam. "Samantha, do you think the two of us could have a moment alone?"

"Sure. I'll get us some tea or something." She paused by the door. "You're allowed tea, right?"

Gabriel smiled and nodded.

"Right. Okay."

"We don't need to hide anything from her," Elliot said, after she'd left.

"Perhaps make that decision after you've heard what I have to say."

Elliot drew a chair up from the side of the room and sat facing the demon hunter, with his elbows on his knees.

"I heard you say something, while we were underground. You've encountered this demon in the past, haven't you?"

The revelation that had hit home when he'd seen Sam hanging from the invisible rope returned. "I don't know why I didn't see it before."

"It was the demon that killed your brother?"

He nodded.

Gabriel shifted awkwardly, trying to sit up straighter. "Elliot, I believe your connection to the Mime, through the Penrose dagger, will be vital. Were I able to confront the demon myself, I do not think I could overcome it." The admission clearly rattled him. "Jack also. But you? You may have a chance."

Elliot nodded, unsure how to respond. Deep down he knew Gabriel was right. Gut instinct told him the demon was his to kill, alone. His inheritance.

Gabriel leaned towards him, grimacing. "I spent years tracking the demon Ka after it killed my father. I know how the need for vengeance can become all-consuming. But it can also be a source of strength."

Vengeance. The word had an appealing ring to it. In the first year after James's death, Elliot had tried to seek out what killed him, but there was so little to go on, and he hadn't known a fraction of what he knew now. *Weird News* had been a way to preserve his own sanity. Resigned to the fact that he'd never find what he was looking for, he'd channelled his energy into making amends for what he'd done the best way he knew how.

It never felt like enough.

He looked Gabriel in the eye. "Does it help? Does it make it easier?"

"In some ways, yes. Does it mend what was broken? Never."

Elliot watched the demon hunter settle back against the pillows as his words sank in.

A few moments later, Sam returned. She set a paper cup on Gabriel's bedside table, along with some sugar packets and a stick. "I couldn't remember how you take your tea."

"That will be fine. Thank you."

She handed a cup to Elliot and ran her hand across his shoulders. Elliot watched Gabriel's eyes, sure the man had noticed the gesture.

"So, is everything okay?" she asked.

Elliot glanced up at her. He'd talk to her about James later, when they were alone. "Gabriel thinks my connection to the Mime, through the dagger, is the key. We're going to have to figure out how."

"Indeed. We must keep our wits and play to our strengths if we are to press our advantage." Gabriel picked up his tea, took a sip and let out a murmur of appreciation. Then his eyes fixed on

Sam's hand, still resting on Elliot's shoulder. Elliot put his own hand over hers.

"My father taught me it was best to work alone. To protect those around me from harm." He directed his words at Elliot, and Elliot snatched his hand away from Sam's. "He even kept me at arm's length, especially towards the end. I regret I never questioned why until it was too late."

"Why was it?" Sam asked.

Gabriel smiled wistfully. "I may never know for certain. But I believe it must have been the trauma of my mother's death." He took another sip of tea, as if giving himself time to marshal his thoughts. "My very existence acted as a constant reminder of the pain of her passing. He grew cold. Closed off. I believe he regretted having ever allowed himself to care about someone."

"And he told you it was safer to keep your distance. Never to risk getting attached?" Sam asked.

Gabriel nodded slowly. "If he were pressed to put it into words, he might have said similar."

"That's sad. You don't really believe that, do you?"

"Not any longer, no. I see something in the two of you that my father never entertained; that to care might be a source of strength instead of weakness. I have seen the two of you overcome terrible odds because of the way you support and inspire each other. You must be sure to use that strength."

Elliot glanced up at Sam. He was fully aware of how dependent on her he'd become, but he'd resisted it, pushing her away when he needed her most, precisely because he feared it made him weak. That was going to change.

Liam and Father Monroe returned with the journals shortly after. Once Father Monroe had consecrated Gabriel's hospital room to keep them safe, it was time to knuckle down and plan how to end the demon.

While Gabriel and Jack gave Elliot a crash course in how to perform an exorcism, Sam staked out a spot under the window with Liam and the journals. Even focusing on the last two to three decades, there was a lot to search through, and an hour in they'd found nothing to explain *how* to use the name. Sam's neck ached like crazy despite the prescription painkillers. All they seemed to be doing was making her drowsy.

"Hey, here's something." Liam checked the front page of the diary in his hands. "This is Daniel's last diary. This entry is nineteen ten. I'll read it. 'It has been confirmed that the ritual must be performed under the full moon, which will present a problem. Once the moon rises the demon may flee back to Hell at any moment, as we know it is wont to do if it feels threatened. It will be a challenge to keep it in this realm long enough for the ritual to work. While Charlie continues his quest for the name in Palestine, I must prepare a way to contain the demon at the appropriate time.'"

"Why write ritual if he meant exorcism? Why not just put exorcism? He must mean something more specific. But what?"

"Good question." He watched her rubbing her bruises for a moment, then set his book aside. He inched closer. "Come here, let me take a look."

She glanced at Elliot reciting memorised Latin to Gabriel at the other end of the room, and then shifted until she sat between Liam's knees.

He pulled her hair aside, put his hands on her skin and gently massaged; his fingers felt so warm. She closed her eyes as the worst of the pain and tension melted away.

After a couple of minutes, he withdrew his hands. "Anything?"

She let out a little moan and he chuckled.

"What did you do?" she asked, touching her neck lightly. Though still tender, the raw soreness and swelling seemed much improved.

"Beats me. I've been trying to picture what I want to do, but I don't know if it's making any difference. Maybe all I have to do is touch."

She twisted round to face him. "It's so weird. You're like Mr Miyagi or something."

He clapped and rubbed his hands together with a grin.

Something was nagging Sam. She eyed the book beside him. "Liam, read that passage again."

He picked up the book and found the page. Sam scooched closer to him so she could see over his shoulder. "There. It says, 'it has been confirmed'. Confirmed by whom?"

"Maybe he just means he figured it out."

Sam shook her head. "You've read the way these guys write. They go out of their way to be specific. If he'd meant that he'd have said 'I have confirmed', or 'the evidence confirms', or 'my research confirms', something. 'It *has been* confirmed' though? Not only is he referencing something or someone, he's assuming it's obvious whom. We're definitely missing something." If there was something important, the Penroses would have put it somewhere safe, like they had with the other items. They wouldn't have made it so difficult to work out. "Elliot?"

Elliot twisted round in his seat.

"What did Ethan say again, when you talked to him?" Sam asked.

"Which bit?"

"Right at the end, when you asked him how to use the name."

"Not much. He was running out of time. He said... 'You have everything you need.'"

Sam's nagging feeling told her that something important lurked on the edge of her mind. Something about when Ethan had possessed her. She strained to remember. Not the second time, the *first* time.

"What was in the chest from the crypt?"

Elliot frowned. "The dagger and Ethan's book."

She shook her head. "No, no, there was something else. I felt something in my hand, but Ethan put it down. What was it?"

Elliot's eyes widened and he turned sharply to Gabriel. "The letters! Did you pick up the letters?"

Gabriel swallowed. "I may have overlooked them in my haste."

"They must be important," Sam said. "They wouldn't have put them in the chest if they weren't. Who would they have been writing... Oh! Oh, of course!"

"You have a theory?" Gabriel asked.

"The Vatican! There's tons of references in the journals to the Penroses writing for advice. What if they sent them instructions?"

Elliot checked his watch. "I'll go," he said. "You keep working here. That's if I can borrow your car, Jack?"

Father Monroe handed over his keys. Elliot nodded. "Good. I'll call when I get there."

He headed for the door. Sam scooped up her bag and followed him. He stopped in the corridor and she ran into his back.

He spun round. "Where are you going?"

"With you."

He glanced briefly over her shoulder, back into the room. "I think perhaps you should stay here."

"Uh uh. No way."

"I don't want you getting hurt. After last time... What if something happened again?"

She folded her arms. "I'm coming with you."

"Sam—"

"Did you even listen to what Gabriel said earlier?

"I know—"

"He said we give each other strength and we should use that."

"Yes, but I—"

"You need me. I'm coming."

"Alright, alright." He threw his hands up in surrender and strode off down the corridor.

44

Father Monroe drove a white Range Rover. Sam wasn't sure why, but that wasn't what she'd expected. Elliot fussed with the seat for a while before he put the key in the ignition. Probably not used to the high driving position after the laid-back seats in his BMW.

She wondered whether he'd reported the crashed car in the ditch yet. Probably not. They'd barely had time to think since the day started. Her laptop was still in the boot. Hopefully it would stay put, and the police wouldn't tow it before Elliot could make arrangements.

"So, do you want to go car shopping this weekend?" she asked, as Elliot pulled out of the hospital and headed north-east towards Okehampton.

He glanced at her, frowning.

She put on her most solemn expression. "I'm very sorry, but you're going to have to let her go. I don't think they'll be able to knock the dents out."

That earned a tiny ghost of a smile. She was determined to get another out of him.

"Or, you know, you could just share my car. I'm sure you'll get used to winding the window down to open the driver's door. And in a couple of months you won't even notice the squeaks."

He finally chuckled. "Are you trying to take my mind off things?"

"Is it working?"

"Yes. Thank you."

He relaxed into his seat and put the radio on. Sam let her mind wander while he drove. She was pretty sure they were together now, after their talk in the waiting room, but as to what that actually meant, there was still a lot to figure out. They'd known each other for so long; what if it felt weird or awkward? Right now, fighting the Mime had to take precedent, but it was reassuring to know that Elliot wanted to figure it out too.

There was no sign of the demon on the journey, which probably meant Gabriel was right; it was playing the waiting game. If Mastho could make it to the end of the day and retreat to Hell, it would have months, if not years, to plan for when it returned at the next conjunction.

At around twenty past four they arrived at St Michael's. Parked cars lined the lane, and every space was taken in the car park beside the church. The volume of cars didn't bode well for sneaking in.

Elliot parked the Range Rover, blocking some other cars in, and they climbed out. Sam felt instantly safer the moment they crossed the line of the consecration, even if it was only psychological.

Elliot tried the door and found it unlocked. He handed Sam the car keys. "Wait here, I shouldn't be long."

He slipped inside, and the door swung softly closed behind him. Sam paced across the steps, worrying her thumbnail between her teeth. They needed those letters. But it would be okay; if someone stopped him, he'd talk his way round them. Of course he would.

She walked a few paces along the wall of the church, sat down on the grass with her back to the sun-warmed stone and tried to relax. Far from the damp start up on the moors that morning, the afternoon was hot and hazy; the kind of day for dozing outside, listening to the birds and insects, glass of iced tea or lemonade to hand.

The churchyard wasn't giving her the same creeping sensation of nearby spirits as it had when they'd arrived yesterday. She wondered whether it was only the Penrose spirits who haunted this particular place. Maybe the other weathered, neglected graves scattered through the grounds were too old. After all, what held a spirit to a place? What happened when they were no longer tethered? Did they cross over to some other place, or fade away to nothing?

The door opened and Elliot stepped out, clutching the bundle of letters in one tense hand. When he spotted her, his grip and his shoulders relaxed.

"There's an event going on in the community room," he said as he walked over. "Church was empty and I managed to sneak down." He lowered himself to sit beside her, one knee drawn up with his arm resting across it. His eyes kept darting around the lane, the car park and the churchyard. Alert to any movement, any threats.

Inside the church might be safer, but they didn't have time for awkward questions. This spot inside the consecration would have to do, but it would be foolish to let their guard down.

"So, what have we got?" Sam asked, indicating the letters. He handed them to her and she removed the tie. Arranged in date order, the correspondence evolved through the century. The oldest, from Giles's time, were folded, with cracked wax seals still stuck to the outside, and were handwritten in elegant, ornate script. The most recent, dated nineteen twelve, was typed on flimsy gilded paper tucked into an envelope postmarked Rome.

She started from the beginning and read out each letter.

It sounded like Giles first contacted the Vatican on the advice of the bishop of his diocese. He wrote asking for help and they agreed to dispatch an agent – some kind of holy special forces. From the subsequent letters it sounded like the Vatican's representative hadn't fared too well. Sam wondered if he'd charged in as Gabriel had at first, overconfident and underprepared.

After that first incident, the Vatican charged Giles and his family with eradicating the demon. The correspondence grew sparser over the next few decades, with terse, short replies to whatever Giles had written, telling him to have faith, to trust in God, and so on.

"No wonder Ethan turned to the occult," Sam muttered. "They weren't exactly big with the practical advice."

She read through a few more, into the mid-nineteenth century, until she hit one addressed to Mordecai Penrose.

"Oh, this is interesting," she said.

Elliot was staring across the churchyard, away from her, and she waited until he looked round.

"I'm listening," he said, though his eyes stayed wary and watchful.

She skipped over the pleasantries at the start and read out the relevant part. "'You conclude correctly. The demon's name would surely facilitate a successful exorcism. However, we cannot support this course of action. The crimes of Edward Penrose, lamentable though they were, have created an opportunity for the warriors of God to strike a blow against the legions of the inferno. Exorcism to sever the connection between the demon and the vessel would merely banish the demon's spirit to Hell. While the connection remains, there is a chance to eradicate it from all existence.'"

Elliot took the letter. "So, that explains why they didn't search for the name sooner. They were counselled against it."

"Do you think that means we shouldn't do an exorcism? Surely it doesn't matter whether the demon is banished or eradicated so long as it stops killing people. Screw the Vatican's agenda."

"Hmm. Well, we know they did start looking for the name later. Maybe the Vatican changed their mind. Keep reading."

Sam quickly opened the next envelope, which contained a copy of Mordecai's sarcastic response, the gist of which inferred that the Vatican were conjuring excuses to cover for the fact they didn't know the name. The Vatican's next response, dated some weeks later, confirmed, in rather stilted language, that no, they didn't have it.

She returned the letter to its envelope and opened the next. Finally, she reached one of the letters addressed to Daniel Penrose, Charlie's father and the youngest of Mordecai's two grandsons.

"'Your observations of the gateway have proved most enlightening,'" she read. "'That the demon may manifest such a portal at any location confirms that it never fully crosses over; a portion of the spirit or essence remains in the inferno as an anchor, and the manifestation in this realm is but an extension. Destruction of the host or vessel in this realm will only ever serve to weaken it.'" She paused and glanced up at Elliot. "'To destroy the demon, you must force it to cross over completely. Only then will it be vulnerable to physical attack.'"

Her mouth felt dry and she tried to read Elliot's closed expression to figure out if he'd reached the same conclusion she had. "They weren't trying to exorcise it or banish it, were they?" she said. "They were trying to *summon* it."

The next few letters dealt mainly with the quest to find the name, but the conclusion gradually grew clearer. To force the demon to cross over, it had to be summoned, and the summoning required the name.

Around the turn of the twentieth century the Vatican sent their best guess at a ritual.

"Oh great," Sam said as she unfolded the paper. "It's in Latin. Do you think it'll matter if we don't know what it means?"

"Let me see."

She handed him the letter.

His eyes flicked back and forth across the page and he mouthed the words, then he glanced at her. "'*Evoco Daemonium*' is something like, I call the demon. '*Dice nomen*', here, I think means say the name. That part's an instruction."

Sam sputtered a laugh.

"What?"

"Oh nothing. It's just of course you read Latin, everyone reads Latin, except me apparently."

He shrugged. "I learnt at school. Honestly I could be getting it completely wrong."

Sam waited while he studied the next line.

"'*Legiones averni sunt testes mei.*'" He blew out a breath. "Legions of something are witnesses of mine, or are my witnesses. At least I think it's witnesses. Testes is the root of testify, so…"

She tilted her head back against the warm stone, watching him, and sighed. There was something really sexy about the way he could do that.

He tensed. "I'm trying, alright."

"Sorry, I didn't mean it like that. Keep going."

He frowned for a moment then a smile tugged at his lips and he refocused on the letter. "I think most of it is words to say out loud. There are a few other directions though."

"How do you…"

He angled the page so she could see. "Some of the verb endings are imperative form. Like this bit, '*cruenta manum tua*'. It's an instruction to do something to your hand. I don't know what that word is though."

"Cut?"

He frowned. "Maybe. *Secare* would be more common. Or *incidere*, like in the next line. '*Incrusta pugionem a sanguine et incide maledictum*'," he read and wet his lips with a nervous dart of his tongue.

"'*Sanguine*' like in exsanguinate? Blood, right?" Sam glanced at Elliot's tense expression.

"Yes. Something about coating a weapon with blood, and then you cut this *maledictum*, which isn't the demon… It must mean the vessel."

"Your blood on the dagger? That would make sense," Sam said.

He nodded, eyes distant. The colour had drained from his face and he took a deep breath. "I should call Gabriel, ask him to translate it in full."

He pushed off the wall and stood up.

"Are you okay?" Sam asked.

"Fine. We just need to understand what we're dealing with here."

He paced away towards the end of the church. Sam curled her knees up to her chin and bit her ragged thumbnail.

———•———

Elliot left Sam to review the remaining letters while he made the call. He walked a short distance away from the church, wary of leaving the consecration, and took a seat on a wooden bench among the headstones. His whole body ached, and he felt like he could sleep for weeks.

When Gabriel answered, he ran him through everything they'd discovered.

"My goodness," the demon hunter said.

"We worked out the gist of some of it, but my Latin is... well, rusty would be an understatement. If I read it to you, do you think you can translate?"

"I shall do my best."

He read the letter line by line and jotted Gabriel's translation down. The details became clear. The ritual appeared deceptively simple, but, as he'd begun to suspect, it would all come down to him. Edward Penrose's blood created the vessel; it would take Penrose blood, *his* blood, to summon the demon fully into it. And the dagger, which bridged the gap between the Mime's invisible powers and reality, would be the tool to channel it.

It wasn't clear what would happen next, or what would happen to the host, but there was no point in thinking too far ahead when even the first step seemed impossible.

Elliot pinched the bridge of his nose, forcing his glasses up. "I don't know if I can do it."

"Nonsense. I have every faith in you."

"But we don't even have a way to find it." He re-settled his glasses and checked his watch. "We've got maybe four hours until moonrise—"

"Now is not the time for doubts," Gabriel said firmly. "We have all the resources and information we require."

"You're right. You're right, we have to try."

"To start with, the ritual you describe – I've seen variants performed in the past. You will have the greatest chance of success at the location where the demon first took possession of the vessel. The veil will already be attuned to the demon's energies at that place."

"The chapel ruins, in the grounds of the Penrose House." At least they were close.

"Precisely."

"Alright, but how do we get the demon there? We haven't seen a trace of it since it attacked you."

"Ah, there we have a hundred years of progress in our favour. Since Daniel Penrose's time, several generations of demon hunters have developed new methods to contain and control demonic entities. In fact, we can go one better."

Elliot rose to pace the short stretch of grass in front of the bench. "How so?"

"With the demon's name we may attempt a translocation ritual. You will need to prepare a simple ritual circle and perform an incantation. The demon will be drawn through the veil to the circle."

"And that'll get it to the location and hold it there?"

"I believe so. Although the containment may not last, so you should wait until shortly before moonrise."

"Alright. What are we going to need for this circle?"

Gabriel began to describe the requirements. Elliot stopped him. "Just email it to me. Or text it."

"Er, yes, certainly," Gabriel said, though the wobble in his voice made it sound like he might not know how to do either of those things. He'd have to figure it out because they needed to get moving.

45

Following a quick detour into Okehampton to buy supplies for the translocation ritual from the shopping list Gabriel had sent, Elliot drove back to the Penrose house. A whole bunch of tyre tracks criss-crossed the lane up to Hunter's Haven. Tracks that hadn't been there the day before. Emergency services, probably. Elliot hesitated to turn up the lane and instead pulled past and parked the Range Rover in a lay-by further down the road.

Sam retrieved their map from her pack and spread it out on the dashboard.

"We're here-ish." She pointed. "This is the house, and this wall must mark the edge of the estate."

Elliot nodded, but it was hard to be sure because according to the map the area enclosed by the wall was subdivided into several fields, and on the far side it straddled a wooded valley. There were acres to search.

"Can we narrow it down at all?" he asked.

"Those newspaper articles we found in Oxford described trees. And they talked about it as being 'down'. I know that's not much to go on, but maybe we could start at the lowest point and work out?"

The shortest route there would take them through the middle of the estate, but those tyre tracks around the entrance to the driveway made Elliot reluctant to go that way. They couldn't afford any delays, and if anyone was still there they'd have too many questions. Another check of the map revealed that a permanent footpath ran along the outside of the wall. They gathered their supplies and set off on foot.

Fifty yards past the gated entrance to the Penrose estate, at the outer corner of the perimeter wall, a kissing gate opened through the adjacent fence into woodland. Multiple footprints, dog tracks and bike tyre impressions overlapped on the well-used path. It sloped gently upwards for a while before levelling out. They kept the tall boundary wall to their right, following it along to the section closest to the house where a few stones had crumbled from the top. Elliot was just tall enough to peer over.

"What do you see?" Sam asked.

"Police. Looks like two cars and a... an ambulance."

"Oh."

It was easy to forget that barely twenty-four hours had passed since they'd sat in Irene's kitchen, poring over the journals. Since the explosion. Since Irene held Elliot's wrist and whispered her dying words. The Mime's manifestations didn't always obey normal physics, so it was quite possible no one further away had heard the blast.

"They may not have been here long," Elliot said.

Sam drew in a tense breath. "You mean her body was there all night?"

He nodded. "Come on, we can't assume they'll leave. Even a routine survey will reveal the explosion didn't come from inside. We should keep moving, avoid the house."

They followed the path north as it skirted the boundary of the estate, until it veered away from the wall. From there, they had to pick their way through the undergrowth. Sam took the lead with the map.

"I wish we'd known more before we came here," she said. "If we'd known what we do now…"

Then Irene might still be alive. "I know."

"I feel like it's our fault she died."

"It *is* my fault." In retrospect, there were a hundred choices he could have made differently. Hindsight was a wonderful thing, though. Logically, they'd taken each step in the necessary order. He'd had to consult Geoff to make the connection to Gabriel. Had to involve Fiona to find Gabriel. Had to come to the Penrose house to discover the journals. But it didn't *feel* that way.

Sam glanced over her shoulder. "Elliot, that's not what I—"

"No, I mean… it's all been because of me. It *started* with me. And I brought each of them into this. Geoff and Irene. Fiona nearly died. Liam did die, technically. And Gabriel… even James." Saying his brother's name out loud left a lump in his throat. Like ripping the scab off a half healed wound.

She stopped, forcing him to stop too, and turned to face him. "I did hear you say that then, in the cave?"

He nodded, and leaned against a tree, suddenly feeling vulnerable and shaky. It was somehow harder to say it to her than to Gabriel, because she reflected his pain back at him with her compassion.

"I'm so sorry." She stepped close, laying her hand gently on his forearm.

He tipped his head to the side, blinking against the prick of tears. "It was always going to find us. It found him first, and I turned my back on him."

"But that doesn't make his death your fault. You had no way of knowing."

"No? I had no way of knowing it would go after Geoff, or that it would destroy the house, but that doesn't stop those things being my fault."

She pursed her lips. "You need to stop this. This demon is evil and powerful, and it kills because that's what it does. You've done everything you could to try and stop it, to save people." She put her hand up to his cheek to force him to look at her. "You saved me."

For a moment, the old self-loathing gut reaction reared its head, telling him he'd be weak and selfish to accept the absolution she offered, the comfort, and he closed his eyes.

"Elliot?"

"You're right. I know you're right. But it's a hard feeling to shake."

"Don't hate yourself. Hate the demon. It did this to you. All of it."

That was true. More so than he'd really stopped to appreciate before.

A faint voice drifted towards them on the breeze, followed by the low bark of a dog. Elliot stood up straight, trying to catch the sound again. A few seconds later another snippet of voice reached them.

"Police?" Sam whispered.

"Possibly." The wall here was in bad repair, some sections standing but others badly crumbled. Elliot put his hand on Sam's arm and urged her towards one of the taller sections. She crouched behind it, while he crept to the edge and peered round. Catching a flash of motion further along, he ducked behind the stone.

"Two officers, one dog," he whispered.

"Just doing a patrol around the crime scene?"

He nodded. Hopefully the dog wouldn't pick up their scent, or they'd have to explain what they were doing off the marked path. Sam slipped her hand into his.

The voices and footsteps grew closer. He glanced at Sam. She had her eyes closed. He held his breath. The footsteps neared, then continued past.

"We can do this," Sam whispered into his ear.

"I know."

———·———

The wall continued to lead them towards the far side of the estate, and soon trees spread out on both sides. Beyond that point the wall became harder to discern, but a fence of posts and wire ran parallel to what remained. The ground sloped steeply downward. Rampant undergrowth clogged the space between the trees, making it virtually impassable.

"Do you hear that?" Sam asked.

"Hear what?"

She paused, listening with her head cocked to the side. "Water."

"We must be getting close to the stream."

Rather than fight their way through the brambles, they crossed inside the line of the wall and followed the valley until they reached a section where it widened, the undergrowth thinned, and they could finally head down towards the watercourse.

The tops of several stone arches appeared from between the trees when they were almost upon them. Suddenly in front of them the ground dropped away, but Sam had her eyes on the map.

"Watch it!" Elliot lunged to grab her as her foot came down on thin air.

She shrieked as he jerked her backwards, and the map fluttered out of her hands and over the three-foot drop. Elliot landed in the leaf litter with Sam hugged to his chest, between his legs.

She glanced over her shoulder. "Thanks."

They crawled to the edge.

"I think we found the ruins," Sam said.

They knelt on top of a crumbling wall which formed one end of a sunken rectangle. Elliot scanned the ruined structure before them, a low level of anxiety tensing his limbs. The place gave off an intense dark vibe. The forest was quiet here, all the natural sounds distant, drowned out by the mental noise emanating from the place. It was shouting, screaming. Silent. Cold, like the crypt.

On the right side, and part of the left, more substantial masonry remained. Window arches reached high into the branches. The tops had caved in, and ivy strangled the stone. Eventually they would topple. At the far end, another low wall bristled with bushes and saplings. A larger tree had taken root at the far left corner, reducing the wall there to a moss-covered mound. But the area enclosed by the ruins – some thirty to forty feet long, and twenty to thirty wide – was barren. Nothing but bare earth, scattered with dead wood and chunks of fallen stone. Nothing green.

Sam scrambled down and retrieved the map, while Elliot picked himself up and brushed dry leaves off his clothes. He watched her as she shivered, rubbed her arms and ran her hand over the ancient stonework. If he was picking up the aura of the place, no doubt she'd be sensing far more.

"I think the floor must have been higher once," she said, indicating where Elliot still stood.

"Makes sense. A lot of the masonry may have been robbed to build other things." He jumped down.

Sam flinched and spun round.

"What is it?" he asked.

She rubbed her neck and shivered. "Spirits."

He moved close to her and tentatively put a hand to her side. "Are you alright?"

She nodded, twisting her head to one side as if she'd heard something. "There's no particular strong presence," she said.

"I can't feel them testing me. They're just... lingering. I think they're stuck here."

She eased away from him, turning in a circle as she moved across the middle of the ruins. She gazed up at the weathered arches. "Do you think there would have been more of the building here in Giles's time?"

"Undoubtedly."

"Look there." She indicated a stone slab propped against the base of the more substantial right-hand side of the ruins. She approached and crouched in front of it. Elliot watched her trace her fingertips over the faint marks of an inscription.

"It's too worn to read," she said. "Edward Penrose murdered twelve people here." She glanced over her shoulder at him. "Do you think they could be buried under...?"

"I doubt it. But maybe."

She touched some of the stones, low in the wall, and pulled her fingertips away blackened.

"There must have been a fire," Elliot said.

Lips parted, eyes unfocused, she stood. He tensed, watching her warily. "Are you sure you're alright?"

She nodded as she moved away from the wall. "They burned the bodies." She sounded distant, as if her voice were not her own. In the centre of the space, she crouched and pressed her palm to the barren dirt. "Do you feel it?" she asked. "There's so much evil here. The spirits still suffer. I don't think anything will ever grow here again."

"Sam, are you... you? Sam?"

She blinked and focused on him, the distance gone from her eyes, and smiled tensely. "Sorry, I'm still me. It's just... I can feel it. The place, I mean, and what happened here. It's weird. It's not like the graveyards, or the crypt. It's more like the mine on the moor. That same general uneasiness, but ten times stronger."

"If you need to go…"

She stood up. "I'll be fine. We should set up the circle."

"Right." Elliot brought up the string of texts Liam had sent earlier with Gabriel's instructions. "It says we should start by marking the circle."

Sam passed him a large bag of salt from her backpack and he tore the corner open with his teeth. He handed the phone to her to read the next step.

"How big do you think it needs to be?" she asked.

"I guess not huge." He started turning in a slow circle, salt pouring from the bag.

Sam sat cross-legged beside the circle and lifted four coloured candles from her pack. She took a small kitchen knife – bought on their supply trip – and began carving the initials of the cardinal points into the wax.

She set Elliot's phone on her knee while she worked. "Next it says we should use the sage and sandalwood to cleanse the circle of negative energy."

Elliot glanced around at the sterile earth within the ruins. "We can *try*. Does it say how?"

"Yep. We burn them inside the circle, then sweep the bad energy away."

"Sweep?"

"Uh… hang on." She set her candle and knife down and picked up the phone to text Gabriel and Liam for clarification. A few seconds later her phone buzzed with the reply. "Oh, apparently if you don't have a broomstick you just use your hands. Make a sweeping motion and visualise pushing the bad energy out and good energy flowing in behind it."

Elliot found the herbs and incense and, careful not to disturb the ring of salt, used a rock to make a shallow depression in the centre of the circle to hold them.

"Hang on a sec." Carving finished, Sam clambered to her feet and brushed the wax chips off her clothes. She positioned the candles at each of the cardinal points, consulting Gabriel's compass.

"This almost looks like we know what we're doing," she said.

"Let's hope we do." Elliot struck a match and offered it to the dried leaves and incense. Sweet scented smoke curled up.

Sam consulted the notes on the phone again. "It says we should sweep counter-clockwise three times." She took up a position on the opposite side of the circle and began to sweep with her hands, as if wafting the smoke away. Elliot copied her and they moved round the circle. She had her eyes closed and an intense look of concentration on her face.

"Is it working?" he asked.

She shrugged. "I have absolutely no idea."

While the incense burned, they continued sweeping until they'd completed three circuits, then stepped back and admired their handiwork.

"Looks ritual to me," Sam said.

"Should we light the candles?"

"Only when we're ready to use it, apparently."

"Alright. I'm going to call Gabriel." He held his hand out and she returned his phone.

Gabriel answered on the third ring. "You've located the nexus?"

"The ruins, yes, we're here. We've set up the circle, it's good to go."

"Excellent, excellent. Now, timing is crucial. Moonrise is fifteen minutes after sunset tonight, at nine forty-five, give or take a few minutes. The summoning must wait until after the moon has risen. Understood?"

"Yes, we've got it." Elliot glanced at his watch – half past six. They had a few hours to kill.

"The translocation should be fairly straightforward," Gabriel continued. "But once you have the demon contained, there's no way to tell how long it will last. I suggest you allow ten to fifteen minutes. Also, there is another minor complication I must—"

Something big and hard slammed into Elliot's back. The phone flew from his hand and hit the floor a moment before he crashed down. He rolled over and shuffled backwards, gasping against the pain. The Mime stood framed in one of the ancient window arches. Whatever the demon had used to hit him had already dissolved. It wasn't playing games.

The Mime's gaze rotated towards Sam.

"Hey! Hey, leave her out of this." Elliot scrambled across the ground, recovered his phone and stood. "Catch." He pitched the phone to Sam and she caught it in both hands.

"Gabriel? Someone turned up uninvited."

Elliot kept his back to her and positioned himself in front of the Mime with the Penrose dagger in hand. The demon stepped off the ledge, landing in a crouch. It rose smoothly to its feet, a smirk on its black-stained lips, as if this were all part of its plan.

Elliot's palms itched, sweaty, and he tightened his grip on the dagger. His legs tensed with nervous energy and the urge to run. No, the urge to *fight*.

The Mime stooped and brought its hands together. Between them a rush of specks coalesced into a stout wooden handle. A heavy, spiked metal ball at one end rested on the dirt.

The demon hefted the weapon into its hands.

"Elliot, Gabriel says you'll have to perform the translocation *now*!"

"I'm a little busy!" His eyes fixed on the mace as the Mime swung it lazily through the air and advanced.

Sliding both hands to the end of the handle the Mime swung the mace in a wide arc, directly at Elliot's head. He ducked, and the Mime pivoted a full circle, lost its balance and stumbled sideways. He seized the moment to glance at Sam. She crouched, lighting the candles, phone still pinned to her shoulder.

"Okay, hold the line, Gabriel. Elliot, how—"

Her mouth kept moving but he suddenly couldn't hear what she was saying. Like he'd instantly gone deaf. Frowning, he stepped towards her and collided with something solid. Invisible. He put his hand out, and a faint reflection moved to meet him. Not invisible, *transparent*.

He frantically felt his way round the box. Solid and seamless, like the one at the music festival. His heart leapt into his throat and he locked eyes with Sam through the glass. She stood, phone clasped tight in her hand.

A black and white movement in the reflection made him flinch. He spun to face the Mime. It stood outside the box with its gloved hands pressed to the glass surface, its mouth open in a shocked "o".

It could drown him, or suffocate him with sand. Suck all the air out or fill the box with poison gas. When it drowned the girl at the festival, there'd been nothing he could do to break or open the tank. Once she was trapped inside, her fate was sealed.

But things had changed since then. He glanced down at the dagger in his hand. A split second of uncertainty showed through the Mime's mocking mask, and that answered his question. He flipped the dagger so he held it point down.

The power comes from the strength of your conviction.

He was not going to die in a cage, not after they'd come so far. The demon didn't make all the rules. Not for him. He raised the dagger high and stabbed at the Mime's hand. The point connected with the glass and the structure shattered under the blow. Chunks of glass flew through the air and rained down around the ruined chapel.

The Mime snatched its hand away before Elliot could skewer it, and staggered away from him, clutching at its chest. Elliot lunged to grab it, restrain it, but it recovered too quickly and twisted out of reach. The mace reappeared in its left hand and its favourite sword in its right.

"Elliot, the translocation!" Sam shouted.

"Read it, I'll repeat."

She called out the first line.

"Now is the hour, mine is the will."

The Mime advanced and he retreated a step. "Through veil and aether to this place, I *entreat* thee, Mastho."

"You have to visualise the circle in your mind," Sam called. "That's the place you're sending it. Concentrate!"

The Mime swung the mace and he jumped aside. His hair ruffled as it parted the air. "Trying!"

Sam continued and he repeated. "Now is the hour, mine is the will. Through veil and aether to this place, I *command* thee, Mastho."

The Mime lunged with the sword. Elliot twisted to the side, grabbed the demon's wrist and shoved it away. It tried to come at him again, but slowed mid-thrust, as if something restrained it.

"Now is the hour, mine is the will. Through veil and aether to this place, I *compel* thee, Mastho."

Threads of mist curled up from the ground around the Mime's feet, winding up the demon's legs.

"Again!" Sam yelled.

Elliot glanced at the salt circle behind him and focused hard on visualising the demon inside. "To this place I *compel* thee, Mastho."

The Mime's features twisted into a silent snarl.

"To this place I *compel* thee, Mastho!" He jabbed the dagger at the circle, pointing.

The mist erupted and engulfed the Mime, then dissipated, leaving nothing. Elliot spun round. Within the confines of the salt the Mime stood, glaring. Breathing heavily, Elliot braced his hands on his knees.

Sam joined him. "Phase one complete," she said, and put Gabriel on loudspeaker.

"What's happening? Is the demon contained?"

"You bet," Sam said. "Worked like a charm."

"Very amusing, but this is not the time for mirth."

She frowned, then rolled her eyes. "No pun intended. So, we have a pissed off demon mime artist in a cage made of salt, candles and wishful thinking. Now what?"

46

Inside the salt circle the Mime poked at the invisible barrier. Sam eyed it warily. She hadn't been this close since it had approached her outside her house in Bristol. Filth crusted its black hoodie, and rusty brown stains trailed down its chin from the corners of its mouth. She wondered whether it had to eat to sustain the host, and what it might consider food.

The demon crowded close to the side of its cage, as if joining in the huddle over the phone. Sam and Elliot edged further away.

"You said something about a complication?" Elliot prompted.

"Right, right," Gabriel said, his voice tinny through the speaker. "We confirmed from the journals that there will be only one way to destroy the vessel once the demon is fully manifested within."

"The dagger?"

"Unfortunately not. No, fire will be the only sure method. The gloves must be incinerated."

There was a long pause. They had candles and matches, but that might not be enough. Sam locked eyes with Elliot.

"You'll have to go," he said.

"What do you mean?"

"I mean one of us has to stay here and babysit while the other goes to find petrol or something to douse the gloves with when the time comes. And since there's no way I'm leaving you here alone with that thing, you have to go."

She shook her head fiercely. "No. You shouldn't be here on your own. What if something happens? You're the only one who can… We'll just use the candles, build a campfire."

"Elliot is right," Gabriel said. "You must be sure, and a suitable accelerant will act as a guarantee."

She handed Elliot the phone. "Fine. But if I don't find anything in half an hour I'm coming back regardless."

"We're on it, Gabriel," Elliot said. "We'll call you if we don't die."

"You have my utmost confidence."

Sam collected her backpack from beside the circle, slung it over both shoulders and returned to Elliot's side. She stepped in close and pressed the letter containing the summoning ritual into his hands, then stretched up and kissed his cheek. "Be careful, okay?"

"You too."

With one last look into his eyes she headed for the bank and scrambled up.

The only place nearby that might have what she needed was the destroyed farmhouse. The one crawling with police. If she couldn't find anything flammable there, Plan B would be to find any bottle and a piece of tubing. With that she could return to the Range Rover and take some petrol. But hopefully it wouldn't come to that. She didn't want to leave Elliot alone with the Mime for too long.

She pushed her way through the woods until the trees petered out and open pasture spread between her and the buildings. There she crouched behind one of the larger trees and took stock.

From the rear, the damage didn't appear as bad as she remembered. The roof sagged where the front wall had collapsed, but the pointed gable ends stood firm. All the windows and doors were blown out, some just the glass, some the frames and surrounding masonry as well. The explosion hadn't touched the outbuildings. With any luck, there would be something stored there she could use.

A police car was just visible, parked on the wide gravel driveway at the front of the house. The ambulance that had been there earlier must have gone. There were no police in sight, so she guessed they must be patrolling around the estate. Or at least she hoped they were. She set off at a run across the field.

On the edge of the yard, she ducked down behind a low wall, panting hard. Two sets of outbuildings faced each other, with the farmhouse itself as the fourth side of the square. On the left stood the barn, with a lower extension on the end nearest her. The building on the right was more like a garage – smaller, newer, with breeze block walls and a corrugated iron roof.

After a few seconds to catch her breath, she scrambled over the wall and scurried across the yard to the first of two doors into the barn extension. The latch clicked up, unlocked, and she slipped inside.

Saddles, bridles, stirrups and other riding tack filled the space, and there was a strong odour of horse and leather polish. A stack of mouldy blankets sat at the back. She wiped a finger through the thick layer of dust on the seat of one saddle, then brushed a little more off and revealed a nameplate: William Penrose III.

"Charlie's grandfather," she whispered, touching the worn leather.

Reading about them in the journals, it was easy to imagine them as characters in a story, but touching something that had belonged to one of Elliot's ancestors was like reaching through time. A tangible connection.

It didn't take much searching to conclude the room contained nothing of use – some wax and polish in a tall cupboard, but no flammable liquids. She was about to walk out when she heard voices, and froze. Her hand hovered halfway to the latch.

"Could have sworn I saw someone," a deep voice said.

"It was probably just another deer. I saw loads this morning." This voice was higher, female.

"I'm just going to check."

Sam drew in a breath and held it. The door to the adjacent room rattled and scraped open. She wouldn't have long.

"There's no one here," the female voice said. "Come on, let's go back. We can sit in the car until the next shift comes on."

Of course, they'd been sitting in the car. That was why she hadn't seen any police, but they'd seen her – or thought they had. Good job they weren't sure.

She tiptoed towards the rear of the room, but hesitated. The fingermarks in the dust could give her away. The police might not notice, but she couldn't take that chance. She hurried to the saddle and scooped a handful of dust from the floor. She shook the dust over the marks, then darted to the stack of blankets.

The adjacent door creaked again as they left. Sam's heart raced and her hands shook, but she forced herself to stay calm as she picked up and quietly shook out one of the blankets.

"I'm just going to take one more look," the male police officer said. "You go back if you want."

Sam squeezed into a gap between some wooden crates, with the blanket draped over her, and checked her feet were tucked in. Dust trickled down through the fibres and she sneezed. For an agonising few moments she feared they'd heard her, but the blanket and the closed door must have muffled the sound.

The latch scraped. The door opened. "Anyone in here?"

Sam kept her breath shallow and concentrated on staying perfectly still. Invisible.

He took a few paces into the room. She heard the scrape of his boots on the gritty flagstones. After what seemed an age, he puffed out a sigh.

"So?" his colleague asked.

"It wasn't a deer," he grumbled. "Go check the other ones. I'm going to take a look round the side." He shut the door as they left.

Sam wondered why they hadn't brought the dog they'd heard with the patrolling officers earlier. A dog could have sniffed her out in no time. Maybe that unit had left earlier, along with the ambulance.

The footsteps and voices receded across the yard. Sam let out a long breath.

She waited a good few minutes, not even daring to crawl out from under the blanket, before she finally convinced herself they weren't coming back. She crossed the room, peered through the crack between the door and the frame and caught sight of a figure in a fluorescent yellow jacket on the far side of the yard.

Shit. They'd obviously decided to stick around and keep an eye out from this side of the building. Now she was trapped.

———·———

In the ruins, Elliot sat on the ground with the ritual text and his notebook out in front of him. He'd reviewed it several times, memorising the sequence and the wording. He watched the Mime fidget within the circle, then checked his watch. Sam had left a little over an hour ago. That was alright. If it took her twenty minutes to reach the farmhouse and then another twenty to search, she wasn't overdue by much. Not time to worry. Not yet.

He sent her a quick text to check she was safe. At least there was no risk she'd be attacked by the demon.

He glanced up, and the Mime narrowed its eyes.

"Comfy in there, Mastho?"

It flinched at the sound of its own name.

When they'd picked up the supplies to make the circle, Sam had insisted they bring snacks. At the time he couldn't fathom how she could think about food, but now lunch seemed a long time ago and his stomach rumbled. He fished a cereal bar from his pocket. As he rose and paced around the salt cage, his prisoner rotated to keep facing him.

"There's a lot of questions I wish I could ask you, but there's not much point, is there?"

Mastho shrugged.

"You killed my brother because he had Penrose blood, didn't you? Because he had the power to destroy you, like I do."

The Mime adopted a wide-eyed expression and covered its mouth with one gloved hand, as if to say "oops".

Elliot shook his head. "They weren't all like that though, were they? Your victims. They weren't all a threat to you."

The Mime held one hand out and rocked it. Some were, some weren't, but more than he thought? He was a direct descendant of Giles Penrose, but there must have been other branches of the family that split off over the years, or even before Edward and Giles were born. Descendants of distant uncles, cousins. How closely related would someone have to be for Ethan's dagger to recognise their blood? To be a threat?

"You were trying to wipe out the line completely?"

Mastho stamped and ground its heel into the mud.

"That's why you came to Bristol. To find me."

The demon grinned malevolently and drew a finger across its throat. To kill him.

Elliot thought back to the days they'd spent in Bristol trying to detect a pattern in the Mime's attacks, to predict its next move. He'd suspected he'd been too lucky, and now he knew why.

It had all been a game, to draw him in.

Well, who had the upper hand now?

He opened the packet in his hand and took a bite. The Mime watched as he continued to pace around the circle. "You know, something clicked earlier." He stopped and folded his arms. "You did this to me. You took my brother. You destroyed my life."

Mastho gave an exaggerated bow.

"That was a mistake."

It looked up, mid-bow, eyebrows raised in a quizzical expression.

"If you hadn't killed James, I would never have left London. Instead, here I am." He held both arms out to the side and the Mime sneered, sending a heady rush of adrenaline through him. "You know you're going to die tonight, right?"

It shrugged again and canted its head to one side.

"We'll see? I guess we will."

He glanced at his watch again – two hours until moonrise. "Not long now, Mastho."

He took great satisfaction in the way it cringed every time he used its name.

47

Sam searched the tack room twice more. There was definitely nothing suitable hidden there. She'd texted Elliot to explain where she was, telling him not to worry, but she was starting to worry herself. Through the thin gap at the side of the door, she watched the male officer pace the yard. His colleague had taken over for a while, but now he was back. They were taking it in turns, which presumably meant one of them would be watching the rear of the house constantly now.

The shadows lengthened across the yard.

She was running out of time. If he didn't get bored and leave soon, she'd either have to make a run for it or talk to him. Both those options sounded way too risky. She couldn't leave Elliot to take on the summoning alone.

The wall that divided the tack room from the room next door only extended to the height of the side walls. Above, the top of the wall and the line of the pitched roof formed a triangular gap. Sam checked on police guy. He was currently strolling along the far side of the yard.

As silently as she could, she stacked up a couple of sturdy wooden crates and used them to climb on top of the tall cupboard. From there she could peer over the wall into the next room.

Rusty tools hung from hooks on the walls, and all manner of junk lay piled in the corners. It didn't look promising in terms of flammable stuff, but it did have one thing the tack room didn't: another exit. Directly opposite where she peered over the wall, a door opened into the main barn.

She stretched to look down. Against the wall stood a workbench, lower than her cupboard but not by too much. She should be able to get down, if not back up. Two doors was a one hundred per cent trade-up on her current situation though, so she gripped the top of the wall, bent her knees and jumped. Coarse grit dug into her palms. She strained to hoist herself up to hip level, then swung her leg up and hooked her knee over.

Lying lengthways along the top of the wall, she blew out a breath. Dust puffed in her face. She coughed as quietly as she could and blinked watering eyes, then swung both legs over to the other side. She lowered herself until her hands were by her waist, elbows locked, but she couldn't touch the workbench with her feet. A spike of alarm tightened her chest. Twisting her hands round, she managed to drop another few inches. Still no bench. Panic welled up, rising fast. She couldn't climb back up from this position and she couldn't just drop – she might tumble off the bench. Her shoulders and biceps screamed, entirely unused to supporting her entire body weight. Her feet scrabbled against the wall. One heel caught something metallic, which clattered to the floor. She let out a squeak as her fingers slipped. Her stomach swooped, but her feet hit the solid workbench and she managed to absorb the drop with her knees.

She crouched there for a moment, waiting for her heart rate to slow, then scrambled down and darted to the door. There was no gap at the side this time, but there was a large keyhole. She peeked through. A flash of yellow on the far side of the yard confirmed police guy hadn't heard the racket. She blew out a long, relieved breath.

The bench she'd dropped onto extended the full length of the wall. Deep lines and dents scored the surface, marks from many years' use. She ran her hand over the dark wood. Perhaps the archaic thing had been there since the nineteenth century. Had Ethan Penrose created the dagger at that bench? Or was it older still? She shivered. Did Edward sit at it to create the gloves?

She hadn't expected the room to provide what she needed, but on a shelf below the workbench were boxes, more tools and some containers. With a jolt of excitement, Sam knelt and wiped off the labels. Mostly paint, but she found some white spirit in a sticky plastic bottle, then, even better, a square metal container of paraffin next to a tarnished Tilley lamp. She picked up the rust-marked tin and shook it. It was heavy and sounded nearly full.

Her hands trembled as she stuffed the paraffin into her backpack, because now sneaking past the police and returning to Elliot became her only priority.

Another quick check at the keyhole. The man currently stood to her right, near the wall across the open end of the yard. There was no way she could slip past him unless he moved round to the front of the house, or even just into the barn so she could skirt the outbuildings and use them to cover her route to the trees. She checked the time on her phone. It was already quarter past nine. Time was slipping away, time she couldn't afford.

"Come on," she muttered.

He wasn't going to move until something made him move… or until *she* made him move.

She tried the door into the barn. The latch clicked up smoothly and the door opened inward. Cooler air tumbled through from the long, shady space. A huge set of double sliding doors on the right stood closed, and the only light came from a few small, unglazed windows high up. Unlike the tack room and the workshop, this space was fairly empty, with a few bales of straw stacked up in one corner, and at the far end a medium-sized tractor.

She hunted round the edges for another door – preferably one that led out the opposite side of the building – but no such luck. She was contemplating setting a fire to draw the police officer's attention when she peered into the cab of the tractor. A shiny set of keys hung from the ignition.

A ready-made distraction. She grinned.

She checked the barn doors weren't locked, secured her backpack straps and reached for the keys. The throaty motor rumbled to life. She sprinted for the workshop, closed the inner door quietly, then crouched by the keyhole in time to see the yellow of the man's jacket whip past. She held her breath.

The rollers of the barn doors squealed.

Cautiously, she twisted the door handle and peered round, in time to see the police officer disappear into the barn. She slipped out silently and hurried on light toes to the end of the building, then broke into a run, angling across the field to keep the farm buildings between her and the yard.

At the treeline she crashed through the undergrowth and dropped down behind an oak. She panted, dragging huge gulps of air down her dry throat, and coughed until she felt sick.

Once she'd caught her breath she crept out from her hiding place and scanned the field for any sign she'd been followed. On the edge of the yard she saw the policeman scanning the field, a radio to his lips, but then he turned and walked the other way.

She puffed out her cheeks. The can of paraffin sloshed in her backpack as she set off through the trees at a jog.

Elliot sat on the crumbling masonry at the side of the chapel. With the sun below the horizon, it was getting dim beneath the canopy of trees, and Sam had the only torch. He checked the time of her last text, then his watch. She should be here.

The candles around the circle still burned, lighting the demon's hooded face from below. The Mime tapped the side of its cage and Elliot tensed.

"Not much fun when you're the one trapped behind an invisible wall, huh?"

The Mime manifested a stick. Elliot hopped down from the wall. He watched the Mime warily as it used the stick to probe higher and higher, extending it like a telescopic aerial.

Some fifteen feet up, the tip met no resistance. The Mime grinned, and the stick collapsed into a shower of glittery sparks.

Gabriel hadn't warned him the cage didn't have a lid.

Elliot drew the dagger and glanced at his watch again. Moonrise was only five minutes away. The longer he waited, the higher the chances of the demon escaping to Hell. Unless Sam returned soon, he'd have to start the ritual without her.

The Mime sat cross-legged on the ground and rested its chin in one hand, index finger tapping against its temple. Elliot wondered what it was waiting for. Was it trying to decide on the best escape route, or was it just an act, designed to keep him second-guessing himself?

Mastho would not want to leave him alive. Neither of them wanted to spend the next three years or more preparing for the demon's return. If that meant the demon didn't flee at the first opportunity, it would be to Elliot's advantage.

He tried to keep his eyes on the Mime while he sent Sam another urgent text. He glanced away for a couple of seconds, and when he looked back Mastho had vanished.

A rope dangled down into the middle of the circle from the overhanging trees above. He caught a flash of white gloves and face as the Mime slipped through the branches and dropped over the arched wall.

"Shit!" Elliot ran towards the edge of the ruins and scrambled up into one of the arches, to see a huge, spherical boulder rolling towards him, an unstoppable force. He dived to one side. The rock crashed into the centre of the ruins, obliterating the salt circle, then collapsed and drifted away into nothingness.

As Elliot scrambled back to his feet, a black blur tackled him from the side, knocking the breath from his lungs. His foot slipped on the crumbling masonry and they tumbled together over the edge of the wall. He slammed into the hard ground with the weight of the Mime on top of him. His head smacked into the dirt and black spots exploded behind his eyes. The demon pinned him down and extended one arm to the side, katana materialising in its grasp.

48

Elliot grabbed the Mime's arm, pushing against it with one hand as it tried to bring the sword to his throat. His head and shoulder throbbed, sapping his strength. He knew he wouldn't be able to hold it for long. The Mime's small stature belied its physical power.

White eyes flashed triumphantly.

Elliot gritted his teeth and with his other hand clawed at the arm holding him down.

A light flickered between the trees. The Mime's expression faltered, like it wanted to look, but it wanted to kill him more.

"Elliot?" Sam's voice, calling across the ruins.

The light swept briefly over where they struggled, then swung back to settle on them, wavering as Sam ran towards them and scrambled down. The Mime twisted to look up into her face, just as she whacked it around the head with her torch.

Its grip slackened. Elliot threw everything into struggling free. The demon was strong but not heavy. He shoved it to one side, scuttled backwards and lashed out with a kick that connected with the demon's shoulder. The Mime crashed onto its side, and Elliot lunged for the dagger, snatching it up from the ground.

Sam grabbed his arm, jerking him to his feet, and they faced the demon crouched in front of them. Its eyes flashed bright with hatred. Then it retreated, scuttling over the wall into the dark of the forest.

Elliot sagged against Sam as a wave of dizziness struck.

"Whoa, careful," she said. "Are you okay?"

He experimentally moved his arm. Pain shot through his shoulder – the old injury from Bristol flaring up – and he groaned. His head was clearing though. He rubbed his shoulder and blinked hard. "I'll live."

"What happened?"

"It escaped."

A shadow flitted across the far side of the ruins. Sam twisted to shine the torch in that direction.

"It's not done with us yet." Elliot clutched at Sam for balance as his head spun. "Please, tell me you found something."

"Oh yes. When I am done with them those gloves will be toast."

Over her shoulder the Mime reappeared, balancing atop one of the higher parts of the wall.

"Find some cover," Elliot said under his breath. "And be ready."

She nodded, then scurried away to crouch behind a piece of fallen arch at the side of the ruins.

Elliot faced the Mime across the bare earth. For a moment neither of them moved. Behind the demon, a sliver of white moon appeared between the branches. Elliot spread his hands to the side, one clasping the dagger. His heart pounded with adrenaline, and the pain only heightened the rush. It all came down to him, in this moment. He'd memorised the words. He knew what he had to do.

"*Evoco daemonium Mastho*," he called into the night. "*Legiones averni sunt testes mei.*"

The Mime scowled and took a step off the wall. It landed on one knee, one hand to the dirt, eyes locked on Elliot.

"*Inhabita maledictum terrae.*" He brought the dagger to his palm, ready to make the cut he needed to coat the blade with his blood, but hesitated, thinking better of it. Blood was blood, after all, and he'd need to be able to use his hand. His sleeve already rolled up, he moved the blade to his forearm, where a cut would be less inconvenient. "*Sanguis viri quis advocat tu primus fluit per vena mei.*"

The Mime charged, hitting Elliot in a rugby tackle that bore them both to the ground. Elliot grabbed the demon, using the momentum to roll back over his shoulder and bring himself out on top of the Mime, straddling its chest. He pinned the demon's wrists with his left hand, the dagger still held in his right. The Mime squirmed.

Elliot returned the blade to his arm and paused to take a breath.

A coating of specks appeared over the Mime's hands and arms, coalescing into a layer of grease. The Mime pulled a slippery arm free and bucked hard. Elliot lost his balance and scored a deep line across his arm with the dagger.

"Shit!"

The Mime manifested a black truncheon in its hand and lashed out. The blow caught Elliot across the face, dislodged his glasses and snapped his head sideways. Mastho wriggled free and crawled away across the clearing.

Elliot recovered his glasses and staggered to his feet. Blood dripped down his arm from the cut and his head throbbed. He dabbed his lip with the back of his right hand, and it came away bloody. He glanced at Sam across the chapel, and she nodded, eyes glinting.

"*Sanguis viri quis advocat tu primus fluit per vena mei,*" he repeated as he held the dagger to his arm and gathered some of his blood on the blade. He'd hoped to keep the Mime in sight the whole time, but he'd make it work, somehow. He cradled his bleeding, bruised left arm to his stomach and rotated a full circle, searching for the demon.

The Mime appeared on the ruined wall, framed in one of the derelict window arches.

"Elliot, there!" Sam called.

"I see him!" He gripped the dagger tighter and pointed it towards the demon. "*Compello tu a potestate sanguinis.*" It owed its entire existence to Penrose blood and that blood held power over it, power he could wield.

A gusty wind picked up, whipping Elliot's hair and sticking his shirt to the sweat between his shoulder blades. Tremors vibrated through the chapel, dislodging loose stones. The Mime jumped down. At its side, the scabbard and hilt of its katana reappeared. The blade that had run through Gabriel. Its last resort. When all else failed, that weapon always turned the tide.

Elliot looked the demon in its lifeless black and white eyes and took a step closer. "*Audi loquo nomen tui et obedi, Mastho!*"

The Mime glared at him and drew the sword.

The rumbling grew louder and, with a harsh screech, bright light flooded the clearing from behind Elliot. He glanced over his shoulder, squinting at the glare. Along the edge of the ruins behind him, light flared from an expanding, spinning disk of purple smoke, boiling with lightning. The middle parted like an iris, but the edges continued to rotate, spilling cold light and jagged sparks into the twilight gloom. The middle of the circle cleared to reveal darkness, then a white flash on the far side lit up barren rocks.

"You're not getting past me that easily!" Elliot snarled. He jabbed the dagger at the demon. "You will cross over, Mastho!"

The Mime charged. Elliot ducked to the side. He slashed the blade of the dagger against the Mime's hand, where it gripped the sword, and sliced. The blood on the blade stained the fibres of the glove, and the Mime dropped its weapon.

A black shape surged from the portal, carrying with it a sulphurous odour, like vinegar and burnt hair. It parted around Elliot where he stood with his back to the opening, and enveloped the human form of the Mime, obscuring it from view. A demonic howl rent the air, and the oily shadow absorbed into the host.

The Mime took two lurching steps towards the portal. Elliot tensed, clutching the dagger tight, unsure what form the demon would take now.

The Mime collapsed to its knees.

For a moment, it huddled on the floor, then it raised both hands and stared at them. Its lips parted and it let out a very human scream, filled with pain and suffering and no small measure of insanity.

The gloves writhed and shifted, inching their way off the host's hands. Elliot watched, frozen to the spot, as they dropped to the ground, skittered away across the chapel like pale spiders and disappeared into a crack in the stonework.

49

Elliot scanned the edge of the ruins in the glare from the portal as it howled and screeched behind him. His eyes watered from the lashing wind. That the gloves would run off on their own after the summoning hadn't occurred to him. They were gloves, for Christ's sake!

The demon had clearly abandoned the host. The man had crawled a few paces and now knelt by their demolished salt circle and rocked on the spot. His haunted eyes stared at nothing.

Sam appeared by Elliot's side and handed him the torch. He caught paraffin fumes, whipped up from the open container in her hands.

A white shape skittered across the top of the wall, level with Elliot's head. He flinched, and searched for it in the torch beam, but it had vanished. The pain from his shoulder and the cut on his arm had dulled enough not to occupy his whole attention, but he felt the blood, sticky and wet, running down his arm. He'd have to resist the urge to do something about it until this was finished.

"Is it just me," Sam yelled over the din, "or is this the weirdest thing you've ever done?"

"It ranks pretty high."

A handful of pebbles tumbled down from the top of the ruins to their right. Elliot spun to face the spot where the stones had been dislodged. Sam clutched the can of paraffin at chest height as he took a step towards the wall. A pale blur streaked from behind the fallen masonry, across the bare earth of the chapel. The host shrieked as the gloves scurried past.

"There!" Elliot pointed with the dagger. He went to take another step away from the portal, but hesitated. The gloves were doing it on purpose, trying to draw him away so they'd have a clear run at the portal. If they got past him it was all over.

"Those things seriously creep me out," Sam said. "I don't even like spiders and those are... gee-argh!"

"Agreed. We can't let them escape." He glanced at the container in her hand. "How much is in that?"

She sloshed the can. "Quite a bit."

"Enough to set a fire across the front of the portal?"

She grinned. "I'm on it."

Elliot stayed close, panning the torch along the walls and guarding the gateway to Hell – or whatever was on the far side – while Sam worked to pile up sticks and branches to give the fire something to latch onto. She poured the paraffin over the wood. Elliot glanced down as she struck a match close to the pile and bright yellow flames leapt up to join the violet light from the portal.

A flash of motion drew his attention to the top of the low ruins directly opposite, twenty feet away. The gloves raised themselves up on their fingers, menacing him. He imagined they gave a feral hiss – unhappy about the flames, no doubt.

"Sam." He nudged her with his elbow.

She turned and drew in a sharp breath when she saw the gloves poised, ready to leap.

"Stay here," he said. "Make sure the fire keeps going. I'll try and grab them. When I've got them, I'll pin them down and you douse them."

"Okay."

He slowly approached the gloves, holding them in the torch beam. They bobbed and swayed, one slightly in front of the other, then the rear glove hopped forwards while the other menaced from behind. He tried to think of them as an intelligent entity. They were, after all, still Mastho, still the same demon who had been controlling the host and manifesting weapons. They seemed strangely pitiful now, bound inside the vessel, but somehow they still exuded menace and hatred.

As he drew closer, they grew more agitated, moving further apart in their war dance. Could they split up, he wondered, so they could attack from two sides? He slipped the dagger into his belt to free up his right hand. His pulse raced, adrenaline and pain making him twitchy as he put his hand out towards them. The gloves tensed. With a couple of deep breaths, he lunged. His hand came down sharply on the stone, and the gloves skittered away along the edge of the ruins.

"Did you get them?" Sam called.

"Not yet!" Damn it, they were fast.

He shone his torch along the wall, but they'd vanished again. He scrambled up and followed the way he'd seen them go.

Behind him, Sam shrieked, and there was a clang as the container of paraffin hit the ground. Elliot spun round. One of the gloves clung to her leg, climbing higher. She tried to push it off, but for an entity made only of fabric it had a fierce grip. The other glove appeared on her shoulder, fingers tangling in her hair.

"Elliot, help! Get them off me!"

He jumped down and stumbled to his knees. By the time he regained his feet, one of the gloves had wriggled onto her left hand. The other choked her, clasped around her bruised throat. She clawed at the one around her neck with her free right hand, gasping, but her left arm hung limp at her side, as if the glove on her hand had paralysed her limb.

Her eyes met his, wide and scared.

"Don't panic!" He rushed to her side, dropping the torch.

Her left leg buckled under her, and she lost her balance and fell. Her left wrist crumpled as it hit the ground and she let out a harsh yelp.

Elliot dropped to his knees beside her and grabbed the glove around her neck. He worked his fingers between the fabric and Sam's skin and prised each finger off.

Tears filled Sam's eyes. "No, no! I can't—"

Her left fist flew at his face and connected with his temple hard enough that he saw stars. She screamed, her back arching off the ground in pure agony. Somehow the glove on her hand was exerting control over her arm. He grabbed her wrist in his left hand as she swung for him again. She shrieked, and he felt the broken bones grind in his grip.

"I'm sorry. I'm sorry!"

Holding her possessed left arm to one side, he pulled the first glove away from her neck. She put her own right hand around her throat to protect it and sucked in deep, ragged breaths. The thumb still hooked around the back of her neck and Elliot levered at it until it slipped free.

Now he had one squirming glove in his grip, but he still needed to get the other off Sam's hand. He pinned the first glove to the ground with his knee.

Sam wrenched her left arm free and struck at him again. As he leaned out of reach, she kicked with her left leg, catching his ankle and sending a sharp jab of pain through the joint.

"I can't stop it!" she cried. Her left hand reached for Elliot, clawing, and she grasped her upper arm with her free hand, trying to restrain it. "Get it off," she snarled through gritted teeth, fingers digging into her arm, eyes screwed shut.

He tried to be gentle, but the demon kept struggling. The

glove on the floor curled its fingers into his leg. He jumped, and Sam yelped as he jolted her broken wrist.

"Anytime now!" she yelled.

He pulled each finger to loosen them, but one by one they wriggled back on before he could do the next. "Oh, come on!" He seized the hem around her wrist and pulled, but the fabric wouldn't fold or turn inside out on itself.

Sam moved her grip to her forearm, closer to her wrist. "Elliot! Just pull the fingers!"

He locked eyes with her. Tears streamed down her cheeks, whipped away by the wind, and she nodded, telling him to do whatever was necessary.

With Sam holding her wrist steady, Elliot pulled the fingers and slowly the glove slid from her hand. Sam's breath came in halting gasps. He could see how much it was hurting her, but they had no choice.

The glove popped free. Elliot fell back. The glove beneath his knee squirmed loose but he pounced before it could escape. He struggled with both writhing gloves, and for a moment the sheer absurdity of what he was doing hit him. If it weren't for the pain, the exhaustion and the shrieking Hell portal a dozen feet away, he might have laughed.

Sam rolled to her knees and cradled her wrist to her stomach. Drawing harsh breaths through clenched teeth, she crawled to the paraffin can. Elliot followed her with the thrashing gloves. He held them down and Sam tipped the liquid over them, dousing his hands in the process. Wet, they became slippery, and he struggled to hold them down. He pinned them under his knee, paraffin soaking into his jeans. Sam pulled a box of matches from her pocket. She worked a match out with her good hand then held the box in her teeth to strike it.

"Ready?" Elliot asked.

She nodded. The match flared to life. The gloves squirmed and strained towards the portal.

The flame guttered in the howling wind and went out.

"Quickly!"

Sam fished out another match and struck, but it blew out immediately. She took the box from her mouth with her injured left hand and, gritting her teeth, tried another with her broken hand cupped around it to shield the flame until it took hold. Elliot stared at her with admiration. She glanced up and nodded.

He released the gloves and she ignited them. The paraffin caught with a whoosh and bright flames leapt up.

The burning gloves shot away, trailing smoke and flame as they streaked for the doorway to Hell, and safety.

Elliot pulled the dagger from his belt and lunged after them on hands and knees. He impaled the gloves with the dagger, pinning them to the dirt a foot from the sparking edge of the portal. The fire leapt to his paraffin-soaked hand and he swatted the flames out against his thigh, feeling the hairs on his arm crackle and singe. He shielded his eyes from the wind and the bright flashes of light. The gloves fought to tug themselves free. The tearing of fabric against the blade was inaudible over the din, but Elliot could see the fibres parting. The flames licked up around the handle.

The smoke thickened, turning blacker as the flames consumed the vessel, and for a moment Elliot half imagined he saw a twisted face, full of agony and rage, swirl up from the gloves, before the wind tore it apart.

Abruptly, the portal began to collapse in on itself. One cloth finger strained towards the closing doorway, then fell limply to the ground. The clearing sank into darkness, lit only by the discarded torch and the soft glow of the paraffin flames.

Mastho was no more.

50

Elliot knelt beside the remains of the gloves and watched them crumble to ash, until a hand on his shoulder made him jump. Sam stood behind him, her arm cradled to her body.

"Are you alright?" he asked.

She shook her head.

He stood, pulled her into a one-armed hug, careful not to crush her wrist, and kissed the side of her head. He could feel her trembling. "You were amazing," he murmured.

Her pain reminded him of his own injuries. He released her, recovered the fallen torch and inspected the cut on his arm. The sight of the blood still seeping and running down to drip from his fingers made him queasy.

"Hands… hands… hands… aren't mine…" the host, previously silent, muttered. He still knelt on the ground, having barely moved since the gloves abandoned him, but the markings on his face were fading.

Sam moved away from Elliot and crouched by the man's side. Holding her injured arm protectively against her stomach, she put her other hand on his shoulder. He flinched and scuttled a few feet away.

Elliot recovered Sam's backpack from where she'd left it at the side of the ruins. He found a dressing and a bandage, left over from the ransacked first aid kit. As he bound his wound, he watched Sam patiently, cautiously, approach the host again.

"It's okay," she said gently. "It's over. We'll take care of you." The hint of strain in her voice was only obvious to Elliot because he knew her. She was hiding her own pain and any residual fear or resentment, trying to put the man at ease. Offering care and compassion because that was what was needed in that moment, no matter what it took to do so. That would always be one of the qualities he admired most in her.

"What's your name?" she asked.

The host stared at her fearfully and shook his head. Elliot wondered whether his experience had left him with amnesia, or if he'd simply lost his sense of self, locked inside while the demon controlled his body. Amnesia might be a mercy.

"Okay," Sam said. "Don't worry, we can—"

"I c-couldn't stop it," the man murmured.

"I know," she said. "It wasn't your fault." She glanced up at Elliot, her eyes filled with tears. No one could understand what the man was going through better than her, and Elliot was sure her own nightmares would be at the forefront of her mind right now.

He collected the dagger from where it stood upright in the ground, surrounded by the last remains of the gloves.

The host's eyes strayed to the smoking embers. "Gone now?"

"That's right," Sam said. "Come on, can you walk?"

Elliot left the smashed remnants of the salt circle and the empty can of paraffin where they lay. He joined Sam, her backpack slung over his shoulder, torch in hand, and helped the host stand. The man rose on unsteady legs and Elliot supported him, but after a moment he seemed to find some strength. His expression remained distracted, vacant but tense.

Sam put an encouraging hand on his upper arm. He stiffened but started moving, and the three of them began the walk back to the car.

Elliot's feet dragged. Adrenaline and tension had kept his exhaustion at bay, but now the fact that he'd had about two hours' sleep in the last thirty-six intense hours made itself felt. It was tempting to take a shortcut directly across the estate, but the police would likely still be at the house, so they couldn't risk it. He craved rest like a dehydrated man craved water, and every part of him hurt.

While Sam guided the trembling host, Elliot called Gabriel. The phone rang and rang. Eventually the demon hunter answered with a muffled, "Elliot?"

"Mission accomplished."

Gabriel sighed. "Well done. The vessel is destroyed?"

Elliot grinned, a touch of chest-swelling pride leaking past his exhaustion. "Completely. Nothing left but ash."

"And the host?"

He glanced at the man stumbling along beside Sam, starting at every sound from the forest. "Traumatised but alive."

"Excellent. We could not have wished for a more satisfactory outcome."

Elliot let that sink in for a few seconds. He'd achieved something pretty extraordinary really. "We're on our way back now. I'll have to tell you the whole story another time."

Gabriel chuckled. "I shall look forward to it, my friend."

He signed off, and they focused on picking their way through the dark woods towards the footpath, then onto the road. They reached the car and Sam helped the host into the rear seat, where he sat, hugging himself and rocking.

She joined Elliot beside the car. "What are we going to do with him?"

"He's going to need psychiatric help. We'll take him to the hospital."

She frowned and hugged her arm again.

"What's wrong?" he asked.

"They won't believe him. But what he went through was real."

"We know, though. We'll keep an eye on him." Elliot opened the passenger door for her. She flashed a brief smile and climbed in. He closed the door and jogged round to the other side. A red stain was already spreading across the bandage on his arm where the blood had soaked through. Not much he could do about that until he got them all back to Plymouth.

As he pulled the Range Rover out onto the road, Sam twisted to face him. "It's over. It's actually over."

"Yeah."

She hugged her broken wrist in her lap and, when he glanced across, quiet tears were leaking down her cheeks, but she had a soft smile on her lips.

———•———

When they arrived at the hospital, Sam was surprised to see so many cars still there, but then she realised it was only about eleven o'clock. It felt like it should be closer to four in the morning.

The sterile waiting room of the accident and emergency department welcomed them back. It was crazy to think they'd only been there that morning. Sam guided the host to a seat while Elliot checked them in. What would the hospital staff think of her, returning barely twelve hours after her neck injury with a broken wrist?

"Sammy!"

She spun round. Liam strode up to her and wrapped her in a bear hug. She yelped as he squashed her wrist, and he dropped her like a hot potato. Hugging her arm, she gritted her teeth until the pain subsided from blinding to bearable.

Liam held his hands out. "Here, let me…"

She extended her arm and he wrapped his hands round her wrist, closed his eyes. The pain gradually melted away to a dull ache.

"Better?"

"Hmm."

He grinned. "So, how's it feel to be a full-on demon hunter?"

"Me? I didn't do much."

She glanced over to where Elliot was talking to the woman on the reception desk.

"You two okay?" Liam asked. He raised an eyebrow, and she realised he wasn't referring to the big demon battle so much as everything else.

"I think so, yeah."

"Good."

A door clanged open at the far end of the waiting room and the host yelped.

Liam did a double take. "Wait, is that…?"

Sam nodded and sat down next to the host. "Shh, it's okay, you're safe."

The host swallowed hard, eyes darting around the room. He was shaking. Liam sat on the man's other side and put a hand on his shoulder. Did his power work on psychological injuries?

He shrugged, as if to say, "worth a try." It could be impossible to tell; but after thirty seconds the host seemed to relax a little.

The man raised his head and focused on Sam. His eyes were returning to a more human, if still tortured, hazel. "How long?"

She patted his hand where it rested on his knee. "About three weeks."

His eyes widened but he didn't say anything.

"It'll help if you can remember your name," she said. "So the doctors can find your family."

"Carl. Carl Prestwick." He shuddered, as if hearing himself speak his own name was an intense, emotional release.

"Listen, Carl," she said, "the doctors will take care of you, but they won't believe you. Do you understand?"

He nodded slowly.

"But you're not crazy. It did happen. You can tell them whatever you want, whatever you *need* to, but if they try to tell you it wasn't real, you don't have to accept that. Not inside. Not deep down."

She shared a look with Liam and he gave her an encouraging nod.

"Just remember that, okay? And remember you're not alone. We know what happened too."

Carl's lips twitched into a half smile. It was the first expression she'd seen from him that wasn't blind fear.

It wasn't fair. He was free, but now he faced an equally daunting challenge. The doctors would treat him like he suffered from psychosis, or schizophrenia or something, when what he really needed was treatment for post-traumatic stress. It shouldn't be like that. There should be a place where people could find help when they'd suffered real supernatural horrors.

She watched Liam holding the man's shoulder. He had his eyes closed, concentrating hard.

———•———

Father Monroe joined them shortly after. Visiting hours were over, so he and Liam had been kicked out of Gabriel's room. They had the journals with them, which they took to the car while Sam waited for *another* X-ray.

It took the best part of three hours to finally get the results. The break was hairline and didn't require a cast, the doctor said.

Something to thank Liam for, no doubt. Instead they gave her a rigid support brace, which fastened with Velcro.

Elliot received seven stitches to his arm and a fresh dressing. He seemed strangely happy about his war wound, like it was a badge of honour or something. Maybe because he'd missed out on the last round of hospital fun.

At a little past two in the morning, the four of them hit the road back to the hotel north of Dartmoor. On the way, they swung by the site of the crash the day before. Elliot's car still lay upside down in the ditch, and they were able to recover their laptops and other things they'd left there.

Another half an hour, and Elliot was swiping their key card on the hotel room door. Sam followed him in cautiously. Everything had been such a whirlwind over the last twenty-four hours it was hard to be sure where they stood.

Elliot kicked off his shoes, slumped down on the end of one of the twin beds and raked both hands through his hair. The bruises across his jaw and cheek had darkened, and his split lip looked angry and sore. He rubbed his eyes under his glasses and covered his mouth as he yawned.

At least she'd snatched a couple of hours' sleep in the hospital coffee shop that afternoon. He hadn't even had that.

She sat down next to him and nudged his shoulder with hers. "Whatcha thinking about?"

He stared vacantly ahead for a moment, then sighed. "What it all means."

"How so?"

He tilted his head towards her. "What's next? For me, for us. What am I supposed to do now?"

When Gabriel had defeated the demon that had killed his father, he'd considered walking away from his calling. Was that what was going through Elliot's mind? He'd vanquished his demon and now there was nothing to give him purpose. Nothing to hold him to the life he'd been living since his brother died.

"Are you thinking you could go back to London now?" Sam asked. "Pick up where you left off?"

He rolled his eyes as if the suggestion were ludicrous. "No. Never. I know it might not seem like it most of the time, but I actually love living in Bristol, chasing weird stories with you. I like not having to worry whether I'm impressing the right people, or who might stab me in the back." He took hold of her hand and gave it a squeeze. "I guess I'm just contemplating how it all fits together. *Weird News* and… and…"

"Being a demon hunter?"

"Yes. Is that crazy?"

Her eyes fixed on her splinted wrist and Elliot's bandages. Anyone would have to be slightly crazy to want *more* of what they'd just been through, but sometimes life didn't give you a choice. Once you knew what was out there, it became harder to ignore the monsters and still sleep at night.

"I made a difference today," Elliot said, staring at the carpet. "It's the first time I've ever really felt that way. Known, without a shadow of doubt, that something I did made the world a better place."

She rested her head on his shoulder. "I think you'd make a great demon hunter."

He slipped his arm round her and kissed her hair.

She gazed up at him. "What do you say? Cross and McBride, paranormal investigators?"

He chuckled and hugged her tighter. "I say let's take it one step at a time."

"Yeah, and the first step should be sleep." She encouraged him onto the bed, then curled up with her head on his shoulder, the wrist brace slightly awkward between them. He reached across and flicked the light switch.

51

The following morning, they met Liam and Father Monroe for breakfast. Then they checked out and hit the road north to Bristol. Elliot took the front seat, with Father Monroe driving, so Sam sat in the back with Liam and told him the whole story of the night before. Recounting it added a sort of distance, made it easier to deal with.

In a little under two hours they turned onto her street and parked up outside her apartment building. She'd not been home since the Mime had confronted her outside, the day before they'd fled Bristol in search of Gabriel. It seemed so long ago that everything took on a faintly alien quality, like returning home after a long holiday. There was a new patch of graffiti on the wall opposite, and some smashed car window glass spread across the pavement. She caught Elliot staring at the spray paint tags, an unreadable, introspective expression on his face.

She unlocked the door and let the boys in with the trunk of journals – Elliot's now, since they contained his heritage. He planned to leave them with her until they had more time to move them. Then they reconvened outside to say their goodbyes.

Elliot shook Father Monroe's hand. "Make sure Gabriel gets home alright, hmm?"

"Of course. And I hope you won't be a stranger."

Elliot shook his head. "I need a few days to straighten everything out, but it'd be good to… debrief."

The priest clapped his sore shoulder, and he winced.

Sam was still watching them when Liam moved in front of her and threw his arms around her shoulders in a tight squeeze. She stuck her left hand out to the side, trying to keep her broken wrist from being squashed, but she returned the hug fiercely with her other arm.

"I'll miss you," he murmured by her ear, sending a shiver through her.

"Put her down," Elliot said.

Liam released her and put his hands up in surrender. Sam eyed the two of them warily as they faced each other. Elliot extended a hand and, after a moment's hesitation, Liam took it to shake. Elliot pulled him forwards, grabbed him round the shoulders and gave him a slap on the back.

"If you need anything."

"Cheers. I'll call."

"Thank you, for everything."

Liam shrugged. "Hey, it was a blast. You know, apart from the dying part." He winked at Sam. "Anyways, you two take care of each other and don't go doing anything I wouldn't, hey?"

Sam laughed. "Like what?"

"If I find something, I'll let you know." He opened the car door and hopped in.

Sam accepted a brief hug from Father Monroe, then stepped back with Elliot while their friends buckled up and drove away.

The engine noise faded until only the general hum of the city remained. She glanced at Elliot, who was watching the car disappear at the end of the road. Suddenly they were alone and there was nothing and no one vying for their time. Her stomach fluttered, a mix of anticipation and anxiety.

She slipped her hand into his, drawing his attention. "Do you want to come in for a coffee?"

He frowned briefly. "Actually, I thought I'd head up to the office. Make sure everything's alright."

She tried not to let the disappointment show in her face, but she clearly failed. With a look of concern, he stepped closer and lifted her hand to his chest. "But I was going to say, how about dinner tonight?"

"Are you asking me out on a date?"

"Yeah, I guess I am. If you'd—"

"I'd love to."

He put his other arm around her shoulders and for a moment they stood there, close and quiet. He pressed an affectionate kiss to her temple and stepped back.

"Meet you here at six thirty?"

"Sounds good."

He started walking. Sam watched him for a few seconds, then headed inside.

She'd spent very little time in the last week *alone*, and the silence, the stillness, was welcome. It gave her some time to think through everything, without any need to mask her emotions.

She'd tried to convince herself that what had happened to her at university could never happen again, but now she knew it was part of her, something she would have to reckon with again, probably many times. She'd seen people she cared about die, nearly died herself, gazed through a portal into Hell. But on the other hand, she'd made new friends, discovered incredible truths, and forged an exciting new future with Elliot.

Sat on her sofa, wrapped in a blanket, safe and solitary, she cried her way through half a box of tissues, just letting it all out – the emotional jumble – until she felt cleansed, ready to face whatever came next.

———•———

The walk through Bristol up to the *Weird News* office in Clifton took Elliot the best part of an hour up some steep climbs, but it felt good. He experienced an odd sense of disconnection as he strode along familiar streets. It had been less than a week since they'd fled Bristol with the demon on their tail, but somehow everything seemed different. He felt like a stranger in his own city. But it was his city, the same home he'd adopted four years ago. It hadn't changed; he had.

The walk helped clear his mind. There was so much to figure out that it was hard to know where to start, but by the time he reached the road outside the office he'd settled on the bones of a plan. First, he was going to document everything and figure out which parts to publish and which to leave out. Then he was going to hit their publication deadline next week.

The rest would all fall into place in time.

He approached the front door of the office, and froze. Blue-and-white tape crossed the door and the lock was splintered. He pulled the tape down and pushed. The door swung in on loose hinges.

Inside, a stale odour permeated the office. No, not stale. Wrong. It stank of chemicals and other people and not its familiar, comforting self. He dropped his laptop bag in the hall and walked through to the main office.

Yellow, numbered tickets peppered the room, clustering thickest on the wall behind his desk where he'd pinned his research on the Mime's victims to the map. The police had tagged and presumably photographed everything, but they hadn't taken it. He wondered why not, if they were considering it evidence.

Yates, of course. No one else seemed inclined to tie him to the demon's crimes. Surely nothing in the evidence would incriminate him. He sat in his desk chair and ran a finger through the fine coating of black fingerprint dust on his desk. They couldn't have prints from the demon, it always wore the white gloves. But they might have lifted his from Geoff's office, or maybe even from the girl at the festival.

He took a deep breath. This was the worst part, like Sam always said. You could vanquish the evil thing, but no one would believe you, and you still had to face the consequences.

A floorboard squeaked in the hall and he glanced up to find Detective Yates standing there, arms folded. Elliot tensed, then stood.

"Here to arrest me?"

For a moment Yates stood stoically in the doorway. Then he let his arms drop to his sides and stepped into the room. "No." There was a weariness about the way he moved, like he'd had a long week.

Elliot glanced over his shoulder at the map on the wall. "You thought you could tie me to—"

"Actually, I thought you might be dead," Yates said. He perched on the end of Sam's desk. "You didn't show at the station; and where you'd been in the thick of every strange incident that landed on my desk, you suddenly vanished."

Maybe that was why they hadn't taken the evidence. They'd broken in searching for a missing person, not a criminal. What must Yates have thought when he saw all the information on the map?

"Right. About that, I—"

"Followed him to Oxford. Yes, I know that *now*."

Elliot eyed him suspiciously. "Followed…"

Yates glanced past him at the map, then pushed off the desk and walked closer. Elliot backpedalled, a spike of apprehension bordering on fear firing his reaction. It was ridiculous; he'd killed a centuries-old demon last night and the detective was being perfectly reasonable. Yates ignored him, reaching past to pull one of Sam's photos of the Mime from the wall.

"This guy. It took me a while, but I caught him on CCTV near some of the attacks. Because they were attacks, weren't they?"

Elliot's mouth was uncomfortably dry. This was not how he'd anticipated this conversation going. Part of him suspected Yates was luring him into a false sense of security.

Yates nodded towards the wall. "You laid it all out. Once I knew what I was looking for…" He sighed. "I owe you an apology. I kept demanding answers, but I wasn't ready to hear them. And you knew that, I think."

Elliot blinked, lost for words.

"So?" Yates prompted.

"What?"

"This is the part where you volunteer some information. Fill in the blanks. What happened in Oxford? Is he still out there? Do we need to—"

"We dealt with it," he said.

Yates ground his teeth, a little of the old frustration showing through this newly open-minded version. Elliot realised he was still being cautiously evasive. Maybe he needed to acknowledge Yates's apology with one of his own. A little trust between them would be no bad thing.

"You're right. I'm sorry. You want the whole story?" he asked, warily.

Yates nodded.

"Alright." Elliot moistened dry lips, considering where to start. He moved past Yates and retrieved his laptop case from the hallway. From it, he removed the Penrose dagger. He set it on his desk, knowing that all Yates would see would be the hilt.

"That is the demon Mastho." Elliot pointed at the photograph. "And I didn't follow it to Oxford. It followed me." He sat in his office chair and launched into the story from the beginning. After a while Yates wheeled Sam's chair over and, to his credit, sat patiently through the whole tale. He even kept it together when Elliot demonstrated what the dagger could do, by cutting a sheet of paper with the blade.

As Elliot finished describing the demon's final moments he reclined in his seat.

Yates did likewise, and let out a long breath. "So, it's definitely dead?"

"Yes."

There followed a tense pause in which Elliot tried to read the man's stony expression.

"And the… the man—"

"The host?"

"Yes. What happened to him?"

Elliot shrugged. "He's alive, but… Well, not particularly coherent." His eyes snapped to Yates in alarm. "You can't arrest him. He's a victim. Arrest me if you have to arrest someone! He doesn't deserve that."

Yates sucked his teeth.

"Detective?"

The man sighed, more of the weariness of a stressful few days showing in his eyes. "I won't be arresting anyone. There's too many inconsistencies."

Elliot let out a tense breath he hadn't realised he'd been holding.

"Too much that can't be explained," Yates added. "Conflicting statements, lack of clear evidence."

"I see."

"Apparently, when that happens, it's policy to go with the simplest, most reasonable explanation."

Elliot watched him carefully. "Which is?"

Yates rose to his feet. "A series of bizarre, unrelated accidents, and a crackpot reporter with a conspiracy theory."

Elliot let that sink in as he considered his hands in his lap. When he worked up the nerve, he raised his eyes to Yates. "I feel like there's a 'but' coming."

"But *I* know what you did. You were trying to do something important, I get that now. But I hope you understand the position I was in."

His mind flashed back to those moments in his apartment in London with James four years ago. If he was ever going to forgive himself, he *had* to forgive Yates. "I do. It's hard to accept until you see it for yourself." He stood as Yates walked to the door.

"Sorry about the mess," Yates said. "You can just ignore all of this." He waved his hand to take in the evidence tickets. When he reached the doorway, he paused and faced Elliot. "If anything like this ever comes up again…"

"What?"

"Expect a call. I might need you."

Elliot rubbed a hand over his mouth. "Sure."

Yates nodded and left. Elliot returned to his desk and sagged into his seat. He exhaled a long breath, contemplating all the implications of that parting remark. The tiniest hint of a smile pulled at the corner of his mouth.

———•———

With Yates gone, Elliot took a moment to clean out the coffee pot – they'd left it sitting when they'd departed Bristol, and it wasn't pretty – and set it brewing.

He pulled down the map, photos and notes from the wall and boxed them up. Then he wiped down his desk to remove the residue of fingerprint powder. Once he'd fixed his coffee, he sat down, opened his laptop and started typing thoughts as they came to him.

Where did responsibility begin and end? He'd blamed himself for James's death for so long. He could wish forever that he'd not turned James away that night. Maybe if he hadn't, they would have learned more sooner. Maybe they could have fought the demon side by side.

Or maybe it would have killed them both in London, and no one would have been left to stop it this time.

He couldn't be responsible for something that might or might not have happened because of a choice he'd made with no way of knowing the consequences. He'd never stop regretting it, but the demon had killed his brother, not him.

With Mastho dead, he'd expected the weight of responsibility to ease, yet it hadn't. It felt different but no lighter. The world felt bigger. His part in it felt bigger.

What was it Ethan had said? He'd had the luxury of a righteous calling, rather than the penance his father had suffered. Maybe now Elliot could exchange his own penance for a calling.

He picked up the Penrose dagger from where it lay on his desk. He'd spent four years trying to distance himself from the man he'd become in London. A man prepared to exploit anything and anyone, no matter the cost, to earn the next promotion, the next accolade, all in pursuit of his father's respect and pride. But in his hand now was hard evidence.

That man was never who he was *meant* to be.

A DEMON HUNTER'S PROMISE

Through the blinds across the interior partition, the lights in the hospital corridor flickered. Gabriel glanced up from the book he was reading by the dim glow of a lamp.

A shadow by the curtain shifted.

Unnatural. The temporary consecration would likely have weakened once Jack Monroe departed the vicinity.

He reached into the satchel hung from the head of the bed and drew forth the ward he'd used against Ka. There was no guarantee that whatever stalked him would be repelled, but the pointed end made a passable weapon.

"Show yourself," he muttered.

The shadow drew darkness from the corners of the room and formed it into a shape. A body.

The petite figure wore a tailored pinstripe jacket, cinched in sharply at a narrow waist, over a matching pencil skirt and traditional stockings. She wore her hair pulled up into a tight twist below an elegant hat, from which a net extended to cover part of her face. Gabriel regarded the woman warily.

"Who are you?"

"Oh, I wouldn't want to make it too easy for you now, would

I, Mr Cushing? Names are such troublesome things for us."

"You're a demon."

"Quite astute of you. But then, daddy dearest did teach you well."

"What do you know of my father?"

She flashed him a sly smile. "Much."

Gabriel shifted himself into a more upright position. He grimaced at the stab of discomfort from the stitches in his side. He held the ward out. "Speak, demon. What do you know?"

"You can't hurt me." She sat in the chair beside the bed and crossed her shapely legs. "I'm not really here. Which I am sure you would have figured out eventually."

Only a psychic projection. That explained how the demon could penetrate the residual consecration. "What do you want?"

She uncrossed her legs and shifted forwards, hands clutching the arms of the chair. "*That* is a much better question. What do I want? Mr Cushing, I want you dead."

Gabriel scoffed. "If you're only an illusion, you cannot hurt me."

The demon sighed and stood. "Quite right. It's an unfortunate fact of existence that we don't always get what we want. At least, not *when* we want it. But I can wait." She paced to the end of the bed and leaned on the rail. "You, Mr Cushing, have been quite the thorn in my side this past year. Generations of your family pursued Ka, but it was you, only you, who destroyed him."

"What is your point, demon?" He spat the word, throwing all the loathing he could muster into it.

"Ka was very dear to me. He was one of my best. And now your little protégé has dispatched another of my followers." She approached him and bent forwards until her face was only inches from his. "This, Mr Cushing, will not be tolerated."

"You have no power here."

The demon ground her teeth. "As we have established. But mark my words, demon hunter, my followers and I will not be so easily tricked in the future. Our Lord Dagon will be restored, and you will fail."

Gabriel met her gaze, unflinching. "No, you mark *my* words, demon. I am Gabriel Cushing, and I swear here and now that I will hunt every one of your demonic followers and destroy them all. I will seek out evil and dedicate my life to removing it from this world as my father did before me."

The demon laughed, and straightened. "We shall see, Mr Cushing. We shall see."

He blinked, and she was gone.

Penrose

Edward Penrose II
1768 - 1794

Edward = Mary
Penrose   Trenton
1747 - 1795 1751 - 1823

Robert = Amelia
Penrose   Postlethwaite
1770 - 1794 1772 - 1828

Jemima
Penrose
1789 - 1857

Giles = Winnie
Penrose   Hooper
1774 - 1836 1775 - 1857

Ethan = Anis
Penrose   Boswell
1796 - 1865 1804 - 1869

Gideon
Penrose
1827 - unknown

Mordecai = Isabella
Penrose   Sanchez
1824 - 1892 1826 - 1884

Joshua Penrose
1845 - 1867 †

Henrietta Penrose = Matthew Prouse
1847 - 1908   1840 - 1905

William Penrose III = Ruth Catchpole
1842 - 1910   1845 - 1911

Ezequiel Penrose = Izabel Crowe
1864 - 1892   1862 - 1888

George Penrose
1888 - 1888

Daniel Penrose = Celia Danes
1866 - 1912   1869 - 1922

Charles Penrose †
1889 - 1915

Emily Penrose = Henry Carter
1892 - 1957   1888 - 1914

Elizabeth Carter
1915 - 1940

Rosemary Carter = Ian Clary
1911 - 1996   1908 - 1990

Sarah Michaels = Oliver Acton
1931 - 2001   1930 - 1999

Paul Clary
1933 - 1940

Judith Acton = Edwin Cross
1953 -   1953 -

Marjorie Acton = Colin Rowland
1960 -   1957 -

James Cross
1977 - 2005

Elliot Cross †
1980 -

Ashley Rowland
1985 -

Lillian Rowland
1987 -

HUNTER'S HAVEN

ACKNOWLEDGEMENTS

This book has been an epic 10-year journey learning how to be a writer. A lot of people have contributed to that journey. I'd like to thank a few of the most important.

Rich, my life buddy. I couldn't have done any of this without your love and support.

Mark and David, who created Gabriel Cushing, way back when we were all still in our 20s, trying to make a movie over a long weekend and setting fire to coats on the beach. Thank you for letting me explore more of his story.

The Kelley Armstrong OWG gang. You were my first step. You were vital. Thank you for staying in touch all these years. Especially Dianne, for seeing my potential, and Steve, for being my role model.

North Bristol Writers, especially Pete. Thank you for pushing me, teaching me, and helping me to become someone who helps and inspires others.

Eve, Addy, James and Stuart, who took a chance beta reading for an unknown author and then became my biggest cheer-leaders. You kept me confident and inspired through the most daunting phase.

Jo, my editor. You helped me reach a finish line that just seemed to keep getting further away.

And finally Marek, Lin and the team at Matador, for all the hard work that went into producing and polishing a book I am immensely proud to call my own.

ABOUT THE AUTHOR

Chrissey Harrison writes varied speculative genre fiction. Books about monsters, magic, action and adventure, and fragile human characters trying to muddle through as best they can. They make mistakes and bad choices sometimes, and they have to learn to recognise their own strengths and weaknesses and turn to their friends and loved ones for help and support.

Her short stories have featured in several anthologies; most recently *Forgotten Sidekicks* from Grimbold Books (Kristell Ink). She is a member of The Alliance of Independent Authors and an avid supporter of local bookshops.

A science geek, gamer and fan of sci-fi, fantasy and horror, Chrissey wears many hats. Metaphorical hats, that is, not so much real hats. Mostly her writer hat, her graphic designer hat and her crafter hat. When she's not working on her fiction she likes to make things – plushies, hand-bound books and random upcycled stuff.

She lives in Clevedon in a creaky old Victorian terrace with her partner and her 18-year-old goldfish, Ambition.

WANT TO READ MORE?

Subscribe to Chrissey's newsletter for exclusive extras – free short story/novella ebooks that tie into the *Weird News* series and other stand-alone short reads. Get your first freebie when you sign up!

You'll also get monthly book recommendations to your inbox, along with news about new releases, event listings and other cool stuff.

Sign up now:
chrisseyharrison.com

FIND CHRISSEY ON SOCIAL MEDIA

Twitter/Instagram: @chrisseywrites
Facebook: /authorchrisseyharrison